A DiFFERENT DAY,
A DiFFERENT DESTiNY

The Snipesville Chronicles, Book 2

Also by Annette Laing:
Don't Know Where, Don't Know When

For Natalie — 🙂

A DiFFERENT DAY,
A DiFFERENT DESTiNY

The Snipesville Chronicles, Book 2

Cheers!

2014

By Annette Laing

CONFUSION
PRESS
Statesboro, Georgia

For my parents, Watson and Audrey, who made possible that first transatlantic trip that set me on the adventure of a lifetime, with much love.

Printed in the U.S.A.

Cover design: Deborah Harvey
Inside design: Kelley Callaway

Author web site: www.AnnetteLaing.com

Contents

A DiFFERENT DAY, A DiFFERENT DESTiNY

The Snipesville Chronicles, Book 2

PROLOGUE

Jupiter wasn't a large planet or a mighty Roman God.

He was a short and burly fifty-one-year old man with a slight limp and grey hair.

And on March 14, 1851, he had a job to do.

He and his fourteen-year-old son, who was also named Jupiter but always called Jupe, were walking barefoot through the cotton fields, past the gnarled brown twigs of last season's crop.

Soon it would be cotton-planting time in South Georgia, and Jupiter was figuring out just how many acres he would assign to each of his workers, depending on their ages and their strength. Jupiter was in charge of the people at Kintyre Plantation, but he wasn't really. Like almost everyone else on the plantation, he wasn't a landowner. He wasn't even employed. He was owned.

Jupiter was a slave. He bossed around the slaves who worked in the fields, a job he had inherited from his own father. Jupiter was rewarded for being willing to order people about: There was extra food for the family, and a better cabin without quite so many holes in the walls. His was, by plantation standards, a cushy job. One day, when he got too old, Jupe would take his place.

But Jupiter hated himself when he had to whip other slaves as runaways and malingerers. These were people he had known all their lives. He had watched them grow up. He celebrated and worshipped with them. He felt sick after a whipping, knew that people were afraid to talk to him like they talked to each other, but he told himself that he had no choice: If he refused, he would lose his job. Worse, his young master might even take him to the slave market in Savannah to be sold, and he would never see or hear from his wife and children again.

Everyone in the slave quarters reckoned the master to be crazy. Actually, Jupiter didn't think that his master was crazy. He thought he was an idiot, and that made him even more dangerous.

So Jupiter kept his head down, and did his job, and tried not to hope for better times, at least in this world. Hope, Jupiter believed, well... Hope hurt. Best to make the best of what he had: A little control over what happened in the fields where he had lived and worked his whole life.

He walked past the old live oak tree, with its massive spreading branches mostly gone now, and thought to himself that it needed to be removed. Digging up the dead tree would clear a little more land for growing cotton.

Suddenly Jupiter stopped in his tracks. He asked himself, who would benefit from a little more cotton? Only the stupid young master, who spent more time playing cards with other "gentlemen" than paying attention to his cotton fields.

That was when Jupiter decided to plant pecan trees instead, four of them… No, six. The master wouldn't notice young pecan trees. In a few years, the slaves would have pecans to eat, and maybe to sell in Savannah at the Sunday markets. He made up his mind to start on the project that very week.

When Jupiter snapped out of his daydream, he was shocked to see a woman standing just a few feet away from him. There would have been nothing surprising to Jupiter about seeing a black woman in the field. But this was a white woman, a lady, perhaps a little older than him, in a bonnet and long dark red dress with its hem coated in beige dust. She was busily scribbling in a notebook, and occasionally pausing to stab her pencil-end repeatedly on a tiny metal box.

Jupiter took off his hat, and tried to look as respectful as possible in front of this stranger. "Beg pardon, missis, but is you needing help? Is you lost? I's Jupiter, and I's the driver here."

She looked up and smiled, before, again, tapping the box with her pencil. "No, I'm not lost. Just running some numbers."

Jupiter squinted at the strange lady. "Numbers, ma'am?"

"Yes," she said. "Would you like to look them over?"

"No, ma'am," Jupiter said hastily, shaking his head. "I can't read no numbers. I can't read at all. Nor write. No, ma'am."

She looked at him mischievously. "Of course you would say that, Jupiter. It's against the law for a slave to be literate. Yet, somehow, you still manage to write those marvelous letters to your sister in New York, and to keep that diary of yours. Amazing, for a man who can't read, really. Miraculous, in fact."

Now, Jupiter was scared. How did she know of his diary and letters?

"How you reckon that?" he asked sharply, before adding, "Ma'am?"

"Oh, please don't ma'am me, Jupiter. I'm not Queen Victoria. Anyway, don't you worry: I won't tell anyone, I promise. I think it's great. Keep going. As I girl I know would say, 'You totally rock.' "

Jupiter was confused, and very apprehensive. The lady, meanwhile, had tossed her pencil and notebook into a small bag she carried.

"All done," she said, mostly to herself. "Hope I got it right. Oh, well, it'll do. Bye, Jupiter. Nice meeting you. Love your writing, by the way. Can't put it down."

She gave a small wave to the baffled Jupiter, and took off toward the piney woods.

"Ma'am?" Jupiter called, gesturing a thumb in the opposite direction. "The road and the big house are that way."

"I know," she said. "But I'm walking back to Snipesville."

Jupiter and Jupe exchanged baffled looks, but when they glanced toward the lady again, she had vanished. Jupiter shivered. Was she real? Or was she a ghost, or a spirit, like his ancient great-grandmother used to describe in her lilting West African accent? He shivered, and decided to head home to sit a spell.

Jupiter didn't notice that the lady had dropped something, quite by mistake. It was a small metallic box, and it lay glinting in the spring sunshine. That afternoon, some boys, dashing through the field on their way home from collecting firewood, would run over and past it without noticing it. One boy even stepped on it, grinding it slightly into the ground.

****

The Professor noticed that she had lost her electronic calculator when she returned to her office at Snipesville State College, just a few miles away, and more than 150 years into the future.

Rummaging through her bag, she muttered under her breath in a vaguely British accent. Now she realized, with a sinking feeling, that the calculator, or part of it, was the mysterious object she had examined just last week at the Victoria and Albert Museum. How had her calculator ended up in present-day London?

Chapter 1:

MEANWHILE, BACK IN SNIPESVILLE

It all started with Hannah Dias' ankle.

More than a hundred and fifty years after Jupiter and his son had met the Professor in a cotton field in Snipes County, Hannah and her brother Alex were playing with their friend Brandon Clark in a forlorn little park in the small town of Snipesville, Georgia.

At least, Alex and Brandon were playing: They had made swords out of sticks, and were laughingly battling each other. Before that, they had examined a colony of fire ants that was busily excavating the sandy soil. Hannah, meanwhile, was slumped on the only bench in the park, examining her fingernails and looking sour.

The day was bright and sunny, but Hannah was in a foul mood. Even though she was a native Californian, she hated hot weather: After all, she had grown up in foggy San Francisco. Meeting up with Brandon had seemed like a good idea that morning when it was still cool, but not now, at mid-day, in the sweltering muggy heat of an August afternoon in southeast Georgia.

Hannah and Alex lived in a remote subdivision in Snipes County, where there were plenty of expensive houses, but almost no other kids. They had moved from San Francisco to Georgia only a few weeks before, soon after their mother had died in a car accident and their father's bank had transferred him to Georgia.

Brandon, a black kid from Snipesville, was Alex and Hannah's only friend in town. He and Alex had hit it off the moment they met, united in their shared hatred of team sports, their love of obscure facts, and their enjoyment of teasing Hannah.

Hannah, Alex and Brandon: Three ordinary kids in an ordinary town, right?

Not quite.

The day that Hannah and Alex first met Brandon seemed like an ordinary day at first. They got together when all of them were playing hooky from summer camps at Snipesville State College. Little did they know that this was to be the last ordinary day of their lives. Without warning, the three kids were transported in an instant from Snipesville to Balesworth, a small town in England. That was strange enough.

But even stranger was this: They arrived during World War Two.

In 1940, to be exact.

Soon, Brandon was separated from the others, and thrown even further back in time. He was still in Balesworth: Only now, he was there in 1915, in the middle of World War One.

And in Balesworth—Alex and Hannah in 1940, and Brandon in 1915--they had stayed for months. They had made friends, gone to school (except for Brandon, who found a job as a dentist's apprentice), and settled down with their English foster families. Finally, after they had rescued an abused foster kid called George Braithwaite, they returned to present-day Snipesville as suddenly as they had left, on the very same day in July. No time at all had passed, and it was as though the entire bizarre experience had simply never happened.

Now it was mid-August, and life in Snipesville seemed to have returned to ordinary, which is to say, dull and miserable. The summer heat was unbearable, especially for Hannah, who really wished she had stayed home with the air-conditioning and the TV, instead of roasting her butt on a park bench.

Alex and Brandon had stopped sword-fighting, and now were standing in front of Hannah looking at her with pity.

"What?" Hannah snapped. She didn't like being stared at, especially pity-ingly.

"Why don't you do something?" her brother demanded.

"Yeah," Brandon backed him up. "You're just sitting there looking all mean and grumpy."

"Well, excuse me for breathing," harrumphed Hannah. "This is so boring." She gave a dramatic sigh. "And it's, like, a gazillion degrees."

Brandon rolled his eyes and, turning to Alex, changed the subject. "Hey, did you know that someone wants to build all over this park?"

Hannah put a hand to her chest in mock shock. "Ooh, I am so sad. Like, I'm supposed to care? At least tell me it's going to be a new mall."

"No, it's not a mall," Brandon said. "They're gonna build houses and apart-ments. C'mon, Hannah, I know it's not much, but this is the only park in the whole of West Snipesville. Look, would you guys sign the petition against the development?"

He pulled a crumpled piece of paper and a stub of a pencil out of his back pocket, and handed them both to Alex, who signed eagerly and sloppily.

But Hannah was too hot and irritable to care at all. "Brandon, like, who is going to listen to some kids with a petition? For real. It's a stupid idea."

Brandon scowled at her. "Nobody's making you sign it. You sure have been a pain in the butt since we got back. Too bad Mrs. D. isn't here to sort you out."

"Yeah," laughed Alex, "Then you'd have a pain in the butt."

Embarrassed, Hannah pouted and looked away. She hated being teased about the time that Mrs. Devenish had whipped her. Mrs. D., as the kids called her, was the stern old lady with whom Hannah and Alex had lived in England in 1940. Although Hannah had thought that she would never, ever recover from the humiliation of her punishment, she had eventually and unpredictably bonded with Mrs. D. She missed Mrs. D. and her granddaughter Verity, who had been Hannah's best friend. She even missed Eric, the mischievous wartime refugee who became Mrs. Devenish's adopted son.

After a long silence, Alex asked his sister, "So what do you want to do this afternoon?"

"I know what, Hannah," said Brandon, a twinkle in his eye. "You should go check out that new girls' clothing store on West Main Street."

"Where?" Hannah gasped, jumping to her feet.

"Right next to the bakery," said Brandon. No sooner had the words left his mouth than Hannah started speed-walking across the park. The boys laughed, and resumed their swordplay. But they had just crossed swords (or sticks) when they heard a shriek, and turned to see Hannah lying sprawled on the ground.

"Trust you to break your ankle," said Alex. He was sitting on his hands on a chair in Dr. George Braithwaite's living room, swinging his legs, while Brandon propped up the wall next to him. Hannah answered her brother with a withering glance.

It was too amazing to be a coincidence: George Braithwaite, the abused little boy in England, now lived in retirement in Snipesville, where he was best known as Snipesville's First Black Doctor. He was also Snipesville's First British Doctor, but nobody in Snipesville, apart from Hannah, Alex and Brandon, found that nearly as interesting.

"It's not broken," Dr. Braithwaite said, as he carefully wrapped Hannah's ankle. His accent still echoed his long-ago upbringing in England. "It's just a sprain. But you will need crutches, Hannah, and you'll need to take good care…"

"Crutches!" Hannah said disdainfully.

"Crutches," Dr. Braithwaite said firmly. "I have a spare pair that you may borrow. Anyhow, you don't have any major plans for this week, do you?"

"We did," said Alex morosely. "Hannah and me are supposed to be going to London with my grandparents on Friday. They're coming all the way from California to get us."

Dr. Braithwaite gave a sympathetic cluck. "That's a pity. Hannah might find it hard to get around in the city. You'd better call and see if they can postpone the trip."

Hannah and Alex were dismayed. The trip had been a wonderful surprise: Grandma had called from California just that past weekend to tell them.

Dr. Braithwaite stood up and admired his handiwork in bracing Hannah's ankle. "Look on the bright side. If your trip were delayed, that would give me time to arrange for you to visit Eric and Verity... if you would like."

He had seen Hannah's hesitation and the doubtful looks that Alex and Brandon had traded.

It was weird enough, Hannah thought, to be friends with old Dr. Braithwaite. Would she want to meet Eric and Verity as old people, too? They had married after World War Two, and were still living in Balesworth, in Mrs. Devenish's old house. Much as Hannah missed Verity, she wasn't sure she wanted to meet her as an old lady. Sitting beside her, Alex was thinking much the same thing about Eric. Brandon, meanwhile, felt guilty for being secretly pleased that the Dias kids would go to England after all, because he was stuck in Snipesville for the summer, and wanted their company.

There was an awkward silence. Fortunately, Dr. Braithwaite's telephone rang. It was Hannah and Alex's dad calling, to say that he was on his way.

"It's a shame," Dr. Braithwaite said as he hung up the phone, "that this might be your first and last experience of our little park, Hannah. By the time you recover, I'm afraid it will probably be gone. But there's still some hope. You see, the city council is meeting this afternoon to decide whether to approve a scheme to develop the land. If you could all come to the meeting to help us oppose the plan..."

"Well, I can't," Hannah said quickly, "Obviously."

Dr. Braithwaite handed her a pair of crutches. "Now you have these," he said, "there's no reason why you can't hobble from the car to the city council chambers."

Hannah scowled at him. Dr. Braithwaite smiled to himself.

In the end, both Hannah and Alex went to the meeting, but not because they wanted to go.

When Mr. Dias collected them from Dr. Braithwaite's house, he told them that he needed to attend the city council meeting before he could take them home.

But that wasn't the worst news he had for them: He had already spoken to Grandma about Hannah's ankle, and she had decided to postpone the London trip. "I always thought this was one of your Grandma's crazy ideas, anyway," said Mr. Dias, as he parked his car and put on the handbrake. "You guys need a chance to get settled here in Snipesville."

Hannah awkwardly hauled herself into the city council building on her crutches. "I am totally embarrassed," she whispered angrily to her brother as they took seats in the back of the meeting room. "This has been one of the worst days of my entire life. If we hadn't gone to that stupid park, we would still be headed to England."

"Hey, don't blame me. Me and Brandon offered to go to the college with you," Alex said reasonably. "We could have played on the computers. You could have gone to Starbucks in the Union. You were the one who didn't want to go."

But Hannah was adamant. "I'm never setting foot on that campus ever again. Not ever. She's there."

"Yeah, so you keep reminding me." Alex groaned. He knew immediately who Hannah was talking about: Dr. Kate Harrower.

People in Snipesville, if they thought about Dr. Harrower at all, knew her as a middle-aged history professor at Snipesville State College. What they did not know, however, was that she also happened to be a time traveler (according to Hannah, an evil time-travelling genius), who had taken (according to Hannah, abducted) the Dias kids and Brandon Clark and spirited them off to World War Two England. Once there, the Professor, as the kids called her, had left them (Hannah: abandoned them) in Balesworth, reappearing only at various times to offer advice or assistance.

But all that was over now. Hannah had no intention of ever repeating the experience.

As the city council meeting came to order, she resentfully settled into her chair, and prepared for a very boring evening.

The meeting dragged on for what felt like centuries. Brandon was dropping into a coma. He had never been so bored, even in math class, and that was really saying something. He tried to stay awake by watching the city councilmen: Five white men, two black men, and no women. He smirked as he remembered the perfect word for the looks on their faces: *Glaikit*. It was a Scottish expression he had learned from Mr. Gordon, the kindly dentist who had employed him as an apprentice in England in 1915. *Glaikit* was a colorful Scottish way of saying that a person has a really stupid look on his face.

About twenty minutes into the meeting, the park development came up.

Brandon followed the discussion with great apprehension. He had grown up playing in the park, and it was hard to imagine it buried under a bunch of apartments.

First, a man in a suit spoke in favor of the project, mostly in incomprehensible lawyer language.

Next up was Carter Howells, one of the two black councilmen. Mr. Howells rumbled in his deep voice, "The property in question is the only park within easy walking distance of West Snipesville, a predominantly African-American neighborhood."

Now Councilman Cassius Shrupp spoke. Shrupp was the other black councilman, who owned a carwash in town. Brandon's dad always called him "Suck-Up Shrupp."

Mr. Shrupp cleared his throat. "If I might intercede… While I appreciate the community's concern for a park, this land hardly qualifies. It has never been officially designated as a park. It's waste land, and it is ripe for development. This project will create jobs for West Snipesville, and I for one intend to vote for it."

Discussion was now opened to the audience, and Dr. Braithwaite rose to his feet, lifting Brandon by the arm from his chair. "I would like to ask you, gentlemen, where you expect this lad and his friends to play?"

The room hushed as the tall, distinguished black Englishman addressed the council. "The only other parks in this town are miles away. And I daresay that any children from our neighborhood who took the time to walk to them would not meet with a warm reception. It is not safe to play in our streets, where the traffic is so heavy and yet the sidewalks so few. Children like young Brandon here need someplace to be."

Brandon was ready to die from embarrassment, but Dr. Braithwaite wasn't done with him. "Brandon is an honors student, a fine young man from whom great things are expected. Will he remember his hometown of Snipesville with fondness, or as a place in which profit was put before children? I implore you, gentlemen, to tell Brandon where you stand."

Brandon died from embarrassment. And his agony wasn't over yet.

Dr. Braithwaite turned to address him. "Brandon, perhaps you could tell the council, in your own words, why they should turn down this proposal?"

Brandon was now burning in Embarrassment Hell. He coughed, and tried to think of something to say. What he said was, "Um. Ahem. Ur."

"Speak up, lad," Dr. Braithwaite encouraged.

Brandon took a deep breath and tried again. "I, um, agree with Dr. Braithwaite. I need somewhere to hang out. And so do my friends." He began to warm to his subject, and his voice grew more confident: "Like, my friends Hannah and Alex. They live out in Magnolia Acres but they have to come to town to play in a park. So lots of kids use the park. And…er… that's all I have to say."

Brandon was about to run back to his seat, but a rush of applause stopped him, and so did the voice of Cassius Shrupp, who had just hurriedly consulted with the other councilmen. "Well, we certainly appreciate you coming to speak with us this evening, young Brian," he said. "Now I'd like to make a motion that we bring this matter to a vote."

Six heads nodded in agreement.

They voted. The plan was approved, six votes to one (Carter Howells casting the only "no" vote), and the park was condemned to be buried under houses and apartments. Dr. Braithwaite looked severely at the councilmen, and slowly shook his head from side to side. Alex's dad sighed heavily, capped his pen, and tucked it into his jacket.

Alex understood why Brandon, Dr. Braithwaite, and Brandon's parents were at the meeting. But he wondered vaguely why his own dad was there.

As they left the meeting hall, Brandon said to Dr. Braithwaite, "Man, you could have warned me."

Dr. Braithwaite gave him a small smile. "And would you have said anything if I had?"

"Probably not," Brandon confessed.

"There you are then. I had faith in you, Brandon. You were magnificent."

Brandon raised his eyebrows. "Thanks. But we still lost. Don't you have any ideas to save the park?"

"Right now, not an earthly," Dr. Braithwaite said. "We can only hope for a sudden change of heart among the councilmen."

On the way home, as Hannah sat hunched in the back seat staring out the window, Alex asked his dad why he had been at the meeting. Mr. Dias breezily waved away the question. "It's just something the boss asked me to do," he said. "Mr. Marshburn likes to stay abreast of anything that might affect property values. Oh, and did I mention, guys? He and Mrs. Marshburn invited us to dinner tonight. They've got two kids, a boy and a girl, so it's a chance for you guys to make friends."

The Marshburns lived in an expensive subdivision without a name that was hidden away in rural Snipes County. Mr. Dias said that the few people who knew about it called it the 'super-secret neighborhood.' He explained, "It's beyond exclusive. You have to have an interview before you're allowed to build there."

Getting to the super-secret neighborhood involved taking a turn onto an unmarked country road, then driving down a long and winding trail into the woods. Finally, the Diases arrived at an automated gate, where Mr. Dias punched in a number code he had written on a sticky note. Instantly, they emerged from piney woods into Beverly Hills. The super-secret neighborhood was dotted with impressive mansions, and centered on a country club with a huge kidney-shaped pool and fancy waterslide, tennis courts, and a volleyball court. The Marshburns' home was in the very back of the subdivision, and it was enormous. Two cement lions stood guard at the front doors.

Mrs. Marshburn opened the door, and beamed at them. Everything about her sparkled: Her eyes, her teeth, her clothes, her nails, her earrings, her necklace, her rings, and even her carefully manicured blonde hair. "Welcome to our home, and welcome to Snipesville," she gushed in a thick Snipes County accent, as she ushered them inside. "It's so nice to finally meet you, Alex and Hannah! Your Dad has told us so much about you. Oh my gosh, Hannah, what happened to your leg, honey?"

Hannah thought about saying something sarcastic, but she just gave Mrs. Marshburn a wan smile as she hobbled into the house on her crutches.

Mrs. Marshburn, meanwhile, was still talking. "Well, y'all just make yourselves at home. We are so glad to have you in our community!"

Hannah wondered how she could be glad to have them living there when she didn't even know them. For all Mrs. Marshburn knew, the Dias family could be a gang of axe murderers. Mrs. Marshburn showed no such concern, however, as she ushered them all into the living room. Fox-hunting prints and deer skulls were mounted on the walls, and all the furniture looked brand new. It reminded Hannah of one of those fake-looking show homes that parents drag kids around when they're looking to buy a new house.

"Would you all like a sweet tea?" Mrs. Marshburn asked, clapping her hands together as if she were about to pray. "My husband and the kids are already in the pool, so y'all just head on out back and introduce yourselves, and I'll bring your drinks." She pointed to the sliding glass doors.

In the back yard, the Marshburn daughter, who looked about fourteen, was sitting at the patio table, with a towel wrapped around her shoulders. She was talking nonstop on her cell phone. "So I can't believe that she said that… and then she's all like, 'it's no big deal, y'all fuss too much. And I'm all, you are such a total two-faced… Yeah."

Hannah flopped into a patio chair, laid her crutches on the cement, and began to inspect her fingernails, just as Mr. Marshburn climbed out of the pool, grabbed an enormous towel, and wiped off his face. "Hey there! Good to see you, Bill. You Hannah and Alex, right?" he boomed in a Georgia accent that was as strong as his wife's. "Hey, Hannah, your dad told me you hurt your ankle. You sure you can't join us in the pool?"

"That's okay. I hate swimming," Hannah said truthfully.

Mr. Marshburn paused a second in toweling himself off. "Well, never mind, Hannah, you just introduce yourself to my daughter Natalie, soon as she gets off the phone, and Alex, you go say hey to Trey."

But Natalie showed no signs of getting off the phone. She glanced at Hannah, looked her up and down with distaste, and returned to her phone conversation with a smirk and a toss of her hair. Hannah slumped down in her seat and wished she had remembered to bring her own phone so she would have something to do, even if it was just to pretend to call a friend.

Trey made a half-hearted effort to converse with Alex, who had joined him in the pool. "So, you're from California, right? Is it true y'all are crazy?"

Alex hadn't a clue how to answer that, so he just gave what he hoped was an amused and sophisticated smile.

Trey stared at him.

It was the beginning of a beautiful friendship. Not.

"Low Country Boil," announced Mrs. Marshburn as she brought to the table an enormous steaming bowl of red potatoes, meaty sausage chunks, bright yellow corn on the cob, and huge pink shrimp.

"Where's the ball?" asked Alex, puzzled.

Even as she smiled, Mrs. Marshburn looked offended, and Mr. Dias hurriedly explained. "That's boil, Alex. Not ball."

Alex's eyes widened. "Oh! Sorry. I'm not used to everyone's accent yet. No offense, Mrs. Marshburn."

CHAPTER ONE

Hannah wrinkled her nose at the steaming shrimp, and groused, "You eat shrimp hot?"

Mrs. Marshburn's smile looked even more firmly welded to her face as she gritted her teeth. "Yes, honey, that's how we like it down here. Why don't you try it?"

Trey was laughing. "You don't know about Low Country Boil?" he whooped. "Man, y'all are backward in California. You got a lot to learn. Where you going to school?"

"We start at Snipes Academy in September," said Alex.

"Is that right?" cooed Mrs. Marshburn. "Well, how about that! Trey and Natalie both attend S.A. It's a very positive school, and I believe that's so important for children, to have a positive learning environment. Don't you, Bill?"

"Absolutely," Mr. Dias hurriedly agreed.

Mrs. Marshburn beamed at Hannah and Alex. "I'm sure the kids at S.A. will make you very welcome. That's the kind of positive place it is. Won't you, kids?"

"Sure," Trey said unconvincingly, suppressing a smirk. "We love Yankees."

Mr. Marshburn had other things on his mind, and he turned to Mr. Dias. "Listen, Bill, I gotta tell you, the Renaissance Project is a major investment opportunity, one of the finest I've seen in many years. You know, I think it's gonna revitalize downtown Snipesville. There's big money there. And it's great to have the city on board with this."

Alex finally saw a chance to participate in the conversation. "Excuse me, Mr. Marshburn? Are you talking about the park in West Snipesville?"

Hannah's eyes grew wide with alarm, and she discreetly drew her finger across her throat. But Alex didn't take the hint. He said, "I don't want it to be destroyed."

Mr. Marshburn looked uncomfortable. "I'm talking about a patch of undeveloped land that some folks call a park, Alex, if that's what you're referring to."

Alex caught a look from his dad, and was beginning to sense that he had shoved his foot in his mouth, but he still couldn't figure out how. He forged on. "Sir, I just don't think it's fair to kids. Our friend Brandon lives in West Snipesville, and he's pretty upset about losing his park."

Mr. Marshburn looked sternly at him, and then said in a steely voice, "Well, Alex, you tell your friend that this park, if you want to call it that, isn't nearly as important to his future as bringing business to downtown Snipesville."

Alex persisted. "Yes, but…"

"Um, okay, Alex, you've made your point," said Mr. Dias, looking embarrassed and a little afraid of his boss.

But Mr. Marshburn had a point of his own to make. "Bill, let me tell you something. I'm excited about this project, because I care about this town. We Marshburns have lived in Snipesville for nearly 200 years. My great-great-great-grandaddy built the first hotel, and we've been here ever since. So I reckon we know a thing or two about what's right for our community, and that's progress."

"It's not progress to have nowhere to play," Alex said stubbornly.

Mr. Marshburn's smile now looked as fixed as his wife's. "Well, I'm sorry you feel that way. But you know, it's always best to think positively."

He turned back to Mr. Dias, and ignored Alex for the rest of the evening.

When they got home that night, Alex told Hannah how, after dinner, he had tried to persuade Trey to support the park. "But he just laughed at me. He had one of those Confederate flags in his bedroom. And you won't believe what he said, Hannah. He said, 'Why should I care about the stupid park? Only the blacks use that park.'"

Hannah wasn't shocked. "Hey, you're surprised? This is the South, stupid. And even if it wasn't, lots of people think like that in California, too. At least Trey was honest, not like his mom. She's the kind of lady that Grandma calls sugar-coated dog poop."

That night, Hannah was sitting in bed when she switched off the TV, and sighed heavily. Returning to Snipesville from her bizarre time-travel journey to England had been such a huge relief. But now, only a few weeks later, she was more bored and miserable than ever. Sometimes, she thought about faraway California, where her mother was buried. But Hannah realized uneasily that, more often, she thought about Mrs. Devenish, her English foster mother. It was painful to think that Mrs. D. was now long dead, and that Verity, her granddaughter and Hannah's best friend, was very old indeed.

Now Hannah was laid up with a stupid sprained ankle, and the one thing she had been looking forward to, her trip to modern-day England, wasn't happening. Life sucks, Hannah thought. That's all there is to it. As if to agree with her, her ankle gave her yet another sharp pain.

Like most people, Hannah sometimes had strange dreams, but that night, her dream was weirder than most. She dreamed that she was floating on a soft fluffy cloud, when suddenly she was shot from a cannon, and her skin peeled away painlessly, as though she were a human banana. And then she awoke, with a huge sigh of relief.

Hannah remembered her ankle, and scowled. Levering herself to sit on the edge of the bed, she gingerly placed both feet on the floor. And felt nothing. No pain.

Lifting her injured foot, Hannah was startled to see that the brace Dr. Braithwaite had put on had somehow vanished: She looked on the bed, but it was nowhere to be found. Puzzled, she reached down for her crutches, but they were no longer by the bedside. So she held onto one of the bedposts, and carefully raised herself to her feet. Her ankle felt fine. She did a little dance just to make sure.

Now Hannah whooped, punched the air, and cried, "It's a miracle! I'm healed!" She dashed downstairs to tell Alex. But he wasn't home. He had gone to Snipesville to meet up with Brandon.

****

Alex and Brandon were on their way from the sandwich shop on Main Street to Brandon's family's funeral home, Clark and Sons Home of Eternal Rest, Inc. They planned to walk the neighborhood together asking people to sign the petition to save the park, but first Brandon had to deliver lunch to his dad. He also needed permission to use the copier in the office to print out the petition. It was always better to ask for such favors when his dad was there, because if Brandon asked his scary Aunt Marcia (or Morticia, as he secretly called her) her answer was guaranteed to be no.

"I've never visited a funeral home before," Alex said, with an excited shiver. "It's kind of creepy, isn't it?"

Brandon shrugged. "Not to me."

In fact, Brandon avoided the family funeral home whenever possible. Not because it creeped him out, but because he was afraid that if he appeared to take any interest at all in the business, everyone in the family would assume he wanted to inherit it one day. That was a terrifying thought.

"Cool building," said Alex as they climbed the wooden steps of the old white house to the wrap-around porch.

"Yeah, thanks," said Brandon. "Most of it's about a hundred years old. Dad and Uncle Sam only bought it a few years ago. Before that, we worked out of that place over there for about forty years." He pointed to an empty squat cinderblock building on the other side of the park.

"Wow, quite a step up," said Alex. "You guys must be pretty successful. Are more people dying, or what?"

"Yes, they are," said Brandon as he opened the door. "A lot of people moved to Snipesville in the past few years, most of them retired folks. They don't live very long."

Just inside the doorway hung a large portrait of a seated gracious-looking black woman smiling sweetly, and a man standing solemnly behind her, with one hand on her shoulder. "Who's that?" Alex asked.

Brandon looked up respectfully at the portrait. "That's my grandparents. They retired from the home, and they live next door."

Alex scrutinized the picture. "Your grandma looks like a nice old lady, but, no offense, your grandpa looks kind of scary."

Brandon laughed. "Other way round, man. Don't trust appearances, Alex. Grandpa is pretty cool. But Grandma, well, don't get me wrong or anything, she's not mean, but I would put her in the same class as Mrs. D. You don't mess with Grandma."

As Alex followed Brandon down the hallway, he inhaled the gentle fragrance of air freshener, and took note of how opulent it all seemed, especially when the neighborhood was so poor. The beige carpet looked brand new, and the walls were lined with antique furnishings, including an ancient organ. "Does that thing work?" asked Alex.

Brandon nodded and said in a whisper, "Aunt Morticia, I mean, Aunt Marcia, plays it. She always plays depressing stuff."

"Where are the dead bodies?" Alex suddenly asked.

Brandon pointed to the double doors ahead of them and smiled. "Straight through there," he said.

Just inside, Alex paused in front of a chalkboard on which someone had written a couple of Bible verses and the stern admonition that *This is a Christian business, and we are here to serve, whether or not our customers can afford to pay.*

"That's kind of crazy," said Alex, gesturing to the sign. "How do you guys make a profit?" He immediately regretted saying it.

"It's not about profits," Brandon said heatedly. "Uncle Sam is the only one who makes a living here, and no way is he getting rich. My aunt's part-time, and my dad helps out when he can. It's just what they do. Kind of like Mr. Gordon in Balesworth. He wasn't in dentistry for the money. He sometimes fixed people's teeth without charging them."

Alex felt sheepish. "Sorry."

"It's okay," Brandon said, patting his friend on the shoulder. "I'm sorry too. I shouldn't have lost it. I just get so tired of people thinking that everybody does everything for money. You know, the funeral home does all right, but it's not like anyone in the family takes fancy vacations or buys big cars... Well, we buy the hearses, of course, but they don't count, because they're only used for funerals. Anyway," he opened the door to the left, "this is the embalming room, where we get the bodies ready for burial."

"Are we allowed in here?" Alex asked uncertainly.

"I think so," said Brandon, a little less confident now. "Do you want to look or not?"

"Um, sure," Alex said, hoping he wouldn't regret it.

The embalming room was a disappointment. It didn't smell of death or pickled frogs, as Alex had expected, but of bleach. It didn't look like a dungeon, as he had secretly hoped, but like a kitchen, with sinks and cabinets. There wasn't a corpse in sight. A long sloping table sat in the middle of the room.

"Is that where they put the bodies?" he asked, pointing to the table. Brandon nodded.

Alex pointed to what looked like a round fish tank on the counter. "And what's that?"

"That's for the embalming fluid. They pipe the stuff into the deceased through those tubes. It stops the body from decomposing."

Just then, the door was flung open. The flinger was Brandon's Aunt Marcia, the funeral home's business manager and receptionist. She scowled at Alex and Brandon. "What are you boys doing here?" She didn't wait for an answer. "Brandon, I want you and your little friend out of here," she snapped. "Right now." She normally looked sour, but Brandon thought that, this morning, she looked like she had drunk a pint of pickle juice.

He knew better than to argue. "Yes, ma'am. Just brought Alex to show him around. I've got Dad's lunch. He's here, right?"

Aunt Morticia jerked her head backward toward the office and grunted.

When Brandon and Alex arrived in Mr. Clark's office, he was peering at a spreadsheet on his computer. He glanced up as he heard them in the doorway, then turned and eagerly clasped his hands on his desk. Usually, Mr. Clark worked across town at his own business, Gordon Clark and Son Insurance of Snipesville. But since Uncle Sam's heart attack, he had been running the funeral home part-time while his brother recovered.

"Hey, boys, how're you doing?" He gave the boys a big smile, his eye firmly fixed on the Jiffy Subs sandwich bag that Brandon was holding. "What do you have for me?"

In reply, Brandon gave him the bag, and he began rustling happily through the contents. "Italian special with extra salami, right?"

"No," Brandon said apologetically. "Sorry, Dad. Mom told me to get you the veggie delight on whole wheat, no mayo. And that's not Coke, it's water. Extra lemon slice and chewy ice." Brandon's mom was a nurse, and she kept the entire family in line: When Brandon's dad was diagnosed with high blood pressure, she had immediately put him on a strict diet.

Mr. Clark unwrapped his sandwich, contemplated it for a moment, and then pulled a face. "I guess it'll do me good," he said, grimacing, and took a large bite. As he chewed, he looked like a camel with bellyache. Through a mouthful of sandwich he said, "You two all set for your adventure? Pretty exciting, huh?"

"I guess we are," Alex said. He hadn't really thought of the petition drive as an adventure, but he supposed it was.

Mr. Clark laughed. "I figured you guys would be more excited than this!"

Now Brandon was looking at his father in absolute confusion. "Dad, are you talking about the petition?"

Mr. Clark, who had been about to take another bite of sandwich, paused. "What petition?"

"To save the park." Brandon said.

But Mr. Clark shook his head. "A petition? Who put you up to that? Seems kind of like jumping the gun to me. The council doesn't even vote on the park proposal until next month."

The boys exchanged puzzled looks, and Brandon opened his mouth to point out that the council had approved the project just last night. But Mr. Clark had moved on. "Anyway, I'm talking about England, dummy. You're going to England tomorrow with Alex and Hannah, remember? Lucky you." He took a sip of his water.

Brandon and Alex were now totally confused. Brandon said, "But their England trip was cancelled. Remember I told you yesterday about Hannah's ankle? And anyway, since when was I supposed to go with them?"

But now Mr. Clark was annoyed with his son. "Is this some joke? Brandon, this isn't funny. It's just irritating. Go on with you now."

It was a bizarre conversation, and Brandon was deeply embarrassed. Was the old man's diet giving him hallucinations?

Hannah, meanwhile, paced about the living room in total frustration. She had tried to reach her dad about five times on his cell phone, but there was no answer. When she finally called his office, his secretary, LaRinda, told Hannah that her dad was in a meeting and couldn't be disturbed.

"But it's an emergency!" Hannah protested.

"What's happened, honey?" LaRinda asked.

"My ankle, it's better!" Hannah cried.

LaRinda informed her that a healthy ankle did not count as an emergency.

When Hannah's cell phone finally rang, she snatched it off the coffee table. It wasn't her dad: It was her Grandma Ellen. Of course! Why hadn't she thought to call Grandma before?

"Grandma!" Hannah yelled excitedly. "My ankle's fine! We can go to London!"

"Hi, sweetheart. I'm sorry, I can't hear you too well. This is a terrible connection. Look, I'm just calling from the airport to let you guys know that Grandpa and I are about to board our flight to Atlanta. How are you? Are you excited yet?"

"You guys decided to come anyway?" Hannah was baffled.

Grandma's tone now grew very serious. "Come on, honey, joke over. Don't be obnoxious. By the way, we heard from your friend Dr. Braithwaite, and he put us in touch with his friends near London. They're going to have us over for tea. Won't that be exciting, to visit real English people in their home?"

Hannah suddenly got chills. "Grandma, what are his friends called?"

"Let's see… Their name is Powell. Verity and Eric Powell."

Verity and Eric: Hannah and Alex's best friends in World War Two England. How had Dr. Braithwaite arranged this so fast? Why had Grandma forgotten that the trip had been cancelled?

Hannah's head was spinning. Just then, she heard the call waiting beep. It was her Dad. She promised to call Grandma back, switched to the other line, and took a deep breath. "Dad, I think Grandma has finally lost it. She says her and Grandpa are on their way from Sacramento, and they're taking me and Alex to England tomorrow. But you know what else is weird? My ankle's okay. It's like it was never hurt."

Mr. Dias sounded distracted. "What are you talking about, Hannah? Since when was something wrong with your ankle? Look, make sure you finish packing before your grandparents get here. And could you call Alex and find out if Brandon's passport arrived yet?"

Now Hannah was completely confused. "Brandon's going with us?"

"Of course he is," said her dad, half-listening, "Why are you being so difficult? Look, I have to go. I have to fetch Alex. Don't worry about the passport thing. I'll call Brandon's dad. Bye for now." And then he hung up.

Twenty minutes later, Alex raced through the front door, and Hannah ran up the hallway to meet him. Simultaneously, they yelled at each other, "YOU'RE NOT GONNA BELIEVE…" and then both of them stopped in their tracks.

"You first," said Alex. "Whoa, what happened to your ankle?"

Hannah told him the story of her miraculously healed ankle, and of her bizarre phone conversations with her dad and grandmother. She saved the strangest part for last: "She even said we were bringing Brandon. I don't think we've ever mentioned Brandon to her. It's too weird. And Dad thinks Brandon's coming with us."

Then it was Alex's turn. He was telling Hannah about the conversation with Brandon's dad, when he saw that his sister's hands were shaking as she anxiously ran her fingers through her long hair. "Come on, Hannah," he said gently. "Come sit down."

Alex took her by the hand and led her down the hall to the living room, where he persuaded her to sit on the sofa. He switched on the TV, hoping to make the day seem normal. But then he saw that the date on the screen was July 12. When he flipped channels, it was the same thing. As Hannah sat silently, Alex ran to the computer in the den and switched it on, only to see "July 12" on the desktop. He logged on… And there it was… July 12… All over the web.

"No," he whispered to himself. "Today is August 17… It's August."

When Alex returned to the living room, he broke the news to Hannah, who was looking very young and very lost. In a small voice, she said, "I thought that if we, like, stayed away from the college, the weirdness wouldn't happen again… Alex, I am so scared."

"Me, too," admitted her brother, "and when I left Brandon, he was pretty freaked as well. I think we'd better call him and tell him what Grandma said. I guess the only good thing about all this is we get to go to England after all, and see Eric and Verity."

"Yeah," said Hannah doubtfully, "but they'll be old people. That's different. I can't imagine Verity as a wrinkly old lady. What will I say to her?"

Before Alex could reply, there was a loud knock on the front door, and he went to answer it. "May I come in?" asked a flustered woman standing on the doorstep. He recognized her at once: She was not very tall, quite thin, and had a heart-shaped face topped off with grey hair. Professor Kate Harrower was not the most likely-looking of time-travelers.

Alex had barely opened his mouth to greet her when the Professor ran down the hall and into the living room.

Chapter 2:
THE MORE THINGS CHANGE

As soon as Hannah clapped eyes on the Professor, she jumped to her feet and exploded in fury. "Get out of our house! How do you even know where we live?"

The Professor ignored Hannah's outburst. She looked very worried as she dropped her purse on the sofa, and shifted uneasily from foot to foot. "Hannah, I just came to ask if everything is okay. Does anything seem different to you?"

"Different!?!" shouted Hannah.

Alex, who was standing behind the Professor, spoke up. "Yeah, you could say that things are kind of different. Hannah twisted her ankle yesterday, and our trip to England with our grandparents got cancelled. Then, this morning, it's like none of that even happened, our grandparents are on their way from California, and now we find out that Brandon's coming with us to London, even though this was news to all of us...."

"AND IT'S JULY AGAIN!" Hannah screamed, making the Professor stagger backward.

Alex added calmly, "Yeah, that too. Can you explain?"

"Oh, dear," said the Professor, grimacing. "I was afraid of this."

"So what, exactly, do you have to do with it?" demanded Hannah, crossing her arms.

"Me? Nothing. Nothing at all." She didn't sound convincing. In fact, she sounded a bit guilty. "Look, I've been wondering if either of you has come across my pocket calculator? It's quite an old one. It's metal, and it has..."

Hannah was about to spontaneously combust. She was so angry, she could barely speak. "Weird stuff is happening, time just went backwards, and you're worried about a crappy old calculator?"

The Professor looked uncomfortable and tried to sound casual. "Well, not particularly... But if it should turn up, could you take good care of it, please? It's a bit fragile, practically an antique really. Try not to damage it. I'm sure it will turn up. Don't worry."

"We won't," Hannah spat.

CHAPTER TWO

As the Professor retreated up the hall under Hannah's stony stare, she said, "Hopefully, Time will right itself soon. I'm just as concerned as you are about what's happening, believe me. And do keep an eye out for my calculator."

Hannah, as Alex later explained to Brandon, used a bad word in reply. But by then, the Professor had already closed the door and fled.

****

The journey from Snipesville to Savannah Airport normally took almost an hour, but at the speed that Alex and Hannah's grandfather drove, it was more like twenty minutes. Grandma spent a lot of time with her fingers pressed against the dashboard, fussing at Grandpa to slow down. Brandon and Alex crouched anxiously in the back seat of the rented minivan, behind Hannah, who spent most of her time silently staring out of the window.

As the traffic slowed on the freeway a few miles from the airport, Grandma turned to the kids. "You guys are quiet. Anyone would think we're taking you to school, not to England. You aren't nervous about flying, are you?"

Brandon thought he should be polite. "Yes, ma'am. Kind of. I've never been to an airport before."

"Well, I'm not surprised to hear that. It is an expensive way to travel," Grandma said.

"Oh, it's not just the money. It's just that mom and dad don't have much time, and Mom says that Snipes County is God's Country, so why would we want to go anywhere else?"

Grandma looked doubtfully at Brandon in her rear view mirror. "Well, that's one way to look at things, I guess. But how do you feel about it?"

Brandon smiled. "I'm excited. It will be so cool to see England again."

Grandma exclaimed, "Again?"

When Alex dug him in the ribs, Brandon realized what he had said, and he added quickly, "I mean, after watching it on TV and stuff."

Soon after they arrived in London, Alex began to feel like he had flu. Grandma said it was jet lag, and she prescribed lots of walking outdoors. Grandpa, meanwhile, had other plans, which involved visiting an insanely long list of attractions, starting immediately. Alex and Brandon soon found themselves on what seemed like a death march around a bunch of dusty museums. Alex envied his sister: Hannah had pouted and demanded to go shopping instead, and, as usual, got her way, while the boys set off for their Educational Experience.

First up was the Science Museum. Grandpa desperately wanted to see the displays on the history of computers, and he convinced himself that Alex and Brandon were as fascinated as he was. He rushed the boys past some very cool science exhibits to get to his first stop, a complicated mechanical device that was eight feet high and eleven feet long.

"Would you believe that this is the first calculator?" Grandpa said grandly, throwing out an arm toward it. "This is Charles Babbage's Difference Engine."

"Where's the motherboard?" asked Alex, peering through the glass at the cogs and dials.

Grandpa had been hoping for a question like this. "Aha! There isn't one. It's mechanical, works like a clock. Amazing. Wow, look! It says here that this was the second version, designed between 1847 and 1849. Babbage didn't ever finish building it himself: This one was put together at the Museum a few years ago."

While Alex examined the impossibly complicated machine, Brandon wandered off. To Brandon, the Difference Engine, with its hundreds of cogs, just looked like machinery, and that wasn't interesting. Meanwhile, Grandpa had moved to the next machine, and he kept on talking, having completely failed to notice that he had lost Brandon's attention. "Now, here's a model of Babbage's analytical engine. This was the very first computer, and it used punch cards instead of disks, but, again, it was never built in his lifetime..."

"Oh, gross!" gasped Brandon. He had found something much more interesting than Charles Babbage's machines. He had found Charles Babbage's brain. Pickled in a jar.

"Why'd they put his brain in a bottle?" Brandon asked breathlessly.

Grandpa peered at the exhibit label. "Says here that the Victorians thought you could learn a lot by dissecting the brains of geniuses."

"Weird. And what's a Victorian, anyway?" asked Alex. "I've always kind of wondered about that."

Now Brandon perked up. He liked history. "Those were the people who lived in the reign of Queen Victoria," he said promptly. "She became Queen in 1837."

Grandpa was impressed with his grandson's friend. "You know your history, Brandon! Good for you. Now, tell you what, guys, let's go look at something more modern. The first Apple computer is right over there." He began to move in the direction of his pointing finger.

"Cheat," Alex whispered to Brandon as they followed. "It's easy for you to remember Victoria, because she was still Queen when you were living in Balesworth."

"She was not, you moron," Brandon protested. "She'd been dead for fourteen years by then!"

"Well, close enough," laughed Alex.

At lunchtime, Grandpa took the boys to a hamburger place. Alex was disappointed. "Hey, next time, can we go get some shepherd's pie, or some sausage rolls?" he asked Grandpa, "You know, real English food?"

"You really wanna eat that stuff?" Grandpa asked with eyebrows raised. "The Brits aren't exactly known for good food."

"That's not fair, sir," Brandon said. "Their food is very good, once you get used to it."

Grandpa looked at Brandon, wondering how on earth he would know. "Okay, if you say so… Maybe some other day we could try their traditional fish and chips. Now, we gotta hurry. Our next stop is Madame Tussaud's Wax Museum."

The boys glanced at each other and then scrunched up their faces in dismay. "Grandpa, what's that?" Alex asked.

"More fun than it sounds," Grandpa said, picking up his umbrella. "You'll see."

Madame Tussaud's Wax Museum, housed in an impressively large stone building, turned out to be pretty cool. Grandpa took pictures of the boys as they posed with the uncannily life-like models of their favorite celebrities. Alex and Brandon grossed themselves out in the Chamber of Horrors, with its gory scenes of torture and execution, and marveled at the wax rendition of the death of a man from the French Revolution called Marat, who had been murdered in his bath. A pale-faced wax Marat lay in the tub with a big knife in his chest.

"This is awesome!" said Alex as they took a ride in a fake black taxi cab through scenes from London's history, and Brandon agreed happily. Their car paused briefly in front of the Great Fire of London, which Alex said was almost as good as Disneyland. But both Alex and Brandon fell silent as they reached the display on World War Two. They were immersed in a confused jumble of sound that was dominated by the wail of an air raid siren and the gravelly voice of Winston Churchill, Britain's wartime prime minister. Brandon pointed to a wax model of Churchill, and said quietly, "Man, that looks just like him."

Grandpa, sitting behind them, agreed that it was a great likeness. Of course, Grandpa could never have suspected that Brandon recognized Churchill because he had met him in person.

As Alex listened to Churchill's words, he felt as though he had been thrust back to 1940, and that he was sitting happily in Mrs. Devenish's drawing room with a mug of cocoa, listening to one of the Prime Minister's broadcasts. He felt his eyes get moist, and he turned away so his grandfather and his friend wouldn't see him choke up.

****

Hannah, meanwhile, was shopping. She hadn't been shopping –really shopping--since she had moved from California to Georgia. Snipesville's tiny "Small" hardly counted: It was the lamest so-called mall ever, and its only clothing store for teens, The Boiled Peanut, was pathetic. So when Grandma proposed a shopping expedition in London, Hannah jumped at the chance.

"This is so totally exciting," Hannah gushed as she walked along Regent Street with Grandma, each of them carrying department store bags. "It's cool to be somewhere where people are into serious shopping… I bet the English had a blast when the War ended."

Grandma looked oddly at her for a second: Hannah had never shown any interest in history before. "Actually, honey, I believe they had a pretty hard time for years after the War, so I don't imagine they went on a spending spree right away." She pulled out her map of central London and examined it closely, then pointed toward a side street. "Hannah, let's go this way. It takes us over to Piccadilly."

Hannah perked up even more. "Is that another cool department store?"

Grandma smiled. "No, honey, it's a street, but it's where we'll find Fortnum and Mason. That's the Royal Family's grocery store."

Hannah shrugged and pulled a face. It sounded boring. Then again, she thought, she might run into one of the handsome princes pushing a cart in the aisles. How cool would that be?

When they reached Fortnum and Mason's, a doorman in a smart blue military-style uniform held open the door for them, much to Grandma's delight. Hannah followed Grandma into the store but, once inside, she came immediately to a screeching halt.

Fortnum and Mason's Food Hall was luxurious. It was actually carpeted, in plush red. The walls were painted a delicate cream color. Huge glittering chandeliers hung from the ceiling.

Hannah gazed on the scene in disbelief. "This is a supermarket?"

But Grandma didn't answer. She had already grabbed a basket, and was loading up with expensive jars of strawberry and champagne preserves. While Hannah waited for her, she glanced around and found that she was standing by an enormous and ancient wooden clock. There was a tiny slot in its side, next to which was a label: *Plays Tunes, 50p.*

Hannah tapped her grandmother's shoulder, and pointed to the sign. "Fifty pounds to play a tune? Wow, prices went up."

"No, dear, that's not pounds. It's pence."

Hannah screwed up her face. "I thought pence was written as 'd.?'"

Grandma was impressed. "How did you know that? Well, it used to be, but that was a long time ago, before England adopted decimal currency, and got rid of shillings. Now, would you like the clock to play some music for you?"

Hannah nodded, and so Grandma gave her a fifty pence coin, which she popped in the slot. When the music began, Grandma recognized the tune, and burst out laughing. She tugged at Hannah's sleeve. "Hannah, it's *Dixie*! They're playing *Dixie* for you!"

Hannah drew a blank. "Huh?"

"*Dixie*! Haven't you ever heard this in Georgia? Oh, for heaven's sake… It's a sort of Southern theme tune." To Hannah's intense embarrassment, Grandma began to sing: "Oh, I wish I was in the land of cotton, old times there are not forgotten…"

"Actually," said a voice from behind them, "the clock plays many tunes, so it's quite a coincidence that it would play this particular selection. May I help you find something, madam?"

The woman wore a smartly-pressed black and white staff uniform with green tie. But Hannah knew straightaway that she wasn't employed by Fortnum and Mason. She was the Professor.

Hannah hissed, "Go away!"

"Hannah, that's rude!" exclaimed Grandma, turning to her in surprise.

The Professor was unfazed. She waved aside Grandma's concern, and urged her to sample the violet creams at the chocolate counter, which Grandma was happy to do. Then the Professor took Hannah aside. "I have a confession," she said urgently in a low voice. "I made a huge mistake, and that's why you must find the calculator. I don't think it's a coincidence that the clock played Dixie. I think that's Time trying to right itself somehow. It's telling us something."

"You are totally creeping me out," Hannah snarled. "Just go away and leave me alone."

The Professor shook her head in despair as Hannah stalked off to join her grandmother at the candy display. Hannah, meanwhile, was shaking, and when another assistant offered her a chocolate sample, she stared at her without seeing or hearing. All Hannah could think was, why me?

The three kids did their best to enjoy London, despite the unnerving feeling they shared that something was very wrong, especially after Hannah told the boys of her bizarre encounter with the Professor. They took a ride on the huge Ferris wheel called the London Eye, witnessed the changing of the guard at Buckingham Palace, and uncomplainingly made more museum visits than they could possibly absorb.

Three days after they arrived, it was time for their trip to Balesworth to visit Verity and Eric, whom they had last seen in 1940.

The kids were already anxious as they climbed out of the large black taxi at Kings Cross Station. After Grandpa bought tickets, they checked the departures board for the next train to Balesworth, and, as Harry Potter fans, were delighted to realize that their train was due to leave from Platform 9. Alex won in the frantic race to be first to pose at the Platform 9 3/4 photo point, and he pretended to push a luggage trolley through the wall as his grandfather snapped his picture. Hannah and Brandon waited impatiently for their turns.

Afterward, they all settled into the first-class compartment at the rear of the small commuter train. Brandon talked nonstop at Grandpa about Harry Potter and the sad demise of steam engines. Meanwhile, Hannah repeatedly flicked her hair, wrinkled her nose at the smell of the engine, and brushed at real and imagined dirt on the seat. Alex tapped his foot rapidly on the floor.

"I don't think much of first-class travel," sniffed Grandma, glancing disdainfully around the tiny compartment. Indeed, their seating area hardly seemed different from the regular seats that they could glimpse through the glass doors. The major difference was the warning signs plastered to the windows advising that anyone sitting in first class who did not hold a first-class ticket might be fined. Brandon wistfully remembered railway travel in 1915 and 1940: The plush seating, small private compartments lining the narrow corridor, and the reassuring chuffing of the steam engine. Now, the experience was modern, and much bleaker: Narrow upright seats were crammed together in tight rows on either side of an open middle aisle, like an airplane.

Just as the engine started up, the automatic doors to the first-class compartment swooshed open. A youngish man in a sharp black suit barged in, and threw himself into the only remaining first-class seat, facing Alex and Hannah. He immediately took occupancy of the table that lay between him and the kids, thumping down his briefcase, and opening up his laptop, even as he fumbled with the cell phone that he held under his chin.

He spoke quickly. "Baz? Yeah, hi, it's me. I'm on the train now, and I should be there about…oh, half an hour, I reckon. Did you get the plans copied? Great, great… Now, look, I won't hang about, got a bit of a personal errand this afternoon…Yeah…but I'll touch base round half past four, yeah? Okay then….Yeah… Cheers."

He hung up, and started tapping away on his laptop.

Alex was fascinated, and stared at the man, who caught him watching.

"God," said the man through clenched teeth. "Look, don't you kiddies belong in the cheap seats? These seats are reserved for first-class passengers."

Suddenly, Alex became aware of his grandfather standing next to him. "Is there a problem?" asked Grandpa, staring down at the man, in a tone that suggested there had better not be a problem.

The man stared right back at him, and said firmly, "This is first class."

"Yes," said Grandpa gravely. "That's right. And your point would be?"

The man sighed heavily, and went back to his laptop, punching furiously at the keypad. Grandpa patted Alex on the shoulder. Just as he returned to his seat, the door slid open, and in walked a short man in his forties with graying blond hair. He was wearing a nametag that said E. Veeriswamy. Calling out,"Tickets, please! All tickets," he waved a small metal ticket punch.

Grandma immediately pulled the tickets out of her purse and offered them for inspection. "Veeriswamy. That's an interesting name. Indian, isn't it? But you're not Indian, are you?"

"No, madam, but one of my ancestors was," said Mr. Veeriswamy as he punched the tickets. "He was from the Punjab, and he was a butler at Balesworth Hall about a hundred and fifty years ago. I'm rather proud of that."

"Oh, how thrilling!" Grandma said. "Did he ever meet Queen Victoria?"

As Mr. Veeriswamy was chatting with Grandma, Alex and Hannah's rude seatmate hastily packed up his briefcase, and made to leave. In a flash, Mr. Veeriswamy blocked the aisle and politely asked for his ticket.

The man was not pleased. "Look, I haven't got time for this rubbish. I have to get off at this station."

But Mr. Veeriswamy wasn't moving. "We won't be arriving in Welwyn for another five minutes. Your ticket, please."

Reluctantly, the man pulled out a ticket, and handed it over. The ticket inspector was not impressed. "This is a standard railpass, sir. It's not applicable for travel in a first-class compartment."

Alex looked at Hannah, and they both smirked. The man grew flustered. "Yes, well, I paid good money for it, and there weren't any seats in standard. I'll have you know that I have asthma."

"I'm sorry to hear that, sir, but as I'm sure you know, this ticket isn't valid."

The man exploded. "Listen to me, you irritating little jobsworth, do you know who I am?"

"Yes, sir," said Mr. Veeriswamy. "You're a passenger without a first-class ticket. The penalty fare is twenty pounds. Please could I have your name and address?"

****

The angry young man finally left the train at Balesworth, and so did Alex, Brandon, Hannah, Grandma, and Grandpa. Mr. Veeriswamy waved cheerfully to them as the train pulled away.

While Grandma stepped into a cafe on the platform to buy bottled water, the kids gazed around them in dismay. They recognized nothing. Hannah was ready to cry. Alex looked bewildered. Brandon searched in vain for something familiar. "What happened to the railway station?" he said finally, in a dull voice, thinking of the old station that looked like a gingerbread house.

Alex was shaking his head in dismay. "I guess this is the new one," he said. "But is this ugly, or what?"

It certainly was. The new station was a grey block, and it wasn't even new: stains and chips all over the concrete suggested that it had been around for some time. Behind the station sprawled a big box mall that would have looked right at home in California, complete with a McDonalds and a bowling alley. In front of the station ran a busy four-lane road, and a huge white building, like an enormous Lego brick, with *Balesworth Leisure Centre* painted on the side.

"Okay, guys, let's go get a cab," said Grandpa.

"No," said Alex. "Let's walk. I wanna see what they've done to Balesworth."

The kids' last visit to Balesworth had happened around seventy years earlier, when it was still a small town surrounded by fields. It wasn't anymore. It was a city, and much of it seemed made from concrete, just like the station. It was very, very grim. Rising up the gentle hill that had once been farmland were thousands of identical houses, row after row of brick, with the occasional bleak concrete block of apartments among them.

As Grandma asked directions, Grandpa turned to Alex, and was astonished to see tears running down his face. "What's wrong, kiddo? Don't you feel well?"

Alex tensed. What on earth would he say? That he was a time traveler, that all three of them were, that here was once a place that they had lived in and loved, and that it had been destroyed? Not likely. Alex shook his head. "No. I'm just sad. Dr. Braithwaite said this was a beautiful old town when he was a kid. I guess it changed."

"Everything changes, Alex," Grandpa said gently.

"This shouldn't have," Alex shot back.

Grandma rejoined them. "Good job I asked the way. We were headed in the wrong direction. Now we'd better hurry, because they're expecting us. C'mon, guys."

Their journey took them out of the town center, and across a long pedestrian bridge that straddled a busy four-lane highway. As they reached the end, they found themselves at the bottom of a narrow tree-lined road. It took the three kids only a second or two to realize that their Balesworth, the old Balesworth, hadn't vanished after all. Alex and Hannah excitedly pointed to the street ahead. Brandon looked eagerly to a row of large old houses. One was an animal hospital, while another housed a lawyer's office. His eyes lit up, and he looked to the left....But the house where he had lived and worked with Mr. Gordon in 1915 was gone. Where it should have been was now a grassy hill leading down to the highway.

Brandon gasped, and to everyone's astonishment, burst into sobs.

Grandma was alarmed. "What on earth... Brandon, what's wrong? What is with you kids?"

But Brandon was just as quick-thinking as Alex. "I'm okay... Just tired, I guess," he sniffled, taking a tissue from Hannah's outstretched hand.

By now, Alex was already well ahead of everyone, trotting up Balesworth High Street toward the church tower. What he found disorienting was that all the shops had changed: The greengrocer's where he had once queued for potatoes, carrots and apples, was now a cell phone store. The grocer's, where, just weeks earlier, he had stood at the counter with Mrs. Devenish while she sorted through the kids' ration books looking for sugar coupons, was gone: Swallowed up, along with the butcher's shop, by a supermarket. But the bakery was still there, and, if the name was anything to go by, it was still owned by the same family. The church they had all attended in 1940 was still standing.

And then Alex realized to his joy that if he looked up, to the second story of the High Street, it really hadn't changed at all. Most of the buildings were still exactly the same. Only the shops had changed.

As the others caught up with Alex, it became Hannah's turn to hurry. She dashed down an alleyway that ran parallel to the High Street, and finally stopped before a ramshackle and ancient wood-beamed white building. In

1940 it had been the Tudor Tea Rooms. Now, it was a coffee house named Balesworth Brews.

Hannah laughed when she saw the name. "Sweet! Hey, you guys, maybe now I can get a Frappuccino in Balesworth!"

Alex and Brandon got the joke, but Grandma ushered them away. "Come on, you guys. We don't have time for coffee. Mr. and Mrs. Powell are expecting us, and I'm still not sure we're going the right way."

As they neared the top of the High Street, Grandma halted uncertainly, and turned to her husband. "Fred? Do you see a tree-lined path here?"

Grandpa shook his head. Alex and Hannah couldn't help Grandma either: The road ahead looked very different than they remembered: Another four-lane highway lay where once there had been fields, hedges and trees. With a sigh, Grandma pulled out her cell phone. She was about to call when Brandon suddenly announced, "It's this way." He led them to a long footpath lined with horse chestnut trees.

As they walked, gravel crunched under their feet. Brandon smiled at that sound, and his memories of gathering shiny horse chestnuts in 1915 with little Oliver Healdstone, Mr. Gordon's nephew. But his smile vanished as he realized that even little Oliver was surely dead by now.

A hundred yards ahead on the path, a tall woman walked toward them under a dense shade of trees. Hannah's eyes widened when she spotted the bobbing grey head, and her breath caught in her throat. She did a double-take, put her hands to her mouth, and suddenly took off at a run.

Even as Hannah got closer to the woman, she couldn't think. If she had, she would have known that what she wanted to believe made no sense. But she could not, would not think that. The clothes were different, but they would be, wouldn't they? And it could be her, couldn't it, because who knows what the time shift has done...

She hurtled right at the woman who was striding toward her.

And before she knew what she was doing, Hannah was throwing herself at Mrs. Devenish.

Chapter 3:
POLES APART

The woman Hannah was hugging had gone stiff. Maybe she had died from shock? Dead or alive, she wasn't Mrs. Devenish, who had been gone for decades.

Hannah let go, and looked up. Now her thoughts were racing even faster. This woman was Mrs. Devenish. She was a Mrs. D. with lipstick, and modern clothes, and... But she couldn't be. The nose wasn't quite right. Neither was the chin. So who was...?

The not-quite-Mrs. Devenish spoke, looking down in astonishment at Hannah. "Hallo, that's quite a greeting, isn't it? How did recognize me?"

"Um, I, like, just recognized you," Hannah said.

The sort-of Mrs. Devenish looked down in puzzlement at Hannah. "But you've never met me before. How extraordinary... Never mind. I'm Verity Powell."

Hannah felt cold adrenaline shooting down her back. She had known all along that Verity would be an old woman when they met, but she hadn't really understood it, not until now. And in her old age, Verity had become the spitting image of her grandmother, Mrs. Devenish.

Now it was Hannah's turn to start crying.

Grandma was embarrassed. "What in the world... Pleased to meet you, Mrs. Powell. I'm Ellen Walker, and this is my husband Fred. I have no idea what's gotten into these children today. It's been one long weepfest since we left the train."

Verity looked uncomfortable. "Really? Well... Welcome to Balesworth, regardless. I was worried you had got lost, so I thought I ought to come down and meet you. And please, do call me Verity." She smiled, and gestured to them to follow her.

As they walked down the chestnut path, Verity quietly asked Hannah, "Are you all right, dear?" But she didn't wait for an answer before turning back to Grandma. "It must be difficult for them, mustn't it? Jet lag, and a different culture. Now, kids, please tell me your names. George never mentioned them in his letter, which was very remiss of him."

Alex and Brandon were now also trotting alongside Verity, struggling to keep up with this tall old Englishwoman. Alex said, with emphasis, "I'm Alex, this is my sister, Hannah…"

Brandon chimed in. "…And I'm Brandon. But some people call me George." He looked at Verity meaningfully, hoping to trigger her memory. But she kept right on walking, leading her visitors up a dizzying spiral stairway to a pedestrian bridge over the busy highway. After a few seconds pause, she said casually, "I must tell you of a funny coincidence. My grandmother looked after several evacuated children during the War. One of them was my husband Eric, and then there was Dr. George Braithwaite. But for a short time, Granny also cared for a brother and sister called Alex and Hannah, who had a friend called Brandon Braithwaite. He was black, and like you, Brandon, he was known as George for some reason. I forget why, now, but there was a lot of confusion between him and Dr. Braithwaite, as you might imagine. Please tell me your name isn't Braithwaite?"

"No," Brandon admitted. "It's Clark."

"Ah-ha," said Verity. "And those children Granny fostered were English, while you, of course, are Americans, so I don't suppose there's any relationship. An odd coincidence, though, isn't it? No wonder Dr. Braithwaite didn't tell me your names. He probably meant to surprise me."

Alex said brightly, "Speaking of surprises, you won't believe this, but we're the same…"

Hannah clamped a hand over his mouth. "Shut up," she hissed in his ear.

As the children entered Mrs. Devenish's old house, which now belonged to Verity and Eric, they looked eagerly around the hall. The hat stand was still there, laden with coats, scarves, boots and shoes. A phone still sat on the same hallway table, although it wasn't the old heavy black rotary dial, but a modern grey cordless set. All in all, though, the hall hadn't changed much.

"My husband's pottering about in the garden," Verity said, kicking off her shoes. "I'll give him a shout and put the kettle on for tea. Now, why don't you make yourselves at home, and have a seat in the living room?"

"The living room?" blurted out Alex. "Don't you mean the drawing room?"

Verity threw back her head and laughed. "Darling, I have no idea what old films you've been watching, but that's terribly old-fashioned, isn't it? No one talks of drawing rooms these days. Tell you what… Why don't you all join me in the kitchen instead? We can all have a lovely chat about your travels while I make the tea."

The kitchen was practically unrecognizable. Gone was the clunky old black 1940s range for cooking. Gone was the deep white ceramic sink where the kids had once helped Mrs. Devenish to wash the dishes. In their places were a gas stove, a modern double sink, a microwave, and, in the old larder, a refrigerator. Luxury of luxuries, there was even a dishwasher, standing where the fireplace had once been. The only familiar furniture was the huge old wooden kitchen table, which looked even more well-worn than they remembered.

Just as Verity was filling the electric tea kettle, the back door opened, and in stepped a stooped bespectacled old man who was rather shorter than his wife. He smiled politely at everyone as he wiped his shoes on the doormat. Brandon's first thought was that he looked like a friendly turtle, but Hannah and Alex simply gawped as they realized that this was their old pal Eric.

Eric barely glanced at the kids, and introduced himself with handshakes to Grandma and Grandpa. As he spoke, Hannah noticed that he sounded much more posh than in 1940, when he had spoken with a thick London accent. Verity, strangely, sounded much less posh in her old age, both in the words she used and the ways in which she pronounced them.

Verity laid a hand on her husband's arm. "Eric, these children are..."

Hannah interrupted. "Hannah and Alex Day... Er, Dias," she said, correcting herself too late. She had stumbled, giving the last name that she and her brother had somehow acquired in 1940 England. She trailed off: "And this is... Brandon..."

Eric stared, but Verity looked annoyed, and said irritably, "Is this someone's idea of a joke?"

Grandma and Grandpa exchanged quizzical looks. "Excuse me," said Grandpa, "But am I missing something? What's the joke?" Nervously, he laughed. Nobody else did.

Verity was examining Hannah's face –really looking—for the first time. Eric, who appeared stunned, was staring at Alex. Brandon, meanwhile, stood to one side and hoped somebody would recognize him, too. He didn't have long to wait: Quickly, both Eric and Verity's eyes switched to him, and grew very wide.

Without shifting her gaze from Brandon, Verity finally replied to Grandpa's question. "I'm terribly sorry, Fred. No joke. It's just that your grandchildren and their friend bear a striking resemblance to the children Eric and I knew during the War... who had the same names as you three. But who would now be around our age, of course..." She faltered.

Grandpa was none the wiser, but he couldn't think of what to say, and neither could anyone else. There was another awkward silence. Suddenly, Verity turned to Eric, and said, in a tone of forced cheerfulness, "Eric? Why don't you give Fred and Ellen a tour of our garden?"

"Eh?" Eric was still gawping at the kids. "Oh. Right. All right. Should I take the children too?"

Verity gave him a very significant look that clearly meant "No. Get a clue."

As soon as the adults were safely outside, Verity dashed upstairs, and, moments later, returned holding a photograph. As the children gathered around her, she looked at them all again, her eyes flitting between each kid and the picture. Finally, in a calm, quiet voice, she asked, "Are you the grandchildren of the kids we knew?"

Alex decided that his moment to speak up had arrived. "Verity, it's really me," he said flatly. "I'm Alex."

Verity shook her head in disbelief, and sank into a kitchen chair. "That's impossible," she said.

"Yes, I know," said Alex, sitting next to her, as Hannah and Brandon took their places across the table. "But it's still true."

Verity briefly rested her chin on the heel of her hand, not sure what to say next. "You're American," she continued stubbornly. "Those children were English."

Brandon said, "We all sounded English to everyone in Britain, except to each other. We don't know why, but we did. It just kind of came with the time travel."

Verity's eyebrows shot up at the words "time travel."

Alex realized that, to convince Verity that they were who they claimed to be, they needed to tell her something that only they would know. He took a deep breath. "Verity, the day Mrs. D. whipped you and Hannah and Eric because you broke Mrs. Smith's window, I wasn't there because I had a cold."

Verity muttered, "That's absurd." But she didn't sound quite so sure.

"We know that," said Brandon. "We know it's crazy. But it still happened."

"Verity?" Hannah said. "Here's something else. We shared a room. That's how I know you have a birthmark on your…"

"Yes, well, that's quite enough," Verity interrupted. "Go on, then. Tell me who you really are."

In a rush, Alex told her the whole story from the very beginning, starting with their move from San Francisco to Snipesville and their meeting with Brandon, and finishing with the story of Hannah's ankle, the shift in time, the reinstated vacation, and the addition of Balesworth to the itinerary.

Alex added, "I mean, it's great to see you and all, but it's totally freaking us out that we're here."

Verity exhaled sharply. "What do you have to say, Hannah?"

Hannah couldn't take her eyes off Verity. In awe, she said, "You so look like Mrs. D."

Verity gave a small smile. "Yes, I do look like Granny. So does my daughter. So did my mother, come to that. This face runs in the family, I'm afraid."

Hannah considered further. "But you have a different accent from her. Your accent even sounds different from the one you used to have."

"Oh, I'm sure it does," Verity said. "That's no miracle. We all sound a bit less posh in England these days. Well, except Eric, of course, who sounds more posh than he did as a child. I blame Granny for that. She was always correcting his accent, as you'll remember…" Suddenly, she gave a cry that sounded halfway between laughter and weeping. "Oh, it's hard to take this in…"

"Tell me about it," said Hannah, smiling at her old friend who was now her *old* friend. She felt incredibly torn: It was wonderful to see Verity and feel as though Mrs. D. had returned from the dead, only as a relaxed and modern person. But Hannah also knew that she had lost forever the Verity of 1940. Then she saw Verity looking at her with…Was that love? It was. Hannah felt a lump form in her throat.

Verity asked gently, "Do your grandparents know about this?"

"No, they don't," Alex said, "They would think we were all insane."

Verity slapped a hand onto the table. "Right then, everyone. We had better keep quiet. But let's see if we can't extend this reunion, shall we? Come on, Hannah, help me take the tea through to the living room."

Alex ran a hand across the microwave door, and asked Verity, "What do you think Mrs. D. would have thought of all this new technology?"

Verity lifted the tea tray. "Alex, I know exactly what she thought, because she told me. In fact, I can just hear her saying it now…" She gave a perfect imitation of Mrs. D's voice: "You must have spent a fortune on all these gadgets."

Alex grinned.

While Verity plotted with the kids to persuade Grandma and Grandpa to leave them in Balesworth for a few days, she set out tea in chipped mugs, and cookies in a plastic package.

"Mrs. D. would be shocked," Alex muttered with a smirk as he waved a finger at her offering.

Verity smiled ruefully. "Too right, Alex. She must be rolling in her grave. Teabag tea without proper cups or saucers, and supermarket biscuits! Not Granny's style at all. In fact, most things today wouldn't be Granny's style. What a mess this country is in." She gave a heavy sigh.

"Mrs. D…" began Hannah, and then she blushed. "Sorry, I mean, Verity… Like, what happened to Balesworth?"

"I suppose you mean the New Town," Verity said. "Well, not quite so new anymore. Our Balesworth is called the Old Town. The Government built so-called New Towns after the War, to house people who had been bombed out of their homes in London. Granny was very torn about it. Don't get me wrong: She was all for modern housing for working-class people, and she thought New Towns were a splendid idea. She just didn't want one in her own back yard. I thought she was a terrible old hypocrite, and I told her so."

"Uh-oh," chorused the kids, before dissolving into giggles. They could well imagine how the formidable Mrs. D. reacted to Verity's remark.

"Quite," said Verity with a chuckle. "She tried to clobber me. But by then I'd learnt how to duck."

The kids laughed, and then Verity continued thoughtfully, "Now, I'm not so sure she was wrong. The New Town is a rough place these days. We had a burglar alarm put in after we were broken into a few years ago. But the town keeps growing, with no regard for what it gobbles up. The council agrees to any development at all, regardless of what it destroys. It looks as though we're the next to be gobbled. We've been told that all the fields around this house will be new houses before long, and the best we can expect is that the council will require us to sell this house to the developers, so it can be demolished. We tried arguing that it should be a listed building, that it should be preserved because it's so old, but it didn't work. The house has been altered too much over the centuries."

Before Alex had a chance to ask her to explain further, his grandparents and Eric returned.

Grandma looked very concerned. "That's a beautiful view of the fields and woodland from your backyard, Verity. But Eric tells us that there are plans to develop that gorgeous landscape, and that you may even lose your home. Is that right?"

"I'm afraid it is," said Verity. "I was just telling the children about it. It's too sad."

"You can say that again," said Eric. "That Mr. Pole," he drew out the name with distaste, "That Mr. Pole the builder and his greedy friends have made a fortune putting up nasty overpriced poorly-built little houses, and they'll stop at nothing. Bunch of shysters, that's what they are."

"Eric!" Verity sounded shocked.

"I'm not ashamed to say it," said Eric firmly. "That young man ought to have more respect. And, anyway, this is an historic house, I'll have you know. Henry Watson once lived in this house."

The Americans gave him blank looks. Eric explained. "He was a famous Victorian writer. He wrote *A Hertfordshire Lad*, and *Notes From Balesworth*."

More blank looks.

Verity said bluntly, "He was amazingly boring. Reading his books is an old English cure for sleeplessness."

"Anyway," Eric persisted, "whatever his merits as an author, or lack thereof, he's very well known in Balesworth. A group of us tried to persuade the council to make a country park out of the land that lies between here and Balesworth Hall, because this area is so closely associated with Henry Watson … But they wouldn't buy it." He shook his head in disgust.

Verity explained. "The trouble is, we can't prove that Henry Watson was born here. It's just an old story Granny said she heard once. Mummy always said it was nonsense. She told me that Watson was born and grew up in Balesworth Hall, where his mother was the cook. So that's that."

At that moment, the doorbell rang. When Verity returned with the visitor, it was the awful man from the train who had cheated on his rail ticket.

Verity shifted awkwardly. "Everyone? This is our son, Mark."

Eric looked away, clearing his throat. When Grandma and Grandpa saw who it was, they looked very embarrassed.

"Hallo," said the newcomer, extending a confident hand to Grandpa. "I'm Marc Pole. That's Marc with a 'c'"

"He's the yuppie formerly known as plain old Mark with a 'k'," grumbled Eric, "and that's Pole spelled P-O-W-E-L-L. Sorry we didn't pronounce it trendily enough for you."

"My dad has quite a sense of humor," said Marc without smiling, and then, more loudly, "Isn't that right, Dad?"

"I'm not deaf," Eric said defensively.

Marc gave him a condescending smile. "No, of course you're not."

Marc tactfully pretended not to recognize Grandpa, Grandma and the kids. "Great to meet you. So, first time across the pond, yeah? Well, I hope you won't be disappointed. England's not all tea, the Queen, and old country houses. I think you'll find that the UK is a modern nation these days. We're a center of global commerce, with state of the art communications and a high-tech…"

Verity snorted. "Honestly, Mark, I don't think we need all the jargon, do you? Are you staying for supper?"

Marc glanced at his very expensive watch. "Sorry, Mum. I've got a meeting this evening, so I'll probably just grab a McDonald's."

Verity bridled at the suggestion. "You'll do no such thing. At least let me make you something to eat."

But Marc wasn't enthusiastic. "Heat me up one of your ready-made supermarket meals in the microwave, you mean? No thanks, Mother." He laughed at her. Alex disliked this man more than ever, and one look at his sister and Brandon confirmed that they felt exactly the same way.

Eric said triumphantly, "Don't think that I don't know you're up to your ears in this development lark. You don't think we're letting you ruin this area without a protest, do you?"

Marc looked pained. "Look, Dad, you and Mum will be offered a lot of money for the house. Why don't you just buy yourselves a nice little cottage out in the country? You're always complaining about the crime in Balesworth."

Eric bristled. "It's nothing to do with money. This is our home. You haven't given any of us the least consideration, not us nor your sister. Lizzie remembers Granny, too, you know."

Marc was visibly irritated now. "Well, I'm sorry, but the old dear's not really relevant, is she, not when she's been dead and buried for decades?"

"More's the pity," said Eric heatedly. "She always said you would be trouble. If she'd been younger when you were a kid, she would have straightened you out with a bloody good hiding. Like I should have done when I had the chance."

Suddenly Alex blurted out, "Mrs. D. wouldn't have wanted this, all you guys fighting."

Everyone stopped in surprise, and Alex's grandmother looked ready to kill him. "Alex, you stay out of this," she hissed. "It's not our business."

But Hannah was on her brother's side, and her loyalty to Mrs. D. and Verity made her brave. "Don't ask me how, okay, but all of us knew Mrs. D., and she was so cool. Marc, it's totally cruel of you to do this to her house, and to your parents."

Marc looked at her in bafflement. "You say you knew my great-grandmother? She's been dead since long before you were born. You must have her confused with my grandmother."

Hannah was about to say more, but Verity stepped in. "Marc, I think you'd better leave. We can discuss this later."

"No, no need," said Grandma hurriedly, gathering up her purse. "We really must be going. Thank you for your hospitality. It was nice to meet you. Come on, kids."

CHAPTER THREE

Grandma and Grandpa looked mortified. The kids were devastated. This wasn't how they wanted the reunion to end.

"Grandma," protested Alex. "We can't leave, not now. We gotta help."

Grandma's face hardened and she pointed at the door. "Young man, you heard me. March."

Alex did as he was told: He marched out of the living room. But he didn't head toward the front door. Instead, he walked quickly in the opposite direction, toward the kitchen and the garden. He wasn't leaving, he thought frantically, not until he saw Mrs. D.'s garden once more. There was nothing happening that he could control, except this. Wrenching open the back door, he could hear his grandmother behind him, calling his name. But it was too late.

He stepped over the threshold, and everything went black.

Brandon and Hannah were right behind him, and even as Brandon saw Alex vanish into thin air, it was too late to stop himself from following... The last thing he heard was Hannah yelling, "Alex!" before she, too, was swallowed up by darkness.

Chapter 4:
BUY ONE, GET TWO FREE

Alex was lying on a hard, uneven surface, and something was poking into his back. His eyes were firmly closed: He was afraid to open them.

His head hurt, and he couldn't think clearly. He could tell he was lying on dirt, and he could hear birds, and he could smell... What was that? Cow poop? And pine trees. Definitely pines.

He was desperately hoping that he was in Verity's back yard, but in his heart he already knew he was somewhere else entirely.

When Alex finally allowed his eyelids to flutter open, his first thought was that he had died and gone to heaven: Two tiny puffy white clouds floated directly over his face. He rubbed his eyes, and focused. The tiny clouds, he now saw, hung on a brown stem. That was odd. He reached up and touched a cloud. It felt solid, and he grasped it more firmly. Suddenly, it pricked him. He snatched back his hand, and saw a drop of blood forming on his finger. Carefully, he felt the cloud again, and as the fog around his mind cleared a little, he realized that it wasn't a cloud at all, but a cotton boll. He had cut himself on the razor-sharp edges of the pod from which the puff of cotton had burst.

Alex sat up. He was in the middle of a cotton field.

The cotton had been picked, and most of the dried brown twigs around him were stripped clean. This looked a lot like Georgia. But where, exactly? The field was virtually silent. All he could hear were the cries of birds, including, he saw with alarm, those of three vultures circling above him. A strong gust of wind blew through, and he shivered. It was pretty cold for July. If this was July.

Alex was afraid to look at his clothes, because they didn't feel like his clothes. When he plucked up the courage, he glanced down. He took in what he was wearing: Unfamiliar black cotton pants, stiff cotton shirt, red woolen vest, heavy black jacket and uncomfortable black leather shoes. Where was he? And most importantly, when was he?

Reaching behind him, Alex grabbed the object that had been digging into his back. It was a small metal box, its front smothered in dried mud. Curious, he rubbed the mud away with his wetted fingers, and was astonished to find in his hand an old pocket calculator. He pushed on the switch with his thumb, and the calculator fluttered to life. Surely this meant he had to be in the late twentieth century, or even in the present day… But what would explain his clothes?

He was considering this question when he spotted a black teenager lurking at the edge of the field, watching him. His heart sank when he saw how the kid was dressed: A worn beige shirt, black trousers that ended at the knee, and no shoes. Alex hoped for the best, but he already knew that he was looking at a slave, and that meant that he had traveled in time. Hastily, he stuffed the calculator into his pants pocket, just as it dawned on him that it must belong to the Professor. Surely, she would soon show up and take him home.

Jupe was watching Alex, wondering why a white boy was sitting in the cotton field, and whether it was safe to ask him for an explanation. Jupe didn't want to offend him. Offended white people were dangerous.

Plucking up courage, he called out, "You okay, massa?"

Alex got to his feet and brushed off the dirt with his good hand. "Yeah, I'm cool, but my name's Alex, not 'massa.' Where am I?"

Jupe answered cautiously. "You're at Kintyre plantation, in Snipes County."

Alex didn't particularly want to know the answer to this next question, because he doubted he would like the answer, but he had to ask. "What year is this?"

Jupe looked blank. He was thinking, 'You don't know what year it is?' But he didn't dare say it. What he said was, "Don't rightly know, massa… Say, you look to me like you need help. I can't take you to the big house, because my massa's gone, and he took the house slaves with him. But I can take you to our cabin, and my daddy can send for the doctor."

Alex rubbed his head. "I'm fine, I think. I could use a glass of water and a lie down for a while, if you don't mind."

Jupe cracked a smile. What an odd kid! He had never met a white boy who spoke so politely to him, not even the poor whites who sometimes came begging for food. And the way this boy was dressed, he was no beggar, even if he did look a little beaten up. He helped Alex to his feet. "C'mon, young massa. I'll take you."

****

At that moment, Brandon woke up in the dark. He was crouched with his back against an uneven and rough wall, and his knees were drawn up to his chin. Opening his eyes, he could see nothing. His glasses were on, his eyes were open, but he could see absolutely nothing at all. He was blind. Whatever had happened had blinded him. He started to panic.

And then he felt something that was almost as bad. Oh, great. He had wet himself.

But, wait, no, he hadn't, because the wetness was only under his bottom. He was sitting in a puddle. But he was still blind. Now he heard voices approach, and a deep, loud, rumbling. Where could he possibly be? Gingerly, he felt around him, running his fingertips across rough stone and dirt. He seemed to be sitting in a tiny alcove. Now his fingers alighted on a thin rope, made of rough twine.

The voices and the rumbling grew ever closer, and suddenly there was a loud shuddering slam just to Brandon's left, followed by curses. He jumped up, pulling on the rope for support, and bumped his head. This knocked him back into a crouch in the alcove, just as a pool of dim light touched him. He could see! But what was he doing in a tunnel? Who was this bare-chested young man carrying a lantern, and leading a pony and cart?

The young man had halted his pony. He swung the lantern higher to throw light onto Brandon. "Some trapper you am! Bit late, were yer? Wake up, young 'un, or me cart will teck your legs off at the knee!" He peered more closely at him. "Eh, look, that be not just the coal dust on yer, bin it? Yo am a darky! Dun yo spake English?"

Brandon groaned. He could barely understand what the man was saying. He reckoned it might be English, so he was probably still in England. But the chances were good that he was no longer in the twenty-first century. Of one thing he was certain: He was not in Verity's garden.

And then he figured it out. He was in a coal mine.

****

Hannah also felt before she saw: A sudden rush of freezing air whipped her face, drying her skin, taking her breath away, and forcing her eyelids closed. When the wind dropped a little, she cautiously opened her eyes. But they were watering, and her vision was blurred. She felt weighed down by something, and so weak that she thought she might faint. Hannah rubbed at her eyes, and when her vision cleared, what she saw shocked her so much, she stepped back and leaned against a tree.

She was looking down from the top of a steep hill. Below her, a road zigzagged back and forth down to three long rows of tall stone buildings, each three or four stories, one behind the other. Beyond the buildings ran a fast-moving river, and to her left, a cascading waterfall. All around was woodland, except for a meadow that lay across the river, on the other side of a footbridge. The skies above her loomed gray and gloomy. Hannah's ears were freezing, and the wind was giving her an earache. When she put her hands to her ears, she felt the brush of coarse fabric from her long sleeve, and looking down, she now saw why she felt so heavy, and she gasped. "No," she cried. "Oh, no, no, no, no, NOOOOOOOOOO!"

Hannah's long brown dress hung all the way to her ankles. A coarse, prickly grey woolen shawl was wrapped around her shoulders. Her hair was pulled tightly into a bun. Her feet were crammed into thick stockings and heavy, uncomfortable shoes. At once, she knew that she had time-traveled, and she was horrified.

She hung her head miserably, and began to cry. At that moment, she felt a light touch on her shoulder, and she spun around in fear.

It was the Professor, and she was dressed just like Hannah.

Hannah couldn't help herself. She ran at the Professor, and started slapping blindly at her, screaming in rage. "I HATE YOU! Take me back. I want to go home. Why won't you leave me alone?"

The Professor grabbed Hannah's wrists. "Calm down, honey. Please. Shhh… I'm so sorry. I don't want you to be here, and I don't want to be here myself. But we are, and that's all there is to it. Now, please, hush, and calm down."

Hannah went limp, and the Professor loosened her grip around the girl's wrists. To her surprise, she fell into the Professor's arms. Hannah closed her eyes and groaned, "But I never went to the college campus… I thought that was why it happened last time. Where are we now? Are we still in England? When are we?"

"Eighteen fifty-one," the Professor replied.

Hannah stepped backward and put a hand over her mouth. She was wide-eyed. "Oh my God… We're in the eighteenth century?"

The Professor rolled her eyes. "No, Hannah. You see, when the year begins with eighteen, it means we're in the nineteenth century. Just like when we're in the twenty-first century, the years start with twenty…"

Hannah screamed, "SHUT…UP! I don't want any of your stupid history lessons. Okay, so we're in eighteen fifty whatever…"

"One. We're in eighteen fifty-one."

"WHATEVER!"

The Professor scratched her head. "Actually, that's pretty important to know…

"I said, WHAT-EVER! Why has this happened again?"

The Professor paused uncertainly, and said in a low voice. "I don't know. I still don't understand what makes us travel in time, but..."

"Oh, yeah, sure," Hannah said sarcastically. "Okay, at least tell me where we are."

"Can't you tell from the gorgeous view? We're in Scotland. Down there is New Lanark, the famous cotton mill village near the city of Glasgow."

Hannah looked at her skeptically. "If it's so famous, how come I've never heard of it?"

The Professor smirked. "Oh, I'm not surprised that you haven't heard of New Lanark, Hannah. But a lot of us have, you know. New Lanark was a clever idea for the early Industrial Revolution: The first owner, David Dale, built a cotton spinning and weaving factory here in the countryside, so the workers could have lots of fresh air, along with a school, clean and well-maintained housing, and all on site... It was the best deal for factory workers at the time, and it made Dale and his son-in-law Robert Owen plenty rich, too, although the current owners, the Walkers, are struggling a bit...It reminds me of China in the early twenty-first century, interestingly enough..."

Hannah waved at the Professor to be quiet. "Okay, okay, T.M.I... I can't believe this is happening to me... Where's my brother and Brandon? What have you done with them?"

The Professor looked primly at the girl. "Perhaps if you were more polite, you would find out."

Hannah put her hands on her hips and curled her lip. "Why should I be polite to you? You're a time travelling criminal witch! Just tell me where they are."

The Professor sighed. "That's the problem. I'm sorry, but I'm not sure. Brandon may be in a coal mine near Birmingham."

"What's Brandon doing in Alabama?" Hannah goggled at the thought.

"No, not that Birmingham. He's close to the original Birmingham, the one in England. Alex is somewhere in South Georgia: Might be Snipes County, might be Savannah. Or he could be in London. Look, I can't be positive about this, because my information is a bit flimsy, to be honest."

Hannah exhaled noisily. "So you're useless, is that it? What else is new? Oh, go away. Leave me alone. I'll manage."

And with that, Hannah defiantly stomped off down the hill, toward the cotton mill. The Professor watched her go, and said quietly, "You won't manage, you know...Well, actually, you will. But it won't be easy. That much I do know."

****

Alex began to drift awake from his stupor. He shifted on the uncomfortable cotton-stuffed mattress beneath him, which was supported only by the floor. His head was pounding and his ears felt as though they were filled with liquid. Hearing voices, he kept his eyes firmly shut.

"Where you find him?" A woman's voice asked the question, and she was African-American by the sound of it.

"I didn't find him," replied a man. "Ask Jupe. He found him, brought him back here."

Jupe spoke up next. "He was in the middle of the big field by the new pecan trees. He was flat on his back in the dirt. I thought he was poor white, but look at his clothes, Mama. He's a gentleman, all right." Alex was surprised: Jupe now sounded so much more sure of himself.

"If he's a gentleman," Jupe's mother said sharply, "What's he doing on his back in the middle of a field?"

Jupe's father laughed loudly at that. "Oh, woman," he said, "You think that's bad, you've not listened to my stories about our master. I've seen that man drunk out of his mind lying in his own vomit in the gutters of Savannah. No, fine clothes or not, they're all poor white trash underneath."

Jupe's mother asked, "So what will you do with him, then?

There was a pause. Alex's blood froze. Would they kill him?

But Jupiter sighed, and said, "Reckon we'll see how he is when he wakes. Then I'll take him home, or else have him write to his people, and leave him at the inn to wait for them. I can't take no chance on leaving him in the big house, in case he steals something. He looks young to me. Maybe he's a runaway."

Jupe spoke, sounding shocked. "White folks run away?"

"Why, sure they do," Jupiter said. "Children run away for all kinds of reasons. Even if you're rich, that won't protect you from a devil of a father, or a cruel master."

Alex slowly opened his eyes, and saw that he was in a bleak, dark wooden cabin, and that everyone in it was staring at him. Immediately, Jupe's mother averted her eyes from his. She made herself busy stirring the kettle that hung over the blazing fireplace.

Jupiter spoke to Alex, but now he sounded different, as though he was speaking to someone older than himself, not to a mere boy. "You feeling better, young massa? My wife here can fetch you a dipper of water, and something to eat. I'm Jupiter, the slave driver here at Kintyre Plantation. You already know my son Jupe, and this here's his mother, Sarie."

"Pleased to meet you all," said Alex. Hearing this, a startled Sarie stirred her cauldron so hard, she slopped some of the contents into the fireplace, where they sizzled loudly. Sarie tasted the soup, and made a clucking noise of approval. Then, grabbing a rough flat piece of wood, she scraped some gray and red ashes out from under the pot, and made a pile of them on the dirt floor. Seizing a thick rag, she carefully lifted the handle of the three-legged pot, and swung it onto the ground, over the glowing embers.

"Soup'll be warm a long while, Massa," she said to Alex. "You just tell me when you want some."

Alex sniffed the air and scrunched up his face. "What is it, if you don't mind me asking? Smells interesting."

"It's chitlins with cabbage," Sarie said matter-of-factly.

"Chitlins?" Alex looked blank.

"You must know chitlins?" exclaimed Jupiter. "Unless you're not from round here…You must be from the North!" Now that explained some things about this strange white boy, Jupiter thought to himself.

"No, not exactly," said Alex. "I'm from the West. From Northern California."

Jupiter smiled at him, and pointed to his jacket and waistcoat. "You must've made your fortune in them gold fields out there, young massa. Look at them fine clothes! Now, where are you headed?"

"Home, I guess," Alex said. "Hey, do you know where Snipesville is?"

Jupiter chuckled. "Know it? Snipesville's just up the hill there. We'll have you there in no time."

Sarie tapped her husband's arm. "You and Jupe take him in the cart, Jupiter. But first, you let him eat."

"What are chitlins, again?" Alex asked.

"They're the bowels of a hog," Jupiter replied bluntly, enjoying what he knew would be Alex's reaction.

Alex blenched. "Um, just water for me, thanks all the same." He got to his feet.

As Alex followed Sarie out to the well, Jupiter, with a grim smile, said quietly to Jupe, "Well, he's a gentleman all right: Won't touch chitlins. We'd best get him to where he needs to go."

Although Alex protested that he felt well enough to walk, they took the cart, driving through the fields and up a gentle forested hill. Jupiter drove, while the two boys sat in the back. Alex worried about his sister and Brandon. Were they here, too? Had Brandon been mistaken for a slave? He got the shivers, and found himself fervently hoping that the Professor would turn up soon, reunite the three of them, and take them home.

The cart soon ground to a halt in a clearing in the woods, in front of a log cabin which had a set of deer antlers affixed over the door and smoke curling from the chimney. "Where are we?" Alex asked.

Jupiter took a deep breath and said, "Well, young Massa Alex, you asked for Snipesville. And this here is Snipesville."

Alex gazed forlornly at the lone building. "But where's the rest of it?"

Jupiter laughed. "You're looking at it, sir. That there's the inn, where Massa and Missis Marshburn live. There was supposed to be more to Snipesville, folks say, but the land in the west of Georgia is a whole lot better than here, and so folks keep on moving out yonder. The Marshburns and their slaves, they're the only people who stay here."

Alex briefly chewed his lip. "Wow. Well, that's that, then. Let's head on to Savannah, I guess."

But Jupiter shook his head. "Oh, too late for that today, sir."

"Why?" Alex asked. "I mean, Savannah's only an hour from here." He immediately realized what he had said: He had been thinking of the journey by car.

"Begging your pardon, Massa Alex," Jupiter said slowly, "But you don't know Georgia right well, do you, young sir? We're more than a day's drive away, even if we start at dawn. Now, you might could take the Macon to Savannah train tomorrow, but it don't pass near here. Closest railroad stop is at Millen."

There was a silence. Alex was running out of ideas. Thoughtlessly, he felt in the recesses of his pocket, and was relieved to find, lodged next to the calculator, a small leather pouch that jingled when he shook it. He pulled out the pouch, and eagerly tipped several coins into his palm. "Tell you what, Jupiter, if I stay the night here, would you drive me to Millen in the morning? I could pay you."

Jupiter had been thinking about this possibility, too. And more. "Might could do that," he said cautiously. "But could I beg a favor? Will you take Jupe with you to Savannah? There's not much for him to do at Kintyre Plantation, what with the massa gone. Maybe he could find a little work in the city, hiring himself out."

Alex nodded. He figured Jupe would be good company. But Jupe sat up in alarm and looked questioningly at his father, who ignored him and said to Alex: "Very good, sir. We see you first light tomorrow." With that, Jupiter shook the reins, and turned the cart around for the return to Kintyre Plantation.

As Jupiter drove slowly down the hill, Jupe could no longer keep quiet. "Daddy, why are you sending me away with that white boy?"

"It's a chance for you," Jupiter said bluntly. "You and him, you might could get away to your Aunt Betsy in Massachusetts, and her abolitionist preacher husband. You persuade Massa Alex to take you there or out to California with him, and you'll be free."

Free. What a powerful word that was. But Jupe couldn't get his head around it, because all he felt was panic. He said desperately, "I might never see you again, you or mama or the rest of them."

But his father was adamant. "There's no certainty in this life, Jupe. We'll all see you in the next life."

Jupe wasn't giving up, and thought desperately for other reasons to stay at Kintyre. "But what will you tell the massa? What will you tell the others about me?"

His father had a ready answer. "I'll tell them you ran away, and somebody saw you fall in the river. Look, if things turn out bad with Massa Alex, you leave him as quick as you can. You can do that, because I'm gonna write you two passes, one that says you belong to him, and one that could take you all the way to North without him. But much better you should stay with Alex, because in the company of a white boy, you won't draw the attention of the slave patrols. Don't you get the passes mixed up, or let Alex see them close up, you hear? And don't you trust this Massa Alex, not for a moment, or he'll sell you down the river soon as look at you. He seems like a nice innocent Yankee boy, but he's white, and he'll soon learn what that means for him. Got that?"

Jupe was forlorn. He knew from the tone of Jupiter's voice that he could not change his father's mind. "Yes, sir. But what will we tell Mama?"

Jupiter said quietly, "The truth. You always tell your mama the truth."

The nineteenth-century Marshburns were a far cry from their descendants, Alex's dad's boss and his family. Mr. Marshburn, the 1851 version, was lying curled up asleep and drunk under the table in the filthy, smelly front parlor. Mrs. Marshburn, wearing a torn and stained dress, was screaming at him to get up, and kicking his shoulder.

Alex, stood awkwardly in the doorway wondering what to do. Finally, he coughed to let them know he was there. "Um, I guess I need a room? How much is it? Is breakfast included? Do you have a restaurant?"

CHAPTER FOUR

Mrs. Marshburn gave her husband a last savage kick, and turned to look at Alex as if he were mad. But she spoke politely to him. "Good evening to you. You know, it's real late, and you look mighty young. You got negroes with you?"

Alex was confused. "Uh, they just left."

Mrs. Marshburn wasn't sure whether to laugh or shriek, so she did both. "Your niggers just left you here? They ran off?"

"No...." Alex hesitated. Then he realized the misunderstanding. "They're not my slaves. They just helped me out. I'm travelling to Savannah."

She nodded, and wiped her hands down the front of her dirty dress. "Well, then, we got a place in back. I'll see what I can scrape up for supper, but there ain't much. Might could give you clabber milk and a crust in the morning. Maybe could boil you a mess of corn and ham for your supper tonight."

Unappealing as the offer was, Alex thought it sounded better than pig gut soup and a mattress on the floor.

Holding out her hand, Mrs. Marshburn said, "It's just a dollar for the tariff." Alex counted out the money in change. He marveled at a huge thick penny stamped with an Indian in braided hair.

Twenty minutes later, Alex was sitting in front of his meal, wishing he were somewhere else. Mr. Marshburn had removed himself-- or been removed -- from under the table, but otherwise, the dining room was still revolting. In one corner, an emaciated dog suckled her newborn litter. Flies hung in the air. The whole room smelled like rotting wood, dog poop, human pee, and whisky. Alex's supper was equally disgusting: A rough wooden bowl containing a thick warm paste of coarse corn grits. A few shreds of salty, stringy ham were mixed into the mush. But Alex was starving, so he ate it anyway. Or, at least, he ate it until he found the crushed remains of an enormous cockroach on his spoon.

After supper, Alex saw his room in the rear of the house, and wished at once that he were back in Jupiter's cabin. Boots and clothes littered the room, and sleeping men shared every small double bed, up to three of them in each. The room stank of whiskey, armpits, flatulence, and sweaty feet. "Where do I sleep?" Alex asked the landlady.

She pointed to a bed next to the window. "In with him," she said, and with that, she left the room. The bed was occupied by a man who appeared to be in his forties, and who was snoring gloriously.

Alex was incredibly embarrassed, but he didn't have much choice. Quietly, he removed his shoes, and tentatively slid into the bed on the window side. He decided against trying to wrench any of the blanket away from his bedmate.

Startling Alex, the man spoke. "Good Lord, what time is it?" he said, struggling to sit up. He had an English accent, and if Alex wasn't mistaken, it was quite upper-class.

Alex had no idea what time it was. He whispered, "It's pretty late. Sorry to wake you."

The man rubbed his head and yawned. Then he said loudly, "That's quite all right. There's not a great deal of sleep to be had in this dreadful lodging anyway."

Others in the room growled at him to be quiet. But he ignored them, and continued to speak to Alex at regular volume. "I do hope you didn't eat the rubbish that ghastly woman was serving."

"Afraid so," admitted Alex. "It was gross. I found a roach in mine."

"I am surprised," the Englishman drawled, "that it wasn't a rat. This must surely qualify as the worst inn in America, and that's no small contest." He stretched his arms. "I cannot sleep, it's hopeless. Would you care for a drink?" He looked closely at Alex through the half-light from the windows. "Oh. You're a bit young for whisky, I suppose. Never mind, do you object if I…?"

"No, go ahead," said Alex. He hoped the man wasn't going to turn out to be a violent drunk. Where was the Professor, he wondered?

The man retrieved a silver flask from the leather bag under his head, un-corked it, took a sip, and shuddered. "Ugh, dreadful stuff. And the landlady would evict me in a minute if she saw it. She's temperance, she says. She doesn't believe in alcohol, and neither does her pig of a husband. Meanwhile, we are supposed to pretend not to notice that her husband is a drunken sot, and that the entire house reeks of spirits. What an odd country this is."

Alex was curious about his bedmate. "You're from England?"

The man wiped his mouth on his hand. "Hmm, yes. I live in Georgia now, for my sins. If the climate does not kill me, I may return home for good one day. Indeed, I already have plans for a sojourn in London this summer, my first in many a year. I shall come back, though. Or perhaps not. It depends on business. And on other things."

"Where are you from in England?" Alex asked pleasantly.

The man exhaled loudly, as though irritated to be asked. "Oh, I very much doubt you will have heard of it. I hail from Balesworth in Hertfordshire. Is that a satisfactory answer?"

Alex gasped. "That's so cool! I lived there once!"

"Did you now," said the man skeptically, and took another sip of whisky. He clearly didn't believe Alex. There was a pause. "I wonder," the man said care-fully, "do you read, write and compute?"

"I know computers, if that's what you mean," Alex replied.

The man looked puzzled and tried again. "I mean, do you know your numbers?"

Alex figured he meant math. Of course. No computers in 1851. "Yeah, sure. I'm okay with numbers, I guess."

The man smiled. "Should you require a position as a clerk, I may have a place for you in Savannah. My name's Thornhill, and you'll find me on the Bay. I make no promises and I cannot pay a great deal, but you will find me there. For now, I think I shall make another attempt at sleep. I must depart early tomorrow." He returned his flask to his bag, lay down, and turned over.

In the early hours of the morning, Alex awoke, his stomach swirling with nausea. He realized that he had no idea where the bathroom was, or if there was one. With no time to spare, he dashed to the open window, stuck out his head, and threw up onto the ground below. When he was done heaving, he realized he was itchy all over, and he held his arm out into the moonlight to see the problem. To his horror, he saw spots of blood. Further frantic self-examination revealed the same spots all over his body. He discovered their source on the bed: Big bloated bedbugs. He and the stranger were sleeping with an entire bedbug colony that had been feasting on them both. Alex decided to spend the rest of the night on the bare floorboards.

Early the next morning, Mrs. Marshburn's slave woman bashed loudly on the door. The sleeping men murmured in protest. Alex lay shivering on the floor, his teeth chattering uncontrollably. He felt sick and filthy, and his mouth tasted like a hamster habitat. With no toothbrush, he pulled a corner of his shirt out of his trousers, and rubbed his teeth with it. It didn't help much.

Suddenly, he realized how he could prove to Mr. Thornhill that he knew Balesworth: Balesworth Hall! During the Second World War, the massive old stone and brick mansion had served as a hospital for soldiers. Alex hadn't visited it, but he knew that Mrs. Devenish had sometimes volunteered there. Surely it had existed long before 1851. Eagerly, he jumped to his feet to tell Mr. Thornhill.

But the bed was empty. Mr. Thornhill was gone. Alex was disappointed, but he remembered the job offer. The idea of holding a job scared him a little, but surely the Professor would rescue him soon?

Once dressed, Alex reluctantly made his way to the dining room, where several men were already eating breakfast. Recalling his supper (and its unpleasant aftermath), he refused the "clabber milk" he was offered, milk that had gone sour while it sat around unrefrigerated. It was thick and lumpy. The slave woman didn't seem offended when he declined to taste it. She simply said, "Okay, then," and poured the milk into a wooden bowl for the dog and its puppies. Alex, trying to be polite, asked her where Mrs. Marshburn was. The slave looked toward the ceiling—or was she rolling her eyes? "She still in bed," she said sourly, and left the room.

Alex needed fresh air, and so he waited for Jupiter and Jupe in the misty clearing in front of the inn. He trembled with cold, and listened anxiously for the clopping and rolling of Jupiter's horse and cart. As the cart emerged from the woods, Jupe waved to him, and Alex felt slightly less anxious. But only slightly. When he had first time-traveled, Hannah had been with him. It was lonely without her. He felt in his pocket once more and made sure he still had the calculator. Where was the Professor? And what had happened to his sister and Brandon?

Chapter 5:
ATTITUDE ADJUSTMENT

Brandon had crouched in the pitch darkness of the coal mine for what felt like forever. Every few minutes, the thunder of an approaching cart broke the silence, and he pulled on the rope to let the cart, pony, and miner through the door.

He fervently hoped that the Professor would show up soon, and tell him what he must do to get home, just as she had in 1915. It was scary underground: Dark, dripping wet, and freezing cold. Occasionally, voices and the clang of metal picks striking rock echoed from the mine shafts. Mostly, the only sounds came from the mine itself, as it creaked and shifted overhead... How deep underground was he?

Nothing distracted Brandon from focusing nervously on his surroundings. The mine was eerie. The darkness closed in on him, and he imagined that fresh air was running low. His breathing became rapid and shallow. He had to get out of here. He needed out. Now.

Without any plan, Brandon crawled from his alcove, climbed uncertainly to his feet in the total darkness, and started to feel his way along the tunnel. When he realized he had no idea where he was going, or how to get back, he began to tremble uncontrollably. Taking one more step, he cried out as he scraped his head against the roof of the mine. Clutching his scalp, he dropped to his knees and wept, more from fear than pain.

A few seconds later, stirred on by panic, Brandon resumed his escape attempt, only to find that his way was blocked. Was he trapped? He swallowed hard, and felt around the blockage, only to realize that he had found another trap door. He knocked loudly on the door and, to his enormous relief, a trapper opened it for him. Stooping down, Brandon struggled through, emerging into an enormous barely-lit underground cavern. He took a deep breath.

A few yards ahead of him, miners were lying on their stomachs underneath a dangerous-looking overhang of earth and rock. About half of the men were completely naked, and all of them were hacking away with pickaxes at the thick coal seam. A huge rock column supported the cavern ceiling, and a cluster of miners was seated around it, having a picnic. Among them was the young man whom Brandon had met earlier. He was holding an enormous round meat pie and a beer, and he called over to Brandon, "Alright?" It was a friendly greeting, and he pronounced it "Oroight."

Brandon nodded curtly. Another miner, an older man, beckoned to him. "Here, coom and sit wi'us while we 'ave our paces." He held up his sandwich, and so Brandon understand what "pace" meant. Lowering himself onto the cold hard ground, Brandon shook his head, as if he were trying to get water out of his ears. He didn't want to think about what he was doing here. Perhaps it was a nightmare. Perhaps he would wake up in modern London in July, or, better still, in Snipesville in August.

The young miner turned to the others, and said through a mouthful of pie, "Here's the darky boy I was telling you about."

Brandon cringed at the word, but it wasn't anything he hadn't heard before, in twentieth-century Balesworth.

The older miner smiled at him. "Right enough, Ben, he is and all! What's thy name, lad? I be Zachariah, but everybody calls me Zach."

"My name's Brandon," Brandon said reluctantly.

The small group of men laughed at his accent. To their ears, he sounded like a native of south-east England. Ben said, "Hark at him, lads, he may look like he belongs here in the Black Country, but he ain't one of us…. You sound like you am from down South, lad."

Zach joked, "Arr, never was spoke a truer word. We'll make a Black Countryman of him yet," and the group laughed. "Welcome to Hitherton, Brandon, the finest town in the Black Country of England. Come have a bit of snap with us."

"I don't have any lunch," Brandon explained sheepishly. "I didn't bring it."

"Here, don't fret, have some of mine," said Ben, breaking off a piece of his pie and handing it to Brandon. Zach leaned over to give Brandon a lump of cheese.

"Thanks, you guys," Brandon said, gratefully chowing down, but his eyes got wide when Ben also offered him a swig of his beer. "I don't drink," he said quietly.

"Get away!" exclaimed Ben in surprise. "Oy, lads, we've got one here who's taken the temperance pledge. Am you a Methodist? Do you go to chapel?"

"Um, yes," said Brandon, figuring it was easiest to agree.

Ben nodded knowingly. "Arr, that explains you not drinking, like."

"Well, just don't come preaching to us," said Zach with a chuckle, "and we'll get on like a house on fire."

CHAPTER FIVE

Brandon didn't know why, but he had adjusted to their strange accent far more quickly than he could have imagined: He understood every word. He wondered about that. Could it be that whatever magic allowed them to hear his voice differently also allowed him to hear and understand them more clearly? He munched his lunch, and glanced nervously at the heavy shelf hanging over the working miners. It was supported only by upright wooden planks that looked about as substantial as matchsticks. "Isn't that kind of dangerous?" he asked.

"Oh, arr, it is," said Zach, "But what can you do? Work's work, and this is ours. We lost a couple of blokes not six month ago. It was sad, because we were just about to call them out to let the shelf drop, when it fell of its own accord. Poor chaps never stood a chance."

Brandon shuddered.

"Don't frighten the lad," Ben said, "He's only a trapper on his first day. Are you coming to the pub with us, Brandon?"

"I think I'm too young to go to a pub," Brandon said, thankful to have an excuse.

"No, lad," said Zach, "You're talking daft. Come with us, we'll see you right."

Just then, a burly man in a bowler hat stopped in front of the group, and looked pointedly at Brandon. "You the new trapper? You're late for work. I was expecting you hours ago."

"Nah, he was on time," Ben said quickly. "He was working when I came through with my first load this morning."

Brandon silently thanked Ben for covering for him.

The man in the bowler hat didn't look convinced. "Well," he said to Brandon, "why aren't you still at the trapdoor now, eh? I never told you it was time for your snap, did I?"

"No sir," Brandon said cautiously. "I guess I got confused."

The man leaned down and pointed a finger in Brandon's face. "You just confuse yourself back to work then. I got an eye on you, I have." With that, he went over to check on the working miners, pausing only to shoot a stern look at Brandon.

"I don't think I know the way back," confessed Brandon to Ben. "And he's the boss, right?"

Ben slapped him on the back. "Don't you worry, our kid, I'll show you where you trap. And that one? That's the doggie, that is."

Brandon looked blank, so Ben explained, "The doggie's the butty's man underground."

Brandon thought, What the heck does that mean? So much for the magic translations…

Very reluctantly, he followed Ben and his lantern back toward the trap door.

"Haven't you got a candle, Brandon?" Ben asked.

"No. Am I supposed to?"

"Well," Ben said, as the trapper opened the door for them, "The trappers that can afford candles usually bring one with them. Of course, the most you afford is one each day, and when it runs out, you're in the dark again. Still, though, it might help you get used to the mine, like." He crouched and ducked into the mine tunnel, holding his lantern ahead of him, and Brandon followed. I don't want to get used to this, he thought desperately. Where's the Professor? I want to go home.

****

Hannah gazed around her at the factory village of New Lanark. It was an odd-looking place. The towns and villages she had seen in England had grown gradually, and the buildings did not match each other: Different styles of buildings jostled together in no particular pattern, large and small, thatched-roofed and slate-roofed, modern and ancient. Hannah had liked that: Those communities were imperfect and alive. They had soul.

New Lanark did not. It reminded her of New Balesworth, except prettier. The tall stone buildings were almost identical in size and appearance, and arranged in straight, neat rows. To Hannah, it all looked a bit creepy, as though no human beings had been involved in the village's creation. She breathed in the smell of wet stone: A heavy rain had recently ended. Although Hannah caught glimpses of people behind windows, nobody else was on the street.

Suddenly, a girl dressed like Hannah touched her on the shoulder, and said, "Lookinfaygaffah?"

Hannah jumped away, startled. "Huh?"

The girl repeated herself. "Yelookinfaygaffah?"

Hannah said slowly, "I Only Speak English."

The girl laughed at her. "Aye, yeedaethat, dafty! Me an a'. Now," she spoke slowly, "Are… ye… lookin'… fur… the… gaffer?"

"Maybe," said Hannah. "What's a gaffer?"

The girl seemed amazed by Hannah's ignorance. "He's heid yin at the mull."

Hannah was none the wiser. "Look, I'm sorry, but I don't understand you. I'm an American. Is there anyone around here who speaks English?"

The teenager looked incredulously at Hannah, and pounded her shoulder with a closed fist. "Ye say ye'er fray Americay? Gaun!" And then she began to speak quickly to Hannah, who couldn't understand a word.

Hannah stared at her in desperation. Then suddenly, the babble from the girl's lips emerged crystal clear, and Hannah found that she could understand. It was very weird. In England in 1940, everything that she had said was mysteriously translated into the accent and language of the time, while she had to fend for herself in understanding what she heard. But now, even though the words spoken to her were in broad Scots, Hannah could somehow, someway, know what was meant. The girl had been asking if she was looking for the factory boss, the head man at the mill.

Hannah now realized that she did not wish to speak with the gaffer. "I'm looking for, like, Child Protective Services," she said. "I need a foster home." It came out in a long string of Scots, although Hannah herself couldn't hear it.

The young woman heard the words in Scots, but "foster home," much less "Child Protective Services," meant nothing at all to her. "I dinnae ken yer meanin'," she said. "I don't know what you mean, but are you needing a place to stay? You could maybe get a place with us yonder, on Wee Row." She pointed to one of the rows of buildings nearby. "Jeannie McKay died yesterday, and Mrs. Nicolson's needing a new lodger for the tenement. And they'll need a new piecer at the mill, too."

Exasperated, Hannah said "I have no idea…" She was about to add, "… what you're talking about," when she heard a cough from behind her.

"No foster care system here, Hannah," said the Professor quietly. "Basically, your two choices are work or the workhouse. It wouldn't be a bad idea to allow Bella here to help you out." She turned to the young woman who was waiting patiently. "Bella, would you take Hannah to Abby Nicolson, who's expecting her, and then to the mill to ask for work?"

"Who's Abby Nicolson?" asked Hannah suspiciously.

The Professor tried to give her a reassuring smile. "She takes boarders, or lodgers as they're called in Britain."

Bella held out a hand to Hannah. "Come on, lassie. What's your name?"

"Hannah Dias."

"Hannah Dow?"

Hannah rolled her eyes. She was used to the Brits mangling her last name. "Yeah, okay, that'll do. Hey, let's go. I'm starving. I gotta eat." Hannah deliberately ignored the Professor as she followed Bella, which is not to say that she wasn't relieved to know that the Professor was still hanging around. But Hannah was not ready to beg the Professor to rescue her. Not yet. She would show that woman what she was made of.

Hannah was out of breath when she reached the third floor of what Bella called the tenement, the apartment block where Mrs. Nicolson lived. Mrs. Nicolson was a small, stooped woman who might have been in her sixties or seventies. Or forties. It was hard to tell. Her face was deeply lined, and she looked like a gnome.

She stood aside to allow Hannah and Bella into a poky little room. The low ceiling was stained to a dull grey by tobacco and fireplace smoke. Two beds hung with shabby curtains stood side by side against the opposite wall, a small kitchen table filled the middle of the room, and two straight chairs faced the kitchen range, in which was burning a blazing fire. A door at the far end completed the room.

"Do I have to sleep in the kitchen?" Hannah asked, amazed. "Or is my room through there?" She pointed at the door in the far wall.

Mrs. Nicolson was astonished. "That's not another room, lass. That's the press, where I keep all my bits and bobs." Hannah understood now that she had pointed to the closet. She also understood she would have to sleep in the same room as Mrs. Nicolson, and who knows who else.

Hannah tossed back her hair, and put a hand on her hip. "I'd rather have my own room, to be honest. Do you know if anyone else has a room for rent?"

Mrs. Nicolson laughed, revealing a couple of missing teeth. "Anyone would think you were a fine lady! Look, there's a wee bit of space for you in the trundle, next to Bella." To demonstrate, she pulled a low cot from under the bed.

Hannah stared at it in dismay. "Like, a camp bed? That sucks."

Mrs. Nicolson ignored her. "Board and lodging is due at week's end. That'll be five shillings."

She didn't ask Hannah if all this was acceptable. Anyway, Hannah knew that, really, she had no choice. But she wasn't happy about it. Perhaps it was time for a conversation with the Professor, after all.

****

Alex was on a train, and Jupe was right beside him. The seats were arranged on either side of a long central aisle, and the large carriage, much bigger than British trains, jolted along noisily, as coal smoke drifted through the unglazed windows. When the great whistle thundered, it drowned out any conversation. Not that either Alex or Jupe felt much like talking.

Now, about three hours into the journey, a young black woman was making her way unsteadily down the carriage, selling fried chicken and warm biscuits. The delicious aroma wafting from her covered basket was tantalizing, and Alex was starving. He called her over, and bought chicken and biscuits for Jupe and himself.

Suddenly, the door leading to the next carriage banged open, and in walked three mean-looking men, one of them bearded and carrying a whip. All of them wore guns tucked into their trousers. The train conductor buzzed anxiously behind them.

"Slave patrol!" snapped the man with the whip. "Any niggers, get your passes out for inspection." Alex could sense Jupe tensing up next to him. Then, quickly, Jupe rummaged in his pocket, and furtively pulled out a folded wad of paper. Glancing sideways, Alex was surprised to see Jupe scanning not one, but two passes. Why did Jupe have two passes? Before Alex had a chance to ask him, Jupe hastily stuffed the second pass into his pocket.

The woman selling food warily pulled out a tatty slip of paper, and handed it to the bearded patrol leader. He spent a long time reading her pass, or pretending to read it, and she grew nervous. Timidly, she said, "My massa gives me permission to work the railroad."

"Does he now?" sneered the man. He grabbed the basket out of her hands, and passed it to his friends, who laughed as they helped themselves to chicken and biscuits. Meekly, the woman took back the now-empty basket from him, nodded, and made her way back down the carriage as quickly as she could.

When the patrol leader saw that Alex and Jupe were together, he assumed that Jupe was Alex's slave, and he only glanced at the pass before moving on. But Alex heard him mutter to the other men, "That boy don't look like he can afford his own nigger, does he?" Jupe was shaking now, but Alex simply stared back at the patrol leader. As soon as the man averted his gaze, Alex sighed heavily and slumped in his seat.

He had thought Jupe would be good company. But Jupe, sitting in strained silence, wasn't company at all. Alex was beginning to think of him as an irksome responsibility.

Across the aisle from them sat a grey-haired stranger. He was tall and well-dressed, in an impeccable grey suit and shiny new stovepipe hat. A stout walking cane lay across the seat facing him. Ignoring Jupe, he smiled indulgently at Alex. "You headed home to Savannah, young man?"

"No, we're going to look for work," Alex replied.

"We?" exclaimed the man, looking for an invisible white boy seated between Alex and Jupe.

Alex suddenly realized what he had said. "I mean, I'm going. With my... um... servant."

"Ah-hah," said the man with mock gravity. "And what line of work would you be in?'

Alex tried to sound important. "I hope to be a clerk."

"Oh ho!" laughed the man. "Well, you choose an interesting time to arrive. Savannah is growing once more. Three new city squares are presently being built, and that's just the beginning. Cotton, young man, cotton and slaves! That's the foundation of our prosperity."

What a weirdo, Alex thought, as he glanced at Jupe to see if he was offended by the mention of slavery. But Jupe looked as impassive as ever. Alex found him such a mystery. Compared to Jupe, he felt like an extrovert.

"That's cool," Alex said unenthusiastically. "Hey, do you have any idea where we could find Mr. Thornhill?"

The man was still smiling. "Jeremy Thornhill, the English attorney? Why, of course. You'll find his offices on Factor's Walk at the Bay. The Bay is our mercantile center. From the railroad station you walk north until you almost reach the Savannah River. At the top of the bluffs is the Bay."

A light went on in Alex's head. "Oh! You mean Bay Street!" He had eaten dinner at a restaurant on Bay Street with Hannah and his dad.

"Call it what you will, boy," said the man. "We call it the Bay." He smiled again, but his eyes were an icy blue, and his smile was just like a shark's. Alex figured he'd offended the stranger, but why was it a big deal just because he had contradicted him?

"Anyhow," the man continued in a genial voice, "I happen to know that Mr. Thornhill is at home today, at his splendid residence by Lafayette Square." He narrowed his eyes and glanced pointedly at Jupe as he spoke to Alex. "But I am curious. Why seek a position when you own this slave? You could sell him and make enough money to live comfortably for quite a while."

Alex shook his head firmly. "No, he's not for sale."

The gentleman breathed out, his nostrils flaring. "If you change your mind, son, call on me at my office. You'll find me on Johnson Square. My name's MacGregor. Mister John MacGregor." As he turned back to his newspaper, MacGregor was inexplicably chuckling to himself, as though he knew something Alex didn't.

Jupe wouldn't even look at Alex, much less thank him for his support, but carried on staring straight ahead. Alex was really starting to resent him. Why was he stuck with this strange kid, who always agreed with him, and wouldn't talk to him like a normal human being? Maybe he should just sell him to Mac-Gregor… As soon as he thought it, Alex felt guilty, and a little scared that he should even think such a thing.

Soon afterward, the train unexpectedly shuddered to a halt. At first, nobody said anything, but a quiet murmur quickly arose among the passengers, who then quieted when heard shouted conversation between the conductor and the driver. The conductor appeared at the end of the carriage. "Ladies and gentlemen, I'm sorry to disturb you, but the engine's looking mighty dangerous. Reckon y'all might should get off the train." He didn't need to say it twice. People grabbed their belongings, and jostled each other as they headed for the doors.

While the engine cooled, everyone stood at a respectful distance. After about twenty minutes, Alex approached the conductor and asked, "When's the next train?"

The conductor, a young white man, tipped his hat back on his head, and thoughtfully stroked his moustache. "Not today, young sir. I sent a boy to the nearest livery to arrange for carriages, but that won't be for a long while yet. I hesitate to suggest it, but I reckon you might want to walk. We're only about four miles from the city, and there's a good trail yonder."

Alex turned to Jupe. "Jupe, should we walk? Is that okay with you?"

Both Jupe and the conductor boggled at Alex. Why, they wondered, was he asking his slave's opinion?

Jupe answered carefully. "That's what you want, Massa Alex?"

Alex was getting impatient with him again. "Yeah, but is that what you want?"

Jupe slowly nodded.

Jupe and Alex weren't more than quarter of a mile from the stalled train when they caught up with a coffle, a procession of slaves. Around twenty young men and women were chained together at the wrists in pairs. A long chain connected them all together. Most people were carrying their few belongings in strips of cloth tied into bundles. The women wore headscarves, while the men sported headwear ranging from simple cotton caps to colonial-style tricorn hats. Their clothes were old, patched, and ragged.

To Jupe's astonishment, Alex walked alongside one slave, and said, "Hi, so, where are you guys headed?"

"Um, Savannah, sir," said the surprised young man, keeping his eyes firmly downcast. "We're going to auction."

"What kind of auction?" Alex asked innocently.

The slave looked at Jupe, silently appealing to be rescued from this crazy white boy. Jupe signaled with a grimace that he knew Alex was crazy, but what could he do about it?

The clip-clop of hooves announced the arrival on horseback of a red-haired white man with a broad-brimmed hat. He was wearing striped pants and a long black coat, but Alex only had eyes for the pistol he had holstered, the rifle strapped across his back, and the long bull whip tucked under his belt. He said to Alex, "Can I help you, sir?"

Alex wasn't sure what surprised him most: To be addressed as "sir" by a man in his thirties, or that the man had an Irish accent. He muttered, "Um, no... No, thanks. I was just asking these guys where they're headed."

"Will you be after buying any of my merchandise, now?" the man asked eagerly. He smiled and waved a hand over the sad procession of men and women, who continued to plod up the rutted dirt road through the pine forest. When Alex didn't answer, the slave trader gestured at Jupe. "Or maybe you want to sell me this boy. He looks young, I say, but likely. How much are you wanting for him? I could sell him for you if you pay me a small commission." To Jupe, he said, "Are you a full field hand, boy?"

Jupe blurted out, "Please don't sell me, Massa Alex."

Alex was alarmed by the turn the conversation had taken, and by Jupe's distress. "No, of course I won't sell you," he said quietly, and then turned back to the slave-trader. " I can't sell him. He doesn't belong to me."

Alex was about to add, 'A person doesn't have the right to own someone,' but the slave trader eagerly interrupted him. "He doesn't belong to you? Then who does he belong to? Is he a runaway?"

Alex thought fast. This man worried him. "No. He belongs to my... uncle. In Virginia. He loaned him to me."

The slave trader licked his lips. "You sure? What with you walking and that, I reckoned you were down on your luck. I'm not trying to cheat you, I just reckoned you should know that this here's a valuable young field hand..."

"No, he's not mine to sell," Alex said truthfully.

The Irishman shrugged and bid Alex a good day, before turning his horse and riding to the back of the coffle.

That left Alex and Jupe once again walking side-by-side with the slaves. Unaware that Alex was in hearing range, one young man was talking to talk to the other slaves around him. He was high-spirited, and he made the sad-eyed men and women laugh with his tales of outwitting his master. "Why, once I stole a chicken, and after I snapped its neck, I tied it to my leg, under my breeches. I took it into the woods and I cooked it… I mean, I worked for that chicken. I fed that thing, and I picked its eggs, so I reckoned it owed me a right tasty meal."

But then, the laughter faded as the man described his return from running away to visit his wife and small daughter, who were slaves on another plantation. "The whipping was bad enough. I'll carry those scars until Judgment Day. But when the man say I was too much trouble, and that he would put an end to my mischief by selling me far away…I really thought I was like to die."

Alex saw the man's lip tremble, and he felt desperately sorry for him. He would probably never see his family again.

Suddenly, Alex realized that he himself might never make it home, might never see Hannah or his father again, that he might … Why was he worrying about these slaves, or, for that matter, Jupe? They would all be long dead by the time he was born. Strange thoughts crossed his mind. Would it really be that big of a deal if he sold Jupe? Slavery would be over soon, wouldn't it? Jupe would be free then, and meanwhile, Alex would be rid of him. Without thinking, he asked Jupe, "When was the Emancipation Proclamation?"

"Eighteen Sixty-Three," answered a woman's voice.

The Professor steered her horse to walk alongside the boys. She drew stares from the slaves and the slave trader, who weren't accustomed to unaccompanied ladies on horseback. "You're lucky," she said to Alex. "I'm the only person in 1851 who could possibly have answered that question. Why do you want to know, anyway?"

Alex guiltily dropped his gaze from her. "No reason… I'm so happy you're here! So hey, where are my sister and Brandon?"

"In Britain," she said bluntly. "It took me forever to find you. Weeks."

"I have your calculator," Alex said, pulling the gadget from his pocket. "Can I go home now?"

But to his disappointment, the Professor waved the calculator away. "No, keep it. I think you're going to need it in your new job. It'll certainly make things easier when you add up Thornhill's accounts. And who is this?" She pointed at Jupe, who was pretending not to listen to the bizarre conversation.

Alex said breezily, "Oh, this is Jupe. His dad asked me to take him to Savannah."

At the mention of Jupe's name, the Professor slapped her forehead, as though something had just dawned on her. She muttered to herself, "So this is what

Jupiter was writing about in his letters to his sister. No wonder he was being cagey, the wily old devil." Leaning down from her horse, she hissed at Alex, "You're taking a huge risk bringing this kid with you. You know you could be arrested for stealing him?"

Alex didn't know that. "But I didn't steal him," he protested. "He just sort of came with me. I couldn't stop him."

"Georgia law doesn't see it that way," the Professor said gravely. "He's considered property, just like land or this horse. And he's not yours. So you had better figure out what to do with him."

Without further comment, she turned her horse, and cantered back in the direction from which she had arrived. Alex called after her to wait, but she kept on riding until she was out of sight.

"I want to go home," he said plaintively.

****

Brandon left the coal mine by climbing a ladder through a narrow vertical shaft. It wasn't the scary climb that he had feared: He had assumed he was miles down, but it took him only a minute to reach the surface.

"It's a drift mine," Ben explained when Brandon mentioned his surprise. "We're lucky not to be down one of the deep pits."

The outside world was almost as dark as the mine. Looking at the blasted landscape, Brandon began to understand why this area was called the Black Country. The miners were black from head to toe, emerging from the pit in coal dust-covered shirts, trousers and caps. Black slag, the dusty refuse from mining, lay all around in huge heaps, while ramshackle buildings and enormous chimneys added to the sinister atmosphere. Brandon coughed as the thick, sooty air invaded his lungs. Soon, he was coughing so hard he was afraid he would throw up.

He followed Ben, Zach, and the others as they trudged through the devastated terrain: Every miner, it seemed, was headed to the pub. As they turned a corner, bursts of red and orange flame and showers of sparks shot from two enormous towers, which looked like a castle on fire. Brandon gasped, "What is that?"

Zach explained. "That be the blast furnace. That's where all the coal from our colliery goes when it leaves the pit. It's used to make iron." As the fireworks exploded spectacularly, Brandon wondered to himself why this place wasn't called the Red and Black Country.

The weary miners tramped in a long line along a muddy footpath, and then arranged themselves in single file as the path narrowed and took them down-hill. It continued alongside a canal, on which were moored brightly decorated narrowboats that made Brandon think of giant floating cigars.

Ben tapped Brandon's shoulder, and gestured up the hill toward a boxy white building. "Welcome, Brandon, to The George and Dragon, the worst public house in all of England!"

The pub actually didn't look that bad. The soot that begrimed it had col-ored it a shade of light gray. Extending over the door, a painted sign portrayed England's patron saint, St. George, clad in armor on horseback, as he valiantly fought a dragon with sword and shield. But nowhere on the building was the name of the pub written. Brandon wondered if this was because the miners couldn't read.

The miners poured into the pub through the narrow whitewashed passage-way, and turned left into a tiny room. The wooden bar with its beer pumps took up about a third of the space, and it was already standing-room only. Many miners were smoking small white clay pipes, and tobacco smoke and coal smoke mingled heavily in the air, along with the sour stench of stale beer. Benches and tables clustered around the walls, but only a handful of lucky miners had arrived in time to find seats. Everyone else stood on the bare wood-en floors. If Ben and Zach hadn't cleared the way for Brandon, he might never have made it past the doorway.

Strangely, nobody was drinking beer. Neither were they waiting at the bar to buy some. Over the hubbub, Brandon yelled to Ben, "Why aren't we ordering drinks?"

Ben laughed loudly at Brandon's question, and he nudged Zach. "Eh, listen to this, Zachariah! This lad said he was teetotal, and now he wants to know why he hasn't had his beer yet! Oi, Brandon, how can we order if we haven't been paid?"

Now Brandon was utterly confused. Why had everyone come to the pub without money?

At that moment, a man standing close to the door cried, "Oi, lads, here comes the butty."

Looking past Zach's elbow, Brandon glimpsed a man in a bowler hat stop-ping in the doorway. He began to call out names. As each miner stepped for-ward when his name was called, he was handed a wad of paper. Brandon asked Zach what was going on.

"Payday," said Zach. He pronounced it 'Pie-die.' "You are new, lad. Now mind, we're not paid in money. We're paid in tommy notes. You can only use them in the butty's shop, to buy your food, like, and in this pub, because the butty owns this, too." He shook his head in disgust.

Brandon was outraged. "Wow, that's terrible. This guy owns the mine?"

But Zach was shaking his head. "No, no, the butty owns the shop and the pub, but he don't own the mine. Lord Chatsfield is the owner. The Earls of Chatsfield have always owned this land, so what's under it belongs to them, or so they say. The Earl gets the butty to run the mine, and the butty hires us. That way, if the government finds out we work too long hours or the mine's dangerous, the butty blames the Earl, and the Earl blames the butty. So neither of them gets blamed, see?"

Just then, the butty yelled, "Brandon Clark." Brandon thought he had misheard, but Zach said, "That'll be you," and shoved him forward. Brandon collected his pay, and found that, sure enough, it was not money he had received, but small printed slips that said they could only be used in the mine shop and the George and Dragon pub. As the butty handed out more wages, a man in the corner of the pub started to sing.

"You charitable friends, I pray, lend an ear, to the miner's petition, which soon you will hear…"

Now everyone in the pub joined in the song, except for Brandon, who didn't know the words. He listened with increasing anxiety to the grim and gory tale of the miner.

Before they've been working scarce half an hour,
A great fall of coals on their bodies doth pour,
Then help it is called for by all who surround
To see where their mangled bodies can be found
Some crushed all to pieces, their brains fly around!
Then pity poor colliers that work underground…

"Oh, gross," groaned Brandon.

But the song wasn't done. The miners continued:

There yet is more danger to which they're exposed,
There is fire, and sulphur, and water likewise,
This fire is quick, also powerful and sharp,
Many a poor collier has been burnt to the heart.

Brandon shuddered. Bad enough that he worked alone in silence, dark, and damp, but now he knew how unsafe his job actually was. He also had a hunch that the song was deliberately chosen as a protest to the butty.

"Come on, Brandon," yelled Ben, waving his tommy notes in Brandon's face. "Let's get some ale."

"I told you," Brandon said firmly. "I don't drink alcohol."

Zach took him aside, and said very firmly in his ear, "Listen, our kid, just a bit of friendly advice, like. The butty and his men are watching, and if you wanna be kept on at the mine, you'll buy at least a half-pint of beer. You don't got to drink it."

"Ar," said Ben, "You can always give it to us!" They laughed.

But Brandon was shocked. He looked toward the bar, where men were crushed three deep, some waiting to be served, and some already holding pewter beer mugs and fighting their way out of the throng. "So the idea is that we all get drunk, and then we spend our money here in the pub?"

Zach looked grim, and nodded. "Ar, you're a clever lad. That's exactly the idea."

"I won't," protested Brandon. "That's a total rip-off." He was furious. When he worked as Mr. Gordon's apprentice in Balesworth in 1915, he earned a fair wage, learned a skill, been mentored by Mr. Gordon, and had a place to live, too. The mine was clearly a very different story.

"Come on, lad," Zach cajoled him. "What will your mum and dad say when they find out you packed in your job, eh?"

Brandon imagined what his parents would say if he told them he had just quit as a coal miner in Victorian England. "They would be shocked," he said truthfully. "But they won't know. I'm leaving."

"You won't get far on tommy notes," said Ben, looking concerned.

But Zach clapped Brandon on the back. "You could do something better than spend your life down the pit. Go on, get yourself down to London." He smiled. "They do say the streets in London are paved with gold, but I wouldn't put much stock in it, if I was you. Good luck and fare you well, Brandon." He raised his beer glass to him.

Brandon had no idea if Zach's words were encouraging or sarcastic.

It was drizzling rain and freezing cold outside. The damp air made Brandon feel he was breathing coal-soaked fluid. Standing in the dark outside the pub, he rocked backward and forward on his heels. When he exhaled, he added a fog to the heavy air. All he could see was the canal shimmering in the moonlight, and beyond that, darkness. The tommy notes in his pocket were useless anywhere apart from Hitherton. He stepped back into the pub's entry hall, so that he was neither really outside, nor really inside. Several men roughly pushed past him as they left the pub, cursing him for getting in their way.

Brandon was afraid of staying outside, and of going back in. He had a horrible feeling of helplessness, of having two choices that weren't really much of a choice, of being trapped. Tears prickled his eyes, and he began to hyperventilate.

He was only dimly aware of a woman who hurried up the canal towpath toward the pub. She clutched a dark shawl around herself, and held up her long skirt to keep it out of the mud as she splashed through the puddles.

But Brandon's heart leapt when she came close enough for him to see her face. "Professor Harrower?" he gasped. "Boy, am I glad to see you!"

She ran past him into the hallway, stopping to pull off her shawl, and shake the rain from her hair. "Hi, Brandon. Sorry I'm late. Oh, I do so hate wool clothes. The minute you get rain on them, they stink. Well, at least they're more waterproof than cotton. Welcome to the Industrial Revolution, by the way. Come on, let's have a drink, and you can tell me how the coal mining's going."

"It's not," said Brandon. "I just decided to quit."

She paused with her hand on the door of the small Select bar, the room where women were allowed. "No, I'm sorry, really I am, but you can't do that. Stick it out for a bit. I'm sure you're supposed to."

Brandon was horrified. "No, ma'am, I can't. Look, can you please find me something else to do?"

She beckoned to him. "Come on, let's find a seat so we can talk."

The Select was almost empty of customers, and quiet despite the shouts and singing from the Public bar next door. The two of them sat at a table, and the Professor handed Brandon a few coins, sending him to fetch two half-pints of beer. He was a bit shocked to be asked to fetch alcohol, but did as he was told.

After Brandon carefully laid the glasses on the table, the Professor took a sip of her drink and grimaced. "Oh, that's dreadful. Repulsive. Don't drink yours, Brandon."

"Don't worry, I won't. I'm underage, remember?"

"Not in 1851, you're not. Look, here's the real problem..." She pressed her knuckle to her lower lip for a moment, and then said quietly, "You can't quit. I need to keep track of you."

"I'll come with you," Brandon said eagerly.

She shook her head. "No, you can't do that. You must stay here."

CHAPTER FIVE

Brandon was upset. "Nothing personal, Professor, but no way am I going back down that mine. I mean, for what? Why can't you help me get a good job?"

But the Professor was angry too. "You're starting to sound like Hannah. Look, I'm not running some time-traveling internship program here, okay? I can't promise you that you'll get useful training so you can make a lot of money when you grow up. You've heard of the Industrial Revolution, right? When most people move from farm work to factory work? Well, here it is, and somebody has to do it. Why shouldn't it be you doing a crummy job? Do you think you're better than those guys in there?" She jerked her head toward the other bar. "None of them wanted to be miners, but that's practically the only way they can make a living. I mean, they could work in the foundries with boiling hot metal and no safety equipment, or they could quarry limestone with no safety equipment, or they can mine with no safety equipment. Or they can starve, because most of the old farming jobs have disappeared. Those are pretty much the choices for most of these men, except the ones lucky enough to know a skilled trade."

Brandon struggled to answer her tirade. She had never spoken to him like this before. "Well, no, I guess I... No, wait! Yes, I am better qualified than this! I can read, and I have a skilled trade. I trained with Mr. Gordon as a dentist's assistant."

"Okay, fine," said the Professor in a resigned voice, as she got to her feet, drawing her shawl around her shoulders. "I'm sure you will have no trouble finding yourself a professional job in the Black Country, as a partly-trained dentist with no certification. Off you go."

Brandon didn't move.

"Go on," said the Professor, folding her arms. "You obviously have loads of opportunities, so why don't take one of them?"

Brandon looked at her with utter loathing. "I can't believe I'm saying this, but I'm starting to think Hannah's right about you. You are mean. You really don't care what happens to us."

"I do care, Brandon," she said, "But not in the way you expect. Look, I'm not in charge here. You're now part of England in 1851. There's only so much I can do for you, and mostly, this is in your hands. You're in a place where everything is changing, people are on the move, and not always out of choice. You can stay in the Black Country, and work in the mine, or you can take your chances somewhere else. But I can't guarantee that if you leave, I'll find you again. Ever."

Brandon took a sharp intake of breath. That was scary. Throughout the kids' adventure in twentieth-century England, the Professor had always reassured them, always promised them that everything would be okay. He asked nervously, "So how are we all going to get home? Is it when one of us finds your calculator? Is that it?"

"I don't know," she said with a sigh. "Alex has already found the calculator, but I still have a lot of questions I need to research. I can't be too hasty." There was an awkward silence. Finally, the Professor clasped her hands, laid them on the rickety table, and looked Brandon in the eye. "Brandon, please stay. Just for a while…"

But Brandon was more and more certain that he could not bear life in Hitherton for another day. "I want to go," he said determinedly. "I'll head to Balesworth, because I'm guessing that's where Alex and Hannah will be…"

"They're not," said the Professor abruptly. "Alex is in Savannah, and his sister is a factory worker in Scotland."

"Hannah? Working in a factory?" Brandon's eyes bulged at the very idea. "Wow, how does she like it?"

The Professor laughed. "Oh, she doesn't like it very much at all, but she's doing it. Please, Brandon, just stick it out for a few days. I'll be back as soon as I can."

"But where will I live?"

"Oh," she said, "Yes. Well. Um."

"It's not good, is it?" he said apprehensively.

"Not terrific, no. But here you go. Here's your address." She handed him a letter, and got to her feet. By the time Brandon had opened the envelope and read the note inside, she was gone, leaving him to wonder what was meant by "The Union Workhouse, Hitherton."

****

Hannah had never in her life heard so much noise. The factory's spinning room was the size of a small gym, and it was lined with row after row of clacking spinning machines called mules. They were all powered by watermills on the River Clyde that gushed past New Lanark.

Every few minutes, the spinners pulled the iron machines backward on their wheels along railroad-like tracks bolted to the floor. While the machines rested, kids and young teens ran down the length of them, pausing here and there to lean over and repair broken threads by gathering them up and quickly rubbing them together. Meanwhile, younger kids scurried on their hands and knees under the machines to clean up dust and oil with brushes, dustpans, and fingers. When the machines started up again with a great screech, the kids scampered away like mice, and the spinners moved the machines forward. Hannah thought that her machine, with its whirring spindles of cotton thread, looked like a giant abacus. The "gaffer", her boss Mr. MacDonald, had introduced her to a red-haired young woman called Elspeth, a spinner, who carried on spinning while she explained to Hannah how the mill worked.

Hannah found it hard to hear Elspeth over the noise, and her attention wandered. She glanced out of the window, and soon was transfixed by the sight of the roaring waters of the Clyde tumbling over the falls below. Suddenly, Elspeth was tugging her arm.

"Ow! Let go of me!" Hannah yelled, batting at Elspeth.

"Well, pay attention then, would you?" Elspeth yelled over the noise, dragging Hannah backward with her as she pulled on the spinning frame.

"I watched what you did and I get it," Hannah shouted confidently. "Just get me started on a machine, okay?"

"But you're not a spinner like me," replied Elspeth, shaking her head in exasperation. "You mustn't copy what I do. You're starting as a piecer."

"And what does a piecer do?" shouted Hannah over the racket.

Elspeth looked exhausted by Hannah. "Have you not been listening to a word I say?"

Hannah shrugged. "I can't hear you!"

Elspeth buried her face in her hands. "Oh, in the name of … Look, Hannah. Look over there, at the wee bairns on the ground." She pointed to the children, who lay flat on their stomachs, keeping their heads down under the machinery as they flailed away at the floorboards with brushes. "They're called the scavengers. Now, look at Bella coming down the row." She pointed to Bella, who was running down the aisle between spinning machines. "She's a piecer. That's what you'll be doing. "

Hannah watched as Bella stopped, reached over, deftly picked up a handful of threads, and rubbed them together, before rushing onward. Suddenly, Elspeth began pulling back on the machine, and she called out to Hannah, "Now, away and follow Bella."

Within an hour, Hannah had started to learn how to piece. As she rubbed the threads together, her hands began to tingle and then sting, and her feet started throbbing from all the standing. Glancing at the wall clock, she realized she still had five more hours of work to go. How would she ever manage?

ATTITUDE ADJUSTMENT

At the end of the day, Hannah staggered from the mill, following Bella amid a large crowd of women, men, boys and girls. Hannah repeatedly looked at her hands and cringed. Her fingers were bright red and agonizingly painful, especially in several patches where the skin had rubbed away. Her whole body ached, and especially her right knee, on which she had leaned her weight as she pieced.

Hannah was exhausted, and as she dragged herself back up the hill toward Mrs. Nicolson's tenement, she began to sob. Her working day would begin again tomorrow at 6 a.m., and she simply couldn't face it, not for an hour more, much less ten and a half hours every day.

When Bella heard Hannah crying, she turned to her. "Come now, Hannah, it'll be all right. You'll get used to it. I've been doing this same work since I was nine, when I started as a half-timer, working six hours a day. It's no so bad."

Hannah cried harder. Bella tried again to cheer her up. "You can go to the school with me at noon. It's only fourpence a month, and you can learn to read and write."

Hannah wailed. "That's the good news? Are you kidding me?"

Before Hannah reached the main door of Mrs. Nicholson's tenement building, she had decided to quit.

Chapter 6:
FiRED UP

Bella pushed open the door to the tenement flat—it had no lock. Mrs. Nicolson was standing at the fireplace, bending forward to stir something in a black cauldron. Even to Hannah, who was very picky about food, whatever she was cooking smelled good. She had worked so very hard, and she was desperately hungry.

"Ah, here you are," said Mrs. Nicolson, straightening up. "Would you girls like a cup of tea? The kettle's just boiled."

Bella smiled gratefully. "Tea? Oh, thank you, Mrs. Nicolson."

Hannah said, "Sure, tea, yeah, okay," and collapsed onto her back on the nearest bed.

"And would you mind sitting in a chair?" grated Mrs. Nicolson. She was already irritated that Hannah had accepted her offer of tea with so little grace. Tea was expensive. Reluctantly, Hannah slid off the bed onto the floor, staggered dramatically to her feet, and threw herself into one of the rickety chairs.

Mrs. Nicolson handed Hannah a cup of tea in a roughhewn pottery mug, and Hannah sipped at it. It was sweet with sugar, and as she drank it, she cheered up a little.

There was a long silence as all three of them quietly ingested their tea. Then Mrs. Nicolson said, "Och, Bella, you're that quiet, you must be tired out this night, are you?"

Hannah now understood why Bella might be tired out tonight, and every night.

"Aye," said Bella sadly, "and I slept through school the day."

Hannah couldn't believe her ears. "And that's a bad thing?"

"Of course," said Bella. "How can I make something of myself if I don't heed my lessons?" Hannah looked at the small, thin, and sad-faced Bella, and wondered what she thought she could grow to up to become. Chat show host? Supermodel? Hannah giggled to herself.

Mrs. Nicolson clearly had a similar thought. With a knowing smile, she said to Bella, "Never mind making something of yourself. You're lucky to be working here."

Hannah thought this was a bit extreme. "Lucky? Are you serious? My hands have been bleeding all day, and my legs are so swelled up, I think they're gonna explode. I mean, look at them! On top of all that, I'm supposed to go to school?"

Mrs. Nicolson looked crossly at Hannah. "No, it's not easy here, I'm not saying that, but the work hours are shorter than ever they were. And New Lanark is famous for the owners' treatment of workers. Men still come from all over the world to see what Mr. Dale and Mr. Owen made here. The gaffers aren't as cruel as some I've heard tell of in Glasgow, and we all learn to read and write. And our houses are provided."

"True…," said Bella. "All so long as the mill makes a profit."

"Aye, if the mill makes a profit," agreed Mrs. Nicolson. "True enough."

Bella continued. "Anyways, I never meant that I wanted a better job. What jobs are there for the likes of me? No, all I want is a few more hours to myself, and a few more books to pass the time, and maybe some more pennies to spend."

"You're a dreamer, lass," tutted Mrs. Nicolson. "By the by, I've heard tell the Walkers are seeking a buyer for the mill. Mind, I'll say this, they've never been as good employers as Mr. Owen. He was famous, was Mr. Robert Owen, and he was a good man, aye, that he was."

Hannah really wasn't interested. "It's all right for you," she said sullenly to Mrs. Nicolson. "You don't have to work in the factory."

Mrs. Nicolson said calmly, "But, Hannah, I did work in the mill. I was a spinner for fifty years. Now, girls, let us have our supper. I must finish cleaning this house before the bug hunters come."

"What's a bug hunter?" asked Hannah, puzzled. "And what house?"

"This house," said Mrs. Nicolson, circling a finger in the air to demonstrate that the room was her house. "The bug hunters are them who inspect to be sure we keep our houses clean."

"That's so rude!" exclaimed Hannah.

"Aye, well," said Mrs. Nicolson quietly, "I've always thought so, too, but the owners think otherwise, since they own the houses."

Hannah was intrigued by the very idea of strangers coming in to check an apartment for cleanliness. She wondered how her mother would have reacted. "So what happens if they find a messy house?"

Mrs. Nicolson said dramatically, "If my house were mucky, I'd be sent to Botany Bay."

"What does that mean?"

Bella answered. "She means that, if her house is found dirty, she'll be sent as a convict to Australia, like a thief or a robber."

Seeing Hannah's shock, Mrs. Nicolson laughed. "Nah, nah, it's just our wee joke, Hannah. Our Botany Bay is a tenement down the street. It's not Australia, mind, but it's cramped and rickety, a grim enough place, and it's where they send the folk who displease the bug hunters. Listen, Hannah, workers must always keep our mouths shut, or else be out on the street. You understand, lass? We don't own the land, or the factories, or the roofs over our heads, so we must bide in silence."

Hannah nodded dumbly. Biding in silence was not something she did naturally. It turned out that she wasn't the only one.

"Nonsense," said Bella suddenly. "Mrs. Nicolson, we're as good as the owners. If we had a union, we would soon turn the tables…Aye, that we would."

Mrs. Nicolson raised her eyebrows. "Bella, I wouldn't be saying that too loudly, if I was you."

Just then, the door opened, and a man in his thirties stomped in. Yanking off his cap, he threw it on a peg behind the door. Hannah wondered who he was.

Silently, the man took his place at the head of the table, and pulled a short, white clay pipe from his jacket pocket, along with a small pouch of tobacco, from which he proceeded to fill the pipe.

"Good evening to you, Charlie," Mrs. Nicolson said.

"Aye, and you, Mother," Charlie replied. He got to his feet again, took a rolled straw of paper from a holder on the wall, and lit it from the fire, before applying the lit paper to his pipe.

As the tobacco smoke swirled around her, Hannah coughed in protest, but she already knew it was pointless to complain. Lots of people smoked in 1851, just as they had in 1940. Although, now that Hannah thought about it, she hadn't yet seen anyone smoking cigarettes. Nor had she seen anyone smoking pipes in the factory. "Why don't people smoke in the mill?" she suddenly asked Bella.

"Don't be daft, girl," growled Charlie. "One spark and the whole mill would be alight." Then he fell silent again.

Mrs. Nicolson brought four steaming wooden bowls to the table, one after the other, starting with Charlie's. "Hannah's the new lodger. Here's your tatties, with a wee bit of milk." When everyone was seated, Charlie said a grace. But Hannah wasn't praying: She was staring through her fingers at the food. Three boiled potatoes and milk? What a weird appetizer.

After they had finished eating in silence, Hannah realized that the potatoes had been supper. All of it. Three boiled potatoes, served with a splash of milk.

Charlie had received a double portion.

After he had eaten, Charlie seemed to mellow a bit. "So you're the new lodger, eh?" he asked Hannah, as he re-lit his pipe. "And where have you come from?"

Hannah waved a hand vaguely, implying that she had come from far away. Charlie looked askance at her, and said warningly, "Are you one of the Catholic Irish? I won't have a Catholic in this house."

"What's wrong with Cath…" Hannah began to say, but Bella kicked her under the table. Fortunately, Charlie had lost interest in Hannah, and was looking out of the window. It was just starting to rain.

"It's a grand view," he said wistfully. "I went with the lads over the river on Sunday to kick a ball around, but we were chased off."

"Aye, well," said Mrs. Nicolson, "That's just as well. Ye shouldn't be playing on the Sabbath anyways. It's a sin."

Charlie stared mournfully out of the window. "Well and good, Mother, but a man needs more from life than standing all day in a mill."

"Don't we all," Hannah grumbled. "So how come you're not allowed to play soccer over there?"

Charlie continued to look out at the river and the green field and trees beyond. "Och, the two old biddies who own the field told the Walkers they don't want us workers on their land, even though the field is just empty pasture. They expect us to keep to the village."

"Hey, fair enough," Hannah said dismissively. "It's their property." What was this guy's problem, she wondered?

Charlie turned and gave her a sidelong look, but said nothing.

****

Late in the night, long after Mrs. Nicolson and Charlie had retired to their curtained beds, and an exhausted Bella had fallen asleep on the trundle on the floor, Hannah was lying wide awake, listening to everyone snoring. Her teeth felt icky: When she had asked Bella for a toothbrush, Bella had handed her a twig. Now she needed to use the bathroom. But there was no bathroom.

Hannah figured it had to be somewhere in the building. In darkness, she shivered her way on bare feet across the rough floorboards, out of the apartment, and onto the freezing cold stone staircase. She was dressed in her shift, a thin cotton garment that was the only underwear she or any of the other girls possessed. Swiftly, she crossed the landing and cautiously opened a door, only to realize that she was entering someone else's apartment. A voice in the gloom yelled at her to get out. She slammed the door shut.

She groped her way up the staircase to the fourth and highest floor, and then turned back, and felt her way downstairs again. In desperation, she looked out the tenement entrance, hoping to spot a nearby outhouse, but she could see nothing that looked likely, and now, she was shivering violently in the night air. Reluctantly, she returned to the flat, and shook Bella awake. "Where's the bathroom?" she hissed.

Bella started. "Eh? What? Oh, there's a closet, at the end of the street. But you won't be going out there the night! Use the chanty. It's over there." She pointed vaguely to a corner of the room, where a chamberpot sat, covered in a cloth rag.

Hannah was grossed out, but desperate. She reluctantly picked up the chamberpot, removing the cloth, and placed it in a far corner of the room. Arranging the two chairs around her and draping her shawl and blanket over them, she made a sort of privacy screen. She used the pot quickly, terrified she would wake the others.

Shortly, Hannah was back in the cot she shared with Bella. She had an uneasy gnawing sensation in her stomach and her tummy growled loudly. Why was it doing that, she wondered? Was she sick? After a few more anxious moments, it dawned on her that she was hungry. And there was nothing she could do about it.

In the early hours of the morning, when it was not yet light, Hannah was woken by a sharp tapping on the window. This was especially startling because the apartment was on the third floor. Hannah jumped up and dashed to the window, just in time to see a man on the street below rapping against the glass with a long pole.

"What the..." Hannah muttered. She knocked hard on the window. "Go away, weirdo! Get lost!"

Mrs. Nicolson poked her head out from the bed curtains and called, "Why are ye shouting at Harry? He's our knocker-up."

Hannah whirled around. "Your what?" she giggled.

Mrs. Nicolson repeated, "Knocker-up. He knocks us up of a morning. We pay him a penny a week."

Hannah fell about laughing now. Mrs. Nicolson, shaking her head in confused irritation, tutted loudly, and disappeared behind the bedcurtains.

"Wow, a human alarm clock," Hannah said. "And what an awesome name... Hey, Mrs. Nicolson, do we, like, get knocked up every morning? Only I don't wanna get knocked up yet." She dissolved into giggles again. But now that she was out from under her thin blanket, she began to shiver. She could see her breath in front of her. Bella was already pulling on her heavy petticoat, skirt, and shawl over her shift.

"Where are the baths?" Hannah asked, as she tied on her skirt.

Bella jerked her head toward the window. "In the bathhouse across the way. Our bath night is Monday."

So that was why the factory workers smelled funny, Hannah thought. Nobody had a bath more than once a week. Yuck.

Hannah was having serious doubts about her decision to quit her job. If she left the factory, she would have to leave Mrs. Nicolson's, and then where would she go? What would she do? For one crazy moment, she imagined she would run away to Balesworth and Mrs. Devenish. But then she remembered that Mrs. D. hadn't even been born yet. And how would she eat on the journey? Food was expensive and she hadn't been paid yet. In 1940, Hannah had thought that her choices were limited. But in 1851, she had no real choices at all.

Mrs. Nicolson was stirring the huge pot in which she had cooked the potatoes the night before. Hannah didn't recall anyone washing the pot, but, to her surprise, she also realized she didn't care much if the pot was dirty. She was hungry. "Mrs. Nicolson," she said, "Are there any other jobs round here aside from the factory? For someone like me, I mean?"

"None as you'd want, I expect," said Mrs. Nicolson. "You could find a job in service in the town."

That meant nothing to Hannah, and her face registered confusion. Mrs. Nicolson, looking up from the cooking pot, said, "I mean you could be a maid."

That sounded good. Hannah could just see herself in a cute little black and white uniform, serving tea and scones. "So how do I do that?"

"I don't know why you would want to be someone's maid-of-all-work," sniffed Mrs. Nicolson. "You'll never have a moment's peace, and only one afternoon off a week, if you're lucky. Scrubbing floors and cooking meals..."

Hannah changed her mind. That sounded dreadful.

Mrs. Nicolson placed four wooden bowls on the table, and filled each with a sticky, grey mess. It was oatmeal. Hannah hated oatmeal, even the super-sweet instant kind with marshmallows.

But right now, in 1851, Hannah could think of nothing that she wanted more than a hot bowl of oatmeal. She could barely wait until Charlie had said grace before digging in with her rough wooden spoon. The oatmeal wasn't sweet, it wasn't smooth, and she didn't care. In Hannah's opinion, this oatmeal was the weirdest version of one of the grossest, most disgusting foods ever invented. And it was delicious.

****

While Hannah was discovering a love of oatmeal in rainy Scotland, Alex was in sunny Savannah, Georgia. He was standing before a large gray brick mansion on a beautiful tree-lined city square.

After a moment's hesitation, he began to climb the curved iron staircase to the entrance on the second floor. But Jupe hung back on the street, reluctant to follow. Alex didn't notice that he was missing until after he had knocked on the door. "Jupe," he hissed, "Come on up!"

Jupe didn't move. "I can't go in the front door, no, sir."

Suddenly, it occurred to Alex that perhaps he, too, as a lowly would-be employee, should have gone to the kitchen door. But it was too late now, because a white woman in a mob cap was looking at him expectantly. "Yes, sir?" Her accent was Irish.

"I'm here to see Mr. Thornhill," Alex said nervously. "He asked me to apply for a job as a clerk?"

The maid didn't seem horrified by his reply, or that he had used the grand main entrance, and she stood aside to allow Alex into the hall. But he held back. "Um, my friend? He's downstairs."

She smiled at him. "Yes, sir, well, he's welcome, too." She stepped outside to beckon to Alex's friend. But when she looked down the steps and saw Jupe hovering nervously, his hat in his hands, her smile vanished. She turned to Alex in confusion. "Where's your friend, sir?"

Alex pointed at Jupe, and the woman's expression now turned very grim indeed. "Your boy can wait there, sir," she said, unsmiling.

"It's okay, Massa Alex," called Jupe, waving to him. "I'll be here."

Alex wasn't happy about this, but he entered the house alone. While the maid disappeared to announce his arrival, he looked around. The hall was luxurious. Plaster oak-leaves and acorns ran in a border along the tops of the walls, which were hung with portraits, including one of Mr. Thornhill himself. The maid soon returned, and she led Alex into an airy and elegant parlor furnished with a dark red chaise, a bookcase filled with leather-bound volumes, and an odd-looking vertical piano, which stood bolt upright with cascades of peach-colored silk covering the strings.

Amid the clutter of furniture and knick-knacks, it took Alex a second to pick out Mr. Thornhill. He was lounging in a chair by the fire, smoking a cigar. Across from him was Mr. MacGregor, the sinister man from the train. Mr. MacGregor glanced at Alex, his eyes widening for a second as he recognized him. Then he smiled slyly to himself, and took a puff on a large cigar.

Mr. Thornhill did not rise, nor did he ask Alex to sit down. During the awkward silence, he removed his cigar from his mouth. "How can I be of assistance to you, lad?"

Alex hoped he hadn't made a terrible mistake by coming here. His words tumbled out. "I hope so, sir. My name's Alex Day. I don't know if you remember me or anything, but we met in Snipesville, and you said you might…"

Mr. Thornhill interrupted, his eyes twinkling. "Of course I remember you. It was only last night, and I wasn't that drunk. Day, allow me to introduce my friend Mr. MacGregor."

Alex nodded. "Yes, sir, I've met Mr. MacGregor before. On the train." Mr. MacGregor cocked his head in greeting, with a faint smile on his face.

Mr. Thornhill gave a short hacking laugh, coughing out cigar smoke. "Well, damn me, that's a coincidence. So, MacGregor, do you think I ought to offer this lad a position?"

"I have no idea," Mr. MacGregor laughed. Alex wondered what was so funny. Mr. MacGregor continued, "As I told Master Day, if he would only sell his slave, he wouldn't need your job."

"Slave?" Mr. Thornhill sat up, furrowed his brow, and tapped ash from his cigar. He turned to Alex. "You had no slave with you at the inn."

There was an awkward silence. Then Alex said, "I met up with him in Millen. He belongs to my uncle… He loaned him to me." Mr. MacGregor was looking at Alex with that same slight smile, curling his lip, but Mr. Thornhill seemed to accept his explanation, and changed the subject. "How's your arithmetic?"

"Math? Um, okay, I guess."

Mr. Thornhill nodded. "Very good. I require a junior clerk. My practice is principally in law, but I also act as the factor, the agent, for certain companies in England and New York. In addition, I do a little… ah… investment in land. I would need you, for instance, to help me take stock at an estate I have recently acquired. Do you believe that such work would suit you, Day?"

Alex had no idea, but he needed a job. "I guess so. What would I do?"

Mr. Thornhill smiled, suspecting that Alex didn't understand what "taking stock" meant. "Very well. You will accompany me to my new property, and write down an account of all that we find there. I wish to know in some detail what it is that I own."

"Sure," said Alex. "I guess I could do that."

"Splendid. I shall have you work with Mr. Baird, my senior clerk."

"Great," Alex said. "Thanks! Have you got any suggestions for where I can live?"

Thornhill waved around him. "You are welcome to board here, Day. Mine is a spacious house…" As soon as he had said it, Mr. Thornhill paused and stared into space for a moment, before collecting himself. "Now, MacGregor, if you'll excuse me for a moment, I must inform the servants of young Day's arrival." He rose, and walked over to a small round object fixed to the wall at waist height. It looked like a large bicycle bell. He pulled back on it, but it made almost no audible sound. Sure enough, however, the Irish maid quickly reappeared, and Mr. Thornhill ordered her to prepare a room.

"Well, I must be off," said Mr. MacGregor, rising to his feet. "Thornhill, would you mind if I had a word with your new clerk on my way out? It's a private matter, pursuant to our conversation on the train." Mr. Thornhill nodded graciously to him.

As soon as they were out of the room, Mr. MacGregor turned to Alex. Quietly, he said, "He doesn't belong to you, does he, this slave?"

Alex was shocked. He held his breath and said nothing.

Mr. MacGregor leaned both hands on his walking stick, and shoved his face close to Alex's. "You could get yourself in a lot of trouble, boy. But I can help you. If you bring him to me, I'll only charge you twenty-five cents a day to hold him in my slave pen. Then I'll make sure he's sold so far away, even God Almighty would find it hard to track him down. But if you decide to keep him, well, I'm sorry, but I might just have to have a word with the patrols. It's my legal obligation as a gentleman. You understand me?"

Alex nodded mutely. He realized that MacGregor was blackmailing him. He hated this man.

Mr. MacGregor stepped back, and picked up his walking stick. "Just think about it. And when you're ready, come and see me. I'll get you a good price for him, too. Unless," and here he gave another short mocking laugh, "you have a better plan, since you're such a smart young man."

****

Hannah wasn't much looking forward to her weekend. She had learned from Bella that church, or "kirk" as the Scots called it, was the only entertainment

open on Sundays. Saturdays weren't much better: She only got part of the afternoon off work. The brightest spot of the whole weekend promised to be Friday, which was the twice-monthly payday.

Late on Friday afternoon, Hannah joined the other workers as they queued to collect their wages at the Counting House on Caithness Row. When she reached the front of the line, she wasn't paid in cash, but was handed a "Wages Ticket" for six shillings: That was two weeks wages. The wages ticket looked a lot like a check. In fact, Hannah realized, it was a check. She could either turn it into cash by standing in another line for the cashier, or spend it in the company-owned store next door.

Now, Hannah thought with excitement, she could go shopping. After about twenty tantalizing minutes in line outside the tiny shop, she stepped through the door to the high-pitched jangling of a bell. Mostly, the wares for sale were in sacks and barrels on the floor: Oatmeal and potatoes, cabbages and carrots. On a rough counter were baskets filled with bread and more vegetables, alongside fish and meat laid directly on the table. Other supplies sat on shelves, including a keg of whiskey, which a shop assistant was tapping into a small bottle for a customer. There were several large wheels of cheese, a whole ham, metal beer mugs, bolts of assorted cloth, and some simple ready-made clothes.

Customers snapped up meat, tea, bread, and even beer. Hannah was mystified by their enthusiasm: The men and women in line were looking eagerly at the merchandise, pointing to the goods on sale.

But since Hannah's food was bought and cooked by Mrs. Nicolson, and there was nothing fun to buy in the shop, she sadly returned to the Counting House, waited in line once more, and exchanged her wages ticket for cash.

It was probably just as well. When Hannah returned to the flat, Mrs. Nicolson asked her for board and lodging money of five shillings, which left her with only a shilling to spend on herself. She was not pleased. "It's kind of a rip-off here, huh? I mean, you even have to buy your food from the factory store."

"I've heard tell of many a swindle in factories," said Mrs. Nicolson, as she placed Hannah's earnings in her pocket. "There are owners who cheat their workers, and mill shops that charge very dear prices. But we are lucky. A friend of mine came from a mill in Glasgow, and she said that our New Lanark shop is the best anywhere. It brings us fresh vegetables and meat and milk from the mill farm, and all cheap. It's a fine thing, and I cannot imagine what we would do without it. If you don't believe me, walk up to the town of Lanark one Saturday, and see how expensive things are there."

"Is the shopping good in the town?" Hannah asked eagerly. "I mean, are there cool shops and stuff?"

"I don't know your meaning, lassie," sighed Mrs. Nicolson, not for the first time.

Hannah still refused to accompany Bella to the New Lanark school, figuring that it offered a very basic education, and that she wasn't likely to learn much. She already knew how to read and write, of course, and the math that Bella showed her was at the level of third-grade arithmetic. Anyway, school wasn't an appealing option at the best of times. At school in California, Hannah had spent most of her time stupefied with boredom.

Hannah didn't enjoy her work in the factory either. It was boring beyond belief. At first, as she got the hang of piecing, she found some satisfaction in fixing broken threads. It was a bit like knitting, or doing some other craft where you do the same thing over and over, except there was nothing relaxing about it. Every spinning mule screeched like a fire alarm crossed with a tractor engine. Elspeth and Bella constantly yelled at her to watch out as the mule moved backward and forward. And then there was the pain. Her hands bled and hurt dreadfully, and she wondered how much it was going to cost her in manicures to get the damage to her nails fixed when (and if) she returned to Snipesville. Over the weekend, her hands began to turn tough and calloused.

On Monday, Hannah was again examining the damage to her nails when she heard a man shout, "You there!"

She looked up to see the supervisor of the spinning works trotting toward her. Bella and Elspeth had spotted him too, and they were working harder than ever: Wisps of Elspeth's blond hair tumbled from under her cap as she pulled the frame backward. Hannah, meanwhile, was standing off to one side, leaning against a pillar, still staring at her fingernails.

"You, lassie, Hannah Dow!" yelled Mr. MacDonald.

She stared back at him. What was the man's problem? "I was just taking a break. My fingers hurt."

Mr. MacDonald, a thin, tall, balding man with glasses, looked pained as he confronted Hannah. He almost pleaded with her. "This isn't the time for resting. Back to work with you, and let this be the last time I warn you."

He reached above her head to a small obelisk-shaped block of wood hanging from a hook, and turned it so that the side painted black, with "No.4" written upon it, faced out toward him.

"What does that mean?" Hannah asked, looking above her.

Mr. MacDonald took off his glasses and polished them with his handkerchief. "What it means, lassie, is that you have a bad conduct mark. Mend your ways today, or there will be another....Ach, did nobody explain this to you?"

"No," said Hannah resentfully.

"Aye well, you'll know now..." he reached up and grasped the small wooden block. "This is the silent monitor. When I turn it so that the blue face, number three, points outward, like so, it signifies that your conduct is indifferent: Not bad, but not very good, either. When it is turned to yellow, number two, your conduct is good. When, as seems unlikely ever to occur, I find your work excellent, I will turn it to number one, which is the white face."

The system reminded Hannah of a kindergarten classroom. "What, do I get a time-out when I get three fours? This is embarrassing. I'm not a baby."

Mr. MacDonald sighed heavily. "Hannah, you know very well that I repeatedly admonished you for your inattention on Friday."

"Yeah," said Hannah. "But I thought that you chewing me out was, like, the punishment. This is... I mean, this is so stupid."

Mr. MacDonald drew himself up. "See here, Hannah, if you wish to take up the matter with Mr. Walker, and appeal my decision to mark you down in the book of character, you may..."

Hannah looked sharply at her boss. "What book did you say?"

"The book of character," repeated Mr. MacDonald. "It is the book in which I record the daily conduct marks."

Hannah was outraged now. "So you've been writing stuff about me, and you only tell me now? That's unreal."

"As I say," Mr. MacDonald said crisply, "You may take it up with the owner if you wish. Now, I have business to which I must attend."

As he walked away, Hannah yelled, "You better believe I will totally appeal this."

Bella sidled up to Hannah. "Don't bother," she whispered. "You know very well that you weren't paying the mule any mind. Come on, Hannah, get to work."

Hannah gasped at her, her face burning. "No! I'm tired! And you're not the boss of me!"

Hannah knew, she just knew, that no good would come of her losing her temper. But she could no longer control her anger. She stomped out of the spinning room, and was about to head downstairs, when she heard a cry behind her. Bella, distracted by Hannah's dramatic departure, had been knocked down when Elspeth drew back the frame.

Hannah was terrified she would be blamed and she didn't know what the consequences might be. She didn't want to get involved, so she turned back toward the stairwell, only to find her way blocked by Mr. MacDonald, who asked, "And where do you think you're going?"

Hannah tried to push past him. "Home! I'm too young to work, and I'm tired, and I've had enough. I'm going home."

He grabbed her wrists and said angrily, "You'll stay here, or you won't be back." Looking over her shoulder, he saw Bella lying on the floor, while Elspeth tried to tend to her. The spinning mule, meanwhile, was becoming hopelessly tangled.

Dropping Hannah's wrists and rushing to help the other girls, Mr. MacDonald yelled back over his shoulder, "That is the final straw! Hannah Dow, your services are no longer required at New Lanark!"

Hannah was aghast. "You're firing me? But you can't do that! I mean, can't you give me one of those bad conduct thingies instead?"

Mr. MacDonald didn't bother to reply.

Outside, standing beneath an overcast iron-grey sky, Hannah asked herself what on earth she would do now. A woman worker carrying a small parcel wrapped in brown paper emerged from the village shop and waved to Hannah, then trotted toward her.

"Hello, I was just picking up some of my favorite oatmeal," said the Professor. "Lovely stuff. Takes longer to cook than rolled oats, but worth the effort… And of course, it's organic, because pesticides haven't been invented yet. Why aren't you at work?"

Hannah wasn't in the mood for a chat. "Where have you been?"

The Professor scratched her head, and said, "Well, as I recall, you told me to get lost. But that's neither here nor there. What's up?"

Hannah said sullenly, "I got fired, that's what."

At this news, the Professor dropped her package, and tiny bits of pinhead oatmeal scattered everywhere. "Blast! Oh, no, are you serious? But, Hannah, you can't have been fired…"

Hannah exhaled sharply. "Yes, I was. It wasn't my fault. It was that stupid gaffer, that MacDonald dude. He blamed me because I got too tired to work. Anyway, it doesn't matter. I'm so sick of this. I shouldn't have to work, because I'm a kid. The mill is awful. In fact, this whole place is an armpit. Come on, take me home. I'm done."

"Hannah, I can't. You think I have that kind of power, and I…"

Hannah interrupted her. "Fine, then take me back to 1940, to Balesworth.

At least let me stay with Verity and Mrs. D."

"Hannah…"

"Yeah, I know. You can't. So find me a decent place to live and then let me know when it's over, okay?"

The Professor rubbed her forehead. "I did find you a good place to live, at Mrs. Nicolson's. And New Lanark is a great place to live and work, believe it or not. But you messed this up, so you're going to have to figure out what to do next. Mrs. Nicolson might have some ideas, but I don't. I'm sorry. I haven't got time to get you sorted out. I'm having enough trouble with Brandon. And now I don't even have my oatmeal. Great."

She walked away, but Hannah followed her, calling out, "Where are you going, witch? Why can't I go with you, huh? Do you have a time machine parked round the corner, or what? C'mon, mystery lady, tell me! And what are you doing to Brandon and my brother?"

Without warning, the Professor roughly pushed her aside, and dashed back into the shop. Hannah tore after her. But by the time she passed through the door, even though she was mere seconds behind, the Professor had vanished. To the consternation of the shopkeeper behind the counter, Hannah searched the premises, but to no avail. The Professor was gone.

Hannah tracked down Mrs. Nicolson to the washhouse, and asked her for advice and the return of her rent money. She certainly got the advice.

"There's not much work here," Mrs. Nicolson said as she scrubbed clothes on the ribbed iron washboard. "You could try Glasgow. Do you know anybody there?"

Hannah shook her head, and Mrs. Nicolson looked at her doubtfully. "Or… well, I don't like to suggest it…But my sister Jessie in Dundee might take you in and help you find work. Her daughters are weavers, every one of them. Maybe they could find you a position in a mill there."

Hannah resented Mrs. Nicolson's lack of enthusiasm. Why was she hesitating to send Hannah to her sister? Sulkily, she said, "Could you at least write a letter to introduce me?"

Mrs. Nicolson wiped at her forehead with a soapy red hand. "Och, no need. You just tell her Abby sent you."

"Okay. What's her address?"

"You'll find her in Castle Lane, by The Vault. That's where she stays. You'll find her there. Just ask folk and they'll know the way."

Hannah couldn't understand how this address would work, but she figured it meant that Dundee was as tiny as New Lanark.

"Can I have my rent money back?"

Mrs. Nicolson stopped scrubbing. "Hannah, you have the cheek of the devil. I spent the last of your rent money on my messages in the shop not two hours hence. No, lass, you go on to Dundee."

Hannah shook her head in despair. "I can't. I've got no money for the train, or hotels, or…"

Mrs. Nicolson rummaged in her apron pocket. "Here's a shilling. It's all I have. Now go and take three of the oatcakes sitting on our table. Mind and don't take them all, or there will be no supper for Charlie, Bella and me."

"Thanks, I guess," said Hannah ungratefully. "Maybe I can get to Dundee on a shilling and three sawdust cookies. How far is Dundee, anyway?"

"How would I know? I've never been there. It's to the north-eastward, that's all I know. Good luck to you, lass."

Mrs. Nicolson began to run the wet clothes through the mangle to squeeze out the washing water. The conversation was over.

****

Back in the present day, the Professor was in the New Lanark archive, frantically paging through the stiff white pages of the leather-bound overseer's book, trying to figure out what had happened. This wasn't supposed to be how things turned out. But the book recorded that Hannah Dow was dismissed for insubordination. The Professor now had to come to terms with the fact that the story she thought she knew was no longer what had happened. The past had changed.

****

Hannah was tired. Very tired. Her feet were soaking because her thin shoes were no match for the mud and water on the roads. Occasionally, she passed a stone marker that told her how many miles she was from Glasgow. She had only herself for company. She had carried her food in a knotted handkerchief, but now the food was gone, and she was starving. She had no spare clothes, and she was pretty sure she smelled bad. Her feet were killing her, and she felt a blister starting.

The farmhouses and hamlets she had passed had not looked inviting, but it was getting late, and she knew she would have to stop soon. Would sixpence get her a night in an inn? How long was it since she had even seen an inn? As if things weren't bleak enough, it started to rain. Hannah pulled her shawl over her head, and kept trudging on.

She cast an eye over the next cottage she saw. It was tiny, but its chimney was belching coal smoke. To the right side of the cottage was a low door. Who lives here, she thought to herself, Scottish munchkins? Nervously, she knocked on the thick wooden door, and heard someone inside rise and unlock it from within.

As soon as the door opened, Hannah felt the wonderful warmth of a fireplace. The young woman who answered had a friendly face and she was carrying a baby on her right arm. "Look at you," she said soothingly in an Irish accent. "You're soaked through! Do you want to stay? Come away in, and let's get you dry."

Hannah was so grateful, she could have cried. She perched herself on a low stool in front of a blazing hearth. The whole room was so tiny, she could practically have touched the walls on each side if she had stood in the middle.

"Have you been tramping for long?" the woman asked, settling down in a chair with the baby in her arms. She casually put the baby back to breastfeed. Hannah was amazed. Who would have thought the Victorians had breastfeeding? Hannah had always heard the Victorians were seriously hung up and embarrassed about everything. She had assumed they fed babies with bottles, just to be polite.

"I've been walking all day," Hannah said. "I'm headed to someplace called Dundee to see if I can find work. I guess it's more far away than I thought."

The woman looked serious. "It's quite a ways indeed. You can stay the night here, but we've no bed for you, so I'll fetch you some straw from the barn, and I have a blanket spare you can use. Oh, and I've a bit of broth you could have. Where are you come from?"

When Hannah told her she was from New Lanark, the woman said, "O'Donnell, my husband, and me, we're from Ireland, from County Clare. During the Famine, we managed to get away on one of the emigrant boats to Liverpool. My husband found a little work there, so we used the money to buy a ticket to America, and took a ship bound for Boston, but the boat sprung a leak, and dropped us in Glasgow. We never got our money back, so we were penniless. I doubt we'll ever see America. Still, we found this land, and my husband built this cottage."

"How did you afford the property?" Hannah wondered aloud.

Mrs. O'Donnell seemed startled by the question. "We don't own it. We're squatters."

Just then, a large man in a heavy coat came in from outside, and shook the rain off himself. "Now, who would you be?" he said to Hannah as he scraped the mud from his boots onto the dirt floor.

"This girl's on the tramp for work," explained Mrs. O'Donnell, reaching over to poke at the fire, her baby tucked in the crook of her other arm. "I said she could stop here the night for a few pennies…"

"Hang on," said Hannah. "You didn't say anything about money. You want me to pay to sleep on straw?"

Mr. O'Donnell gave her a hard look. "We're not the casual ward of the workhouse, now."

"I have no idea what that means," said Hannah. "But I'm so not paying to sleep on straw."

"Then you'll have to see how sleeping under a hedge suits you," said Mr. O'Donnell, opening the door and gesturing at her to leave his house. "Be off with you."

Hannah didn't get far. There was nowhere to go, and the dark evening was now pitch black. Fortunately, it had stopped raining, and she picked out a fairly dry spot under a bushy hedge by a potato field next to the O'Donnells' house. She brushed away some twigs, and tucked herself under the low branches, nestling into the dirt. She was so exhausted, so utterly cold and hungry, it actually felt good to cry.

Hannah was awoken by a foot gently nudging her in the shoulder in the bleak half-light of the morning. "Here," Mrs. O' Donnell said softly, crouching down to hand Hannah something wrapped in a piece of cloth. Stiff from cold and bleary-eyed, Hannah rolled out from under the hedge, and sat up. She opened the packet to gaze in wonderment at a soft grey lump. "'Tis porridge," whispered Mrs. O'Donnell, "for your journey. I saw you were still here when I came out to milk the cow. Now I'd be best getting along before himself sees me talking to you."

With that, she scurried away. Hannah, after watching her disappear into the house, looked at the grey cold oatmeal lump for only a second before sinking her teeth into it and wolfing it down.

As she was scraping the remains of the cereal off her teeth, a voice said, "Funny how much less picky you are when you're really hungry."

The Professor leaned down and handed Hannah three shillings, followed by two items that were totally out of place in 1851 Scotland: A metal travel mug filled with coffee, and an individually-wrapped granola bar. "Here, breakfast. It's all I was able to grab for you."

Hannah looked at the mug sourly. "I don't like coffee."

The Professor's eyebrows shot up. "Oh, I thought you did. I mean, you love Starbucks."

"Only the strawberry Frappuccinos," said Hannah, sniffing at the coffee with a scrunched-up nose.

The Professor pursed her lips. "Yes, well, girl with expensive tastes, this will have to do. And try to make as much progress as you can toward Dundee today, because I don't know when or if I can help out again."

Hannah tore open the chocolate chip granola bar, and gulped it down in a few bites, chewing greedily, and licking the stickiness from her fingers. When she looked up again, the Professor was gone. "Typical!" she said, through a mouthful of oatmeal crumbs.

****

At first, through the darkness, all Brandon could see of the Hitherton Union Workhouse was an imposing silhouette. Approaching it took him through a vegetable garden toward the large brick building with a forbidding entrance of white stone. He climbed the steps, and pulled on the bell at the gate. When he was greeted with silence, he rang again.

Eventually, the door opened to reveal a small man in a stained brown suit. He had thinning red hair, and a pale white pock-marked face, against which his ginger moustache stood out in sharp relief. He looked furious.

"What do you want?" he said accusingly in a London accent. "And how dare you use the Guardians' entrance?"

Brandon could see no alternative but to bluff his way in. "Um, I think I live here?"

The man wasn't impressed. "Not anymore you don't. I'll meet you round the back." He gestured fiercely to his right, and slammed the door in Brandon's face.

Brandon was confused, but he stumbled back down the steps, and made his way to the rear of the building. His first instinct was to tell the man that he'd never been here in his life, but then he decided it might be wiser to see how things played out.

When he reached the gate at the back of the workhouse, he found a family waiting to be admitted. The man's clothes were ragged, and he held his hat in his hands as he stared hopelessly at the ground. His desperately thin wife was wearing a filthy, soaking dress. Her wet hair was falling in rats' tails from under her bonnet, and she cried and held tightly to her wailing baby. They all looked so miserable that Brandon looked away, embarrassed for them.

Soon, the workhouse man unlocked the gate with an enormous jangling set of keys. "Casual ward or admission?" he growled.

"We need to stay longer than a night, sir," the ragged father whispered humbly. "Thank you, sir."

"You want admitted, then. Name?"

"Weaver, sir, John Weaver and family. I tried to find work, sir, honestly I did. I'm a nailmaker come down from Sheffield, but there isn't no work here neither..."

The workhouse man wouldn't let John Weaver finish his story. "Never mind that. You're here, and that's all that concerns me. I'm the Master of this workhouse, and the Matron will be here in a minute to take charge of your wife and child. Go into the wash house, Weaver. You too, lad." He directed a worried Brandon to follow John Weaver into a grim whitewashed building with bricked-in windows.

As the Master followed them, he said, "What do you want back here then, Brandon Clark? Have you lost your job already?"

"No, sir," Brandon stammered. How did this guy know his name?

"That's as well, then. I suppose you never found yourself lodgings, is that it?"

Brandon seized on this. "That's right, sir. I couldn't find a place to live. So I'm, er, back."

The Master shook his head. "You can't live here, not now you've been discharged. I would put you in the workhouse casual ward, since you're only here for the night, but it's full up. So I'll put you in the able-bodied men's dormitory tonight, and you'll need to find yourself other lodgings on the morrow."

The paint was caked thickly on the bare brick walls of the washhouse. Weaver was soon standing naked in a large shallow rectangular pool, up to his ankles in cold and dirty water, trying to bathe, and weeping to himself. But Brandon was resisting taking off his clothes. He said lightly, "Hey, I'll just take a shower tomorrow morning..."

The Master puffed out his cheeks. "Don't be insolent, Clark. It's regulations that every pauper admitted has a bath. Get on with it." He waited until Brandon and Weaver finished bathing, and had dressed in the ugly grey workhouse uniform. Then he ordered them to follow him outside.

Brandon and Weaver trudged across a courtyard, surrounded by high walls and the forbidding main building. Apart from a water pump in the center, the yard's only distinguishing feature was a pile of broken rocks, to which the Master pointed. "Tomorrow morning, Clark, I ought to put you to rock-breaking to earn your keep. But you're a puny little lad, so you can paint a bit of the stairwell instead." He laughed. Brandon was not amused.

The Master opened a door to the main building of the workhouse. It smelled of boiled oatmeal and human bodies. The walls were freshly painted in two different colors, dark green on the top half, and darker green below. The floors were stone. Brandon thought desperately that he had checked himself into a prison.

"Can't I see my wife and baby?" mumbled Weaver as the three of them tramped upstairs.

"No," said the Master, who Brandon now thought of as the jailer. "It's against regulations." He opened a door into a room packed with narrow beds, most of which were already occupied.

"You're lucky," said the Master, jerking his head toward two empty beds. He left without another word, closing the door firmly behind him.

Brandon threw himself onto a bed but promptly jumped up again, crying out in pain. Peeking under the mattress, he found that the bed was made from iron bars, topped with a thin straw mattress. Brandon carefully reclined on it, feeling the bars poking through the mattress and bedcovers, and laid his head on the hard thin pillow. The room was freezing, and although he knew he would miss the additional padding, he slipped himself under the coarse grey blanket and thin sheet. Everything felt rough, sore, and generally miserable. Which was pretty much how Brandon felt about himself. He was in a prison for poor people. Now what, he wondered?

Chapter 7:
LIFE IN THE CITY

Hannah finally glimpsed the thicket of smoky chimneys that was the skyline of Dundee, and not a moment too soon. By this time, she could think of nothing but food. Her stomach felt like it was trying to eat itself. Early that morning, she had struggled to persuade herself to get up from the comfortable straw of the stone barn in which she had spent the night, until she realized that it was too tempting to lie there and die of starvation.

Now she was standing on a hillside in the tiny village of Ferryport-on-Craig. Dundee lay only a mile and a half away. The problem was that between Hannah and Dundee lay the broad estuary of the River Tay, and she had no money to pay for the ferry. Desperately, she wondered if she could swim across. Then she had a better idea. Why not beg? And why hadn't she thought of this before? She had always been good at school fundraisers, selling junk like wrapping paper and bad candy …

With a burst of enthusiasm, Hannah approached the first man she saw, and asked him for money. He told her that begging was a sin, and that she should go home to her mother. If only, she thought bitterly. Next, she wandered up to an older woman who was beating a rug outside her cottage, and said brightly, "Hi, got any spare change?"

"Eh?" The woman squinted at her.

Hannah rubbed her fingers together to demonstrate. "Change? Like, money left over from spending a shilling? You got any?"

The woman held up her rug beater threateningly and advanced on Hannah. "Away with you! Rob me, would you, you besom?"

Hannah ran. Clearly, her sales pitch needed some work.

Finally, she knocked at the door of the minister's house next to the church, and told her tale of woe. It worked. The minister's wife took pity on her, gave her a penny for the ferry, and even handed her a chunk of bread to eat. Hannah demolished the bread on the doorstep.

Within an hour, Hannah was hunkered down in a tiny boat, watching the green fields behind grow smaller and smaller. Turning to look the other way, she watched nervously as Dundee grew ever nearer. The city—and it was a city, not a village as she had hoped-- crouched ominously at the foot of a very steep hill. The closer Hannah got to Dundee, the worse it looked: Plumes of smoke poured from dozens of factory chimneys, and a brown fog hung over the whole place.

At the dock, seagulls squawked and circled overhead. Hannah carefully climbed the scary stone steps that jutted from the harbor wall, then set off aimlessly down the dockside. Grey stone buildings fronted the harbor, facing dozens of sailing ships that lay at anchor, their garishly-painted prows pointing over the street, and their billowing sails drawn up to the rigging. Among the ships were steamers, with great paddle wheels on either side, but even these modern ships had sails to serve them when their engines ran out of coal or the winds were good.

Hannah was overwhelmed by the deafening din of the city: Horses' hooves and massive wagon wheels clattered on the cobbles; a man walked by pushing a handcart with squeaky wheels; four dockworkers in shirt-sleeves and broad-brimmed hats shouted and cursed each other as they pulled an enormous barrel with thick ropes; a herd of cattle waiting to board a ship lowed in their iron pen; and the constant screech of seagulls ripped the air. Everywhere Hannah stepped, her feet squelched in foul-smelling muddy stuff. Judging by the stench it gave, much of it was poo. Worse, it smelled like people poo. But that couldn't be right, could it?

On the dockside, construction workers were building what looked like the entrance to a castle: One massive stone archway, flanked by two smaller arches, was already complete. When Hannah paused to inspect this odd structure, she leaned against a huge cloth-wrapped bale. Trickling out of it was a fiber, but it wasn't cotton. Curious, she pulled out a tangle of prickly golden threads, and sniffed at them, inhaling their musty scent. One of the construction workers had propped a clay bottle of drink on another bale, and he was watching her with amusement.

"It's jute," he said. "It comes all the way from India."

Hannah nodded, and then asked, "Why are you guys building a castle? Is there a war?"

The man burst out laughing. "A castle? Nah, nah, lass, this isn't a castle. This is the Royal Arch, to celebrate Her Majesty's visit to Dundee."

Hannah was thrilled, because maybe her stay in Dundee would have an upside. A royal visit! She would see Queen Victoria! "She's coming here? When?"

"Four years ago." He laughed.

"Very funny," Hannah said sarcastically. "Hey, can you tell me where I could find some lady called Jessie who lives in a castle? In a vault?"

He laughed again. "Eh, lass, you're fankled, you're muddled... I think you're wanting Castle Lane, for it's by a close called The Vault. I don't know your Jessie, but I'm sure you'll find her there. Oh, and take her a bow and arrow, will you? She'll need it, living in a castle."

"Ha. Ha. Ha," said Hannah unsmilingly.

He grinned at her, and then pointed a finger at the city that rose behind them. "Och, just go up yon hill," (he pronounced it "hull") "That's Castle Street, and carry on till you get to the High Street, then turn left. You'll find the Vault next to the Pillars, that's what we ca' the Town House, that's yon great big building with pillars in the front. You canna miss it."

Following his directions took Hannah steeply uphill on slippery stone cobbles, and past long rows of grey stone buildings. Everything in Dundee seemed to be grey or brown or black, from the sky to the ground.

And it was a busy place: Lady shoppers in bonnets held up their long skirts to keep them out of the muck; A couple of rich-looking gentlemen carrying walking canes were discussing warehouses as they passed Hannah by. As it started to rain, a grand-looking horse-drawn carriage halted. The coachman jumped down and pulled the hood over the pale young woman and little boy seated inside.

Most of the people Hannah saw looked poor. Men and women shuffled past on foot, holding their heads down as the rain fell. The women draped heavy woolen plaid shawls around their shoulders or over their heads, the men wore caps, and all of them clomped along in heavy worn-out shoes.

Ahead to the right, Hannah spied a massive stone church with a huge square tower, and facing it, McNaughtan's Royal Hotel. Most impressive of all was the Town House, a huge building with a spire and classical columns. Hannah almost missed it, having mistaken it for a church. Seven arches opened into a covered walkway, where two elegantly-dressed gentlemen in tall hats quietly discussed business, standing close together so nobody could hear what they were saying. Poor men loitered under the archways, and three bare-footed boys kicked around a large pebble. They almost knocked down a gentleman: When he yelled at them, they swore back at him.

Hannah's hope that she might be headed to the fancy part of town evaporated when she spotted the street called The Vault. Reluctantly, she entered the narrow dark alleyway. All sorts of revolting filth was strewn across it. A dead cat lay on the cobbles, and Hannah hurried past it. She emerged into a small courtyard, in which lay an evil-smelling heap that looked and smelled like dung and rotting meat. Holding her hand to her nose to try to shut out the disgusting stink, she bolted through another archway into a short tunnel. As she emerged, a sign on the wall announced that she had arrived in Castle Lane.

Castle Lane wasn't actually a lane, but a triangular courtyard. The ramshackle tall buildings that surrounded it on three sides met each other at crazy angles. Strings of drying laundry hung haphazardly on washing lines that ran from windows. Window panes were thickly begrimed with soot. Stone, smoke, chimneys, filthy windows, and hideous smells: This was Hannah's first impression of Dundee in 1851.

Bells tolled, and Hannah guessed that they came from the large church nearby. But then several men and women in millworkers' costume dashed past her, and she realized that it was a factory bell she had heard chiming, just like the one in New Lanark. When a bunch of young women came running from a doorway that sat between a liquor store and a pub, Hannah took off after them, yelling, "Hey, I have a question!"

One woman turned her head only long enough to yell back, "Eh, well, come on and ask me, but I canna be late for my work!"

Hannah ran alongside her. "I'm looking for an old woman called Jessie… She works at a mill, or something?"

"Is that right?" puffed the young woman. "Maybe it'll be Jessie Gordon you're wanting. That's my mother. Go in the door you saw me come out, and up tae the third landing."

Hannah stopped, winded, as the woman disappeared around the corner. Gordon? That name sounded familiar.

Entering the dark tenement stairwell, Hannah was followed by a woman smoking a short white clay tobacco pipe, and carrying on her back an enormous basket filled to the brim with fresh fish. Hannah and the fisherwoman exchanged no words, but their footsteps echoed as they walked up the stone steps. On the third floor, Hannah knocked on a door, hoping it was the right one. Almost immediately, it flung open, letting a blast of light into the gloom of the landing.

A short stout woman with graying brown hair knotted into a bun filled the doorway, her arms akimbo. To Hannah's alarm, she started yelling. "Did I not tell you I don't want your rotten stinking fish again…." Then she stopped short, looked Hannah up and down, and said, "You're not the fishwife." She looked past Hannah to the terrified fisherwoman, who was already rapidly disappearing down the stairs, and shook her fist. "Aye, be gone with you, and dinna darken my door again or I'll give you a right kick up the erse!" She returned her attention to Hannah, and barked, "Anyways, who are you?"

Hannah shrank away from her, and hoped desperately that she'd knocked on the wrong door. She began to gabble. "Mrs. Gordon? I'm Hannah… er … Dow? Your sister, Abby Nicolson, she is your sister, yeah? She told me to come ask you for help finding a job and maybe I could stay with you, but if that's not cool with you, hey…"

Suddenly, the woman gave a brilliant smile, and reached out a hand to beckon Hannah inside. "Och, why did you not say? I'm old Jessie, indeed. Come away in the house, Hannah, and have a seat before the fire."

The "house" turned out to be two tiny rooms, the first of which was like Mrs. Nicolson's, only smaller. It had a single curtained-off bed and a tiny fireplace, in which a pot and a kettle sat on either side of the coals. Glimpsing the second room, Hannah spotted two more beds, lying side-by-side. The low ceiling was stained with smoke and cracked in places, exposing wooden ribs through the plaster. The apartment smelled strongly of too many people packed in too small a space, as well as coal smoke and reeking tallow candles. Hannah caught a whiff of the suffocating stench of raw sewage blended with cold damp mist that wafted in from the courtyard through the broken window panes that were stuffed with rags in a losing effort to keep out the cold. The windows that were not broken were filthy. Damp and mold were flaking dark red paint off the walls. The only covering on the stone floors was a thin old rug in front of the fireplace.

It was all Hannah could do not to flee in disgust. Instead, she sat down across from Jessie, and tried to pull her chair as close as she could to the tiny guttering fire.

"So how come you live here instead of with your sister?" Hannah asked, amazed that anyone would choose Dundee over New Lanark.

Jessie sighed. "Aye, well…My man, Bobby, he's been dead and buried these past three years. It were him that brought me to Dundee. Oh, I was greeting and wailing for days after I saw this place, it was that grim. But it's getting better, bit by bit. My man was an overseer in the weaving shed at Suttie's… That's Sutherland's Mill… and he saw to it that all the girls got jobs in the factory. So we get by. I've five daughters and a grandson to cook and wash for, mind. But Mina's getting married soon, and I've no doubt I'll have Mary, Mem, and Betty off my hands by and by, so I dinna mind taking you in as a lodger. It will be a bit tight until Mina goes, but, ach, we'll manage."

Hannah looked around. "So where's your grandson? Does he work in the mill, too?"

"Ach, no, John's but seven years old. And how would I ken where he is? He's only home for dinner and tea, and between times, he's roaming the streets. You know how laddies are."

Hannah did not know how "laddies" were. In her experience, "laddies" stayed home, watched TV, played computer games, went to school, and belonged to soccer teams. They lived under the stern gaze of grown-ups, or parked in front of a screen. They did not wander the streets at all. Looking around the room, Hannah wasn't so surprised that John was expected to make himself scarce. How did all these people fit in here?

"Can your girls find work for me?" Hannah asked abruptly.

Jessie narrowed her eyes thoughtfully. "You're a cotton spinner, are you?"

"No, well, not yet… I'm a piecer."

"Aye," said Jessie. "But you're a cotton worker all the same. You'll have to learn the jute to work in Suttie's Mill. Jute is what sacks are made with. It's brown and coarse, not like cotton at all. Dinna mind, they'll soon learn you. You'll make three shillings a week, and I'll need two shillings an' sixpence for your room and board."

Hannah resentfully agreed to the arrangement. What else could she do?

Sharing a bed with three of Jessie's teenage daughters was hardly comfortable: Hannah was kicked awake several times, and she fell out of bed twice. Still, it was better than sleeping under a hedge, and her bedmates kept her warm. She was embarrassed about smelling bad from her journey, but everyone else smelled like they could have used a bath, too. The tin tub that hung outside the building was borrowed by a different family every night, and judging from the smell in the bedroom, it had been a few days since the Gordons had had their turn.

There was another reason for the stinkiness that night: The chamberpot was full, almost to the brim. Hannah shook Mem awake to ask her what to do about it. Mem mumbled, "Och, just chuck it oot the window." Hannah pulled a face as she picked up the pot, quickly pushed open the window, and flung the chamberpot's contents into the night. Almost immediately, shouting and cursing wafted up from the courtyard. She peered nervously through the window: She had splashed two drunken women and a man who were staggering home from the pub. Before they could spot her, she ducked back inside.

Early the next morning, after a breakfast of thick oatmeal, Hannah and the Gordon girls hurried with the crowds of workers headed for the jute mills through Dundee's dingy, narrow, and smelly streets and alleys. Hannah shivered in the thick cold mist, and tried not to slip: A few streets were cobblestoned, but most were muddy tracks, and she quickly learned that it was impossible to avoid stepping in filth.

Jessie's eldest daughter Mina, a young woman in her mid-twenties who was as short and plump as her mother, took Hannah to apply for work. In the office of Sutherland's Mill, two clerks stood at their tall desks, scribbling with ink pens. Mina loudly cleared her throat. One of the men stopped writing, and, after a deliberate pause, looked up sourly. "Yes?"

"This here's my cousin and she needs a job," Mina said, jerking her head at Hannah.

"Indeed," said the clerk skeptically. "And what can she do?"

"She's a piecer, and a good one," Mina said emphatically. Hannah, standing next to her, tried not to giggle at Mina's brazen fibs.

The man looked at Mina's determined broad face, and decided that it was easier not to argue with her. "Very well, but she'll work here on probation, mind. Name?"

Hannah was coached by Maggie O'Leary, a skinny little Irish girl of her own age, and it didn't take her long to learn to piece the jute as the machine spun it into rough string. But jute made her hands more sore and itchy than ever.

Mr. Mitchell, the spinning room gaffer, was a short burly man who looked like a pug dog, and who sweated profusely in the heat of the mill. He constantly flitted among the machines yelling at workers, and stopping occasionally to cuff someone about the head, especially the children who worked as scavengers. Maggie told Hannah that his nickname was Tom the Devil, or, as she pronounced it, Tam the Deil.

"He's a menace," Maggie yelled to Hannah over the noise, as she helped Hannah fix a handful of threads. "He has all the girls greeting, and some of the boys, too. He's always giving someone a swearing or a skelping, and they say he broke a girl's arm last year. Don't give him reason to look at you." Suddenly, her eyes widened, and she whispered "Oh, Jesus, Mary, and Joseph," before putting her head down and busying herself with the piecing. When Hannah looked up, Mr. Mitchell was standing uncomfortably close to her. Worse, he was smiling at her. It was very creepy.

He said to Hannah, "You're new."

Afraid to say the wrong thing, she nodded.

Suddenly, his smile turned into a scowl, and he wagged a finger in her face. "Aye, well, I just saw you talking. The rule is silence. You just watch your lip, lassie, or I'll be after you."

Hannah didn't like the sound of that, but she said nothing. To her surprise, as soon as Tam the Deil's back was turned, Maggie straightened up, and stuck out her tongue at him. An older spinner nearby saw her do it and laughed, and Maggie winked back at her.

At the end of a very long morning, the factory bell clanged, and as the spinning mules shut down, the workers literally ran for the doors. Hannah was confused. Was this a fire drill? She struggled to keep up behind Maggie as the Irish girl tore through the factory yard, and out of the huge wooden doors into the narrow alleyway.

"Why are we running?" puffed Hannah. "Where are we going?"

"We're away home for our dinner, now, and there's not much time," Maggie gasped. "Where do you stay?"

Hannah puffed, "In Castle Lane, I guess. It's a dump."

"By The Vault? Oh, that's not so bad. We stay on Whitehall Close. Here, I'll show you." Maggie led Hannah into a tiny alleyway between two buildings on the High Street.

When Hannah slipped into Whitehall Close, she was aghast. "You're kidding me…"

It was impossibly narrow: An adult standing in the middle of it could easily have touched both sides at once. The alley gave Hannah the creeps: The stone buildings were crumbling, and wide gaps yawned beneath the decaying wooden doors that led into people's ground-floor apartments, so that there was nothing to keep out the rain, the rats, and whatever was in the filthy gutter that ran down one side. There were almost no windows on either side of the street. Hannah gagged as they passed a decaying dog's corpse. Finally, she reluctantly followed Maggie as she ducked into a tiny room with no windows, furniture, light or air. The floor was bare dirt, the air was as damp and freezing as it was outside, and the smell was indescribable. As Hannah's eyes adjusted to the gloom, she focused on a filthy pile of straw and rags in a corner. It moved.

"What will ye be wantin' now?" growled a man's voice, his words slurred, as he looked up from the rag pile.

"Nothing, Dad," said Maggie. "Just a wee visit, like. Go back to sleep, won't you?"

As Maggie closed the door behind them, she said to a shocked Hannah, "Now you know why I never take my dinner at home. C'mon, and let's away for a mutton pie."

"But I haven't got any money…" Hannah said, still reeling from the sight of

CHAPTER SEVEN

Maggie's "house" and father.

Maggie pulled some coins from her pocket. "Then I'll treat you. Just this once, mind."

The girls walked back along the busy and dirty High Street, until they came to a canopied stall loaded down with steaming stacks of small round pies, each with a hole in its pastry lid. Maggie handed over some coins, and soon she and Hannah were carrying warm pies wrapped in greasy sheets of newspaper. Hannah's mouth watered, but her feet were killing her. She needed to rest. She said wistfully to Maggie, "Is there a park or anything close by? I want to sit down."

"A park?" said Maggie, furrowing her brow.

"Yeah," said Hannah. "You know… Grass, duck ponds, frisbees, somewhere we can sit with our pies? Anywhere?"

Maggie said, "We could sit on the church steps, I suppose."

As the two girls squatted on the steps of the Episcopal Church, Hannah unpacked her pie, and took her first bite. The pastry was tough but tasty, and she got a mouthful of a rich meaty gravy with it. It was so delicious that within a few minutes it was gone, leaving Hannah to lick her oily fingers wistfully.

As she waited for Maggie to finish her meal, Hannah started reading the grease-stained newspaper in which her pie had been wrapped. Maggie was impressed. "You can read?"

Hannah said, "Sure, can't you?" But Maggie shook her head. Hannah was astonished: She thought everyone could read. She looked over the front page of the *Dundee, Perth, and Cupar Advertiser*, and quickly lost interest. It was all about people, places, and things she had never heard of. But just as she was about to drop the paper on the ground, something on the back page caught her eye: A crude drawing of a ship.

She picked it up and read: *FOR SAN FRANCISCO DIRECT, The Beautiful British Built Clipper Barque 'SALEM', CAPTAIN B. HAGUE.* Hannah pored through the advertisement, and became very excited. *…has very superior cabin accommodation for passengers, and presents in every respect a most eligible conveyance.* She wasn't sure what "a most eligible conveyance" might be, but it sounded very luxurious. Finally, the ad gave an address in Liverpool, where people could write for tickets.

This had to be some sort of sign! How cool would that be, to go home to California? Of course, she would get home in 1851, but maybe the Professor would bring her back to the present in the city… And then a thought struck her. Wouldn't that be the time of the Gold Rush? Why be poor in Dundee when she could be rich in San Francisco? Excitedly, Hannah scanned the ad to see how much tickets cost, but no price was mentioned. It was then that she spotted another ad below it on the same page:

CHEAP CONVEYANCE BETWEEN DUNDEE AND LONDON DURING THE GREAT EXHIBITION, WITH BOARD AND LODGING WHILE IN LONDON.

This was interesting, too…

The DIRECTORS of the DUNDEE, PERTH, and LONDON SHIPPING COMPANY, desirous of affording all classes an opportunity of visiting London during the EXHIBITION have resolved to make the Fares by their Steamers (unrivalled for speed and comfort) during the ensuing season, and commencing upon the 1st of May next, at the following moderate scale, viz:-
 Main Cabin £5 5 0
 Second do. £ 3 13 6

Now Hannah's heart sank. Five pounds, five shillings! Three pounds, thirteen shillings and sixpence! And only to go so far as London? If that was typical, there was no way she would be able to afford San Francisco unless she robbed a bank. She was only making three shillings a week at Sutherland's Mill, and most of that would go to Jessie for her rent and food. She thought about taking a second job… But when would she have time to work a second job? Downcast, she nonetheless carried on reading.

This charge shall include all Fees to servants, (Hannah guessed that this meant tips to the crew),*and Provisions on the Voyage up and down* (Meals, Hannah guessed again), *and BED and BREAKFAST on Board while the Vessel remains in London. By this arrangement, parties securing Berths will have FIVE DAYS IN LONDON, with every accommodation on board equal to the first Hotels, and without further charge—thereby avoiding all imposition which strangers in London are often exposed to* (People could stay on board and avoid tourist trap hotels.)

Hannah ripped the page out of the newspaper, folded it carefully, and put it in her pocket. Maybe she would find a five-pound note lying on the street. Or something. Both ads seemed to be calling her name.

She turned to Maggie. "So, how about dessert?"

"Come on, then," said Maggie. "You talked me into it. Let's split a rhubarb pie."

Hannah rose and followed her new friend into a small bakery, where the air was rich and sweet and buttery, with a slight tang of cooking fruit. Soon, Maggie was holding a warm pastry that looked exactly the same as the meat pies the girls had eaten, only with a pinkish ooze leaking from the top crust. Ladled on top was a generous dollop of yellow cream: It was almost as thick as butter.

"You know how you were asking about a park," said Maggie doubtfully. "Well, we haven't much time, mind, but we could go to the Magdalen Green, although…"

"Come on," Hannah said, grabbing her hand and pulling her. "Show me. I can't believe I'm saying this, but I want fresh air."

They found a bench in the riverfront park. Hannah had no idea why Maggie hadn't suggested this earlier: It had a beautiful view of the River Tay, and the green fields of the county of Fife beyond. The rhubarb pie made a messy but marvelous feast, and the girls laughed as they fought each other for each morsel of rich pastry, each dribble of sweet sauce. Hannah wished she had bought one just for herself.

"This is the land o'cakes, the Scots say," Maggie sighed as she licked her fingers. "And I believe them. We could never afford wee treats like this at home in Ireland. My Da brought us here from County Kerry during the Famine, after we were evicted from our cottage. Da heard there was work here for a laboring man, but he never was able to find much, and he lost the jobs he got building roads, what with his drinking. So we live on my wages, and I buy him his whisky to keep him quiet."

Hannah remembered Mrs. O'Donnell mentioning something similar. "What is this Fanning thing you guys keep talking about?"

Maggie blinked. "The Famine? All of us Irish living here in Dundee, and you've never heard of the Famine?"

Hannah felt awkward. "Um, no, but I'm kinda new here."

Maggie looked sideways at her, and said simply, "The common folk in Ireland, we eat tatties… potatoes. Four years ago, we dug the tatties, and they were black. They had rotted. We starved."

Hannah was shocked. "We starved? You mean your whole family?"

"Ma, my brother and sister, they all died by the roadside on the way to the boat. Not just my family, though. People died like flies, Hannah, thousands of people, and the government in London never lifted a finger to save us. Sometimes, I think I hate the English even more than the Scots do."

"But couldn't you guys eat oatmeal, or something like that, or go to a restaurant? I mean, don't they sell pies in Ireland?"

Maggie looked incredulously at her. "Hannah, we only had the potatoes. Don't you understand? There were no jobs for us to make money. We grew potatoes, because it was the only thing we could grow on our tiny wee plots of land that would feed all of us. When the crop died, so did we. We couldn't even stay in our houses because we couldn't pay the rent. The landlords evicted us, and burned our cottages."

At that moment, a policeman wearing a blue uniform, top hat, and stern look approached the girls. He jabbed a thumb in the direction of the city. "Lassies, away with you if you canna behave. You're disturbing thon respectable folk over yonder." He jerked his head toward a small and elegant group of well-dressed people who were eating a picnic on a blanket nearby. They were attended by servants, among them a man with black hair.

But Hannah wasn't going to leave without a fight. "How exactly are we disturbing them?" she asked through a mouthful of rhubarb pie.

The young policeman sighed. "Look, lass, dinna give me trouble, eh?" He was almost pleading. "That's Mr. Sutherland and his visitors…"

Hannah was surprised. "Like, Sutherland of Sutherland's Mill?"

The policeman rolled his eyes. "Aye, that's the one. Would you move along? They said that you two tearing into your pie is putting them off their ain food."

Hannah pulled a face. "How rude! Tell them not to look at us, then."

But Maggie had already got to her feet. "Come on, Hannah. Let's go."

Hannah hated—hated—being told what to do, especially when it was unfair. She didn't move. "This is a public park, right? And we're the public. It's not like we're poisoning the pigeons or spray-painting the sidewalks."

But Maggie had already abandoned her, and even Hannah lost courage when she realized she was alone with the policeman.

"Okay, I'm leaving," she announced. But before she headed for the road, she marched up to the startled picnicking group and announced, "I hope you're happy!"

"How dare you!" replied a tall elegantly-dressed Englishwoman sitting upright on the picnic blanket. Looking for support, she turned to the elderly man next to her who said to her calmly in a soft Scots accent, "Understand that this is why those of you who live in the country are fortunate, Emma, for you do not live cheek by jowl with the working classes as do we in the city."

The policeman had seized Hannah's arm. "Should I place her under arrest,

Mr. Sutherland?"

The old man shook his head gravely, "No, no, constable, that won't be necessary. What's your name, girl?"

Hannah returned his gaze with suspicion. She hesitated. So this was Mr. Sutherland, her employer. If he figured out that she worked in his factory, she could be fired. Reluctantly, she said, "I'm Hannah."

"Well, Hannah," said Mr. Sutherland. "May I introduce you to Lady Chatsfield? Now, permit me to ask you a question: Do you think that the working classes need a park of your own, where you may enjoy fresh air and leisure?"

Hannah scrunched up her face. "Um, okay, but what's wrong with us sharing this park with you rich people?"

It clearly wasn't the answer that Mr. Sutherland had expected, and he stifled a laugh, while Lady Chatsfield looked shocked.

Mr. Sutherland shook his head. "You see again, Emma. This girl's answer only makes me more determined to see the establishment of Sutherland's Park for the working classes of Dundee. When they recognize injustice, the people become impudent and even rebellious. It is not enough for privileged folk to threaten them with the workhouse or the prison. We must better attend to the people's welfare, or else expect consequences…"

"You fear your workers?" asked Lady Chatsfield, her eyebrow raised. "That is what is wrong with the new order of things. I have no fear of the workers on my estate. Agriculture is the natural order, Cousin Tom. It is your factories that cause discontent."

Suddenly, they both realized that they were speaking in front of Hannah, and Mr. Sutherland dismissed her, laughing, with, "Be off with you, you impudent girl!"

Hannah shrugged. "Don't worry, I'm outta here. Excuse me if I, like, scare you. I was just out here trying to breathe air that doesn't smell like poop." Her head held high, Hannah swept off.

As she walked back into town, Hannah thought over what had happened in the park. She realized then that, in Dundee, she was afraid in a way that she had never been in Balesworth. Sure, she had been scared of certain people in Balesworth, like Mrs. Archer and Mr. Smedley. But here in Dundee, the fear was all around her. It was a fear of death always lurking around the corner, and a living death for those who survived. It was an oppressive, soul-destroying fear of this place, of this whole dark, dirty, suffocating, and wretched way of life.

That night, when Hannah trudged into the Gordons' crowded flat, Mina was sitting with her elbows on the table, and to Hannah's surprise, she was reading a book. She caught Hannah's look of shock and amazement. Defensively, she said, "What are you looking at?"

Hannah smirked. "Nothing. I just didn't know you liked reading books."

"Aye," said Mina determinedly, "and what else would I be reading? Whisky bottles? Some of us have brains that we need to feed. You ought to learn to read, Hannah…"

"Of course I can read!" Hannah said indignantly.

Mina looked surprised. "Is that so? Funny, I havna seen you reading yet."

"I just don't like books," Hannah said. "They're boring. I mean, there's other stuff I like to do, like texting my friends, or watching TV, or hanging out at the mall…"

Everyone was giving her blank looks, so Hannah tried to explain. "I like to write letters, or go to movies…no, wait, no movies in 1851 …um, I mean, I like to go to the theatre, and go shopping."

"Fancy tastes," tutted Mina's sister Mary, who was knitting in a corner. "I've never seen you write, neither. Has anyone else seen Hannah writing? And where do you find the money for the theatre, or for going to grand shops?"

Hannah thought about this. Mary had a point. Sixpence a week was all she had left after she paid Jessie for her room and board, and that wouldn't buy her more than a few pies. She had been so stressed since she arrived in nineteenth-century Scotland, she hadn't even realized how bored she was. One day seemed to slip into another, without any escape, kind of like how she felt in Snipesville. Surely there was more to life than this?

"So how can you afford books?" she asked Mina, curiously.

"I dinna buy books," Mina said, turning a page. "Sometimes I'm lent them by the minister, and I pay a penny a week's subscription to the workers' library. There's a lot more to talk about in Dundee than just gossiping about the go-ings-on at Suttie's Mill. A few years ago, we even had a speaker all the way from America, a Mr. Ralph Waldo Emerson, the philosopher. Fascinating gentleman with a peculiar name."

With a smile, Mina's youngest sister Mem said, "I heard a rumor today, Hannah, that the police chased you out of the Magdalen Green."

Mina looked at Hannah with new interest. "Is that right?"

Reluctantly, Hannah nodded, and hesitantly she told her eager listeners what had happened.

When Hannah concluded her story, Mina said abruptly, "Well, that was wrong."

"Yeah, I'm sorry," Hannah said sheepishly. "I'm kind of embarrassed about it now…"

But that wasn't what Mina had meant at all. "Nah, nah, Hannah, you did nothing wrong. The Magdalen Green's for the people, always has been."

Her sister Janet weighed in disapprovingly. "Aye, Mina, that's all very well, but the Green is right in front of the millowners' villas. You can hardly expect the likes of Mr. Sutherland to sit in the company of dirty mill girls. You'll need to put on your Sunday best clothes and act respectable if you want to be seen there, Hannah."

"Janet, you're a snob," Mina said to her sister. But then she turned back to Hannah and sighed. "Mind you, she's right. We have to show those people that we're just as good as them."

"Great," said Hannah. "But I don't have nice clothes, and I can't afford them when all I get is sixpence a week. I bet you guys make more than I do, right?"

"Aye, we do that," piped up Janet. "But if you work hard, you could be a weaver like us one day…"

"Och, hud yer wheest, Janet," said Mina irritably, telling her sister to shut up. "Ye ken well that we dinna make much money either, and that it's no easy job finding a place as a weaver…"

"We found places," said Janet stoutly.

Hannah wasn't going to stand for that. "Yeah, it was your dad who got you those jobs, because he was a gaffer. Am I right?"

Janet looked deflated, but the other girls laughed.

Mina said, "Ach, you're both right. Hannah, you need to save your pennies for Sunday clothes instead of buying pies with yon Irish lassie, and we need higher wages, and parks where we're welcome. We'll have to fight old Sutherland for the wages, but I heard that he supports us having a park. And I hear the council is to open a park at the old army barracks in Dudhope, just for us."

Betty, Jessie's youngest daughter, piped up, "What about the Balgay Hill? That could be a park, too."

"Aye, true enough," said Mina, "and soon enough… You know, maybe it's no such a bad thing that Hannah swore out old Sutherland."

"It isn't?" Hannah asked in surprise.

"Nooo… It keeps the millowners on their toes if they're that wee bit afraid of us. Makes them worry about libraries, and lectures, and parks for the workers. If we canna get them to gie us decent wages and places to live, we can at least get them to spend the money they take from our labor the way we want, eh? Maybe we need more folk like Hannah to remind the bosses how the rest of us live." Her eyes twinkled.

"That's not respectable talk, Mina Gordon," Janet sniffed.

"Isn't it?" Mina asked with a sly smile, as she put down her book, and gave Hannah a wink as she rose to her feet. "I think Hannah might have the makings of a fine political agitator."

Hannah wasn't sure what that meant, but she knew she was being complimented. Adults didn't usually compliment her for speaking her mind. It made a nice change to be appreciated.

****

Mr. Thornhill lived alone. Except, that is, for his maids, butler, driver, cook, and their children, all of whom, except the Irish maid, were slaves.

Jupe considered himself lucky: As Alex's manservant, he could sleep in his master's comfortable room, while other slaves lived in the cramped space of the carriage house, above the stables. The downside was that his situation put distance between him and the other slaves, some of whom grumbled that Jupe clearly wasn't a house servant, and didn't have any domestic skills. One afternoon, when Mr. Thornhill rang the bell for tea, the cook sent Jupe with the tea tray. While he was trying to open the parlor door, he dropped the tray with a huge crash, denting the silver teapot and destroying the expensive teacups. Angry, Mr. Thornhill rang for Ezekiel and told him to punish Jupe. Later, when Alex tried to find out what had happened, Jupe wouldn't tell him.

It was a grand house. Four bedrooms upstairs, and even an indoor bathroom, supplied with rainwater collected in barrels. Ezekiel the butler said that the bathroom made the house the talk of the city. But Alex noticed that the barrels were full of mosquito larvae, and reported this to Mr. Thornhill at breakfast.

"Oh, mosquitoes, they're a nuisance," Mr. Thornhill said, helping himself to more scrambled eggs from a silver dish that Ezekiel held out to him. "Don't worry. The servants dispose of the eggs and hatchlings eventually."

"But aren't you scared of malaria or yellow fever?" Alex blurted out. He remembered reading in one of his nature books that mosquitoes were the carriers of illnesses that had killed thousands of nineteenth-century Southerners.

"What have mosquitoes to do with malaria or yellow fever?" Mr. Thornhill said with a laugh. "Everyone knows that the fevers are caused by miasma. That's why the city is cleaning up the streets, to lessen the impurities released into the air."

Something in this explanation didn't sound right to Alex, but he let it go.

CHAPTER SEVEN

That morning, Alex and Jupe accompanied Mr. Thornhill to his office. It was only a few blocks away, but they travelled by coach and horses. Alex soon figured out why they didn't walk: The sandy roads had absorbed a heavy rain-storm in the early hours of the morning, and they were now quagmires. Pedestrians struggled through the boggy sand as though they had ten pound weights strapped to their ankles.

Before reaching the office, Mr. Thornhill stopped the coach at a large store that sold gentlemen's clothing. Jupe and the coach driver remained outside, while Mr. Thornhill took Alex to be fitted for new made-to-measure clothes. He also bought him some outfits that were ready to wear. Alex was delighted by his expensive new clothes. He was happy to think, as they settled back in the carriage, that Mr. Thornhill clearly intended to keep him around for a while. As though reading his mind, Mr. Thornhill said, "You had better prove your worth as a clerk, young Day, now that I have invested so heavily in you." Alex gave a wan smile.

Soon, the coach and horses pulled up on Bay Street, and Mr. Thornhill and the two boys got out. On foot, they crossed over a gully on a cast-iron bridge that led to Factors' Walk, a squat row of brick and green-painted buildings. Alex, having visited Factors' Walk in the twenty-first century, knew that there was more to this strange row of offices and shops than first appeared: It was built directly onto a cliff-face, so that if you walked on the other side, along the docks of the Savannah River, you could see that the Factors' Walk buildings each had five floors, several of which warehoused cotton that awaited shipment to the North and across the Atlantic Ocean.

On the Bay Street side, Mr. Thornhill led the boys into an office that appeared to be on the first floor, but was actually on the fourth. When he walked in, the clerk, a tall and portly man with white hair and red cheeks, was taken by surprise. He jumped up from a chair next to the fireplace, where he had been warming himself.

"Good morning, Baird," said Mr. Thornhill, tossing his tall hat onto a stand. "I see that you're working hard. I have brought this lad with me, by the name of Alexander Day. I've taken him on as a clerk of sorts. Teach him the accounts, would you, and he will accompany me in your place to take stock on the estate tomorrow, if that would suit you."

"Very good, sir," said Baird, who had a Scottish accent. "Yes, that would certainly suit me, Mr. Thornhill. I have no desire to go trachling out to the ends of the earth at my age."

Thornhill replied with a sly smile, "Well, I'm sure young Day would be glad to 'trachle' in your place. Wouldn't you, Day?"

"I would if I knew what that meant, sir," said Alex.

"Oh, it's another of Mr. Baird's curious Scottish expressions. Add 'trachling' to your curriculum for Day, would you, Baird?" said Mr. Thornhill, his eyes twinkling, as he opened the door to his office.

"Yes, sir," said Mr. Baird. "But before you go, would you mind telling me what's to be done with this nigger lad?" He waved a finger toward Jupe.

Thornhill paused in the doorway. "Oh, that's young Day's manservant. His name is Jupe. Not terribly accomplished yet, are you, Jupe?"

"No, sir," Jupe said quickly. It was always best to agree with white gentlemen.

Mr. Thornhill continued. "You can send him over to MacGregor's offices with these final deeds of sale once you have them drawn up, and send Day with him."

Alex pored over the impossibly huge books of handwritten accounts, and although he was at first tickled to realize that this was surely where the expression "book-keeping" came from, he soon got bored and tired. For whatever reason, both he and Mr. Baird worked standing up at tall desks. When he asked for a stool, Mr. Baird just chuckled.

Alex found himself wishing that he had some modern technology. The ink pen he used was hard to write with, and he had to repeatedly dip it into the inkwell on the desk. Then he overfilled it, and made a huge blot on the paper. Mr. Baird tutted and slapped his hand as he gave him blotting paper to clean up the mess.

A computer would come in really handy right now, Alex thought… which was when he remembered the Professor's calculator, tucked into the pocket of his clean new trousers.

As Mr. Baird worked at the other desk copying out letters by hand, Alex furtively totted up the numbers on the calculator. Suddenly, Mr. Thornhill's door opened. Alex tried to slide the calculator back into his pocket, but he wasn't used to his new trousers, and he fumbled a moment too long.

"What's that you have there?" said Mr. Thornhill sharply, furrowing his brow and pausing in his office doorway.

"Nothing," said Alex, and immediately regretted it, because it was so obviously a lie. He corrected himself. "Nothing much. Just a little gizmo I have with me, not really interesting…"

Mr. Thornhill stepped forward, grabbed Alex's wrist and pried the calculator from his fingers. "What the devil is this?" he muttered, and he punched the numbers and symbols. Peering at the tiny screen, he exclaimed, "Good God..." He turned the calculator over and over in his hands, and even tried to open the battery compartment.

Alex was alarmed. "Um, sir, please don't do that, because it might break."

"What is this?" Mr. Thornhill asked him in bafflement.

"It's a calculator. It does math," Alex said cautiously. He held out his hand for the calculator, but Mr. Thornhill didn't take the hint, and continued to inspect it.

"Where did you get it?" he asked.

"I found it," Alex said truthfully.

"By God, there's money in this. I wish to know how it operates," said Mr. Thornhill. "Day, may I borrow your calculating machine for a day or two?"

Alex was reluctant, not least because he would now have to go back to doing the accounts without it, but he agreed. What else could he do?

That same afternoon, Mr. Baird sent Alex and Jupe to Mr. MacGregor's office to deliver a bundle of documents. He gave them directions to Johnson Square, which was only a couple of blocks away. Alex was quite looking forward to a walk through 1851 Savannah. On the carriage ride to the office, he had noticed how rough the squares appeared, compared with the beautiful gardens of the twenty-first century city. Flower beds were few, most trees were young, and the squares lacked the sidewalks and grand monuments they would later acquire. Alex smiled to himself, as he thought of the upside: There weren't any noisy tour buses, either.

But when he and Jupe arrived at Johnson Square, they were both dismayed to see Mr. MacGregor's place of business. A large sign proclaimed, *J. MacGregor, Slave Auction and Sales.*

Alex decided to take the documents in by himself, and Jupe seemed relieved to be left outside. Alex couldn't blame him.

A bell rang when he walked in, and the clerk glanced up. "I'll attend to you presently," he said to Alex, "soon as I'm done with this fella here. Take a seat there." He pointed with his pen to an upright wooden chair in the corner. As Alex sat down, he could hear voices seeping up from the basement beneath the floor boards. With shock, he recognized one of them: It was the voice of the storytelling slave whom he and Jupe had met on their way into Savannah. Now he was recounting his sad tale for a new audience. What were they doing in the basement?

Alex also recognized the man speaking with the clerk as the Irish slave trader whom he and Jupe had met on the road. The Irishman was arguing with the clerk, saying heatedly, "I told MacGregor that I needed him to auction off this gang today, because I need the cash, and I'm headed back to Atlanta tomorrow."

But the clerk was shaking his head. "I realize that, sir, but Mr. MacGregor says it's too short notice… His most generous offer is to buy the slaves from you outright."

The Irishman snorted. "Yes, at a fraction of their market value. What does the man take me for now, a fool?"

Mr. MacGregor emerged suddenly from his office, where he had evidently been listening to the conversation. "I took you, Riley, for a sensible fellow," he said in a charming yet sinister voice. "Now we don't need a fuss, so you just let Smithson here write out a bill of sale, and you can be on your way to Terminus, or Atlanta, or whatever that little place calls itself now."

Riley seemed thrown off guard by Mr. MacGregor's appearance. The differences between them were considerable: Mr. MacGregor was tall, while Riley was short; Mr. MacGregor was clean-shaven and dressed in an expensive, finely-cut suit, while Riley was bearded and wore torn trousers and a filthy shirt. Riley was out of place in the elegantly-furnished office, and he knew it. Mr. MacGregor took a slow puff from his cigar, never averting his gaze from Riley.

But Riley tried once more. "You promised, sir, that you would hold an auction soon as I arrived with the merchandise…"

"Circumstances changed since we exchanged letters," said Mr. MacGregor, flicking ash from his cigar. "And judging from the condition of some of those negroes in my slave pen downstairs, you're lucky I'm willing to take them off your hands."

There was a silence, and then Mr. MacGregor said quietly and firmly to the clerk, "Draw up the bill of sale."

The clerk scurried to comply, while Riley stood by angrily, shifting from foot to foot. It was then that Mr. MacGregor spotted Alex, and invited him into his office, a summons that Alex didn't dare refuse.

Mr. MacGregor closed the door behind them, and motioned for Alex to take a seat before sitting down behind his desk. "Now then, how do you find Mr. Thornhill's employ?"

Alex said guardedly that he was happy to work for Mr. Thornhill.

"And your negro, what is his name?"

Without thinking, Alex told him.

Mr. MacGregor sat back in his chair. "Jupe, is that? Short for Jupiter? And you say you borrowed him from your uncle. What was his name, now?"

But Alex had decided that he had to stand up to Mr. MacGregor. Looking him in the eye, he said, "Nothing personal, sir, but is that your business?"

Mr. MacGregor's eyes flashed in anger, but still he smiled that sly smile. "Your insolence does you no credit, boy. You brought papers for me? Just hand them to Smithson on your way out the door."

As Alex made to leave, MacGregor said chillingly, "I've got my eye on you, boy, and on that young buck Jupiter. And you had better be telling me the damn truth."

When Alex left the building, Jupe was talking to two black men, who hurriedly left when they saw Alex. "Who were those guys?" Alex asked.

"Those men, Massa Alex, they're carpenters, and they invite me to the First African Baptist Church." Then, very quietly, he added, "Massa Alex, that Mr. MacGregor? He's not an honest gentleman, that's what those men say. They said they done some work for that Mr. MacGregor in the slave pen, and he never paid them."

"But why would he pay slaves?" Alex asked.

"No, sir, they're free men. Anyways, they heard Mr. MacGregor takes negroes no questions asked.... And the slaves down in the basement? They said that some of them were stolen, and that Mr. Riley forged the papers."

"Wow," said Alex. "That explains a lot. I'll tell you something else about Mr. MacGregor, Jupe: He scares me."

Alex's upstairs room at Mr. Thornhill's was light and airy, and sun poured into it through large windows. Jupe made his bed on the floor of Alex's room, while Alex climbed up a wooden step-stool into his elaborate four-poster bed with silk canopy. Alex had offered to share the bed, but Jupe refused, and Alex was beginning to tire of trying to find ways to treat him as an equal.

What Alex could not know was that Jupe feared being accused of not knowing his place, even though the floor was hard and cold and the bed looked warm and inviting. What Jupe could not know that Alex genuinely wanted to be his friend.

In the darkness, Alex explained to Jupe that he did not believe in slavery, and did not want to think of him as property. As he spoke, he could hear Jupe's breath catch in his throat, but in the anonymity of the dark, he felt braver about being honest. "Look, nothing personal, but I have no idea why you're here with me," he whispered. "I can't do anything for you, and I'm worried because Mr. McGregor knows you don't belong to me. I don't need a servant, anyway. Why can't you just go home?"

There was a very long silence. And then, in a forthright voice, Jupe said, "Because I'm running away."

In those few words, Jupe shed his fearful, cautious shell, and showed his true self. Alex was stunned, but Jupe was relieved to have told him the truth. "My dad said to stick with you if I could, and head north to my aunt's if I couldn't. But you seem like good folks, Massa Alex, and I want to stay with you if I can. Mostly, I just want to be free. I trust you to keep this secret, and I ain't never trusted a white man before. My daddy would call me crazy, and maybe I am… But will you help me?"

Jupe's honesty made Alex afraid. It was the first time that Jupe had spoken to him as an equal. It was as though he had spent all this time in the company of an actor, and only now was seeing his real personality.

Alex now realized what a huge responsibility he had. His head swam. He desperately tried to remember if the Underground Railroad existed in 1851: Even if it did, how would he make contact with it? Perhaps he could simply leave Mr. Thornhill, and take Jupe north with him, but that might rouse suspicion, and put the slave patrol on their tails… Alex wanted so badly for the Professor to show up and explain what should happen next.

What he said was, "Jupe, I'll help you any way I can. But we gotta think about what we're gonna do. Let's hang out here until we decide what's best."

"We decide, Massa Alex?"

"We. Not just me. You, too. And don't call me Massa, or at least not when we're alone. You know what, Jupe, I have a secret, too. I'm not from here, either. I'm from the future, from more than a hundred and fifty years from now. I don't know how or why, but I've traveled in time. I'm not crazy. I'm just out of my own time."

Jupe, who believed in the ghosts that haunted buildings and the spirits of the woods, as well as in the certainty that he would go to a Christian heaven when he died, didn't find this so hard to believe. And, after all, it made sense out of Alex's behavior. Alex's confession encouraged him to make another of his own. He cleared his throat.

"After I broke the teacups, you asked me what happened. Well, I'll tell you now. Massa Thornhill meant for Ezekiel to whip me, but Ezekiel just pretend to do it, and tell Massa Thornhill that he punished me. Ezekiel's a good man."

Alex agreed with Jupe that Ezekiel was a good man. But what did it say about Mr. Thornhill that he wanted Jupe whipped for a mere accident? Alex felt uneasy, and not for the first time.

****

In the early hours of the next morning, Brandon was lying awake at the work-house. He was bitterly cold. The only window, an arched square divided into small panes, was dripping condensation. The wall behind his head was oozing damp and mold, and the room smelled musty. It was still dark outside.

Just as Brandon was persuading himself to drift back to sleep, the door banged open, and an old man ambled slowly down the length of the room, ringing a loud handbell. Men and boys in the surrounding beds began to cough, scratch, stretch, and swing their legs onto the floor.

Brandon grabbed his shapeless uniform from the hook on the wall, and threw it on. He began to follow the others, but the old man with the bell stopped him. "Master says you've to paint a bit o' the stairwell," he said creak-ily. "I'll show you the paint and brushes."

"Don't I get breakfast?" Brandon said in dismay.

But the old man was firm. "Not until you've worked an hour. Them's the rules."

An hour later, a paint-spattered Brandon was sitting glumly on a bench, con-templating a truly revolting breakfast of dry whole wheat bread and thin oat-meal. Painting was a very boring job, made more so by the fact that the stair-well clearly didn't need painting: It was already thick with several previous coats. Brandon was certain that he was doing busywork, to make him work for the sake of working. He was right.

His oatmeal was an unappetizing grey concoction without milk or sugar, served in a wooden bowl with a large wooden spoon. It looked and smelled like dirty dishwater.

"What is this junk?" he whispered to Weaver.

"Gruel," whispered Weaver. "Haven't you never had gruel where you come from, lad?"

Brandon shook his head and sipped the gruel. It tasted foul, as though nei-ther the water from which it was made, nor the pot in which it had boiled, were entirely clean.

He looked up, and saw a beam, running the width of the ceiling, on which someone had helpfully painted God is Good. What sort of people would build a place like this, he wondered, and then preach at the inmates? It was beyond cruel.

When Brandon had finished his breakfast, having eaten all of the bread but very little of the gruel, the old man told him to collect bowls and spoons and take them to the kitchen. One of the women working at the kitchen fireplace pointed him to the scullery next door. An old pauper woman, her hair in a bonnet, was at the sink, scrubbing at the dishes with cold water, but she looked up as he entered. It was the Professor.

She straightened up. "Glad you're here, Brandon. Well, not really, of course, but…Oh, you know what I mean. I checked myself in last night, but I was hoping I wouldn't have to stay long. These places are quite dreadful, aren't they?"

"Hi. What kind of jail is this, anyway?"

The Professor dried her hands. "It's not a jail, not exactly. Anyone can leave, so long as they tell the Master they're leaving. You only get into trouble if you hop over the wall without giving notice, because that's against regulations, and then you get whipped. This is a workhouse. It's a great way to help unemployed people, isn't it? Not to mention senior citizens, orphans, people with disabilities, and the homeless."

"No," said Brandon. "It's not a great way to help anyone. It sucks. Why does it have to be so nasty?"

The Professor began scrubbing at an oatmeal-encrusted bowl. "The idea is to discourage people from seeking help. The 1834 Poor Law says that everything in here must be worse than it is for the poorest people outside, including the food, the beds, and the clothes. Everything's strictly regimented, as you see. And families aren't allowed to stay together: Men, women, and small children are kept strictly separate. Kids can see their mothers only for a short time on Sundays, in the presence of the Matron or Master. Fathers can't see their kids at all."

Brandon was shocked. "Man, that's harsh!"

"It's meant to be. This way, the poor won't ask to be admitted until they're absolutely starving, which saves the taxpayers money. It's quite successful… if you like that kind of thing. The Victorians think that everyone with a problem should be locked up in a great big building."

"That's awful…" said Brandon. "I thought people were supposed to be nicer back in the day?"

The Professor said softly, "Depends which day. Depends which people."

Brandon said. "Look, how come they know me already, like I've been here before?"

"I don't know, and it's worrying me," she said with a furrowed brow. "I've been asking around, and they seem to know you as an orphan who lived here for a while. It must have something to do with whatever's gone wrong with Time. But, really, there's no point in worrying about it. And I think it's time for you to go to work, isn't it?"

Brandon thought about arguing with her, but he realized it would be no use. He decided that it was time he took matters into his own hands. After he exchanged his workhouse uniform for his ordinary clothes, he headed back toward the canal near the George and Dragon. There, he persuaded a bargeman to take him to London, in exchange for his tommy notes.

Chapter 8:
A QUESTION OF RESPECTABILITY

Late on Wednesday afternoon, the horse-drawn barge slowly glided up the Thames toward the town of Windsor. Brandon was sitting on top of the boat, worrying. It had been a long journey, but the boat was drawing closer to London now, which meant he would have to start making decisions. Maybe he had made a huge mistake leaving his job at the mine. Would the Professor be able to find him? And what would he do for a living in London? It was all very well to think positively, but he knew that what he really needed was to *think*. When he had visited London in the twentieth century, it was a huge, scary city. What would it be like in 1851? He dreaded finding out.

His thoughts were interrupted by the breathtaking sight of an enormous castle looming over the river. "What is that?" he gasped, pointing.

"That's Windsor Castle," grinned Arthur the bargeman. "Home of Her Majesty Queen Victoria, the Prince Consort, and Prince Edward, Prince of Wales."

"Coooool!" Brandon exclaimed, as he scrambled forward for a closer look.

"Don't fall in the drink," Arthur laughed. Then he nodded at the long line of barges they were about to join. "And fear not, you'll have plenty of time to admire it, because we're going to be here quite a while."

Brandon already knew why they were waiting: There was a lock ahead. This hadn't been a speedy journey of the best of times, because the horse on the towpath pulled the boat at walking speed. But locks slowed them down even more. The Thames was a natural river, but much of it had been turned into a canal, an artificial waterway. A lock was a sealed chamber that allowed canals to go uphill or downhill quickly. There were a lot of locks, and it took a long time to go through each one. Every time they reached a lock, Arthur's son, Will, and Brandon jumped down to the canalside, carrying a crank to unlock the gates. With the help of the lock-keeper, the boys pushed with their backs against the massive balance beam to open the heavy gates. Finally, Arthur would steer the barge into the lock chamber, and wait as water was released into it. Once the water was at the level of the next stretch of canal, Will and Brandon jumped aboard, and the gates opened to let them through. Brandon had long ago lost count of the number of locks they had traveled through.

CHAPTER EIGHT

As the long line of boats waited for the lock at Windsor, the sun was beginning to set, and Arthur made a decision. "Best we moor here the night, and wait til morn," he called to Will and Brandon, as he steered the boat toward the side of the canal. His son grabbed a rope, jumped onto shore and pulled the barge to its mooring.

From the riverbank in the grey dusk, the castle looked like something from a fantasy novel. Soon it would be dark, but Brandon couldn't resist making an expedition to see where the Queen lived. He asked Will if he wanted to come with him, but Will and Arthur were more interested in visiting a pub on the riverside for beer and supper, and so Brandon walked up the hill alone.

Windsor was quiet. He passed only a handful of people, one of them a soldier who was walking downhill in red uniform and a tall bearskin hat. As Brandon slowly progressed along the road that curled up and around the castle, he began to see how massive it was, and how ancient it seemed. He imagined medieval archers in chainmail helmets, peering through the arrow slits and crenellations atop the towering walls. He glanced to his right at the shops facing the castle, and immediately came to a halt.

What had grabbed his attention was nothing especially remarkable. It was a brick building with several arched windows, and double doors of black-painted wooden planks, above which sat a large sign in raised white letters: *J.M. Spencer, Cabinet-Maker, Upholsterer, Undertaker &c.* To most twenty-first century people, what this business actually did might have remained a mystery. But the sign made Brandon's heart leap. If he wasn't mistaken, that word "undertaker" meant that he had just found a funeral home. Then again, if he was mistaken, he had found a furniture factory. There was only one way to be sure.

One of the huge double doors stood open, and Brandon cautiously stole a look inside. It seemed, after all, that this was only a furniture workshop. Wood shavings and sawdust littered the floor. Cartwheels, chairs, tables, and wardrobes in various stages of construction lay about the room. Brandon, thinking he had made a mistake, was about to slip out quietly. But then he spotted the three coffins stacked against the wall.

He called out, "Hello?"

Seconds later, a sandy-haired mustachioed man in a leather apron and rolled-up sleeves popped his head round the door at the back of the workshop. "Can I help you?" he asked.

Brandon still wasn't sure that he was in the right place. "Hi, yeah, well, no, probably not. Maybe you can tell me where to go. I need the kind of undertakers who arrange funerals…"

The man rushed to reassure him. "Oh, aye, that's what we do. Well, that is one of the services we perform."

Brandon looked around doubtfully.

The man added, "I'm Daniel, I'm a journeyman cabinet-maker. The master here is Mr. Spencer. Would you like a word with him?"

Brandon was feeling a bit out of his depth, but he figured he might as well talk to the boss. He followed Daniel upstairs to an office, where a middle-aged man in shirtsleeves and tie was poking at the fireplace. His rough hands showed that he was used to hard work, but his tidy clothes suggested that his days of hard labor were behind him. He looked curiously at Brandon as Daniel introduced him. "Mr. Spencer, sir? This is Master Clark, and he's enquiring about a funeral."

Mr. Spencer straightened up and put on his most sympathetic face. "Oh, yes? Thank you, Daniel, you may go. I'm sorry to hear about your bereavement, young sir. May we be of assistance at this difficult time?"

Now Brandon felt really awkward. "Oh, I haven't lost anyone. I just came to see about a job. I have experience. My family owns an undertaker's shop in, er, London."

Mr. Spencer was delighted to hear this. "Well, you might well suit my requirements for a mourner and assistant. I reckon our customers would love to see you at a funeral. You'd bring us good fortune, wouldn't you?"

"Would I?" Brandon was mystified.

"Certainly you would. It's good luck, isn't it, having a black at a funeral?"

Brandon had to suppress a smirk and a groan, all at once. "Like having a black cat cross your path?"

"Yes, well, something like that. And you said your family are undertakers in London? Well, I never. In North London, are they?"

Brandon nodded. When in doubt, he reminded himself, agree with adults.

Mr. Spencer asked eagerly, "Did you ever arrange a funeral at Kensal Green Cemetery?"

"Sure, all the cemeteries," Brandon fibbed. "You'll find us there."

This answer pleased Mr. Spencer. "Splendid, because I haven't ever conducted arrangements at Kensal Green, and if I ever have the honor of doing so, I might need your help operating the modern equipment in the chapel. Do you believe you could assist me?"

"Sure," said Brandon, crossing his fingers behind his back. "It's just...I mean...I need someplace to live, too."

"That's no trouble, no trouble at all," said Mr. Spencer. "Plenty of space

CHAPTER EIGHT

downstairs in the workshop for a limber young fellow like you. I'll have our maid fetch you a blanket and pillow, and you can find a quiet corner to sleep. You look about the same size as the last boy I employed as a mourner, so I trust you'll fit into his suit."

Brandon couldn't believe how happy he was to find a job he had always dreaded: Working in a funeral home.

He spent an uncomfortable night in the freezing workshop, lying on some straw-filled sacks he had arranged under a table. The maid gave him an old blanket that was full of holes, but the promised pillow was never delivered. He could not sleep, and as the dawn crept through the undraped windows, he took a walk down to the river, to bid farewell to the bargemen, and reassure them that he hadn't fallen in the Thames.

But the mooring spot was empty. Sadly, Brandon guessed that Arthur and Will were probably well on their way to London by now, and he hoped they hadn't worried about his failure to return. Then he had to remind himself that, in 1851, he wasn't really a child: He was an employed young adult, and to the bargeman and his son, he was just a stranger. They probably hadn't given much thought to his sudden departure.

Over the next week, Brandon learned the ropes of the funeral business in mid-Victorian Britain. Mr. Spencer had inherited the carpentry and furniture-making firm, including coffin manufacture, from his father. Now, however, he had greater ambitions, and he was happy to explain these at length to Brandon. "You need money these days, Brandon, money and respectability," he said, returning from a meeting with a bereaved customer. "Indeed, to get respectability, you had better have money. My wife is a fine woman, or should I say a fine lady, and she needs to put pretty things on the table and on her person to mix in the sort of respectable company to which we belong. For how else, I ask you, do persons such as ourselves, persons of humble beginnings, rise in the esteem of our betters? Money, that's how. And there's no better way to make money, I say, than in supplying a need that won't never go out of fashion, and that's death."

"But aren't you providing a community service, too?" Brandon asked.

"Why, of course, of course we are, of course," Mr. Spencer added hurriedly. "Indeed, more today than ever before. People today wish to have their loved ones consigned to the grave with respectability, in the proper new fashion, and we are happy to assist them in achieving their desire. Take these, for example." He handed Brandon a greeting card that announced a person's death and funeral. It was elaborately engraved in black on white card, with a picture of a weeping woman sitting under a weeping willow, and Brandon supposed that it was very expensive. He made vague admiring noises, and Mr. Spencer continued. "There's also a great deal of interest, I've learned from canvassing my customers, in American cast-iron coffins with glass face-plates, which allow the face of the deceased to be seen until the moment of interment." Brandon shuddered, thinking how creepy that sounded, but Mr. Spencer didn't notice. "However, I have yet to locate a supplier in this country, since such a coffin is beyond Daniel's capabilities. But I do know of a man in Telford what makes cast-iron gravestones. I'm considering stocking those, because they wouldn't wear away over time like stone does."

"No, that's true," agreed Brandon. "But they would rust."

Mr. Spencer hadn't thought of that. He looked admiringly at Brandon. "You learned a great deal from your family, Brandon. I'm surprised you didn't apprentice to your own father. Family quarrel, was it?"

"Yes," said Brandon, with a slight shrug. "Something like that."

The following Saturday afternoon was Brandon's half-day off. By now, he was itching to take a closer look at Windsor Castle. But as he approached the gate, he saw with disappointment that it was firmly closed, with red-coated guards stationed on either side. He was about to turn back, when he saw an ordinary woman carrying a basket wander unchallenged through a massive stone archway that led inside the castle. The archway was not gated, and, after a moment's hesitation, Brandon followed her. Neither soldier on duty stopped him.

Inside, just as on the outside, Windsor Castle was like something from a fairy tale. But while it looked solid and impenetrable from the outside, on the inside was a little village crammed together within the walls. A row of small stone houses with carefully-tended flower gardens led up the hill. A clergyman in robes, carrying a stack of books, was walking briskly from the large stone church. Ahead of Brandon squatted the massive round tower on a steep mound of grass-covered earth, surrounded by a dry moat.

Meanwhile, the woman carrying the basket had turned to stare at Brandon. "Motte and bailey," she said.

Brandon gave her a big smile. "You found me!"

The Professor looked sharply at him. "I am very annoyed with you. You shouldn't have left Hitherton, and you're very lucky I tracked you down. Fortunately, Windsor Castle isn't a huge tourist attraction yet, and a black kid in town does stand out a bit in the records for 1851. Want to help me deliver these eggs?"

Muttering apologies, Brandon took the basket from her, and they began slowly to walk up the hill. "What did you mean by moat and… whatever you said?"

"Not moat. Motte. As in motte and bailey," the Professor corrected him. "It's a type of castle design, cheap and built in a hurry."

"This doesn't look like it was built in a hurry," Brandon said, sweeping a hand across the view.

"Oh, the original castle was, I promise. King William I, otherwise known as William the Conqueror, built it. The motte isn't another way to pronounce moat. The motte was the big earth mound on which William built a wooden tower. The bailey was the yard next to it. If invaders managed to break into the bailey, everyone inside could retreat to the tower. Pretty nifty, eh?"

"So how old is the stone tower?" Brandon asked.

"Not very. That isn't even the original stone tower. In fact, most of what we see only dates back a few years. Queen Victoria's uncle did a bunch of remodeling, and remade the place to look more romantic and imposing, like people expect castles to be. But it's hardly an authentic representation of how the place looked in the Middle Ages."

Brandon felt cheated. "Man, I thought I was seeing it exactly like it looked in the Middle Ages."

"One thing I have learned from history," said the Professor, "is that very little if anything is as it first appears… So, how's life with the Spencers?"

Brandon was taken aback. How did the Professor know about his new job? "Er, pretty good, I guess, although Mr. and Mrs. Spencer have a kind of funny way of talking. It's like they're reading from a script or something."

"In a way they are," said the Professor, "They want to make sure that they fit in with the right people. Things are changing so fast in England in 1851, people are desperately trying to show that they're educated…Even if they're not. That's why Mr. Spencer talks like he ate a thesaurus. He's hoping to cash in on Victorian England's obsession with funerals. And, along the way, people like him invent the modern funeral industry of which your family's a part."

"I never thought of it as an industry," Brandon objected. "More as a community service."

The Professor smiled. "Oh, I think you've already figured out that Mr. Spencer sees it as more than that. It's his ticket to wealth and respectability, to a place in the new order of things. He gets to rub shoulders with important people, you see, by burying their dead in style. And everyone needs his services, don't they?"

"Maybe even the Queen herself," laughed Brandon.

"No. Her Majesty already has her own undertaker to make funeral arrangements, as she will need to do in about ten years."

Brandon was startled. "Why?"

The Professor shook her head. "Oh dear, no, that would be telling. Look it up later. Impressive place the Castle, isn't it?"

As they approached a grand stone archway next to the Round Tower, they happened on a gentleman who was carefully carving his name into the stone wall.

"Hey," an outraged Brandon whispered to the Professor. "Aren't you going to tell that guy to stop doing graffiti?"

"Why would I do that?" she replied blandly. "Nobody else has a problem with it. Of course, I wouldn't recommend doing the same in the twenty-first century. You'd get arrested."

The Professor paused as they reached a large courtyard. "This is where the Royal Family lives. Give me the basket, because I have to go pop into the kitchens with my eggs. Here, take a couple for Mr. Spencer."

Brandon carefully lifted two eggs from the basket. "Don't you have any advice for me? Or news about Hannah and Alex?"

She said casually, "Oh, Alex and Hannah are fine, I think. I suggest, Brandon, that from here on, you just let life happen, and do what you're inclined to do. Honestly, I shouldn't really be annoyed that you left Hitherton, because, apparently, that was what you should have done. Now, your job is just to go with the flow."

Brandon was dismayed. "But that's what you said when I was in 1915! I feel like I'm being totally useless."

The Professor patted his shoulder. "Rubbish. You're not useless. You helped produce coal, didn't you? Coal is what powers this brave new world of industrial Britain. You helped the coal on its way to London on the canal barge, and so perhaps now, knowing just some of the work that goes into making modern life, you won't take it for granted, and you'll encourage others to think about it too…"

But Brandon was fed up with her lecturing. "Honestly, I just want to go home to Snipesville."

She looked at him skeptically. "What, back to a future at the funeral home?"

"Why not?" Brandon said heatedly. "That's all I'm doing here, working in a funeral home, just getting by until you let me go."

She looked at him sympathetically. "Sometimes, just like this castle, things aren't exactly as they appear. Good luck on the journey, Brandon."

Then she knocked on a door, to be admitted by a male servant in a smart uniform. Brandon was still staring at the closed door when a balding man with dark hair and moustache collided with him. He was almost knocked off his feet, and the rolled documents that the man was carrying fell to the ground.

"Look where you are going, young man," the man said sternly. He had a German accent.

"Sorry, sir," said Brandon, scrambling to retrieve the rolls of paper, even as he wondered vaguely how the accident could have been his fault when he was standing still, and why the man wasn't helping him pick up his own stuff. As Brandon lifted one of the rolls, it uncurled slightly, and he noticed that it was titled The Great Exhibition. That sounded very familiar: Everywhere he had been, Brandon had heard a buzz about this event, whatever it was.

The documents had got a little wet, and Brandon apologized again as he prepared to hand them over. "Sorry, sir," he said.

The man irritably corrected him. "Sorry, Your Royal Highness."

Brandon was mystified, and repeated the phrase as a question. "Sorry, Your Royal Highness?"

The man glared at him. "You do not know who I am?"

Just then, a thought, both dreadful and wonderful, occurred to Brandon. "You're…You're not King Albert, are you, sir?"

The man was even more offended. "Prince Albert, foolish boy," he said, "I am Prince Albert, the Prince Consort."

"I'm sorry," stammered Brandon, handing the papers to the prince. "I thought you were Queen Victoria's husband, but I guess she must be your momma."

Prince Albert muttered "stupid boy" under his breath, and swept into the building. Brandon knew he had stuck his foot in his mouth, but how?

And then he heard laughter. The Professor had returned. "Way to go, Brandon. You just insulted Queen Victoria's husband, and you managed to knock down a bunch of papers about his pet project. Well, at least now I know why some of the documents were in a dreadful state in the archive…"

Brandon was indignant. "Hey, *he* bumped into *me*. Anyway, why's he called Prince, not King?"

"Here's a book," said the Professor by way of an answer, reaching into her basket and pulling out a slim volume. "Go read it."

Brandon inspected the book cover which announced *The History of Hert-*

fordshire, by Nathanael Salmon. Even before he opened it, Brandon guessed that the cover bore no relationship to the contents. Sure enough, it contained a very modern history of Victorian Britain written for kids, complete with cartoon illustrations. He tucked the book inside his jacket, and opened his mouth to thank the Professor. But she was already gone.

****

Alex grew to enjoy Mr. Thornhill's company, and wondered why he had ever doubted him. Mr. Thornhill had a great sense of humor, and his house was amazing. Alex had felt guilty at first about being waited on by so many slaves, but when he went to the kitchen to fetch himself a drink, the cook scolded him for not ringing for a servant. After that, he had begun to enjoy letting other people take care of him. What's more, the house slaves were friendly, and he convinced himself that their lives weren't so bad after all.

He liked working in the office, too. The more he understood about legal work, the more interest he took in it, especially when he got to meet the clients. Most importantly, Mr. Baird and Mr. Thornhill were kindly to him, and there was a constant stream of visitors to enliven their days. In the evenings, Alex sometimes had dinner and played cards with Mr. Thornhill, who even taught him to play poker.

Jupe, meanwhile, had made friends among the slaves in Mr. Thornhill's household. He was growing accustomed to life in the city, and, late one Sunday night, he confided to Alex that the sophisticated city-dwelling free people and slaves at his new church had gently teased him for his "country" speech and ways, and made him feel welcome. They also had good advice for him, as he explained. "You know, Alex, some Savannah slaves are hired out by their masters to make money for them. They work as craftsmen, and they get a lot of freedom from their masters. It ain't easy for them, Lord knows, but it's better than being on a plantation. Maybe I could do that for you one day."

Encouraged by Jupe's optimism, Alex explained his new take on the slaves in Mr. Thornhill's household. "You know, I always thought slaves were all miserable and sad. But Mr. Thornhill's slaves are really happy! And I haven't seen him whip anyone. I thought slaves were whipped all the time. Maybe slavery's not that bad."

In the long silence in the darkness, it slowly dawned on Alex that he had stuck his foot in his mouth. Majorly.

Jupe lay in the dark, weighing whether or not it was a good idea to argue with Alex, and finally he decided to go for it. "Alex, it ain't what it looks like. I promise. Slaves have to smile and laugh with white folks, or white folks make their lives miserable…"

"But I wouldn't do that," Alex protested.

"No, I don't believe you would. But most white folks, they don't hesitate. And so black folks, well, we smile and laugh with you… even when we got nothing to smile about. That's because if we don't, you might get mad at us."

Alex thought about this. "Huh. I hadn't thought about that before… What's everybody afraid of anyway? I mean, like I said, I haven't seen anybody get whipped."

Alex couldn't see it, but Jupe was shaking his head slowly. "You most likely won't see it, neither," he said quietly. "It doesn't happen every day. It doesn't have to: When a slave gets whipped, it's like a warning to the rest of us. Anyhow, you think a fine gentleman like Mr. Thornhill's gonna get blood on his nice clothes? No, sir. But his slaves get whipped just the same…"

Jupe was about to explain further when he suddenly recalled that he had something important to tell Alex. "Say, Cook told me something about Massa Thornhill," he whispered. "His wife died in England, and he brought his boys to Savannah, and they died from fever when they were just young men."

Alex was taken aback. "Wow, I didn't know that. How old were his sons?"

Jupe shrugged. "I don't rightly know, but one was about the same age as me, Cook says. The other one was all grown up. He was supposed to go to college in the north, then one day, take over from Massa Thornhill. But both of them died. Cook said how Massa Thornhill has a new wife and family on his plantation south of Savannah, but she doesn't know nothing about that, on account of she's not supposed to go meddling in his affairs. She did say he doesn't go down there to visit them too often anyway. He's too busy."

Alex wasn't sure he had understood Jupe's story. If Mr. Thornhill had remarried and had more children, then why didn't he bring his family to Savannah? Perhaps it was because the city was such an unhealthy place. Mr. Baird had told Alex about the city's fearful epidemics, including the terrible Yellow Fever outbreak of 1820, which had killed Mr. Baird's wife and a thousand other people. No wonder Mr. Thornhill wanted to keep his family far away. All the same, Alex thought, it was strange that in all of their conversations at the card table, he had never once mentioned either of his families.

A sharp rap on the door awoke Alex and Jupe early the next morning. "Begging your pardon, sir," Ezekiel the butler called through the door. "The master asked me to wake you early, and present yourself for breakfast at the earliest opportunity." Alex wondered what the occasion was, as he and Jupe struggled into their clothes.

A bleary-eyed Alex found Mr. Thornhill already at the dining table, wolfing down ham and eggs. A small brown paper package was at Alex's place. Alex carefully removed the string and unwrapped it, as Jupe, who was serving, craned his neck to see what was inside.

It was a colorfully-decorated wooden box with holes drilled in the front.

The boys looked quizzically at Mr. Thornhill, who was pressing a finger against his lips, watching Alex's reaction with amusement. "See this," he said, and he pushed his finger into one of the holes. A light went on in the largest hole, and now Alex recognized the object. It was the Professor's calculator.

"What did you do to it?" he said, aghast.

"Oh, don't take on so," tutted Mr. Thornhill, prodding at the calculator buttons through the wooden cover. "The mechanic to whom I took it for examination opened it, and then was unable to replace the cover… and, by the by, he said he could make neither head nor tail of this machine… So I had him convey it to a carpenter who made a cover to my instructions. I think it looks much more pleasing in its new attire, and it will be perfect for the Great Exhibition, where I intend to show it as a curiosity. It is too late to enter it for the catalog, of course, but it will serve as a good conversation piece to draw the attention of men of business."

Alex looked blank. What was Mr. Thornhill talking about?

"Didn't I mention?" Mr. Thornhill said. "I am sailing to London for The Great Exhibition of the Industry of All Nations. It promises to be quite an event. Apparently, an enormous glass and iron edifice is under construction to house it, and it will be dismantled as soon as the Exhibition ends. Baird will remain here to manage my business, but I'm taking you with me, Day."

Mr. Thornhill reached into his coat pocket, and tossed something to Alex. "Here, take the original cover. Have it as a keepsake until I return the calculating engine to you."

Alex tucked the calculator cover into his pocket, and wondered what the Professor would say when she found out. But she could hardly be mad at him under the circumstances. And why, he wondered, did he care what she thought? He hadn't asked for the responsibility, or, indeed, to be transported to 1851. He briefly considered tossing the cover away. But then he decided it would do no harm to keep it.

Meanwhile, Mr. Thornhill was happily playing with the calculator. "This really is the most extraordinary thing," he said. "It might come in useful this afternoon. You may be wondering why I had Ezekiel awaken you so early this morning. We are going to take a look at the estate I have acquired, and we shall take inventory of its contents. It's some fifty miles from here, so Tom will convey us to the railway station, and we will take the train. It will be a long day, so Cook has prepared food for the journey. We will bring Jupe along to serve us our meals."

They left Savannah at 8 a.m., and the journey took all morning and beyond. It was 2 p.m. by the time the train drew up to its eighth stop, and it was here that Mr. Thornhill suddenly stood up and announced that they were disembarking. Alex and Jupe grew nervous when they saw where were getting off: They were in Millen. It was too close to Kintyre Plantation for comfort. They were positively alarmed when they walked out of the station and saw Jupiter waiting for them.

As he greeted Mr. Thornhill and loaded up the bags in the wagon, Jupiter avoided looking at the boys, and they, in turn, avoided looking at him. Then Jupe climbed up onto the carriage to sit behind his father, who flinched slightly. Since there were no seats in the wagon, Mr. Thornhill sat in front, next to Jupiter.

"Massa Thornhill," Jupiter said. "Everyone at Kintyre is asking me what your plans are, and I say I don't know. What can I tell them?"

Mr. Thornhill said impatiently, "I have no idea, Jupiter. They must wait until I have decided whether Kintyre can be made profitable."

Jupiter protested, "But it is a profitable plantation, sir, yes, it sure is…"

"Perhaps, but that is for me to decide. I cannot make any decisions until I've looked over the estate and accounts. As soon as we arrive, assemble the slaves in front of the house."

It took the carriage another three hours to reach Kintyre Plantation. Halfway, they stopped briefly for a picnic by the roadside. Jupiter and Jupe pretended not to know each other as they ate biscuits and ham some distance away from Mr. Thornhill and Alex, for whom Jupe had set out a lavish cold meal of ham, biscuits, cheeses, fruit, and cake.

On his first visit to Kintyre, Alex had not seen the house, and he was shocked that it was a very plain two-story farmhouse. He had imagined that a plantation would have a mansion with tall classical columns, and be painted all in white, kind of like the White House. But this house was small, and it was painted a robin's egg blue.

"Aren't you surprised it's so teeny-tiny?" he blurted out to Mr. Thornhill as they walked up the steps to the porch.

"Not in the least," said Thornhill. "In Virginia, perhaps, or even Charleston, I might have expected more, but not in Georgia, and especially not in Snipes County. This land is poor, Day. The soil is mostly good for pine trees. Nobody makes a handsome profit here. It barely makes enough to support a man who owns slaves."

Thornhill pushed open the door, and Alex followed him. Jupe remained outside.

The front parlor and dining room were furnished, to Alex's surprise. "Why did the last owner leave his furniture? I didn't think that was part of the deal."

Mr. Thornhill raised an eyebrow. "It wasn't. House, land, and field hands," said Mr. Thornhill, looking down at the dining table and running a finger across it. "That was all I won. But the former owner has another house in South Carolina, and I understand it's much larger than this. I suppose he didn't need the furniture, and didn't have time to sell it before I took possession, so it is mine now... Except that I'm not sure that I want it. Come along, and let us see if he left his account books. He told me that he would."

"So you won the plantation in an auction?" Alex asked, as Mr. Thornhill rummaged through the drawers of the tall desk they found in a back room.

"Hmm? An auction?" Mr. Thornhill was now leafing through a leather-bound book. "No, no," he said distractedly. "I won it in a poker game, sitting at that very table in the dining room. I rather think young Gordon had had a few too many whiskies, but he should have known better than to wager such an enormous prize on a game of cards."

For all his calm and easygoing manner, Alex thought, Mr. Thornhill could be a pretty ruthless businessman. He wasn't sure whether to find that impressive or scary.

"Now, this is interesting," Mr. Thornhill said slowly, running his finger along a line in the accounts book. "Day, bring this book along, and mark the page so we don't lose it."

"Where are we going?" Alex asked.

"Outside," said Mr. Thornhill.

Jupiter had gathered the twenty field slaves in the dirt yard in front of the house. Most were newly returned from the fields. They were wiping the sweat from their foreheads, and shading their eyes from the sun as they anxiously watched Mr. Thornhill and Alex emerge onto the porch.

"Is everyone assembled?" Thornhill asked Jupiter, who nodded in reply.

"Very well. When you hear your name, raise your hand. Day, read the names from the book."

Alex held open the account book to the marked page, and Mr. Thornhill stepped over and placed his finger on the list of slaves. As Alex hesitantly began to read aloud the names, Mr. Thornhill watched the assembled slaves closely.

"Um… George," Alex said. A wiry and muscular man raised his hand.

"Cuffee." Another man, this one a burly guy in his thirties, lifted up his hand.

"Jupiter… Sarie…. Little Jupiter…"

"Stop," Mr. Thornhill said, holding up his hand. "Where is Little Jupiter?"

The adults looked off into the distance or down at the ground. But several of the children glanced at Jupe, and Mr. Thornhill saw them do it. The game was up.

Jupiter desperately tried to save the situation. "Massa Thornhill, Little Jupiter died…"

Mr. Thornhill waved at him to stop talking. "Little Jupiter, who I believe is your son, is my property, and now works in my household. I believe you sent him to find work in Savannah while your former master was absent?"

"Yes, sir," said a crestfallen Jupiter, looking sadly at Jupe. Sarie burst into tears, aware that Mr. Thornhill was signaling that he was not planning to punish the family. Disappointed though he was, Jupiter looked back gratefully at Mr. Thornhill, knowing that he could well have accused Jupe of running away, and his parents of helping him. All three of them could have been whipped and sold. But Mr. Thornhill said nothing more, except to tell Alex to continue calling the names.

Alex's mind was racing. How had Mr. Thornhill guessed?

When the inventory was complete, Mr. Thornhill dismissed the slaves, and returned to the house, calling in Jupiter and Alex as he did so. He poured himself a whisky, before taking a seat in the small parlor. Alex waited to be asked to sit down, but no invitation was forthcoming. Jupiter waited gravely for Mr. Thornhill's judgment on Kintyre Plantation's future, and his own.

Mr. Thornhill took a sip of his whisky, and then said, "I will sell George, since he is surplus to the labor requirements of the plantation."

"Sir, George is my brother….." said Jupiter helplessly.

Thornhill gave him a hard look. "Jupiter, I have already granted you a singular favor today. Do not ask me for another. Now, as I was saying, George goes to auction. You will manage with the remaining hands."

Jupiter looked utterly defeated. "Yes, sir."

Alex shuddered, thinking of poor Jupiter and George, doomed never to see each other again. He felt queasy.

Mr. Thornhill continued. "Jupiter, I noticed a young pecan orchard occupying part of a cotton field. Why is that? Pecans fetch nothing compared to cotton."

Jupiter looked at the ground. "I reckoned it was a pretty poor corner for cotton planting, sir. The pecans will be mighty good to eat, and they will give us slaves something to sell at market..."

"You made that decision?" Mr. Thornhill said in surprise. Jupiter looked as though he wished he hadn't opened his mouth.

Mr. Thornhill said briskly, "Georgia law requires that a master either supervises his plantation, or that he appoints a white man as overseer to act in his place. But it is practically impossible to find a man willing to do such work this far from Savannah, and even harder to keep him for long. Be that as it may, I doubt many lawmakers are paying much attention to this godforsaken part of the state. Jupiter, can you write?"

Jupiter hesitated, considered his answer, and then nodded.

Mr Thornhill said, "Good. Then you can run the place and keep accounts while I advertise for an overseer. I warn you, it might be a while. I shall drop in from time and time, and, meanwhile, you must send me weekly reports, is that clear? You may keep the orchard, but the pecans must be sold for my profit, or else counted into the slaves' food allowance."

After he had dismissed Jupiter, Mr. Thornhill turned to Alex, and said severely, "You have been extremely foolish. By rights, I should flog you senseless."

Alex swallowed. "Sir?"

Mr. Thornhill stared hard at him. "Don't play innocent with me, Alexander Day. You aided Jupe in his escape from Kintyre. You do know that that is a capital crime? You could be hanged."

Alex was stunned, and he stammered, "I had no idea... That's scary."

"It certainly ought to make you afraid. What on earth possessed you?"

"I don't know," shrugged Alex. "He just kind of came with me. I didn't ask him to, or anything..." Then it occurred to Alex what he was saying to Mr. Thornhill, and he didn't like it. "Look, I don't even believe in slavery..."

Mr. Thornhill gave a grim smile. "Oh, it exists, I assure you."

Alex tried to explain. "No, what I mean is..."

Mr. Thornhill looked as though he was barely containing his fury. "We won't discuss what you think of slavery. In fact, you would be well advised never to raise the subject again. And I mean never. You would cause me great embarrassment, and place yourself in terrible danger."

"What about the First Amendment?" Alex blurted out. "I thought the Constitution says we have free speech?"

"In the South, the Constitution does not apply to a discussion of the demerits of slavery. And you are only a boy, hardly a free citizen of these United States. For so long as you remain within my household, you will keep silent on the subject of slavery."

But this command only angered Alex more. He was not the most talkative of kids, and when he did give an opinion, even Hannah usually respected it. He didn't like being told to shut up, especially on a subject about which he knew he was right.

They caught the train from Millen at 1 a.m., and reached Savannah before dawn. Alex could not sleep on the train, and when he got home, he sank into bed with a grateful sigh.

He didn't sleep for long. Early in the morning, he was awoken by a woman crying, and a man's voice pleading. Alex hurriedly dressed, and anxiously tiptoed downstairs, to find Mr. Thornhill alone in the parlor, sitting on the edge of a chair and looking irate. "No breakfast this morning, Day," he snapped. "We will have to take our victuals at the office. I shall send out Jupe to fetch us something to eat."

"What's wrong?" Alex asked.

Mr. Thornhill ran his hand through his hair. "When we returned last night, I caught Ezekiel and Martha the cook stealing a ham from the kitchen, to give to a poor relation of theirs, a free Negro."

"Maybe he was hungry," said Alex.

Mr. Thornhill almost yelled at him. "That is hardly the point! It was theft from my kitchen. That is the point. I have sent them both to be whipped." Alex's stomach lurched. He didn't want to know the details. He hurriedly made excuses and retreated upstairs.

Back in the bedroom, Jupe was tidying away Alex's nightshirt. Alex told Jupe what had happened, and begged him to explain. "You told me that Mr. Thornhill wouldn't whip his slaves, but he said he's going to have Ezekiel and Cook whipped. What does that mean?"

Jupe looked down at his hands, and then into Alex's eyes. That had taken a lot of effort. He didn't like to look any white man in the eye, even Alex. He took a deep breath, and said, "He sent them to the Chatham County Jail House. That's where Savannah masters send their slaves to be punished. They don't do the whipping themselves, and they don't like to see it done. So Mr. Thornhill sends Ezekiel and Martha to the jail, and the jail man will whip them bloody."

Alex was trying to wrap his head around this. He struggled with his feelings: Loyalty to Mr. Thornhill, who was so kind to him, and revulsion against what he was doing to his slaves.

"But... Hey, they did steal a ham..." Alex said uncertainly.

"Yes, sir, they sure did," Jupe replied. He looked as though he wanted to say more, and there was an awkward silence while he struggled with his thoughts. Finally, he spoke again, weighing his words carefully. "It's like some folks say... negroes, that is... they say that we do all the work, and white people take everything. So when we got a chance to take some wages, it ain't stealing. Otherwise, we get nothing. Leastways, that's what some folks say... I don't hold with it myself."

Alex stared into space for quite some time, considering what Jupe had said. And then he thought about Ezekiel and Martha, tortured and humiliated in a filthy jail, out of sight and out of mind. He felt sick.

****

Hannah found work at the jute factory in Dundee was much like work at the cotton factory in New Lanark. But apart from the work itself, factory life was quite different. There was no system of silent monitors. Instead, there was Tam the Deil, who made up the rules to suit his mood. At first, he was nice to Hannah in a sinister sort of way, standing next to her and asking how she was settling in. Hannah couldn't help notice the older women who worked around her exchanging looks, and trying to distract Tam from her. But as Hannah ignored him, only giving brief answers, and only when she had to, Tam's attitude turned nasty.

He stood to one side watching Hannah work, which made her nervous. She began to make mistakes. Tam walked toward her, shaking his head, and took her aside while the frame was resting. "You're too slow," he said, his face in hers. "You don't know anything about piecing, do ye?"

Hannah stepped away from him, but she managed not to lose her nerve. "Yes, I do. I was a piecer in New Lanark."

He sneered at her. "Aye, but that was cotton. And anyway, you left there, didn't you? Were you given the sack?"

Hannah didn't know how to answer. Yes, she had been fired, but not because her work was bad. It was because she took a break when she was tired... and yes, okay, she had been a bit rude to the gaffer. But maybe she wasn't good at the work, easy though it was? She tried to pull herself together, and remind herself that she had only recently learned to piece, and why did she care anyway? She wasn't even supposed to be here. She was supposed to be in twenty-first-century America.

Hannah and Maggie stayed together through the dinner break, so called because the mid-day meal was the biggest meal of the day. As usual, they bought meat pies, and went window-shopping.

Hannah sighed, as she looked at a plain but new white dress in the window of Moon and Langlands' store. "Maybe Mina's right, and I should quit buying pies and save my money. I wish I could afford something new to wear. I'm so sick of this crummy dress. It's filthy. Jessie only ever washes my shift, because this is my only dress."

"And you're planning to die of an unwashed dress?" said Maggie with a sly smile.

"Well, I mind being filthy, even if you don't," said Hannah. "I wish I had more money. It's so not fair that someone like Tam the Deil makes, like, way more than me, when all he does is to walk around yelling at people and attacking them. And Mina says the owners like Sutherland live off the backs of the workers, with their grand houses."

"Aye, Mina's quite the radical, now," said Maggie. "But I'd rather spend my money on what I can afford, like my pies, and do without what I can't afford. My pal Bella Swan tried to help herself to something she fancied, and she pinched forty yards of printed cotton cloth from the draper's doorstep on Reform Street."

"Wow. What happened to her?"

"She was sent to the prison for eight months. She was lucky that they didn't send her on a convict boat to Australia. I tell you, Hannah, there's no sense in wishing for a better day. Might as well enjoy what we can. And maybe one day we can find men to marry me, then we can maybe leave the mill." She shook her head sadly.

"Wow, I wouldn't wait that long to quit Suttie's," Hannah said. "New Lanark was bad enough, but this..."

"Tell me about New Lanark," Maggie interrupted.

So Hannah did. She told Maggie about the clean tenements and streets, and the school for workers, and the shop that sold cheap food, and the silent monitors. Even though she put a negative spin on all of it, Maggie's eyes got wide.

"And you left all that to come to Dundee? Are you daft?"

Hannah got defensive. "Well, it wasn't that great. I hated it. And…" She hesitated to tell Maggie that she had been fired. "I… I wasn't going to stand there and be insulted by the gaffer with his stupid silent monitor."

Maggie narrowed her eyes at Hannah and poked her in the chest. "You're a fool, Hannah Dow, that you are. Oh, what I would give to work in a place like that! If I could afford it, I would leave tomorrow. But it's too risky. Mem Gordon says you almost starved to death on the way here. The Devil himself must have possessed you to make you leave there and come to Dundee. You should have known when you were lucky, that you should. Pity me, for I'll never have a chance like that, not as long as I live."

In a flash, Hannah suddenly saw the future through Maggie's eyes: Trapped in a filthy slum, in a job without prospects. Good jobs in the mill went to people like the Gordons, whose family members were gaffers, and gaffers were never Irish. Who would marry Maggie when she had so little to offer, and when she had to support her drunken dad? Hannah had never thought of her own future like this… Or maybe she had. Her life in California never seemed to have any plan, beyond escape. And Snipesville seemed to her like a black hole, sucking away even her vague hopes for better times when she grew up. Her sympathy for Maggie rapidly ebbed away in a tide of self-pity.

Early that evening, Hannah forlornly trailed home in the rain along a busy street called the Cowgate. It was dark, and the only light came from the tall sputtering gas lamps next to the sidewalk. She was wet, which didn't improve her mood. Suddenly two people ran up next to her, laughing and splashing her with muddy water as they landed in a puddle by her side: One of them was Mina, and the other was a young man Hannah didn't recognize.

Mina linked arms with Hannah and pulled her close, almost knocking her off her feet. "Good evening to you, Hannah! I thought it was you I spied. Now, meet my intended, my soon-to-be husband, Jack MacLean. Jack, this is our wee lodger, Hannah Dow. She's got the cheek of the devil… So she's all right with me."

Jack was already on the other side of Hannah, and he wrapped an arm around her shoulders and planted a big kiss on her cheek. Hannah was so embarrassed she didn't know where to look, but Jack and Mina just laughed at her bashfulness. Then Mina grabbed Hannah by the hand. "Come on, we're away to the pub. Would you no join us?"

"Um, sure. I guess," Hannah said. She had never been to a pub. "But I'm

CHAPTER EIGHT

too young."

Mina dismissed her worry. "Och, no. It's a right old spit and sawdust bar, but it's friendly enough. Just dinna tell Janet we were there, ye ken? She wouldn't approve." Mina launched into a wicked impersonation of her straitlaced sister. "Ooh, no, what would the minister say? That's not respectable, Mina Gordon." All three of them laughed.

"Mind you," Mina said, "I'd be much obliged if you'd join me in ducking behind a building if you see the minister coming up the street."

Hannah joked, "What if we see him coming out of the pub?" Mina and Jack fell about laughing at that, and Hannah felt like the life and soul of their little party.

She followed the young couple down the High Street to the Nethergate. Then they turned right onto Lindsay Street, walking between the office of the dentist who specialized in false teeth, and the massive church known as the Old Steeple. A little ways farther along, they came to a humble building, to which Jack gestured grandly. "Here it is, my place of employ, the Clarence Theatre, better known to one and all as Fizzy Gow's!"

Hannah was agog. "You're an actor? Wow, how cool is that?"

Jack bowed with a flourish. "I am indeed, miss, an actor and entertainer, known to discerning audiences from Dundee to Glasgow, and much appreciated from Aberdeen to Ecclefechan."

Mina wasn't going to let this go to his head. "Ach, awa' wi' ye! Hannah, he's a just a singing clown in a penny gaff."

"Eh?" Hannah needed this translating.

"A penny gaff," Mina explained. "It's a cheap wee place of amusement for us common folk. It's a good laugh. Jack here acts, tells jokes, sings, and plays his banjo."

"I'll have you know I've performed Shakespeare at Fizzy's," Jack protested.

Mina whispered with a wink to Hannah, "Aye, the quick version of Hamlet, which lasted but a quarter of an hour." They giggled as they followed Jack into the pub next door to the theatre.

Hannah turned down Jack's offer of beer, and so did Mina. As Jack went to the bar for drinks, Mina muttered, "He knows fine that I abstain from liquor."

Hannah was actually surprised: Mina had always seemed to be a bit of a party girl. "Why don't you drink beer?"

"Well, my minister and church dinna approve of liquor," Mina said. "But that's not really why I won't touch the stuff. You see, I reckon that if the work-

❖ 136 ❖

ers in Dundee spent as much time reading books as they did getting drunk, they would have a chance of standing up to the millowners. I hate to agree with my sister Janet, but for once, she's right: The folk who drink to excess demean themselves, and lessen the respectability of all the common folk. Mind you, this isn't a sentiment I express to Jack too often, although you may be sure I wouldn't marry him if he were a drunkard."

Just then Jack returned with the glasses. "Right then, lassies. A pint o' stout for me, and twa ginger beers for you twa."

"Oh, um, I didn't want beer." Hannah stammered.

Mina and Jack chuckled at that. "Ginger beer, Hannah," Jack reassured her. "So pure that the minister himself would not hesitate to lift a glass."

"Now then," he said, as he pulled up his chair. "Tell me why you're for temperance, Hannah?"

Hannah stared at him open-mouthed. "What?"

"Why do you forswear the demon alcohol? And more importantly, why do you think others should do the same?" Jack waved an arm in the air. "Let us hear your argument in this place of ill-repute!"

Hannah didn't know what to say. She was too young to drink, she knew that, but clearly she wasn't too young to drink in 1851. And Jack was asking for her opinion. Hardly anyone asked Hannah's opinion about anything. Ever. She tried to think of what to say. "Um, because I might get drunk instead of, ah, reading books and stuff? And then I wouldn't be able to stand up to the millowners?"

"Oh, you've been talking to Miss Gordon here," Jack said, with a wink at Mina. "Anyway, from what I hear, you have no trouble standing up to millowners, lass. I hear you gave old Tom Sutherland a piece of your mind."

Hannah smiled proudly. Yes, she had, hadn't she? She preened. Wow, she was proud of herself. And now here she was, hanging out with a real actor. "So are you guys gonna find a place to live closer to the theatre when you get married?"

"Aha," Jack said, "We won't be in Dundee. We're striking out for new opportunities."

"What, you're going to Glasgow?" Hannah didn't mean it as a joke, but Mina and Jack laughed all the same.

"No, Hannah," Mina said. "We've made up our minds. We're going to New York."

Hannah's jaw dropped. "New York? Like, in America?"

"The very one," Jack said. "There, I shall entertain those Yankees with a wee song, and a tune on my banjo." With a flourish, he strummed an imaginary instrument.

Mina smirked. "Pretty funny when you think he learned the banjo from the Virginia Minstrels during their tour through Scotland. He's going to take their own music back to them."

Jack added, "Aye, well, afore we go, I'm to give a wee performance at our church's Anti-Slavery Soiree. Why don't you come, Hannah? It'll be an evening to remember, I promise you that."

Hannah was confused. Life was hard in Scotland, but she had no idea that slavery was a problem here, and she said so.

Mina shook her head. "No, not in Scotland. Slavery in America. Ye ken, Jack, about five years past, we had a visit at St. George's Chapel from yon Frederick Douglass? He gave a braw speech, do you remember? Very moving. He showed us the shackles and whips and whatnot that are used on the poor slaves. But whit a sense o' humor, too! A fine gentleman."

Even Hannah had heard of Frederick Douglass: The school always put up his picture for Black History Month. Wasn't he a former slave or something? And imagine people like Mina knowing all about him!

Jack said, "My brother Jamie saw him in Arbroath. Do ye remember how Mr. Douglass complained that the Free Church of Scotland was taking donations from Presbyterian churches in the slave states? After he heard Douglass speak, Jamie was so angry, he went out and painted 'No silver from the blood of slaves' on the church wall."

Hannah was shocked. "You must be so embarrassed!"

But Mina and Jack misunderstood her, thinking she was shocked by the donations from the American churches, not the graffiti. Mina said, "Aye, well, it was pretty embarrassing for our minister, George Lewis. He had travelled all over the South raising money."

"The South? You mean England?" Hannah was confused again.

"Och, no," Mina said. "The American South. The Free Church is a new church, and most of our members are poor. The minister went to ask the Presbyterians in the South for some help. He wrote a book about his travels, and he lent me a copy. It was very interesting. I remember reading about him going to a plantation near the city of Savannah, and how the negroes all worked more like convicts than free men..."

"Savannah?" Hannah exclaimed.

"Aye," continued Mina. "It's a city in...where was it, Jack, was it Alabama? No, Georgia. Och, anyways, Mr. Lewis said that one negro lad had to wear a spiked collar with bells on because he had run away so often. What a shame, eh? Terrible cruel. But many of the Negroes go to church, and like us workers, they have their own. Mr. Lewis met with a colored minister in the city. Mind you, I think he got awfully fond of the white folk he met there, and believed too much what they telt him about the negroes. I reckon if he had spent more time with the colored folk, he would not have been so quick to take money from the whites."

Hannah kept thinking how smart Mina was. She was kind of round, and she wasn't all that pretty, but everyone liked to be with her. Mina's stories were always so interesting. She hated to think of Mina leaving for America. But anyway, Hannah thought, it wasn't like she herself would be in Dundee forever. She, too, would be on her way to America soon, wouldn't she? And that was what she wanted… Wasn't it?

Chapter 9:
HOW THE OTHER HALF LIVES (AND DIES)

Hannah was sorry she had let Mina and Jack talk her into attending the church soiree. The congregation sang a hymn, and then one speaker after another rose to his feet to give excruciatingly boring speeches on the evils of slavery. More than once, Hannah was tempted to jump up and point out that slavery would end in less than fifteen years, with or without long-winded speechifying in a Scottish church.

Finally, the collection basket was passed. Hannah, having only three pennies to her name, dropped in a farthing, a coin worth one quarter-penny. With relief, she now saw everyone get their feet, suggesting that the event was over... But no, it was only an intermission. However, she cheered up enormously when Mina pointed out the tea and cakes, and told her that the second half of the evening was mostly entertainment, including Jack's performance.

When Jack walked onto the platform, Hannah almost dropped her teacup in amazement. He was wearing a ragged-looking outfit and carrying a banjo, but what really got Hannah's attention was that his face and hands were covered in black make-up. He launched into song, accompanying himself in a plaintive version of *Swing Low, Sweet Chariot*. Hannah tried not to laugh, and ended up making snorting noises.

"What's wrong with you?" Mina whispered angrily.

"He's pretending to be black! He can't do that!" Hannah was half-shocked, half-laughing. She could just imagine the look on Brandon's face if he were there.

Mina shushed her, and Hannah did her best to keep a straight face as Jack performed. She reminded herself that Jack wasn't trying to make fun of black people: He was trying to help them. Scotland, Hannah decided, was a very weird place.

On the way home from work the next evening, Hannah stopped to gaze through the windows of Moon and Langlands' store, thinking wistfully of her London shopping trip with her Grandma. Then, she had thought nothing of walking into even the grandest department stores, and buying lots of lovely clothes. Now, she was a little afraid even to enter the modest premises of Moon and Langlands'. She was filthy. She was poor.

She looked sadly at the wonderful dresses and hats she glimpsed through the window. The fashions were so very different from those in modern America, but she loved the bright colors and ribbons… The dresses were so romantic! But just one of those dresses would cost her four months wages, an impossible sum. Even if, miraculously, she found the money, where could she wear the dress? Certainly not in Dundee: The Gordon girls would only laugh at her for wasting so much money, and the police would probably decide that she had stolen it.

When one of Moon and Langlands' clerks spotted Hannah pressing her nose to the window, he angrily shooed her away. Embarrassed, she stepped backward, and the clerk quickly returned his attention to an elegant lady customer. Standing near the open doorway, Hannah could hear the lady commanding the clerk in an English accent to send her the bill for her purchase, telling him that she had to hurry, for she had a train to catch. Then, as Hannah watched, she left the store carrying a package, and a taxi driver waiting outside helped her into his horse-drawn cab. It was at that moment Hannah caught sight of the lady's face for the first time. It was Mr. Sutherland's cousin Lady Chatsfield, the woman at the picnic on the Magdalen Green.

Behind Hannah, the store clerk locked the door, turned the OPEN sign to read CLOSED, and lowered the blinds.

Lady Chatsfield's cab was only a few yards up the road when a great crack rang out, and the entire vehicle slumped to a halt. The axle had broken. The cabdriver jumped down, and swore under his breath when he saw the damage. He opened the door and spoke briefly to Lady Chatsfield, before helping her out onto the street. She stood on the road looking lost. First, she looked for another cab, but only two passed her, and they were both occupied. Then she caught sight of Hannah.

"You, girl, come over here," she ordered.

Hannah's stomach turned to ice. Had she been recognized?

But Lady Chatsfield handed her shopping to Hannah, and said, "I must be on the railway station platform in twenty minutes, or I shall miss my train from Edinburgh to London. If you will carry this and show me the way, I shall reward you with a shilling."

That was more than a day's wages, a week's worth of meat pies and cakes. Hannah didn't hesitate. "Yeah, sure, right this way," she said brightly. Lady Chatsfield hadn't recognized her after all. That figures, Hannah thought: To rich people, all mill girls must look alike.

CHAPTER NINE

Now she had an idea. Why should women like this Lady What's-her-face wear lovely dresses, ride on trains, and eat delicious picnics, while she, Hannah, had only dirty, drab clothes, worked in a miserable factory, ate gristly pies on church steps, and waded through streets covered in mud and poop? Hannah decided it was time Lady Chatsfield saw how Dundee people really lived. As she led her unwitting victim toward the entrance to The Vault, she smiled to herself, feeling more cheerful than she had for days. She would show her, all right.

Lady Chatsfield hesitated as they entered the alleyway. "Are you certain that this is the right street?"

"Oh, yes," Hannah lied. "This is the fastest way. I want to make sure we get there on time."

But Lady Chatsfield remained distinctly nervous, and she was right to be. As they turned into a narrow lane, a woman shouted at them from a window. She was looking straight at Lady Chatsfield. "Hey, you," she slurred drunkenly, "I know you, all dressed up like some grand lady. You're a deserter from the Queen's army, that's what you are, dressed like a woman."

Ooo-kay, Hannah thought, she's nuts. But then things rapidly spiraled out of control. To Hannah's horror, the drunken woman lurched out of a doorway, and followed them, cursing and yelling. Worse, she began to attract followers: Bare-footed boys and girls, young and old women, none of whom seemed to share their drunken leader's bizarre idea that Lady Chatsfield was a man in disguise, but all of whom were enjoying the show. Hannah knew they weren't used to seeing wealthy people in their neighborhood, and, judging from their boos and catcalls, they resented Lady Chatsfield for even being there.

Hannah was now very afraid, and she grabbed Lady Chatsfield's hand, urging her to move faster, which she did, picking up her skirt with one hand and holding on to her bonnet with the other as they hurried along. By the time they reached the Greenmarket, the crowd baying behind them was at least a hundred strong, all shouting, cursing and jeering.

Desperate, Hannah dragged Lady Chatsfield into the doorway of a grocery store that had just closed for the evening. The shopkeeper, Mr. Harris, a sandy-haired man in a white apron, saw them immediately, and flung open the door to let them in. He blocked the doorway to stop the crowd from following.

"If I get any trouble," he yelled to the mob, "I will tell the police and the magistrates I saw you, Bella McKay, and you, Mary Ellis, and you, Tommy McConnell. Be off with you, now."

The crowd fell back from the shop entrance, but did not disperse. People lingered outside, laughing and jeering. Hannah was crestfallen. What had she done?

Lady Chatsfield was near to tears, and the shopkeeper brought her a wooden chair in which to sit, out of sight of the mob. His wife stood by, anxiously wringing her hands.

Lady Chatsfield said forlornly to Mr. Harris, "I've been staying with Mr. Thomas Sutherland at Roseangle, and I'm supposed to depart on the railway train from Dundee in twenty minutes. I left my servant at the station with all the luggage, and now he will have no idea what has become of me." She pointed angrily at Hannah. "This wretched girl took me on a fool's errand. She said she would escort me directly to the station, and instead she has led me through the most dreadful slums."

Mr. Harris gave Lady Chatsfield a slight bow, and spoke to her in painstaking English with only a slight Scots accent. "Please calm down, madam. I'm sure the neighbors will have sent for the police." He glanced over at his wife for confirmation, and she nodded.

He now turned his attention to Hannah, and suddenly, his accent became very Scottish again. "And aren't you the lass who lodges with Jessie Gordon?" he said angrily. Hannah nodded dumbly, and Mr. Harris slapped her hard across the back of the head, then pointed a finger in her face. "You! Find a cab. And if you pass a constable, you ask him to make his way here directly. Got that? Now, get out. And if a cab's not here in the next five minutes, I'll send a constable after you."

Hannah, her ears still ringing from the slap, pushed her way through the jeering crowd.

Once Hannah had found a cab for Lady Chatsfield, she started home on foot. She felt so dumb. She had meant to give Lady Chatsfield a taste of the lives of the losers of the Industrial Revolution. But the lesson had gotten completely out of hand. Hannah didn't belong in Lady Chatsfield's upper-class world, but she didn't feel much like she belonged with a drunken and cruel mob, either. She wished she had never left New Lanark. Things had been less complicated there.

Dragging her feet, Hannah took a very long time walking home. She was not looking forward to returning to the Gordons' apartment. The more she walked, the more she worried. She knew she would be in huge trouble for bringing shame on the household. That was a lesson she had learned in 1940: After a police constable had knocked on Mrs. Devenish's door to tell her that

Hannah, Verity, and Eric had been caught breaking a window, Mrs. D. had whipped the three of them. Hannah shuddered at the thought that Jessie might now do the same. "I am so dead," she mumbled to herself.

As she quietly slipped through the door, Mina was holding everyone's attention, standing in front of the fireplace, addressing her mother and sisters. "Those women put on airs and would have us all as their slaves if they could."

Catching sight of Hannah, she swept a fist through the air in a supportive gesture. "Good evening, Hannah. I was just telling everybody about your escapade this afternoon."

Hannah was horrified that her role in the near-riot was common knowledge, but the only member of the family who seemed upset was Janet. "I think it's shocking," she said in an anguished voice. "What will the neighbors say?"

"Oh, you and your neighbors," scoffed Jessie. "I canna say I would have encouraged Hannah to lead thon woman up our street, but Mina's right that folk like that ought to see where the money comes from. It's the workers' money they live off, right enough."

Hannah was astonished. Not only was she not to be punished, but to Jessie and her daughters (except for Janet) she was suddenly a hero. Emboldened, she said proudly, "Did you hear that Mr. Harris hit me?"

"Damn cheek," blustered Mina. "Did you hit him back?"

"Now, Mina," Jessie warned. "Enough of that. I get my messages at Harrises, and I don't need him telling me my custom's no wanted. Where else would I buy my oats and tea?"

Just then, a great shrieking broke out in the street. The girls rushed to the window, except for Mina, who grimaced, and Janet, who looked offended as usual.

"It's twa lassies fighting!" Betty reported back excitedly. There was a general rush for the door, and Hannah, mystified but caught up in the moment, raced down the stone steps with the others. As she ran into the darkened courtyard, she was almost knocked down by two screaming women grappling with each other. Judging by their slurred yells and a strong smell of whisky, they had been drinking heavily. A large crowd quickly gathered around to watch, women with folded arms shaking their heads, yelling encouragement, or both, and men waving their caps and laughing. Several people were hanging out of their windows to watch.

This, Hannah thought, must be what people do in 1851 instead of watching reality shows on TV. She tried to enjoy the fight, but she became more and more uncomfortable with the spectacle, which seemed so tacky. What kind of place had she landed in, she asked herself? The woman standing next to her was yelling "Bite her!" to the contestants, and Hannah, startled, turned to stare at her.

Of course, it was the Professor.

"You!" Hannah yelled.

"Yes, me," said the Professor with a cheery smile, pulling Hannah aside, away from the action. "So, how are things?"

"Bizarre," Hannah said sullenly.

"Would you like a mutton pie? My treat."

Hannah pulled a face. "No. I'm kind of sick of them right now. It's like eating a burger every day."

The Professor was pleased to have an opportunity to explain something. "Funny you should say that. You see, the mutton pie was a Victorian ancestor of the burger: It's cheap, hot, tasty and fast. It's no coincidence that the jute mill girls eat so much fast food. Like a lot of people in our century, they haven't got the time to cook, and meat pies are filling, especially when you eat one with a sweet cup of tea…" She trailed off when she saw Hannah's troubled expression. "Look, I understand you were involved in a bit of a disturbance this afternoon, is that right? Good for you."

Hannah was appalled. "Good for me? It so was not. I was totally scared, and I never meant for people to follow me."

"I suppose that's true," said the Professor, "but you did what you were meant to."

Hannah blinked. "I did?"

"Oh, yes."

Hannah didn't want to confide in the Professor, but she had nobody else to talk with about what was bothering her. Hesitantly, she said, "This is so different from Balesworth."

The Professor looked away from her and recited, "Different place, different time, different people."

Hannah struggled with that. "Yeah, but… I kind of learned how to deal with England when I was in Balesworth… Like I knew how to be English. But in Scotland I can't seem to figure out the rules."

The fight and the jeering crowd were moving in their direction, so they stepped away again as the Professor spoke. "Scotland is part of Britain, Hannah, but it's also a separate country with its own culture. Plus, you're in an industrial city in 1851, not a small market town in 1940, and you're staying with a working-class family, not a middle-class one. Everywhere and everyone is different at every time. Foreignness upon foreignness, that's what you're dealing with."

Hannah shivered in the cold, trying to process the Professor's words, and she watched as the brawl draw to a close. One woman was knocked unconscious, blood streaming from her nose, and her friends were carrying her away.

She turned back to the Professor. "Dundee is the grossest, most disgusting place I've ever been, and half the people are drunks. People are always getting in fights. There's hardly any shops, and I can't afford them anyway, even if I was allowed in the door, which I so am not. I never get any, like, privacy. So, yeah, it sucks... Except..."

Except. Hannah didn't know how to put it, and she paused for a moment.

"Except...?" prompted the Professor.

"I don't know... The Gordons are nice. I felt like Mrs. D. was so cool, but now I think the Gordons are easier to live with. Jessie doesn't nag, and she doesn't seem to mind much what I do. Mina's awesome. But if Mrs. D. was here, she would be, like, totally shocked."

The Professor smiled knowingly. "Never mind Mrs. D. She hasn't been born yet. It's you I want to hear from. Are you scared?"

Hannah nodded reluctantly, and struggled to put her feelings into words. "I don't know how...I mean... I guess..."

The Professor seemed pleased. "You don't know what to think, do you? I mean, if you judge this place by the standards of America in our time, or Mrs. Devenish's England, then it's dreadful. Actually, by practically any standard, it's dreadful. But..."

"But," interrupted Hannah, "there's something neat here, too. I just don't know how to explain." She immediately regretted saying that. What did she mean? She wasn't sure, but to her surprise, she wanted to understand. "Everything here is nasty. But I feel like it's... Real. Yeah, that's the word. It's real. Like not pretend. Like not totally fake."

"Mrs. D. wasn't totally fake, was she?" The Professor asked gently.

"No...yeah...no...wait...Sort of. I mean, she didn't always say what she meant, and you kinda had to learn how to read her. But Jessie and the girls, it's like what you see is what you get. That's way cool."

"So you prefer that?" The Professor looked intrigued.

But Hannah was once again grumpy and suspicious. "What do you care? I don't even know why I'm telling you all this."

The Professor gave her a knowing look. "Maybe I can help you to understand. You don't have privacy, but you're never lonely here, either. You can't go shopping, but so what? Here, you don't have to worry all the time about how you look. The work's awful, but you have friends there, especially Maggie. And when bad things happen, there are always people willing to help you out."

Hannah pondered this in silence.

"Think about it," said the Professor, tightening her shawl around her shoulders. "I'll be in touch soon, Hannah. And don't worry. I'm pretty sure that things are working out as planned. There's light at the end of the tunnel." The crowd had melted away, and the Professor's footsteps echoed in the empty close. Left alone in the darkness, Hannah turned and hurried back to the tenement.

All in all, Hannah was feeling pretty good about herself, reveling in her new status as the brave mill girl who stood up to rich people. But she was also sad that Mina would be leaving. She thought a lot about Mina's impending departure over the next few days. In fact, she was daydreaming on that very subject when Tam the Deil spotted her.

He stalked over to her, waving a finger. "Hannah Dow, look lively! You're holding up the work as usual, and... What is this?" He briefly grabbed at a handful of broken threads, and immediately shut down the machine.

"Fix them!" He yelled at Hannah, and stood over her while she hurriedly pieced the threads.

Suddenly, Tam was distracted by the whole room erupting in laughter. Hannah at first thought the laughter was directed at her, but it wasn't.

Mina had just made a grand entrance draped in colored paper streamers, and carrying a chamberpot filled with rock salt. She gave her audience a goofy smile and an exaggerated curtsey. All the Gordon sisters had come with her, and, indeed, it seemed that they had brought every other weaver in with them. Everyone in the spinning shed immediately stopped work. As the machines powered down into silence, the room filled with the sounds of women's laughter, giggles, chatter, and jokes.

"We're creeling the bride!' cried Maggie excitedly.

To Hannah's surprise, a sour-faced Tam the Deil only tutted in exasperation, before making a quick exit.

"Hey," Hannah said to Maggie, "Why doesn't he put a stop to this?"

Maggie shrugged, smiling. "He'd be taking his life in his hands, so he would. It's a tradition, and he daren't interfere. There would be a riot if he even tried."

Hannah liked that, and she also liked the raucous joy of everyone around her. She remembered how different things were at the office parties her mom had sometimes dragged her to in San Francisco. There, everyone ate nasty su-per-sweet brightly-colored cake with frosting that tasted weirdly chemical, and that was the big highlight. Otherwise, the "partiers" stood around awkwardly, pretending to enjoy themselves while not really saying much of anything, and after twenty minutes or so, they all made excuses and left, while lying about the wonderful time they had had.

This was not that kind of party. There was no cake, but everybody was loud and happy, and they even held a sort of karaoke, where people took turns get-ting up to sing. Mina's sister Mem warbled a sad song about a young woman from long ago whose father had forbidden her to marry her true love. Before she had even finished the first verse, her sister Mary had started sniffling. By the time Mem came to the end of the very long song, the young woman and her lover were both dead, and practically everyone in the room was in floods of tears, including Hannah.

"Och, look at you all girning," cried Mina. "It's my wedding, not my fu-neral. We need a bit of cheering up. Gie's a song, Hannah."

Hannah, sitting on the floor, was startled to be called upon, and she em-phatically shook her head. "Oh, I can't sing. I am so awful at it."

But the partygoers wouldn't buy that, and the Gordon sisters pulled Hannah to her feet, shoving her forward while the whole room chanted "Sing! Sing! Sing!"

She was so mortified, she didn't know where to look. What would she sing? She could just imagine the stunned silence if she broke into rap. So she settled for a song she had learned in 1940, a silly song with a catchy chorus about run-ning rabbits. It was a bit off key, but everyone seemed happy with her effort, and she sat down afterward to much applause. Hannah felt strangely proud of her star turn, as she sat wedged between Mem and Mary. She joined in the cho-ruses of the next song, and laughed at the jokes even when she didn't entirely understand them.

Betty, the quietest of the Gordon sisters, surprised Hannah by leading the most boisterous song of all, a song about weavers:

Aye, we're a' met together here to sit and to crack,
Wi' oor glasses in oor hands, and oor work upon oor back,
There's no a man amang them a' could neither mend nor mak,
If it wasnae for the work of the weavers.

By now the whole room had joined in, and Hannah sang along with them:

HOW THE OTHER HALF LIVES (AND DIES)

If it wasnae for the weavers, what would they do?
They wouldna hae clothes made o' wool.
They wouldna hae a coat, no, neither black nor blue,
If it wasnae for the work o' the weavers.

"Now then, a'body" said Mina, jumping to her feet as the applause died down. "Let's collect pennies!" She rushed toward the door, carrying the chamberpot, and all the girls and young women ran after her. Out in the mill courtyard, the group dashed toward the first man they saw, who broke into a broad grin when he got a good look at Mina. He gave her a peck on the cheek, then reached into his pocket and dropped a coin into the chamberpot. As the gang of women once more took off, Maggie grabbed Hannah's hand, and they ran laughing together toward the jute warehouse. At this moment, Hannah forgot the hard work, the filth, the cold, the hunger, the tiredness, and even the fear that she would never get home… or feel at home anywhere.

****

Brandon normally felt like a bit of a dork, but today he felt like an utter, total, uber-dork. He was a dork among dorks, the prince of dorks. His dorkiness was to an Olympic Gold standard.

He was wearing his new mourning clothes. His black trousers were way too big for him, and were held up with suspenders and a belt. Worse, his tall black hat was draped by a black crape cloth that came to a point on top of his head, and then trailed down his back in a foot-wide black sash that made him look like Miss Witchy Dorkiness of 1851. In his hand, he carried a sort of flag that looked like a black cloth-covered broomstick. Worst of all, he was wearing a long black overcoat that was more like a dress.

The overall effect was dreadful. Mr. Spencer was very pleased.

Over the past two weeks, Brandon had settled into life at Mr. Spencer's. Early on, he had resigned himself to his little nest in the workshop. Mrs. Spencer's maid brought over plenty of food, and it wasn't bad, for it included meats, vegetables, fruits, cheeses and even, to Brandon's joy, desserts, including a heavy fruit cake stuffed with raisins. All the same, he couldn't help wondering if he would ever be invited to eat at the Spencers' table in the house behind the business, just as Daniel did.

That question was settled one day at supper time, when the Spencers' young son came into the workshop to invite Brandon to supper. Over roasted chicken and vegetables, Mrs. Spencer warmed to Brandon, and suggested he make his bed in the attic room that was next to Daniel's.

Today, the day on which Brandon put on his humiliating costume, was the day on which he would be officiating for the first time as a "mute", or silent professional mourner. His job was to assume a gloomy expression and walk behind the coffin at a funeral.

As he followed Mr. Spencer downstairs, Brandon was still thinking happily about the book the Professor had loaned him. He had been reading about the Great Exhibition of 1851. When Mr. Spencer caught sight of Brandon's goofy faraway smile, he gently reminded him to look sad.

"Sorry, sir," Brandon said, and told him what he was thinking about.

"Oh, I do applaud your enthusiasm, Brandon," Mr. Spencer declared. "The newspapers have been full of it for months, and what descriptions they give! It is truly to be a modern wonder of the world. And it opens on May Day, just weeks from now. Perhaps once the crowd settles down a bit, you can go up to London. Mind you, the admission prices are expensive, for the Exhibition is intended for an audience of quality. You'll have to hope that the Prince Consort and his committee do indeed arrange cheap days for the working classes, as some eminent gentlemen have proposed."

"Oh, they will," Brandon said. He had read about the Exhibition's "shilling days" in his history book.

On Sunday Brandon was at breakfast with the Spencers, when the mail arrived. The maid brought in a letter on a platter.

"You get mail on Sunday?" Brandon asked. He'd never seen that before, not in England or in America.

Mr. Spencer smiled. "Do you not know, Brandon? Lord Ashley's law last year, banning Sunday deliveries, proved temporary. We have been getting Sunday post since September. Now, mind, Mrs. Spencer does not approve of breaking the Sabbath..."

"Indeed, I do not," Mrs. Spencer said timidly.

"...But I believe that business must come first. After all, in my profession, there is no such thing as a day of rest. And I hardly think that one delivery on Sunday is excessive. Wouldn't you agree, my dear?"

Mrs. Spencer inclined her head slightly, making it difficult to tell whether she agreed with her husband or not. Brandon had already noticed that the postman, who resembled a giant ladybug in his red uniform and tall black hat, visited the house up to eight times in a day.

Mr. Spencer, meanwhile, had opened the mail, and his lips were moving as he read the letter. Folding it up, he beamed at Brandon. "You have brought me good luck after all, my boy. This letter contains news that is at once sad and happy, for it will provide my most genteel funeral yet. Old Mrs. Wentworth, that distinguished lady of Windsor, died yesterday afternoon. She is to be buried in London. Her brother has asked me to visit her residence this morning and prepare the body, and then to accompany the coffin to the funeral. What's more, it will take place at Kensal Green Cemetery." The name of the cemetery sounded vaguely familiar, but Brandon couldn't remember why. He just nodded.

Mr. Spencer continued. "I am not, alas, arranging the funeral procession, for a London firm has been appointed to that task, but I am to escort the coffin until it's committed to the ground. I shall need you to help me. I am delighted that you know the workings at the Church of England chapel at Kensal Green, because I am rather nervous about it, to be honest with you."

Brandon had no idea what Mr. Spencer was talking about, but he had a very queasy feeling that it would, perhaps, have been better not to have exaggerated his qualifications at his job interview.

From Windsor to London by rail was a long and dull journey, during which Mr. Spencer talked almost nonstop about how this funeral might boost his business. "This is quite the opportunity to make a favorable impression upon many important personages of quality," he said proudly. He spoke, Brandon thought, as though he had not only swallowed a thesaurus, but digested it, and was now pushing out the contents from the other end.

At the railway station, they met Mr. Perkins, the Important London Undertaker, whose men took charge of the coffin, and loaded it onto a wagon bound for Mr. Perkins' shop, where final preparations would be made.

When Brandon and Mr. Spencer finally arrived at Kensal Green Cemetery, Mr. Spencer stood awed before the huge park-like graveyard that spread before them. Brandon tried to seem impressed, but to him, it looked like every cemetery in modern America. They waited at the grand stone archway for the deceased's relatives, for Mr. Perkins, and for the deceased herself.

"Mrs. Wentworth, may she rest in peace, was a person of quality," said Mr. Spencer to nobody in particular, as he continued to congratulate himself on landing such an important funeral. "She was a lady of great gentility, and much esteemed in Windsor."

Brandon had long ago guessed what this sort of talk really meant, and finally, sick of Mr. Spencer going on and on, he said it. "So she was rich?"

Mr. Spencer was shocked. "We should not discuss her means, Brandon, and especially not immediately after the honorable lady's demise. She was, I repeat, a genteel person, kin to the aristocracy, and that, I'm sure you would agree, is the salient point."

Brandon couldn't agree because he didn't know what "salient point" meant, but he nodded gravely.

At the sound of rolling wheels, they turned and saw several open carriages approaching. In the first was a lady carrying a parasol, and accompanied by her maid. The carriage paused in front of Mr. Spencer and Brandon, and the lady asked if she was addressing Mr. Perkins.

Mr. Spencer fumbled apologetically with his hat. "No, madam, my name is Spencer. Mr. Perkins will be along shortly with the…"

"Mr. Spencer," the lady interrupted. "I am Lady Chatsfield. I am the cousin of the late Mrs. Wentworth. You may recall that we corresponded."

Mr. Spencer groveled before her, bowing so low that Brandon was afraid he would scrape his nose on the ground. "Yes, my lady, of course I recall the favor of your ladyship's letter."

Brandon wondered, since he was dressed like the Beauty Queen of Death, whether he should curtsey, and he began to get the giggles thinking about it. A sharp look from Lady Chatsfield shut him up.

"I intend to follow the procession," she announced in a voice that invited no argument.

Mr. Spencer gulped slightly and bowed again. "As Your Ladyship wishes."

While her coach driver helped her down from the carriage, Brandon whispered to his boss, "What's wrong, Mr. Spencer?"

Mr. Spencer shuffled awkwardly. "Nothing, nothing at all. But… It is a modern idea, this, ladies following funerals, is it not?" He didn't wait for an answer. "Still, I suppose we can get used to it," he added, doing his best to look as modern as possible.

At that moment, a horse-drawn hearse pulled up to the gates. Atop it was a glass enclosure, and within, a highly polished wooden coffin: It certainly wasn't the pine box in which the body had travelled from Windsor. Mr. Spencer muttered to Brandon, "That coffin is the sort of manufacture I would expect from a fine London firm such as Mr. Perkins'. I must speak with Daniel about drawing up plans to build a coffin like that. Just look at the craftsmanship!"

As everyone assembled for the short procession to the Anglican Chapel, Brandon caught Lady Chatsfield looking him up and down. When he returned her gaze, she didn't avert her eyes as he had expected, but instead stared back at him. Then she pulled a veil over her face. Now a second veiled woman joined the procession, and Brandon saw Mr. Spencer shaking his head in bewilderment.

They made their way through the spacious park-like cemetery, past some of the grandest gravestones Brandon had ever seen. Among them were obelisks, as well as a mausoleum that looked like an enormous drinking fountain. Most eye-catching of all was an elaborate grave marker with Greek columns, angels… and were those Egyptian sphinxes at the base? Good grief.

The second veiled woman saw Brandon's astonishment, and whispered to him, "That was built for Andrew Ducrow. He owned a circus. A bit over the top isn't it? It cost him three thousand pounds."

"You!" Brandon yelped in surprise. Mr. Spencer, walking behind, cringed at his outburst, and Mr. Perkins glowered.

The Professor didn't spot the outrage she had provoked. She ploughed on, whispering to Brandon, "Yes, this is the fashionable place to be buried, ever since the Duke of Sussex chose to be interred here seven years ago. Now anyone who is anyone wants to be buried at Kensal Green. Much nicer than having your remains crammed into one of London's overcrowded burial grounds, which are, honestly, revolting." She added, mysteriously, "Of course, Mrs. Wentworth is being buried in the catacombs."

As the funeral party processed up the steps of the Anglican Chapel, the Professor fell back to walk alongside Lady Chatsfield, who asked her, "Do I know you?"

"Not yet," said the Professor. Before Lady Chatsfield could ask more questions, they entered the hushed, dark chapel. The Professor took a pew in the back while Lady Chatsfield continued down the aisle to the front row.

As they reached the chapel porch, Mr. Spencer and Brandon detoured sharply left, and down a narrow spiral stairway into the catacombs.

The basement catacombs were gloomy, dank, and smelly. Narrow coffins were untidily stacked at odd angles on shelves along both sides of the narrow brick passageways. Some coffins lay in tiny open rooms, guarded behind metal bars, as though zombies or vampires might otherwise escape from them. Cobwebs and dust shrouded everything, and the only light that pierced the eerie gloom filtered through air shafts at the ends of each passageway. Brandon almost tripped on the uneven floor. "This is creeping me out," he said to Mr. Spencer. "It stinks. And what the heck is that?" He pointed to a puddle of black tar oozing from one of the coffins.

"You don't want to know…" Mr. Spencer muttered ominously. And then he said suspiciously, "I thought you said you have been here before?"

"Yeah, course, sure," said Brandon, sounding as dishonest as he felt.

They paused in front of a peculiar cast-iron contraption. It was a thick metal pole stretching to the ceiling, loaded with massive gears, and anchored by a large metal turning wheel. "Right then," said Mr. Spencer. "This is the device, is it?"

"Sure," Brandon said uncertainly. He didn't have a clue.

Mr. Spencer nodded glumly. "I told Mr. Perkins that he need not assist us, because you're familiar with the hydraulic lift engine. I hope you know what you're doing, lad."

So do I, Brandon thought, mentally crossing his fingers.

Now a knock echoed from the ceiling, as someone rapped on the chapel floor above. "That's our signal," said Mr. Spencer. "On you go."

"What?" Brandon felt the first stirrings of utter panic.

Mr. Spencer stared at him in disbelief. "Lower the coffin, boy! Hurry!"

Brandon shook his head in bewilderment, then grabbed the turning wheel, and pushed on it. Nothing. He tried pulling. Nothing. He pulled harder. Then pushed harder. Still… Nothing. There was another, more urgent knock from the chapel above.

"Here, let me," cried a frantic Mr. Spencer, who now tried to turn the wheel. He couldn't shift it either. He let out a long string of curses, many of them directed at Brandon.

Within seconds, footsteps raced down the stairs, and Mr. Perkins appeared with his men, all of them carrying their top hats. "What the devil has happened?" Mr. Perkins raged as he raced toward Brandon and Mr. Spencer. He rapidly glanced over the machine, shoved Brandon out of the way, and reached behind him to pull a lever.

"You never took off the brake!" he said accusingly to Mr. Spencer, who looked absolutely mortified, and began to stammer apologies as he nervously fumbled with his hat. But Mr. Perkins had already started the wheel and turned over the job to the largest of his men, who pulled it as fast as he could. Looking at the top of the metal pole, Brandon watched the coffin begin to descend toward them. Apart from the creaking and grinding of the mechanism, everything was silent as the coffin lowered, until finally, the trap doors in the chapel above closed overhead.

Mr. Perkins was seething, and he rounded on Mr. Spencer. "You, sir, gave me your word that you were capable of operating this machinery. As a professional undertaker, I should have known better than to trust the word of a provincial carpenter with aspirations to grandeur. Kindly leave the premises, Mr. Spencer. My men and I will take charge. Good day to you." By this time, his assistants had lifted the coffin, and were carrying it to its place in the catacombs.

Stunned, Mr. Spencer and Brandon watched them all disappear around a corner. Uh-oh, Brandon thought, as Mr. Spencer glowered at him. Smoke was practically pouring from his boss's ears.

"You are dismissed," the undertaker finally managed to say. "Get out of my sight..."

"But..."

"NOW!"

Brandon ran for his life.

He emerged blinking into the sunlight, just as the funeral service drew to a close, and he leaned against a tree to catch his breath. The Professor was the first mourner to leave the chapel, and she looked enquiringly at him as she approached.

"I got canned!" he gasped, stepping forward to meet her. "I totally screwed up, and Mr. Spencer fired me! I'm such a loser. I can't believe I told him I could work that contraption. What am I going to do now?"

But before the Professor could answer, Lady Chatsfield interrupted. She had heard the conversation, and she called over to Brandon, "You there. Did you say that you have been released from employment?"

"Yes, ma'am," said Brandon in surprise.

"Then follow me," she commanded. With that, she turned and walked off in the direction of her carriage, where her maid and coachman were waiting. Brandon looked back questioningly to the Professor, who shrugged her shoulders as though to say "Why not?"

The Professor followed Brandon at a distance, watching with a contented smile as he and Lady Chatsfield held a discussion, at the end of which Brandon rushed back to the Professor. "You won't believe this, but I got a new job already! It's totally unreal. And you will never guess where it is."

The Professor was not surprised. "Try me. I would guess that Lady Chatsfield is interested in hiring you, and she's prepared to overlook the fact that you just got fired, especially because you so charmingly explained that it was based on a misunderstanding. And she lives in Balesworth Hall."

Brandon's face fell. "How did you know all that?"

The Professor simply smiled back. "Well done, Brandon. Now, off you go with your new mistress, and get settled in. The others should be joining you shortly, with a bit of luck."

This got Brandon's attention. "The others?" he squeaked. "You mean Hannah and Alex?"

Again, she smiled, but said nothing. She lowered her veil over her face, and walked briskly in the opposite direction. Brandon contemplated following her, before deciding that it would probably be best not to miss his ride to Balesworth in Lady Chatsfield's coach.

As he climbed aboard, the maid moved aside to let him sit down. "Hello," she said. "What's your name? I'm Flora." Brandon had the oddest feeling that they had met before.

****

Mr. Thornhill hung his hat on the hat stand, then tugged a sheaf of papers from his coat pocket, and flourished them in the air. "Alexander, I have made the arrangements. Here are three tickets for London via transatlantic steamboat, arriving in late April."

"So is Mr. Baird coming with us?" Alex asked.

Mr. Thornhill shook his head. "As I told you, Baird's staying here to mind the business. The third ticket is for an acquaintance."

Alex's heart sank. Surely he wouldn't have to share the entire journey with the awful Mr. MacGregor? He dropped lots of hints, but Mr. Thornhill refused to tell him who the third passenger was.

The cook was still in jail, and so Alex and Mr. Thornhill dined once again in a local tavern. Shortly after their return, they were sitting by the parlor fireplace when the Irish maid announced the arrival of Mr. MacGregor. Alex's alarm only increased when Mr. MacGregor's first words were, "I think it would be best for us to speak alone, Thornhill."

Alex had learned from Jupe that if he put his head into the fireplace in their bedroom, he could hear conversations in the drawing room. After discreetly leaving the parlor, he frantically raced upstairs, and stuck his head over the cold grate, just in time to hear Mr. MacGregor say, "I will tell you plainly, Thornhill: I have just had a very interesting meeting with James Gordon, who brought me slaves for auction. Gordon is a planter near Charleston, but he also holds a small plantation out in Snipes County that he inherited some few years ago. He is frequently absent from his Georgia estate. When he returned there recently, his slave driver claimed that one of the slaves, his own son, had drowned in the river. But the description he gave me of the boy fits Day's manservant perfectly, and I have offered to arrest him. Gordon plans to sell up in Georgia, so, as you may imagine, he's very grateful for my assistance."

There was a long silence.

"Well, how very interesting," said Mr. Thornhill slowly. "James Gordon, you say? And this plantation, would it be Kintyre?"

"It certainly would," Mr. MacGregor said in surprise. Alex could just imagine his cruel smile.

"I hate to disappoint you, old man, but the slave boy, runaway or no, doesn't belong to Gordon. Would you care for a whisky?"

There was a pause, and when Mr. MacGregor spoke, he sounded disappointed. "Why, sure I would, but how do you reckon that?"

Mr. Thornhill explained. "Young Jupiter belongs to Kintyre Plantation, and Kintyre Plantation, as it happens, now belongs to me. I won it from Gordon in a poker game, fair and square. Mind you, I am hardly surprised that the wretch would attempt to cheat me by stealing the boy. He didn't even allow me to sleep in the house after our card game. He just took off in a huff along with his house slaves and locked the door behind him, so I was forced to shift for myself in a ghastly inn in Snipesville. I should have told you all about this episode, MacGregor, but it quite slipped my mind. I am now the master of Kintyre, and all of its field hands. Here... Here's the deed, countersigned by Gordon.... Go on, look it over."

Alex held his breath, but there was only silence. He ducked out of the fireplace and left the bedroom to sit on the upstairs landing, waiting until he heard Mr. MacGregor leave by the front door. After a respectable interval, he returned to the drawing room. Mr. Thornhill was sitting by the fireplace, staring into the embers. "Mr. Thornhill? What will become of Jupe?"

Mr. Thornhill gave him a sharp look. "Good God, boy, haven't you caused enough trouble? Jupe is my property, and I will dispose of him as I see fit."

Alex didn't want to anger Mr. Thornhill, but he knew he couldn't live with himself if he didn't press his point. "Sir, I didn't want Jupe to come with me, and I understand what you told me about not speaking on slavery... But please tell me you won't sell him."

Mr. Thornhill saw Alex's distress, and softened slightly. He sighed. "No, I will not sell him. I have other plans for Jupe."

Alex saw this as an opportunity to try to push further. "You're a nice guy. How come you got yourself mixed up in buying and selling slaves? I mean, you have a nice house here, with everything you need. You have to be one of the richest men in Savannah. Why do you need any more? Why don't you free the Kintyre slaves?"

CHAPTER NINE

Shocked at what he saw as Alex's outburst, Mr. Thornhill rose to his feet, and advanced on him, raising his hand as though to hit him. "You insolent little..." But then he suddenly regained control. He dropped his hand, and said coldly, "Alexander Day, I will not debate a mere boy over matters that are not his concern. Go to your room."

Alex left the parlor with very mixed feelings. He was disgusted with Mr. Thornhill, with Mr. MacGregor, with all these men who got rich off the work and misery of people like Jupe and his family. But he felt very bad about offending Mr. Thornhill, and he wanted to apologize to him. It was all so confusing.

Chapter 10:
HARD TIMES

The morning after Mina's "creeling" to celebrate her coming marriage, Hannah caught herself humming as she walked to the mill. She could not get the songs she had learned out of her head. And the songs were so desperately uncool. She vowed to herself that she would not bring them back with her to the twenty-first century.

Meanwhile, she kept on humming happily. So happily, in fact, that she almost arrived late for work. She had to run to get inside before the factory gates slammed shut, or she would have been forced to take an unpaid day off work.

In her happiness that morning, Hannah forgot about Tam the Deil.

From the moment she arrived in the spinning shed, Tam watched her so constantly that she became more and more nervous and unsure of herself. Finally, she tripped as she ran toward some broken threads, and found herself sprawled on the floor.

"Oh, in the name of..." yelled Tam, rushing to her. He picked her up by the arm and shook her. "You're no much use to anybody, are you? You're that clumsy. You've nothing to say for yourself, eh?"

Hannah flushed red and began to stammer excuses at him. "Th... That's mean. I just tripped, that's all. I mean, I have issues and stuff, but I'm doing my best. Why are you picking on m... me?"

He shoved her away, muttering, "Useless, pathetic," and wiped his hands on his waistcoat as though touching Hannah had made them dirty.

Maggie said to Hannah, "Pay him no heed," but a couple of the younger girls laughed behind their hands. Hannah dropped her head. She was excruciatingly embarrassed.

As she worked at the spinning frame, she wept uncontrollably, but she continued to try to work, afraid to lose her job. Time passed in a daze, and her stomach was tied in knots.

But Hannah was not alone. Every time Maggie passed her, she asked how she was doing, or made some sympathetic remark. She suggested ideas for revenge on Tam. "I have another notion for what we could do," Maggie yelled over the noise. "We could tie him to a spindle, and watch him go round and round all day!" Hannah laughed, and felt much better.

Hannah was just gathering threads and giggling to herself over Maggie's latest joke, when something smashed into her head. Reeling, she dropped to her hands and knees, then collapsed completely, stunned and nauseous. She cried out, but nobody rushed to her aid as she lay on the floor, Hannah tried to gather her wits as her head pounded.

"Get up, you lazy damn wench," cried a voice that was familiar and yet slurred. "On your feet, I tell you, or I'll damn you to hell."

She opened her eyes to find Tam standing unsteadily over her. He was holding a heavy stick. Even as she lay in crippling pain, it dawned on Hannah that Tam had hit her with the stick, and that he was drunk. In horror, she looked at his scowling face, and at the shocked faces of the girls and women behind him.

"Get up, you worthless besom, and do your work," Tam growled. "Or I'll see to it that you're cast out, and you never work in a Dundee mill again. You're the laziest, most insolent girl in the mill. You're worthless. Even the other lassies canna stand you."

Hannah closed her eyes, and, once again, began to cry. She was exhausted, utterly devastated, living in a nightmare of dirt and disease, far from her brother, far from home. Now even her ability to make a living was threatened. And she began to wonder if what Tam said was true: Was she really worthless?

As a parting shot, Tam growled, "You disgust me." He spat on the ground, before staggering away, shouting "On with your work!" at the mill girls, who hastily returned their attention to the spinning frames.

Hannah's head was pounding, and she was afraid she might throw up. The moment Tam left, Maggie rushed over to her and sat her up, while another girl brought her a cup of water. Within minutes, Mina arrived, brought by one of the spinners who had run to the weaving shed to fetch her. Mina kneeled down, wiped Hannah's face with a damp rag, and said quietly, "You're better than him, lass. He's a wee nyaff."

Just then, the factory whistle sounded for the noon dinner, and the machines ground to a halt. The spinners gathered round as Mina and Maggie helped Hannah stagger to her feet.

"I'll fix Tam the Deil," Mina said ominously, her arm around Hannah's shoulders.

An older woman, standing with her arms crossed, said to her warningly, "Mind you dinna lose your job, Mina Gordon."

But Mina would have none of it. "I'm getting married this week, and then Jack and me are sailing to New York. Tam used to treat me terrible cruel, like all the lassies he took a dislike to. It would be a pleasure to gie him a piece of my mind. He's skulking around here somewhere, I'm certain. Well, I'll be back this afternoon, you mark my words. Now, Hannah, you look awfy. Let's get you home."

Hours later, Hannah awoke as she heard the door open. She was in bed, buried under several blankets. Her head was pounding. She screwed up her closed eyes in pain, and started to moan softly to herself, through her closed mouth.

Betty, Mem, Janet, and Mary were all laughing about something as they walked in, but Jessie shushed them all. Hannah felt Jessie's hand touch her forehead. "You're awake then, lassie?

Hannah didn't want to speak. Carefully, she felt the back of her head, where she found a great knot. All she could manage to say was "Hurts."

Jessie said, "Aye, lass, it must."

"Tylenol?" Hannah croaked.

"What's she blethering aboot?" interrupted Jessie's grandson, John, who was crouching in the corner of the room, tossing a pebble from hand to hand.

"Hud yer wheest, you," Jessie chided him, then, louder to Hannah, she said, "What's that you're wanting, pet?"

By then, Hannah had remembered that Tylenol didn't yet exist. "My head hurts," she whimpered. Her chin trembled from the pain.

Jessie clasped her hand. "Mrs. Gow said there was nothing broken. You just need your bed. And she made this draught for you, to help you get to sleep. Drink it." Jessie gently lifted her head, and pressed a rough clay cup to her lips. Hannah sipped the bitter-tasting liquid and scrunched up her face in disgust. But Jessie wouldn't remove the cup from her mouth until she drank it all.

Mrs. Gow was the midwife, and Jessie had sent John to fetch her as soon as Hannah had arrived home on Mina's arm. Hannah hoped that Mrs. Gow's medical knowledge went beyond delivering babies, because doctors were out of the question: They cost too much. Hannah didn't know if doctors in 1851 knew what they were doing, anyway. Jessie swore by Mrs. Gow's healing skills, but how reliable was she? Hannah wondered if she had concussion, and wasn't it dangerous to go to sleep with concussion? But Mrs. Gow's drink quickly took effect, and, soon, Hannah was unconscious.

When she awoke, it was with a raging thirst. She was feeling very irritable, but her head felt much better. Jessie was sitting in front of the fire, sewing a patch onto a dress. At that moment, Mina walked in, pulling off her bonnet. "Well, that's him sorted oot," she exclaimed, collapsing into the chair across from her mother. Jessie looked quizzically at her.

"Tam the Deil!" explained Mina. "I've made sure he won't trouble any lassies again."

Jessie, shocked, put her hand to her face. "Mina, what did you do to the man?"

Mina laughed. "Don't worry, Mother, he won't have the police to me. I didna hurt him. I just telt him to leave Hannah and the other lassies be, or else a few big pals of mine would see to him."

"And what big pals would they be?" Jessie asked skeptically.

Mina laughed. "No idea. But the thing is, Tam disnae know that."

Jessie smiled and so did Hannah. She was still afraid of returning to work, but Tam never said a word to her on the day of her return, or the day after that. Better yet, all the spinners were more kindly toward her than ever.

On Saturday afternoon, Hannah returned to the apartment after taking a walk with Maggie, only to find it empty. She wondered where everyone was. She hung around forlornly, bored out of her mind, wishing she had something to watch, or even something to read. Finally, with relief, she heard the echo of several pairs of feet pattering up the stairs. Jessie and her daughters burst in, along with Mina's boyfriend, Jack. He and Mina were hand in hand and laughing.

"Hannah!" cried Mina, giving a startled Hannah a resounding kiss on the cheek. "Well, we did it! We tied the knot!"

Hannah was confused. "You mean… You got married? When did that happen? Where was the wedding?" And, she asked herself silently, why wasn't I invited?

"We married at Jack's hoose this afternoon!" Mina cried. "Oh, dinna look so sorry for yourself, Hannah, you're invited to the party, of course! We're all ready for a wee bit of dancing and song, are we not?"

Her mother, sisters, and new husband cheered in agreement. "And I daresay now is the time," said Jack, pulling a whisky bottle out from under his coat, "to celebrate with a wee dram for old time's sake."

Janet hissed at him, "Put that away before the minister arrives."

"Oh, the minister's not coming here to this humble abode," Jack said, unplugging the green glass bottle. "We're not posh enough for his company at our wee celebration. A health!" He raised the whisky to his lips, took a swig, and immediately started to cough. "Urghh… Och, that's terrible stuff."

"Aye, well," Mina said sourly, "Serves you right. Now, make us some music, Jack. Betty, fetch up Old Eck MacIntosh and his wife, and see if he would bring his fiddle. "

As Jack began to pull his banjo out of its case, Hannah took Mem aside.

"What's Mina's new name?" she whispered.

Mem looked puzzled. "What do you mean?"

"Her new name? Jack's last name?"

Mem smirked. "Eh, Hannah, I dinna know how they do things in your part of Scotland, but in Dundee and anywhere else I know, the women keep their own name. So she's still Mina Gordon. But Jack's name is Strachan. Now let's celebrate while we can, because they're off to Glasgow in two days to meet the boat to America!"

Strachan? Where had Hannah heard that name before? She had that weird feeling behind the eyes you get when you're trying to remember something, and it's just out of the reach of your memory... The name, for some reason, made her think of her mother in San Francisco. But why? It wasn't her mother's name. When Jack grabbed Hannah for a dance, she forgot all about it.

The morning Mina and Jack left for Glasgow, to meet the ship that would take them to America, Mary could barely speak to say goodbye, because she was crying her eyes out. In fact, the only member of the family who wasn't crying at the train station was Mina. They all stood shivering in the dark of the early morning. All that is, except for Jessie, who had complained that morning of pains in her arms, and had stayed at home.

"I dinna trust these newfangled railway trains," Janet said anxiously. "Mina, mind you and Jack dinna go deaf when you go through the tunnels."

Mina tutted. "We won't go deaf, Janet, that's a lot of nonsense. Better you worry I dinna get seasick, because that's what's troubling us, isn't it, Jack?" She shook her new husband's arm to get his attention. "Pay me heed, Jack, would you?"

Jack was standing next to their travelling trunk, clutching his beloved banjo to his chest, and looking very downcast. "Sorry, Mina. I was just thinking about what a long way from home we'll be."

"Aye well," said Mina firmly, "It's too late to fret now, our tickets are bought and paid for. And we'll be back in a few years, no doubt, wi' all our riches from America."

Mem tapped Jack's arm. "And both of you watch out for all thae wild Red Indians."

Hannah thought how offensive that was, but she tried to remember that she was in a time and place before the world's peoples knew much at all about each other.

"Aye," said Mina. "Dinna you worry, it's them red Indians as will have more to fear from me!"

Everyone laughed, but the laughter suddenly trailed away as a steam train approached the station. Mary said quickly to her oldest sister, "Dinna forget to write us a few lines, lassie."

Now Hannah could see the tears in Mina's eyes, as she said, "Och, dinna be daft. Of course I'll write."

When the train pulled into the station, Hannah, desperate to play a role in this drama, rushed toward a carriage intending to open the door for Mina and Jack, but Janet stopped her, telling her that it was reserved for first-class passengers. So Hannah ran down the platform, but the next several carriages were for second-class passengers only. All that was left were third-class carriages: Three open wagons. And it was toward these that Mina and Jack were heading.

"You'll get wet!" Hannah cried as the other girls helped Jack load in their baggage.

"It's only a bit of water," Mina exclaimed as she climbed in, and wiped a puddle off a hard bench seat. "And we'll get there in the end, same as them who paid first-class."

Hannah smiled, thinking of how her mom had always said the same thing when the family travelled on airplanes in economy class.

As the train pulled away, the Gordon sisters waved, and carried on waving until long after Mina and Jack had disappeared into the haar, the mist that rolled off the River Tay.

Hannah was preoccupied with Mina's departure, but she didn't think about what it might mean for her to lose Mina's protection at the jute mill. She was also distracted by Jessie's illness: Three days after Mina left, Jessie was still in bed, so Janet had taken unpaid time from work, and had taken over all the shopping, cooking and cleaning.

When Hannah went to work that morning, Tam the Deil stopped her at the gate, and told her with barely-concealed glee that her services were no longer required at Sutherland's Mill. What was more, he informed her triumphantly, she was blacklisted as a troublemaker by all the Dundee jute mills, meaning that she would never again find work as a piecer in the city.

Hannah, to her astonishment, had been fired.

She cried as she walked home in the pouring rain. What would she do to earn a living if she couldn't work in the mills? She might starve to death before she saw the Professor again. But then she took comfort from knowing that she had the support of the Gordons. They wouldn't let her starve, and so long as she belonged to their family, she knew she was safe.

Hannah found Jessie lying in bed and Janet peeling potatoes. She delivered the news with maximum drama. "Tam the Deil fired me!" she sobbed, flinging herself face-down on the nearest bed, which happened to be Jessie's. Jessie groaned as Hannah landed on her. Unconcerned, Hannah sat up and continued her tale of woe. "And he says he's going to make sure I don't get a job at another jute mill in Dundee."

If Hannah had expected sympathy, it wasn't forthcoming.

Jessie sighed. "Aye, well, I telt Mina it was a bad idea to cross that man," she said weakly. "You'll have to start looking for work today."

"Today?" Hannah lifted her head from the blanket in astonishment.

Janet laid down her peeling knife, and wiped her hands on her dress. "Aye, today, of course," she said sharply. "With Mother not well, we can barely make ends meet as it is, and we canna support a lodger who hasn't a penny to her name. I'm sorry, Hannah, but that's that."

Hannah was stunned. "Are you seriously telling me you will kick me out if I don't find another job?"

Jessie coughed and looked uncomfortable. "Well, let us hope it disnae come to that, eh? You're a clever lass, Hannah. I'm sure you'll find something."

Hannah went from shock to hurt to anger in a split second. "Okay, that's it," she yelled, and she ran out of the door, and didn't stop running until she was back on the High Street. Her head was spinning. She had thought Jessie cared about her, that she thought of Hannah as one of the family. But now that Hannah was down on her luck, Jessie was prepared to throw her out on the street. Hannah wasn't sure what was worse: Being homeless, or being rejected by the Gordons.

Hannah desperately wanted to leave Dundee behind. The morning rain had given way to bright sunshine, and, even though it was a little windy, she decided to walk up the Law, the massive extinct volcano around which the city was built. As she climbed, Hannah began to persuade herself that nobody in Dundee was really her friend. As she reached the summit, she was tempted to keep on walking, down the other side of the Law and across the Sidlaws, the hills that lay to the north, to take a chance somewhere else in Scotland. Maybe Aberdeen was nicer. But maybe she would starve to death before she even got there.

Hannah felt so sad, it actually hurt to think. She sighed heavily, gave one last look toward the Sidlaws, and reluctantly turned back toward Dundee, walking awkwardly through the long grass. The wind was picking up, combing across the surface of the hill. With a shiver, Hannah pulled her shawl more tightly around her shoulders. She was just starting down the dirt path, when she saw an old gentleman walking briskly uphill toward her, carrying a long walking pole. As he drew closer, Hannah gasped: It was Mr. Sutherland, the mill owner. She stopped and stared at him, but he never gave her a second look as he passed her.

Hannah suddenly felt angry. Very, out-of-control, crazily angry. She yelled his name. Startled, Mr. Sutherland wheeled around.

Hannah shouted, "Do you know what it's like for people who work at your factory?" Without waiting for an answer, she continued. "We're poor, and our food is totally unhealthy, and our apartments are, like, horrible. And you hire some of the meanest men as gaffers. That Mr. Mitchell? We call him Tam the Deil, and he's a total drunk, and he's cruel to all...."

Mr. Sutherland quietly interrupted her. "Have I not met you before?"

Suddenly, Hannah was on the defensive. She pulled a face. "Maybe."

He leaned on his walking stick. "You're the girl I met in the park, aren't you? What's your name?"

Reluctantly, she reminded him.

"Well, Hannah Dow," he said. "Be gone, and leave me to walk in peace."

"Wait a minute!" Hannah cried. "What about everything I said? About Mr. Mitchell, and, I mean, you live in a really nice house and have lots of money, and we're all poor."

Mr. Sutherland looked at her in puzzlement. "But that is the way of the world. Some are born simply to be hewers of wood and drawers of water. That is in your Bible: The Book of Joshua, chapter nine, verse twenty-three. If you are dissatisfied with your employment at my factory, you can seek a position elsewhere."

Hannah's brain was working overtime now. None of this sounded right to her, but where to start? "Yeah, but all the jobs are really bad, and all the mills pay the same, so where do we go? Anyway, I got fired today."

But Mr. Sutherland didn't reply. He simply walked away.

Hannah was bewildered. She knew what this meant. To him, what she said was unimportant. Her life was unimportant. Now her rage exploded. "I'm NOT NOTHING!" she shouted. "I'm a person! I'm a kid!"

But Mr. Sutherland kept right on walking up the Law. Hannah was drained. She was no longer the Brave Girl Who Stood Up to Rich People. She was a puny little nobody.

Slouched in defeat, Hannah was walking along the Nethergate when suddenly she felt an urgent tap on her shoulder.

It was Maggie, who was in tears. "Hannah, I'm sorry, I had to find you. This came for you at the mill, but a quarter-hour ago." She handed her a thick envelope sealed with a small blob of hard red wax.

In alarm, Hannah took it from her. "What is it? Did it come from one of the Gordon sisters? Or is this the official letter firing me?"

"Eh, no, I know all those sisters, and this was from none of them. No, this was a biddy I'd never clapped eyes on in my life. Said she was a friend of yours, and her name was Harrower."

Opening the packet, Hannah discovered a note wrapped around a bundle of documents. She read the note first, which said, "For your voyage, wherever it may take you, KDGH." The documents turned out to be five one-pound notes.

"What does it say?" Maggie asked.

In reply, Hannah hugged her and then did a small victory dance. "It says I'm free! I can leave Dundee."

Maggie was taken aback, but Hannah didn't explain. She felt so incredibly relieved, and suddenly, everything seemed so much better. In a rush, she said, "Maggie, it's been awesome knowing you, and I hope your life gets better. But I gotta go."

With that, she turned away. But she hadn't walked more than three paces when she felt overcome with guilt. Reaching into her pocket, she pulled out her last two penny coins, and handed them to Maggie. "Here, go buy yourself something. I'm sorry. Really, I am. And have this, too." She handed Maggie one of the pound notes. Maggie stared at it: She had never seen a pound note before.

Hannah explained. "It's a pound. Take it to a bank, and they'll give you twenty shillings for it."

Maggie laughed and put a hand to her mouth. "Don't be daft, Hannah."

"No, really," Hannah said. "I know it seems like a lot of money, but it won't go far. Maybe you can use it to eat some better food or something." Maggie just stared at her. Hannah felt helpless to do more. Even if she gave her the whole five pounds, the money would run out, and then what? And most of it would probably go to buy her father more whisky. How much could charity help Maggie, the Gordons, or any of these people? How could they help themselves when even the better jobs barely gave them enough to survive? It was overwhelming. Hannah did not like to be overwhelmed.

CHAPTER TEN

She broke eye contact with Maggie. "Anyway, I'm going. Take care. Have a nice life. It's been great knowing you. I'm sorry. Enjoy your pound."

"But Hannah, why are you leaving?" Maggie asked in dismay. "Where will you go? Here, have your money back so you can stay here."

She offered back Hannah the pound note. Hannah saw the tears in Maggie's eyes, and knew then that she really did like her just for herself. She gave her friend a hug, and tried to explain. "I can't stay here, Maggie. I have to find a way home."

"And where's that?" Maggie asked, wiping her eyes. "New Lanark?"

"No, not New Lanark. It's a lot farther away than that. My home's in…" And then she stopped. What would she say? Snipesville? San Francisco? With her grandparents in Sacramento? With Mrs. Devenish in Balesworth in 1940? She finished the sentence lamely: "…in a faraway place."

Hannah didn't know what else to say. She bid Maggie an awkward goodbye, and the last she saw of her, Maggie was standing in the street, sadly watching her walk away.

From her pocket, Hannah pulled out the crumpled and torn newspaper sheet with the travel ads. She already knew that she had to sail to London, because she still didn't have enough money for San Francisco. What choice would she have had without the Professor's cash? She would have been in deep trouble.

****

It was hard for Alex to believe, but the moment had arrived for him to leave Georgia for England. Standing on the cobbled dockside of the Savannah River, in the shadow of Mr. Thornhill's office building, he watched as slaves loaded travel chests and bundles onboard the steamer. The night before, he had said farewell to Jupe, who looked thoroughly downcast. Alex had no idea what to tell him, and so their farewell had been extremely awkward.

Now, Alex felt very alone, and very anxious. The closest he had ever come to an ocean voyage was a ride on a small boat across the San Francisco Bay. That hardly counted. How would he manage for several weeks on the Atlantic Ocean? And it worried him that he was leaving America. Didn't that put him farther away from home? Worse, he was expecting Mr. MacGregor as a travel companion.

"I know what you're thinking," said a voice beside him. "But it's all right. You're doing what you're supposed to be doing. I should know, because I'm an historian."

❖ 168 ❖

HARD TIMES

The Professor, holding a small bag, looked ready to board the steamer. "I'm going with you," she explained. "I'm rather curious about it, actually. I've never been on an early steamship before. Would you like some seasickness pills?"

"Yes, please!" Alex held out his hand, and she deposited two modern white tablets into his palm. He put them in his pocket.

"I'm Miss Davies, by the way," she said. "At least for the duration of this voyage."

Just then, Alex saw Mr. Thornhill striding toward them and, trailing uncertainly behind him, Jupe, who did not look happy.

Mr. Thornhill tipped his hat to the Professor, who nodded demurely, like a proper Victorian lady. Then, quietly and firmly, he said, "Jupe, get on board."

Jupe did as he was told, and reluctantly walked up the gangplank.

Alex was astonished. "But Mr. Thornhill, Jupe isn't…" At once, both Mr. Thornhill and the Professor shushed him. A startled Mr. Thornhill looked at the Professor in confusion. She ignored the look, and, without another word, lifted her skirts, and followed after Jupe.

"In time, I will tell you what is taking place," Mr. Thornhill whispered to Alex. "For now, say nothing."

Alex soon found the Professor standing on deck at the railing.

"This is a modern, up-to-date ship in 1851," she told him. "Don't worry: Steam ships have been crossing the Atlantic since the SS Savannah left here for England in 1813. The ships almost never sink."

"Almost?" Alex was wide-eyed.

"Almost," repeated the Professor firmly. "Nothing is perfect. If it were, we would have invented uncrashable planes. And do you remember the only ship that was ever described as unsinkable?"

"You mean the Titanic?"

"Exactly."

Alex shuddered. Suddenly, he remembered the calculator, and began to rummage around in his pockets. "Look, do you want your calculator now? I don't need it anymore. The only problem is that Mr. Thornhill kind of… broke it."

The Professor looked intrigued. "How did he manage that?" ·

Alex told her, and as he finished the story, she looked strangely pleased. "Well," she said with a smile, "that's all right then. No, Alex, you keep the calculator for now, please. I don't think I'm supposed to have it just yet…." There was a great groan as the massive steam engines fired up. "Gosh, it looks like we're almost ready to get going. I think I had better hurry."

That was the last time Alex saw her on the voyage. A couple of hours after they set sail, the ship began to pitch back and forth, up and down. It was then that Alex realized he had lost his seasickness pills. He searched the ship for "Miss Davies," but he could find her nowhere. When he asked an officer for help, he was told that no such person was listed as a passenger.

By the end of the first day, Alex felt very confident that he was going to survive the voyage without getting sick. He spent his time walking on deck, and reading in the gentlemen's lounge. He felt sorry for Jupe, who was stuck on the third-class deck, clutching his stomach and groaning. Alex visited him, but it was really nasty: Passengers in third-class bunked in a large dormitory, and lots of people were throwing up. The smell was atrocious, and Alex didn't linger. He couldn't help feeling a bit smug when he saw what bad shape his friend was in: Obviously, he thought, Jupe lacked his own superior seamanship.

On the second day, the storm struck. The ship was tossed about on the Atlantic, violently pitching and rolling, and sending anything that wasn't nailed down hurtling and crashing around the decks. Alex did not feel well. Not at all. He retreated to his cabin, where he clutched a bucket to his chest, and wished for death. And that was pretty much how he stayed for the next two days.

On the fifth day, sitting in the gentlemen's lounge, Alex allowed himself to think he might, possibly, survive the journey. If only he could have the lounge to himself, without the tobacco-chewing American men, who spat long streams of revolting black liquid into spittoons, and the cigar-smoking British men, who filled the lounge with a vile-smelling fog. He was feeling up to some company, but Mr. Thornhill, as usual, was playing cards with a group of other gentlemen. He wondered how Jupe was doing. Finally, he decided to brave the third-class cabin to find out.

Things had calmed down in third class, but it still smelled dreadful, despite the sailors' best efforts with mops and vinegar. However, Jupe was definitely feeling better, so Alex invited him to come walk with him on the deck.

The ocean roared loudly as she ship plowed along, and the boys silently watched the waves wash by, as the mighty paddle wheels churned. Then they ran to the ship's stern, and Jupe pointed to the seagulls that were flying in their wake. "You think those birds followed us from Savannah?"

"Maybe," said Alex.

There was a pause. Then Jupe said, "Wonder if I'll ever see Mama and Daddy again?"

Alex didn't know what to say, and there was a brief silence. Then he changed the subject, asking Jupe the question he had been dying to ask ever since they had boarded: "Why did Mr. Thornhill bring you along? I mean, I'm glad he did, but he won't tell me why. And why is it all so secret?"

Jupe looked at him coyly. "You really don't know?"

"No." Alex shook his head.

"You promise to say nothing about it to nobody?"

Alex nodded.

"He set me free," Jupe said.

Alex gawped. "Wow!"

Jupe smiled. "He explained it to me. He say that when we arrive in England, I'm free, and I stay free until I die, unless I go back to Georgia. He even found me a job."

Alex was amazed by this revelation. Mr. Thornhill had never shown the slightest interest in freeing any slaves, much less Jupe. He suddenly felt a warm rush of gratitude and affection for his boss, tempered only by the uncomfortable realization that he really didn't know him that well. Why had Mr. Thornhill freed Jupe? He hadn't said, and Alex knew that it would not be a good idea to ask him. Jupe, if he knew the answer, wasn't saying.

Jupe had his own worries: He couldn't imagine what England was like, but he knew from Mr. Thornhill that the ocean between Savannah and London was vast beyond imagination. He knew very little about his future, except that he had paid work waiting for him. What that work was, however, remained a mystery.

****

On the Great North Road out of London, the traffic was very heavy or, at least, that's what the coachdriver told Brandon. Brandon thought the horse-drawn traffic was nothing compared to the crush of automobiles, trucks, and buses that ran through modern England. However, the trip from London to the northern part of the neighboring county of Hertfordshire was a much longer journey in 1851 than it would be in the twenty-first century. Brandon sat with the driver and watched the fields roll by, thinking to himself that he was in the nineteenth century equivalent of a car. He wondered if "car" was short for "carriage."

In the late evening, after a long ride, the carriage turned off the Great North Road. It bumped along a rutted track through woods and fields. Brandon wondered where Balesworth had gone, but the driver told him that Balesworth Hall was several miles south-west of the town.

When Brandon finally caught sight of his new home, he was impressed. It was the largest house he had ever seen, apart from Windsor Castle. A grand but simple rectangle, it was surrounded by a huge park of vast lawns and long avenues of trees. The house and the park were reserved for the exclusive use of Lady Chatsfield and her family.

A butler rushed out to greet the carriage as it trundled up the mile-long driveway. After he helped out Lady Chatsfield, she swept into the house with Flora the maid trotting behind her. Brandon found himself standing awkward-ly next to the carriage, wondering just what he was supposed to do next.

The butler, a small thin man with thick black hair, beckoned impatiently to him. Brandon thought he was being invited to follow Lady Chatsfield into the house, but when he moved toward the grand doorway, the butler stopped him with a hand to his chest.

"You are Brandon, yes? I am Mr. Veeriswamy, the butler." He had a slight Indian accent. "Lady Chatsfield informs me that you have no training as a footman, but I shall see what can be done with you." He looked over Brandon's shoulder and called to the carriage driver, "Roberts!"

"Yes, Mr. Veeriswamy?" replied Roberts.

"Show Brandon to the servants' entrance at once, if you please. Brandon, wait for me in the servants' hall, and I shall talk with you as soon as I have at-tended to Her Ladyship."

As he relaxed in the butler's sitting room, Brandon smiled to himself. He re-membered meeting Mr. Veeriswamy's blond descendant, the ticket inspector, on the train to Balesworth. The 1851 Mr. Veeriswamy turned out to be as chatty as his great-great-great-great-grandson. Brandon asked him about the history of the house, and Mr. Veeriswamy, pleasantly surprised by his interest, told him the astounding news that only a few years earlier, it had been four times the size. He drew a sketch to illustrate. "It was a square building arranged around a courtyard, you see. Three wings of the house were torn down, and the fourth changed most drastically. But it had to be done. The house was simply too large for old Lord Chatsfield."

"So there's a new Lord Chatsfield?" asked Brandon. Mr. Veeriswamy looked uncomfortable, and an awkward silence fell between them.

"What's wrong?" asked Brandon. "Is he dead? Are they divorced?"

Mr. Veeriswamy looked shocked. "No, no, no, no. The family's affairs are hardly the business of our new junior footman. You are clearly intelligent and well-educated, but you must know your place, Brandon. Now, as to terms... You will receive twelve pounds each year, your board, and supplies of tea and sugar. You must purchase your own candles and soap, since it is not our custom in this house to provide those. I will of course also deduct from your wages the cost of your uniform. Come with me, and we shall begin your training in the kitchen. Have you polished silver before?"

Brandon had never polished silver before, but by the following morning, he was becoming an expert. His right arm ached, the nauseating ammonia smell of the polish lingered in his nostrils, and the skin on his hands felt tight and dry. The red polish wouldn't budge from under his fingernails. He had blistered his right thumb and forefinger, and pronged his hand on a fork hard enough to draw blood. And he was only halfway done. He sighed heavily as he saw the mountain of knives, forks, spoons and serving plates he still had to do.

When Brandon asked Mr. Veeriswamy if he could take a break, the butler told him bluntly that he must go on with the job, and assured him that his hands would become tougher over time. Great, thought Brandon, but how much would he suffer meanwhile?

He was just starting on a large tablespoon when he heard a sharp rap on the kitchen door. A small boy peered through the window, cupping his hands around his face so he could see inside. Brandon wiped his hands on his apron, and was just rising to open the door, when Mrs. Watson, the cook, got there first.

Speaking to Mrs. Watson, the boy pointed to Brandon. "Who's this?"

"That's the new footman," Mrs. Watson said.

Brandon was irked that the boy had not spoken directly to him. "My name's Brandon," he said curtly.

He was about to ask the boy for his name, when the boy asked, "Are you related to Mr. Veeriswamy?"

Brandon looked at him warily. "No. Why do you think that?"

"Because you're both brown," said the boy. Brandon shook his head. He was really tired of Brits in the past who went on and on about his skin color, and he wasn't all that interested in talking to this kid anyway. He didn't bother to ask the boy's name, but the boy sat waiting for him to ask, and finally said, "I'm Henry. Mrs. Watson's my mother."

"Uh-huh," said Brandon noncommittally, without looking at Henry. But he was thinking how strange it was that the boy sounded much posher than his mother, who spoke with a Hertfordshire accent. And that name… Henry Watson. Why did that name seem familiar? He tried to remember, but it wouldn't come to him. So he gave up, and carried on polishing silver.

Henry was undeterred. "Can you read?" he asked suddenly.

"Well, yeah," said Brandon huffily.

Henry grinned. "You should see the library here. It's extraordinary."

"I've been to a library tons of times," said Brandon grudgingly. "And anyway, I've already been to the one in Balesworth." He didn't mention that his public library visits had taken place in 1915.

"I don't know what you're talking about," said Henry, puzzled. "I had no idea anyone else in Balesworth kept a library. I'm talking about Lady Chatsfield's library, here, in Balesworth Hall. Her Ladyship said I can use it."

Brandon looked at him with new interest. "She has her own library? That's cool. Can you show it to me? I need something to read."

Now Henry looked very pleased with himself. "No, you're not allowed. I got permission especially. Just me."

Brandon was already fed up with this kid. He returned his attention to the silver spoon. "Look, I'm kind of busy right now, okay?"

"All right," said Henry, sliding off his chair. He said it, Brandon thought, like Hannah said "Whatever." He went running up the servants' staircase.

As soon as Henry left, Brandon remembered. Henry Watson... Of course! The writer! Verity and Eric had mentioned him. But why? Was it important? He furrowed his brow, but nothing would come to him. That conversation seemed so long ago. Perhaps if he talked to Henry, he would find out. On impulse, he threw down his polishing cloth, tore off his apron, and followed the sound of the boy's footsteps.

Brandon caught up with Henry in the massive library, where he was already plucking a book from a shelf, while balancing precariously on a tall ladder. When Brandon entered, Henry hissed at him, "What are you doing? I told you, you're not allowed in here."

"Oh, drop the attitude," Brandon said, scowling. "I just have some questions for you."

Henry climbed down. "Don't blame me if you are caught in here and lose your position. I won't defend you."

Brandon wanted to punch him. Instead, he said, "So, tell me about yourself."

Henry preened. He liked talking about himself. "I am Mrs. Watson's son, as I told you, but Her Ladyship has taken a particular interest in my education, and she intends to obtain a place for me at the East India College when I am older, and then I shall be an officer in the East India Company. Lady

Chatsfield's father was an officer with the East India Company, you see, and he brought Mr. Veeriswamy back to England with him."

Brandon had no idea what Henry was talking about. He was more interested in figuring out what he was supposed to remember about this obnoxious boy. But Henry had moved on to talk about his favorite subject, apart from himself: The Chatsfield family. Brandon wasn't especially interested in family history, and at first he tuned Henry out. As he chattered on, Henry settled himself in a comfortable chair, and began to swing his legs as he talked. "You know, Lady Chatsfield only took possession of Balesworth Hall this year."

Now he had Brandon's attention. Henry eagerly seized on his interest, and explained, "She arrived with only her daughter Sarah, and Mr. Veeriswamy. And then she dismissed most of the servants who were already here. Luckily, Mother was kept on, because she's the best cook in Hertfordshire." He added, in a conspiratorial whisper, "The rumor is that they had to sack so many servants because the estate isn't paying very well. Lady Chatsfield doesn't know how to manage it."

Brandon was puzzled. "What do you mean by 'the estate'? Like the land and the farming and stuff?"

Henry nodded.

Brandon asked carefully, "So where's Lord Chatsfield in all of this?"

Henry was not as discreet as Mr. Veeriswamy. "Oh, he's not here. He never expected to be Viscount Lord Chatsfield, you see, because his elder brother inherited the title and the estate. That's called primogeniture, which I wouldn't expect you to understand. I read about it in a law book. It means that the oldest son inherits everything, and the younger sons have to find their own careers. But old Lord Chatsfield's eldest son died without leaving children, and then the middle brother died without children too, so Lady Chatsfield's husband, the youngest brother, is now the heir."

Brandon found this confusing. But now Henry told him something that made his ears perk up. "I don't think anyone approves of the new Lord Chatsfield, not even his own wife. He left her years and years ago to go abroad and he took two of their children with him. Mr. Veeriswamy told my mother that both of their sons have since died, and that Lady Chatsfield has been unable to contact her husband to tell him that he is the new Viscount."

At that moment, the huge door to the library creaked open, and in walked a young girl in a blue dress. She was shocked to see Brandon, and she immediately turned to Henry for an explanation. "Henry, who is this?"

Brandon decided to answer on his own behalf. "I'm Brandon. I work here.

CHAPTER TEN

Who are you?"

She looked at him coldly, and somehow she seemed very familiar, except that she had the most exotic look, as though she were a gypsy. Once again, he found himself struggling to remember something…

But she was already speaking to him sternly. "I assume that you are Brandon, the new footman. I am Miss Sarah Chatsfield. Your place is below stairs. Leave here at once, or I shall summon Mr. Veeriswamy, and you will be held to account."

Who does she think she is, Brandon thought? She's only a kid. He felt his temper rise. He wasn't about to let some little kid make him feel like a cockroach. "So how come it's okay for Henry to be in here?" Brandon demanded.

"That's not your business," said the girl snappishly. "Come along, Henry," she ordered. "We shall play a game of cards. Brandon, you must return to the kitchen."

Remembering what he had learned about the French Revolution, Brandon wondered why the British hadn't revolted, too, and chopped off the heads of the likes of Sarah.

But suddenly, as she turned to leave, he saw her in profile against the sunshine pouring through the windows, and it was then he realized who she reminded him of.

It was Verity. She reminded him of Verity as she had been in 1940, bossy and sure of herself, although Sarah certainly would have beaten her in a Miss Junior Bossy Hertfordshire contest. It must be something in the Hertfordshire water, he thought, that makes girls act like this.

Later, when Brandon went upstairs to collect more silver, he looked longingly out of the window at the beautiful gardens. It was a sunny and slightly warm day, which made it a stunningly rare day in England in April. He longed to be outside. He watched as a small figure ran across the lawn toward the fountain. Sarah was wearing a large wide hat bedecked with ribbons, which she was holding onto with one hand as she sprinted across the grass. Brandon felt a pang of envy.

Shortly, he was back in the kitchen, taking out his frustration on the silverware by polishing it within an inch of its life. A hesitant rap on the window made him look up, but he couldn't see anyone, and assumed it must be Henry. Since nobody else was around to answer, he reluctantly got up, and wrenched open the door.

But it wasn't Henry. It was the Professor, and she was carrying a basket filled with straw, in which rested a number of eggs and, more surprisingly, a can of Coke. Wordlessly, she handed the Coke to Brandon with a mischievous smile. He did a double-take, and then giggled at the sight of this object from the future. Popping it open, he took a big swig. It was lukewarm, but he didn't mind.

"That's better," said the Professor. "So how is life in service?"

Brandon exhaled sharply and shook his head slowly from side to side, giving a little burp. "Huh," he said. "Time travel was so amazing the first time, but I just don't know about this. You know, it's so boring to just do stuff like dig coal and polish silver, while kids like Sarah and Henry get to play and do whatever they like. And I miss my family. Nobody loves me here. Heck, nobody even likes me here. Last time, I had Oliver to look after, but now I don't even have him. Henry is obnoxious."

The Professor smiled gently at him as she sat down. "Henry is obnoxious, I entirely agree, but don't be too hard on him. Like you, Henry is living in a world in which he doesn't belong. Have a heart, Brandon. He's a clever kid, but he's a cook's son, and if Lady Chatsfield hadn't arrived this year, he would probably have been destined to work as a servant, or in the fields. She's offered him a way out. But the price he's paying is that, if things carry on as they are, he will be sent off to India at the age of eighteen, and that's not good."

"Why isn't it good?" Brandon asked, then took a slurp from his Coke.

"Because it isn't supposed to happen," the Professor said. "And I think the reason you're here is to prevent it happening."

Brandon was taken aback. "But why would you want me to stop him from having a chance to do something with his life. I mean, you just said…"

"Oh, I know what I said, but don't you remember? Henry Watson doesn't grow up to be an officer in the East India Company, which will pretty much go out of business in about six years anyway."

But Brandon had another question. "Why is Lady Chatsfield interested in Henry? Or…" Brandon hesitated.

"Or you?" The Professor finished his question for him. "She's a complicated woman, and I don't think it's a good idea for me to guess at all her motives just yet. Trust me, they will soon become clear. Has she told you her little plan for you to speak to her anti-slavery ladies?" He shook his head, and she continued, "I see. Well, she will. I'll be honest: She doesn't see you the same way she sees Henry. She just considers you useful. But you might be able to turn the tables on her. I think you'll find you can make her very useful to us, as time will tell. I have a pretty good idea of what's going on now, I think, and I can advise you to be patient and hang in there. Keep polishing your silver, and doing your chores, and don't let Henry annoy you. Remember, he's very insecure: He's a kid from a humble background who has been raised to believe that he's practically a separate species from the likes of Lady Chatsfield. If you play your cards right, her taking an interest in him won't work out as she intends, but she has already given him the skills and confidence to become a famous novelist..."

Slapping the table, Brandon cried, "I remember now! He was born in Verity's house, except Eric couldn't prove it, or wasn't sure, or something..."

The Professor nodded. "Exactly. Now you have the perfect opportunity to settle once and for all whether Henry Watson was born in their house, or whether he was born here in Balesworth Hall."

The mention of Verity's name reminded Brandon of something he wanted to ask. "You know, Sarah Chatsfield looks a lot like Verity. Are they, like, related?"

The Professor gave a small smile. "Oh, yes. Absolutely. You see, Sarah Chatsfield is Verity's great-grandmother."

Brandon's eyes practically fell out on stalks. "She is? So she must be Mrs. D.'s mother. Wow... That's... Wow. Maaaan..."

"Of course, you have met her before."

Brandon's mind really boggled at this. "I have?"

"You met her when she was called Mrs. Hughes," said the Professor. Brandon gasped as he remembered meeting Sarah in 1915, when she was in her seventies. She had become a very proper and snobbish Victorian, who often argued with her headstrong, independent, and thoroughly modern daughter, Elizabeth Devenish... Brandon's head was spinning.

"Mrs. D. never said anything about being Lady Chatsfield's granddaughter," he said wonderingly.

"No, I know she didn't," said the Professor, and Brandon asked himself how she could be sure, as she continued speaking. "Just as Henry moved up in the world, Sarah moved down, and it was something to which she didn't draw much attention if she could help it. By the time Mrs. D. was born, in 1885, Sarah's parents were both dead, and things at Balesworth Hall had... changed. Sarah Hughes, as she was by then, considered Balesworth Hall very firmly part of her past."

"But how did Sarah become poor?"

"Oh, not poor," laughed the Professor. "You saw her house in Bedfordshire in 1915, didn't you? But as an adult, Sarah was no longer upper-class, just middle-class."

"Okay, so why?"

"That's something else for you to find out," said the Professor.

Brandon had to admit to himself that he was intrigued, and strangely excited. He asked, "And then will I get to go home?"

"Oh, I should think so, but you have work to do first. Now finish up that Coke, because I need to take the can with me. Don't want to confuse the poor old archeologists, do we?"

After she had gone, Brandon felt giddy with relief. His first time-travel adventure in the twentieth century had been so exhilarating. He had felt confident when he had returned to Snipesville, so sure of himself in learning new things and dealing with new people. But that feeling had slipped through his fingers, faded with his past. In 1851, he had felt uncertain of himself, unable to much improve his own circumstances, and, worst of all, despised as a member of the lower classes. But at this moment, for the first time in weeks, he felt cheerfully optimistic.

Chapter 11:
A CHANGE OF SCENE

Hannah stood at the head of the queue in the ticket office of the Dundee, Perth and London Shipping Company, wondering what the problem was. She had presented the money for her fare, so why was the ticket clerk giving her grief?

Leaning forward with his hands on the counter, he looked down on Hannah with contempt. "I cannot possibly allow you to board one of our steamers in that state. Look at yourself. You're filthy. And how someone like you came about this great sum of money, well… I cannot believe you did it honestly. I am tempted to send for the police. Move along now, lass."

Hannah was outraged, and stamped her foot. "You see if I ever ride on one of your stupid boats again!"

The ticket clerk repeated firmly, "Move along or I will send for a constable."

Hannah charged out of the office, pushing through the crowd. But now she felt scared and vulnerable: Lots of people had overheard her say that she was carrying a large amount of cash, and that wasn't safe in a city like Dundee. She screwed up her face, and tried to look fierce and possibly dangerous as she headed up an alleyway toward the city center. At that moment, she felt a heavy hand landing on her shoulder.

She flailed her arms and gibbered in panic.

"Calm down, calm down, it's me! Here to save the day!" The Professor turned Hannah around to face her.

Hannah struggled, wild-eyed and hyperventilating, until she focused on the Professor's face and recognized her. "Don't DO that! I thought you were trying to rob me. Oh my God, I almost wet myself."

"I'm sorry. Look, I just reckoned you would need help getting on board the steamship."

Hannah threw up her hands. "What can you do? That moron wouldn't let me on board even if you bought the ticket for me."

The Professor gave her a patient smile, and ushered her back toward the bustling main street. "Of course he won't. Working class people aren't welcome on the Great Exhibition steamer. And that is why you must become middle class. Hannah, it is time for your transformation. Oh, and my name is Miss Davies, by the way. I am your governess."

Hannah curled her lip. "You're my… Whoozie whatsit?"

"Your governess. Don't you know what that means? Your tutor. Your home-school teacher."

"Whatever," Hannah said, waving a dismissive hand at her. "Look, I don't care if you're, like, my personal tooth-flosser. Just get me out of this dump."

"Come along, then," said the Professor. "Let's get you cleaned up."

Hannah followed her to the High Street. To her amazement, the Professor walked toward McNaughtan's Royal Hotel. "I can't go in there," she said. "That's a seriously posh place. I'll get kicked out."

"No, you won't," said the Professor, taking her by the hand. "Just stay with me, and let me do the talking."

As they paraded through the hotel lobby, past gilded chandeliers and potted palms, the desk clerk looked on in amazement as his grandly-dressed guest Miss Davies entered with a ragamuffin girl. He opened his mouth to object, but the Professor silenced him with a firm "Good afternoon," as she guided Hannah by the elbow and hustled her toward the stairs. The clerk recovered his voice enough to call after her, "Madam, unregistered guests are not permitted in the hotel…." But by that time, the Professor was steaming full speed ahead, room key at the ready.

Two narrow beds took up much of the room. Hannah asked, "Where's the restroom?"

The Professor was removing her bonnet, untying the strings under her chin that held it on. "Oh, there's no separate room for the loo," she said. "If you want to use the one in here, it's behind the screen."

A folding screen stood in the corner, and Hannah ducked her head around it. "No, there's only a small table," she said to the Professor, with more than a touch of annoyance.

The Professor nodded. "That's it. Just lift the top."

Hannah turned back to the odd bit of furniture, lifted the lid, squinted, and pursed her lips. "Um, it's just a hole in a piece of wood over a chamberpot."

"Uh-huh. That's right."

"I thought the Gordons don't have real toilets because they're poor. What gives? Doesn't anyone have flushing toilets yet?"

"Oh, they've been invented," said the Professor. "But most people can't afford them, and even people who can afford them often don't want them: Some doctors are convinced that it's unhealthy to have flushing loos in bedrooms. The early Victorians didn't understand that germs cause disease, you see. They thought that epidemics started with smelly, dirty air, which they called miasma, and since early toilets often belched up sewer gas, it was assumed that they were part of the problem. But probably the main reason why rich Victorians refused to install loos was that it cost more to do that than it did just to have servants empty out chamberpots."

Hannah sighed heavily. "Whatever. TMI. So what do I do with this porta-potty when I'm done?"

"You ring the bell pull," said the Professor, and she did it to demonstrate. "Now a servant will come and take the slops, as they're called, to the slop room. There, some lucky person will wash out the chamberpot, and someone else will return it. There's a servant for practically every task. It's not so bad being well-off in 1851, is it?"

By the time the footman arrived, Hannah was washing her hands in the wash-basin. As he carried the chamberpot toward the door, he asked, "Will there be anything else, madam?"

"Man, I hope not," said Hannah with feeling. She wondered how he could bear spending his days carrying around other people's poo.

"Actually, there is something else," the Professor said swiftly. "Draw a hot bath for this young lady."

The footman took his first good look at Hannah, and his eyes grew wide when he saw her poor and ragged state. Whatever he was thinking, however, remained unspoken. Instead, he bowed stiffly, and said, "Very good, madam."

An hour later, as a fire blazed cheerfully in the fireplace, Hannah was taking a lovely warm bath in a copper hip tub that the servants had filled with steaming kettles. "Got any bubble bath?" she asked the Professor, who was sitting on the bed, reading a book.

The Professor smiled in amusement as she put her book down. "No, dear. Here's the soap."

Hannah accepted the greasy brown bar from the Professor's outstretched hand, and wrinkled her nose. "Ugh, this stuff smells disgusting. Couldn't you have brought some nice soap from Body Bonanza in Snipesville Mall?"

The Professor returned to her book and muttered, "Just count your blessings, Hannah."

Hannah lazily washed off her arm. "Oh, yeah, I am so blessed. I'm living in the armpit of Scotland, and I'm sharing a room with a psychopath..."

"Now, now," said the Professor warningly. "That will do. Finish your bath, and we'll go shopping."

Hannah looked up in surprise. "What, you ran out of oatmeal?"

The Professor turned a page in her book. "No, I meant clothes shopping."

Now Hannah slid herself upright in the bath, and sloshed soapy water onto the rug. "For real?" she screeched with delight, hardly believing her ears. Then she got suspicious. "Like, shopping at the Victorian Goodwill? Or real shopping for new clothes?"

The Professor laid down her book. "New clothes for your new self. You are now Hannah Day, a middle-class child, and you are returning to London for the Great Exhibition. We must dress you accordingly."

When Hannah and the Professor walked back through the lobby, the desk clerk tried once more to protest, but the Professor shut him down. "This is Miss Hannah Day, my charge," she said imperiously as she marched Hannah through the small lobby. "I am a governess. Now kindly add Miss Day's name to the hotel register and cease from your harassment, or I shall have words with the management."

On this visit to Moon and Langlands', Hannah actually went inside. Her dirty mill-girl clothes drew shocked stares from the shop clerks. One of the staff, a short man in a long gray coat, hurried forward from the back of the store to greet the Professor and her odd little companion.

"Here comes the floorwalker," the Professor muttered to Hannah.

"The what?" said Hannah.

"The department manager," the Professor said under her breath, before wishing the floorwalker a gracious "Good afternoon."

"Good afternoon, madam," he replied with a deep bow. "May I be of assistance?" He gave a pointed look at Hannah.

The Professor clasped her hands before her waist, and looked down her nose at him. "Yes, you may indeed. I am Miss Davies, and I am governess to this child, Miss Hannah Day. As you can see, she has met with a mishap, and I must purchase new clothing for her. How quickly can clothes be made to measure?"

"As quickly as you require, madam." The floorwalker bowed his head again.

"I shall require them by tonight," the Professor said firmly.

He blew out his cheeks. "Hmm....Ah....Well, we shall do our utmost, to be sure, but our ability to provide bespoke service at such short notice may rather depend on the extent of your requirements, madam. Perhaps I can show you some of our ready-made articles, which may be altered to suit?"

"Very well," the Professor said. She and Hannah settled into upholstered chairs, and the staff began a parade, bringing clothes for their inspection. By the time it was over, Hannah had picked out three dresses, along with bonnets, gloves, petticoats, and shoes. A very pretty pink dress seemed to be a good fit, and she disappeared into a private changing room to try it on, with one of the female staff assisting her. Soon, she reappeared in the dress, feeling very glamorous, and the Professor agreed that she should keep it on. As the Professor paid the bill, the floor-walker bowed again, practically wiping his nose on the ground, and murmuring promises that the remainder of the order would be delivered to the hotel that very evening.

As she left the store, Hannah almost collided with a shabby little figure, who stepped back and glared at her. Hannah grabbed her by the arm and said, "Maggie, it's me!"

Maggie jumped like a startled rabbit, and glanced at Hannah only for an instant, before wrenching her arm free. Then she disappeared into the fast-moving crowd of workers hurrying home for their noon dinner.

"Why doesn't she know who I am?" Hannah said forlornly.

The Professor gestured to Hannah's new outfit. "You're all cleaned up, and you're not dressed as she would expect. In these clothes, you see, you're no longer Hannah Dow. You're Hannah Day."

Hannah felt strangely empty. Who was Hannah Day? Or Hannah Dow? Were either of them the same girl as Hannah Dias?

That night, Hannah slept the sleep of the dead. The hotel's mattress was not as comfortable as a modern bed, but compared to her bed at the Gordons', it was a vast improvement. After all this time, though, it felt odd to sleep alone.

In the morning, after breakfast, she waited impatiently while the Professor pored through a stack of documents. Finally, noticing Hannah's boredom, she said, "Come on. Let's go have some tea."

Hannah had never had the money to visit a tea shop in Dundee, so she was very excited to be taken to Lamb's Tea Gardens.

Glancing around the elegant café, she asked, "Where are the sheep? I mean, I figure if you call a place 'Lamb's Tea Gardens', you have to have a lamb. Or at least a garden."

"I see your point," said the Professor. "But no. It's named for Mr. Lamb. He also owns Lamb's Dundee Coffeehouse on the Murraygate, and by next year, he will open his temperance hotel, restaurant, and coffee shop on Reform Street. He's quite a businessman. I'm surprised Mina never mentioned him to you, because she's quite a fan. His establishments don't offer alcohol, and they're meant as a nice alternative to all the pubs."

"Urgh… umm…" said Hannah in reply. She had just crammed an enormous jam and cream-slathered scone into her mouth.

The Professor tutted. "Hannah, your manners need work."

"I'm starving," Hannah shot back through a mouthful of scone, which she chased down with a swig of tea. "Can we get some more of these? And what are those cold pancake things?" She pointed to a plate of buttered flapjacks.

The Professor offered them to her. "They're dropped scones, also known as Scotch pancakes. I'm rather partial to them, myself. They're really good with butter and jam. Why don't you…"

Hannah had already grabbed three pancakes, piled two on her plate, and sunk her teeth into the third.

Twenty minutes later, when the waiter had removed the last empty plate, Hannah licked her jammy fingers and groaned happily. "Ohhh….That was awesome. The pastries here are to die for. They're the only thing from Dundee I'll miss…"

"I'm surprised to hear you say that," said the Professor, digging out money to pay the bill. "Won't you miss the people? What about your friends?"

Hannah sat in silence, the scones and pancakes suddenly feeling lead-like in the pit of her stomach. "I don't have any friends," she said quietly. She didn't want to tell the Professor that the Gordons had threatened to throw her out if she couldn't find another job.

But the Professor, somehow, already knew. "You're upset because the Gordons can't afford to keep you, aren't you?"

Hannah looked at her in astonishment. "How did you know that? Are you, like, psychic or something?"

The Professor ignored the question. "It's true, though, Hannah, isn't it?"

Hannah nodded, and her eyes welled up. She wiped at them and sniffed noisily. "I thought they liked me… And I had this awful day, and they weren't nice to me. Jessie just told me to go look for a job. It was so mean. I'm only a kid."

The Professor said gently, "But you're not really a kid here, are you? You have to work for a living. And the Gordons literally cannot afford to support you, Hannah. You know how poor they are. Jessie's sick, and Janet is worried that they might have to pay for a doctor. They do like you, very much in fact, and they would help you if they could, but they're barely getting by themselves. Most of their money goes to rent and food. And once all the others are married, Jessie will only have Janet to help her pay rent and raise John."

CHAPTER ELEVEN

A question suddenly occurred to Hannah. "So who's John's mother, anyway?"

"You didn't know? He's Janet's son. Janet's husband died in the cholera epidemic two years ago. Janet can't afford to support John by herself, so she works at the mill while Jessie keeps house, or at least she will until Jessie…makes other arrangements."

Hannah thought about this, and about all the ways in which the Gordons were trapped. "How can Maggie and the Gordons get out of this?" She swept a hand in the direction of the window, and the street beyond.

"Out of Dundee, you mean?" The Professor asked innocently.

Hannah shook her head. "No, not necessarily. I mean out of being poor. I mean, what am I missing here? My mom always said that people are poor because they just don't work hard enough, and they waste the money they do get, but all these guys work their tails off."

"But isn't it true that they waste money?" The Professor arched an eyebrow. "How is Maggie going to help herself if she spends the pound you gave her on whisky for her dad and pies for herself? Shouldn't she save it?"

"Yeah, but then what?" Hannah said urgently. "I mean, nobody I know here has bank accounts, because they're too poor, and, it's like you said, all the money we're paid goes on food and rent. Maggie can't read, and she doesn't have time to go to school, even if there was a school that would take her, and they won't because she's too old. She has to buy pies because she has nowhere to cook, and no time to do it. So what can she do?"

"Do you need me to answer that question?" asked the Professor.

"Well, duh!" Hannah yelled.

The Professor sat back. "Oh, I don't think you do. I don't feel like telling you what to think, as it happens. Anyway, don't shout at me. Well-brought-up Victorian girls don't shout at their governesses."

Hannah glowered at her, and the Professor seemed to relent a little. "Look, why don't you go and say goodbye to the Gordons? Tell them the truth about yourself, or at least something close to it that they can understand."

The Professor insisted on escorting Hannah to the Gordons' tenement. At first, Hannah was annoyed by her company, but once she saw the weird looks they got in her old neighborhood, as two well-dressed women in one of the city's nastiest slums, she was glad she had not gone alone. The two of them picked their way through the alleyways, trying to avoid stepping in the open sewers that ran down each street.

But when they reached the building, the Professor urged Hannah to go up to the apartment alone. Hannah held back, saying, "Why won't you come with me? Are you gonna leave me here?"

"No, I promise I won't," The Professor said firmly. "I will wait for you, but you must go alone."

Janet opened the door to Hannah's tentative knock, and it was obvious that she had been crying. Her cheeks were wet and puffy, and her eyes were red. She was wiping her nose on her apron when Hannah greeted her.

Janet did not recognize the young lady who stood before her, and she was astonished to see such a person at her door. "Can I help you, miss?" she asked humbly.

Hannah pointed to herself, and said, "Janet, it's me. Hannah."

Janet stared at her. "Begging pardon, miss, but you're…who?"

"Hannah. Hannah Dow."

Janet looked at her closely, and was clearly struggling to reconcile the face to the clothes. "Come away in, quickly," she said, hustling Hannah into the flat. She closed the door, and then grabbed Hannah by the shoulders and shook her. "Where did you steal these clothes?" she hissed at her.

"I didn't," Hannah cried. "I got them from my…" Suddenly, she stopped cold. "What's wrong with Jessie?" Jessie was lying asleep on the bed, and her face was ashen.

"She died last night," Janet said quietly. "Mrs. Gow the midwife came to her, but there was nothing she could do. She thinks Mother's heart gave out."

Hannah gasped in horror. Jessie was dead. And her dead body was right there, in the room. Hannah had only seen a corpse once before, when her Great-Aunt Mae in California had died, and there was an open-casket funeral at the church. Even then, the undertaker gussied up Aunt Mae so much, Grandma had muttered that she looked ready for a night on the town. Jessie, however, just looked dead.

"But I came to say goodbye," Hannah said helplessly.

"Aye, well, It's too late for that," Janet said tersely. "And where were you last night? Ma was that worried about you. She thought we'd been too hard on you after you lost your job."

Hannah's lip trembled. The Gordons did care about her, after all. But Jessie was dead, and she could never, ever say goodbye to her.

"I'm sorry," she said, tearing up. "Something came up. I have a new job, and I'm leaving."

"So you say," Janet said, looking at Hannah's clothes with suspicion. "I daren't ask what you will do."

Hannah couldn't imagine why Janet was so skeptical, but she let it go. "Will you say goodbye to everyone for me? I'm sorry about Jessie. Honest, I am."

Janet gave a brisk nod, and said nothing more. Hannah left the apartment feeling rotten. By the time she reached the bottom of the stairs, she was crying, and the Professor tentatively put an arm around her shoulders as she began to walk her back to the High Street.

Suddenly, Hannah stopped. "But what about Maggie?" she asked. "Can't we do anything for Maggie?"

"I didn't mean to tell you this, but I know you're having a hard time, so I will," the Professor said, giving Hannah a small hug. "Maggie's father will die in November this year. She will be given a place to live by the Dundee Lodging House Association, who have recently opened a home for young women, funded by donations. There, she'll learn to read and write."

"How do you know all that?" Hannah asked, sniffing.

The Professor paused, and Hannah could swear she saw her choke up. Then she said, "Because it's in the records. And because I arranged for it to happen."

Hannah thought of asking how she had done that, but she decided against it. She was feeling very insecure, and she didn't want to give the Professor any reason to abandon her now. She felt strangely vulnerable in her fancy new outfit. She certainly no longer felt that she belonged in a Dundee slum. For some reason, that made her feel very sad.

That afternoon, the same ticketing clerk who had snubbed Hannah Dow warmly invited Hannah Day and the Professor to board the sail-assisted steamship named Perth for the voyage to London. Hannah eagerly seized on her new persona as a respectable middle-class girl, chaperoned by her governess. As she got a look at the opulent first-class dining room, she smiled broadly. "This is more like it," she told the Professor with a giggle. "I have no problem with being a Victorian lady. Bring it on."

"You have had a change of tune," the Professor said. "I thought you quite liked Dundee, for all of its faults." Hannah pretended not to hear her.

Soon, Hannah was enjoying the steamer voyage. Her first-class cabin, next door to the Professor's, was tiny but very comfortable, and she made herself at home. Fortunately, the North Sea was calm, which the Professor told her was a huge stroke of luck, for the voyage down the east coast of Britain in a paddle steamer was often very choppy.

She loved her new pink dress, difficult though it was to move around in, with its many petticoats. Without TV or radio to entertain her, she amused herself by ringing the cabin crew to bring her tea and snacks. She also luxuriated in ordering a hot bath. This meant that servants had to carry buckets of hot water up and down steep flights of stairs, but Hannah didn't worry about that. After all, she didn't have to do the work.

That night, Hannah and the Professor dined in the first-class passengers' lounge. The Professor was tucking into a type of boiled seafood that Hannah had never seen before, piled on a china platter that bore the name *Dundee, Perth, & London Shipping Company*, and a drawing of their ship. The shellfish were called langoustines, and they looked like a cross between shrimp and small lobsters. The Professor snapped their heads off and sucked out the insides before doing the same to the claws and bodies. Hannah winced and said, "Do you have to eat like that?"

"Yes," said the Professor as she teased some meat from a shell, "Don't be silly. They're my favorite, and this is how you eat them. You ought to try one before you pass judgment."

"Fat chance," Hannah said. "They look gross. I'll just have some more of this soup. It's pretty good."

The Professor peered into a langoustine's body. "Suit yourself. Mind you, I'm surprised that at this point you would turn your nose up at anything, since you've mostly been living on oatmeal and potatoes."

Hannah shrugged dismissively and slurped at her soup, wiping her mouth on her sleeve.

"Hannah," said the Professor sternly, "Sit up straight and use your napkin."

"Okay, okay," grumbled Hannah, lifting her napkin and wiping her mouth. "No need to get too into character, Miss Davies."

"It's nothing to do with being in character," said the Professor. "You're grossing me out."

"Hey, at least I'm not sucking on insects." Hannah glanced at the Professor's langoustines and shuddered.

There was a momentary lull in the conversation, and Hannah craned her head to look around the first-class lounge. Ladies were banned from here, except at mealtimes. At all other times, the room was open only to gentlemen, who smoked and played cards here. For recreation, the ladies had only the deck (when the weather was pleasant, and when the sails were not in use) and their own tiny cabins.

Hannah pouted at the Professor as she cracked open another langoustine.

"I don't know why you couldn't have shown up sooner and at least bought me some nice clothes."

The Professor shrugged her shoulders. "And how would you have looked showing up at Sutherland's Mill or at the Gordons' flat dressed like Cinderella, belle of the ball?"

Hannah shot back, "Better than looking like Cinderella, the sad-sack maid."

"You wouldn't have fit in."

"I didn't fit in anyway," Hannah groused.

"That's not what you said last time we met, was it?"

Hannah scowled.

"You know, Hannah," the Professor said carefully, "You actually did fit in with the Gordons. Things ended badly because, well, you expected too much from them."

Hannah felt herself go rigid. The Professor was about to say something seriously embarrassing, she could tell. She tried to stop her by calling over the waiter to bring more soup. But the Professor wasn't about to be deterred from saying what she had to say.

"You expected too much from the relationship with the family, didn't you? Especially with Jessie and Mina. It's not your fault, you know. It's just that you and all your issues arrived at a time and place when people had little enough to spare for their immediate families."

"I don't want to talk about it," Hannah muttered into her soup

"Okay..." The Professor cracked another crustacean. She watched Hannah thoughtfully for a while. "I just have to ask this, so don't flip out... Do you miss your mother, Hannah?"

"I DON'T want to talk about it," yelled Hannah. Several of the other passengers looked over at them to see what the commotion was about.

Hannah sunk in her chair and rapidly drummed her dirty soupspoon on the tablecloth. "Don't talk to me about it, okay?" she hissed.

The Professor put down a langoustine shell. "Look, I know better than you can imagine that I've touched a raw nerve, and I'm sorry. I just want to help."

Hannah growled at her, "Well, don't. You can't. Okay?"

The waiter arrived with Hannah's second bowl of soup. She didn't even look up when he put it in front of her. The Professor thanked him with a smile, and then turned back to Hannah. "Hannah?"

"What now?" Hannah said without enthusiasm.

"You didn't say thank you."

Hannah was now extremely grumpy. "Don't need a lesson in manners from you. At least I don't go around stealing people's lives and stuff. Anyway, it's his job. It's not like he's doing me a favor or anything."

The Professor regarded Hannah coolly. "A few weeks ago, you led a rich woman on a wild goose chase through Dundee just because you thought she ought to see how most people were living, while she lived in luxury on the profits from their work. I'm sorry to ask again, but what I really want to know is why you've suddenly changed your tune about Dundee?"

Hannah was silent. She knew the answer, of course. Because how people live in Dundee isn't my problem anymore. Because I don't want it to be. Because I don't want to feel guilty. Because nothing I can do will help anyway. What she said was, "Hey, I got out. They should, too."

The Professor exploded. "You got out because I paid for you to do it! It's certainly not because you achieved anything by your own efforts, is it? My God, you're a selfish little…"

Hannah picked up the soup bowl, and flung the contents at the Professor's face. Luckily, the soup wasn't very hot, and she missed, instead landing a vivid splatter across the front of the Professor's dress.

Now the entire room was silent, and everyone was staring.

The Professor calmly began to wipe off her dress, and said imperiously, in her Miss Davies voice, "Hannah, you will return to your cabin this instant."

Hannah spat out, "With pleasure. Like I really want to be around you? Yeah, right."

The Professor now sounded coldly furious. "Wait for me there. I shall deal with you presently."

Hannah threw down her napkin, and darted from the room.

In her cabin, a seething Hannah waited for the Professor to knock, because she was ready for her. She had locked the door, and shoved the chair under the door handle. She was prepared to claim to the cabin crew that Miss Davies was not her governess, but her kidnapper. Whatever happened, she was determined not to listen to another of the Professor's lectures.

But the knock never came, and Hannah eventually lay down on her bed and cried about losing Jessie and Mina, until she drifted off to sleep.

In the morning, forty hours after they had left Dundee, Hannah awoke to find bright light streaming through the cabin porthole. The ship's engines had shut down, and the vessel was barely moving. It was then she realized that the steamer had docked in London.

But when she knocked on the Professor's door, there was no answer. Hannah hunted down the cabin steward, who told her that the Professor had already disembarked. "She must be in quite a hurry to see the Exhibition, Miss, if she left without you! Don't worry. I'm sure she'll be back on board this evening, if not sooner."

Hannah hoped he was right, and rummaged in her purse for the money that the Professor had originally given her in Dundee: She had forgotten to ask for it back.

Smiling smugly to herself, she unwrapped the pound notes, thinking what fun she could have in London. Her ticket included five days of accommodations and meals on board, and so, if the Professor had gone off to sulk, it was no big deal. Unless, of course, she never came back... Hannah dismissed that thought with a shudder.

She decided to change into her blue dress before she went out. Unclasping the latches of her travel trunk, she flung open the hinged lid. On top of the clothes lay a sack, and she pulled it aside. That was when she realized that it wasn't a sack: It was a tatty old skirt. Puzzled, Hannah peered into the trunk, and drew out a rough woolen shawl. She began to have a very bad feeling about this. Next, out came a grey, shapeless blouse. Perhaps she had the wrong trunk? No. There was her name, carefully written in black ink on the inside of the trunk lid. She threw aside the blouse and rummaged deeper, but all she found was the bottom of the trunk. In panic, Hannah searched the room. Nothing.

"That witch!" she wailed. "She stole my dresses!"

****

The ship sailed up the estuary where the River Thames meets the sea, and Alex and Jupe watched the riverbank go by, dashing from one side of the deck to the other and back again so that they wouldn't miss anything.

As Alex watched the south bank, Mr. Thornhill joined him. "Behold the mighty River Thames," he said, smiling. "We're almost there."

Alex suddenly had an awful thought, and he blurted out, "Mr. Thornhill, I don't have a passport!"

Mr. Thornhill leaned down to hear him better, and said, "A what?"

Alex frantically gestured with his fingers. "You know, a passport? To get into England?"

"I don't know what you're talking about," said Mr. Thornhill, returning his gaze to the river.

So, Alex thought, passports haven't been invented yet. Phew.

At that moment, a great cheer went up from the passengers on deck. Alex struggled to see what the fuss was about, and finally asked Mr. Thornhill.

"There's Gravesend," said Mr. Thornhill, smiling and nodding ahead of them to a crowded town with steamships and sailing ships clustered in its harbor. The steamer passed a rowing boat, and the passengers waved enthusiastically with hats and handkerchiefs.

Mr. Thornhill removed his hat and leaned on the guardrail. "Here is our point of arrival for London. Do you know, I have learned that we may now take a railway train from here to London Bridge? What a remarkable age we live in!"

Alex smiled. It was hard for him to be as impressed with trains as Mr. Thornhill was, but he tried to understand: To Mr. Thornhill, trains were state-of-the-art technology. His enthusiasm reminded Alex of his Grandpa's fascination with computers.

Mr. Thornhill pulled out a cigar, and then dug around in his pockets for something, muttering, "Confound it! Where are my Lucifers? Oh... wait... here they are."

He held up a box of matches. Striking one on the guard rail, he lit his cigar, protecting the match from the wind with a cupped hand. He blew out a puff of acrid smoke and said, "I have arranged rooms for us at Carhart's Hotel, although I was fortunate to find them. Accommodations are in high demand because of the Exhibition, and Carhart's is the finest in all of London. I don't know whether that speaks well of it or not, but I would hazard that it's no worse than Johnson's Inn in Snipesville."

Alex laughed, and Mr. Thornhill allowed himself a smile at his own joke.

Alex, Jupe, and Mr. Thornhill stood unsteadily on the quayside, trying to get used to solid land again, as they waited for porters to finish loading their trunks.

"Once I have seen to the luggage, we will take a train into town," said Mr. Thornhill, tossing his cigar butt onto the quayside. "Hopefully, our trunks will arrive at the hotel in good time."

"Massa Thornhill?" Jupe said, "Where we going?"

"We are going into London, Jupe. And don't call me Master," said Mr. Thornhill abruptly. "You are free. You may call me Mr. Thornhill or sir, as you please."

As Mr. Thornhill went to give instructions to the carters who were loading the trunks into a wagon, Jupe looked ready to cry. Alex, alarmed, asked if he was okay.

"I don't know," said Jupe, his lip trembling. "I don't know. I'll tell you later, Massa Alex. But I got to think a spell. I don't even know where I am!"

Alex whispered, "Jupe, it's okay! It's gonna be okay! Remember what I told you? You, your family, every slave in Georgia, you're all gonna be free in just a few years!"

Jupe stepped away, looking skeptically at him, and said politely, "Thanks, Massa Alex…"

Alex knew then that Jupe thought he was crazy, but he tried to bridge the gap between them even still. "Please, call me Alex. Just Alex."

"Well, thank you, sir, all the same," Jupe said. Then he looked downriver, as though he could somehow retrace the ship's voyage, back along the English Channel, across the Atlantic Ocean, and all the way home to Snipes County, far from this strange place and Alex the madman.

To Alex, Carhart's Hotel looked less like a grand resort, and more like five houses that had been knocked together, which was exactly what it was. Mr. Thornhill had rented a suite of four small rooms, three bedrooms and a sitting room. All the rooms were much smaller than in the hotels where Alex had stayed with his parents. He said so to Mr. Thornhill, who was very surprised to hear it.

In Alex's room, he found what passed for a bathroom: A wooden washstand with a jug of cold water and a basin, soap, sponge, and a water glass. On the lower shelf was another bowl for waste water.

While Alex found the accommodations a bit primitive, Jupe seemed overwhelmed by the luxury of it all. He had spent the entire journey to the hotel by train and horse-drawn cab with his mouth open, gaping at the sheer size of London. Now he was sitting on his bed, taking it all in.

Alex returned to the sitting room, where Mr. Thornhill was reclining in an armchair, smoking yet another cigar, and pouring himself a glass of whisky. "I must confess to you, Alex, that returning to London has made me feel as though I have traveled through time," chuckled Mr. Thornhill. "So much has changed here that I feel quite dizzy. But I don't suppose you have the first idea of what I'm talking about."

Alex thought, man, you don't know the half of it.

Suddenly, Mr. Thornhill sat up. "I expect you would like to see the sights? There is so much to see in London. Now, I propose that we pay a visit to…"

As soon as he began to speak, Alex found himself mentally flipping through a slideshow of London attractions: Buckingham Palace! Westminster Abbey!

The Houses of Parliament!

"...the Thames Tunnel!" exclaimed Mr. Thornhill. "Let us cast our eyes upon Marc Brunel's astonishing feat of engineering."

Alex looked crestfallen. Mr. Thornhill added hurriedly, "Well, perhaps Madame Tussaud's Waxworks would be best."

"It already exists?" Alex blurted out. Mr. Thornhill gave him an odd look, and so Alex added, "Can Jupe come?"

"If you wish," Mr. Thornhill said unenthusiastically. But Alex did wish to bring him, and Jupe was both surprised and delighted to be invited along.

Madame Tussaud's Waxworks, 1851 version, was much smaller than it would be in the twenty-first century. It sat on the second floor of its building, above a salesroom for horse-drawn carriages. Alex, Jupe and Mr. Thornhill entered through a narrow doorway on the ground floor, and climbed a grand staircase, to be met by a young man guarding a black metal cash box on a table. He brightened up when he saw them approach, and greeted Mr. Thornhill warmly. "Good morning, sir! That will be a shilling each for you, the young gentleman, and your servant, and an extra sixpence for the catalog of the exhibition. Will you be seeing the Napoleon Rooms and the Separate Room on this occasion, sir?"

"I suppose so," said Mr. Thornhill uncertainly, but Alex was already nodding excitedly.

The man extended his hand. "In that case, sir, that will be an extra sixpence per person, for a total of five shillings."

Mr. Thornhill dropped the coins into his outstretched palm and asked, "Is Madame unwell today? Her absence is to be lamented."

The attendant's expression instantly changed to one of great solemnity. "Madame? No, sir. I'm sorry, sir, but sad to say, Madame Tussaud is no longer with us. She died last year at the venerable age of 90."

"I had no idea," said Mr. Thornhill politely. "I have been abroad. Come along, Alex."

The three of them entered what appeared to be an enormous formal living room: Mirrors and drapes lined the walls, and the room was lit with hissing gas lamps. Alex, remembering the teeming crowds at Tussaud's in the twenty-first century, was surprised by how quiet the place was. The wax models outnumbered the real people. And unlike the casually-attired tourist crowd at the modern Tussauds, the few other customers in 1851 were formally dressed and looked wealthy.

CHAPTER ELEVEN

The two boys followed Mr. Thornhill through to the Hall of Kings to admire the Royal Family of Queen Victoria, Prince Albert, and their seven children. Alex decided to step onto the platform and see how tall he was compared with the tiny Queen. But as he did so, Mr. Thornhill grabbed his arm and yanked him back to the ground. "What are you doing?" he hissed.

"I'm sorry. I thought we were allowed to do that," Alex said sheepishly. He and Brandon had taken each others' photos with the waxworks in the twenty-first century, and he had no idea that this was a new privilege. Now, in 1851, he looked about him doubtfully, and said, "So what can we do here?"

"We shall admire the many celebrated people modeled in wax," said Mr. Thornhill, adding testily under his breath, "I should have thought that was obvious."

As Mr. Thornhill turned away, Alex circled his index finger in the air, and muttered, "Woo-hoo." But then he had an idea. He said to Jupe, "Let's check out the Chamber of Horrors!"

Mr. Thornhill had overheard him, but was confused. He turned to an attendant standing nearby. "Where is the, er, Chamber of Horrors?"

"We don't actually like calling it that, sir," the attendant replied in a hushed voice. "That name was a joke in poor taste that appeared in Punch magazine. We call it the Separate Room. We do advise that it's not suitable for ladies, sir."

Mr. Thornhill raised an eyebrow at him. "As you can plainly see, there are no ladies in our company. Lead us to the Separate Room."

The Separate Room (otherwise known as the Chamber of Horrors) was a major disappointment, at least to Alex. Gone was all the really scary stuff, like the torture and execution scenes. Instead the highlight was a display of lifesize wax models of "Celebrated Murderers," who queued up like ordinary men waiting for a bus. The only exhibit that impressed Alex was that of French revolutionary Jean-Paul Marat, the man who was stabbed in his bath. Even then, he was mainly impressed because he had seen the same waxwork two centuries into the future.

Jupe, meanwhile, was dumbstruck by the wax models of the guillotined heads of French Revolutionaries. "What are those?" he whispered, pointing with a trembling finger.

Mr. Thornhill overheard him, and came to join the boys. He pointed to the wax heads and said, "These men advocated liberty and equality for all in France, even for the most ignorant peasants. But their so-called revolution led only to lawlessness, and then to tyranny, as the Napoleon Rooms will show us. The rebels paid for their sins by becoming victims of the rabble. They are evidence of the ill-effects of too much freedom."

Alex followed this wordy lecture, but it bothered him. He spoke up. "Mr. Thornhill, how can there be too much freedom? I mean, Jupe is free now, and that's only a good thing. And you made that happen."

Mr. Thornhill looked coldly at him. "I can only repeat, Alexander, that too much freedom leads to a collapse of the proper order of things. I don't expect a mere child to understand this, or indeed to understand that true freedom is possible only with capital, by which I mean property and money, something that neither you nor Jupe has."

An uneasy feeling spread through Alex's stomach. There was something very chilling about Mr. Thornhill's words, and also about how he had said them, as though he knew something that he was not prepared to reveal to the boys. Uncomfortably, Alex thought, not for the first time, that he knew very little about Mr. Thornhill and his plans.

****

Brandon finished polishing the last shoe in Balesworth Hall just in time for the beginning of his half-day off. Every Saturday between 2 p.m. and 10 p.m., plus every other Sunday afternoon, his time was his own to do as he pleased. Brandon was dying to do something, anything, that wasn't mind-numbing work, just to use his brain a bit. But there was not much to do in rural Hertfordshire in 1851, especially not by himself. If nothing else, he thought, he could take a walk in the country, and get the smells of shoe polish and silver polish out of his nostrils. The weather was gloomy and overcast, as it so often was in England, but he didn't think it was likely he would get soaked through. When the rain came, it rarely rained as heavily here as it did in Georgia. Anyway, he would chance it, because he was keen to see what the town of Balesworth looked like in 1851.

He planned to walk along the Great North Road until Mr. Veeriswamy suggested that he take a footpath through the fields and woods instead. Brandon had forgotten that what the English meant by "footpath" in the countryside was an unmarked dirt trail. Several times, he stopped in the fields and woodlands thinking he was lost, but each time he decided to carry on. Finally, he emerged from the woods just in time to see a steam train draw up at Balesworth Station. He had arrived.

When Brandon finally reached the High Street, he was excited to find the weekly open-air market in progress. In 1915, he had often shopped at a booth selling used books, and he hoped it was in business in 1851. But his hope was immediately dashed, for the market was not much as he remembered it. Although a few stalls here and there sold fruit and vegetables, most of the activity involved serious-looking men smoking pipes and muttering to each other as they clustered around penned-in herds of cattle.

Hesitantly, Brandon approached an elderly farmer with long puffy white sideburns who was hovering at the edge of a conversation. "Excuse me, sir, but can you tell me if anyone ever sells books at this market?"

"You're not from here, are you?" the old man said with a smile, leaning forward on his cane. "Well, lad, you won't find no books here. You're all mizzle-mozzled, you see! This here is Balesworth's cattle market. You want a fair with hawkers and peddlers and that? You best be coming back for the Fair in September, I reckon. Mind you, I don't say you'll find what you're looking for, because nothing in town has been the same since that Great Northern Railway opened here last year. It's like to put an end to the Balesworth cattle market, because now the Smithfield butchers can get their cattle from anywhere, can't they? They don't have to come here. I tell you, lad, this here railway will be the ruination of Balesworth. The inns ain't doing half the business they was, and that's a fact. We hardly seen any coaches these days, and they get fewer all the time. And dangerous the railway is, too. They had a collision not twelvemonth ago, right outside Balesworth Station. I wouldn't travel on it, not me." He rubbed his foot in the dust of the road and shook his head.

"Well, er, thanks," said Brandon, thinking to himself that this old man really liked talking. "That's, er, interesting."

Suddenly, the old man looked up, and spoke again. "Now, if it's books you're after, well, you'll have to go to James Cotter's shop."

"You have a bookshop?" Brandon exclaimed. He didn't remember a bookstore in twentieth-century Balesworth.

The old farmer looked mock-offended. "Arr, we do that. We ain't all joskins in Balesworth, you know. Some of us is book-learned."

"Joskins?" Brandon said blankly.

"Joskins!" laughed the farmer. "That's what we call country bumpkins. Now skedaddle, and get you down to Mr. Cotter's. You'll find he's by the Balesworth Arms. He'll welcome a customer, what with business being so slow and that, and he'd be happy to help a young man of letters such as yourself."

The tiny bookshop was in the front room of Mr. Cotter's house. A bell rang when Brandon entered, and soon Mrs. Cotter appeared. She was taken aback to see that her customer was a black boy, but she quickly recovered herself, apologized for Mr. Cotter's being indisposed, and asked if she might assist him? Brandon didn't know what he wanted, which seemed a great relief to Mrs. Cotter, who sat down behind a small counter and resumed work on a sewing project.

Brandon spent a long time browsing, but none of the books appealed much to him. All were hardbacks, and far too expensive for the shilling in his pocket. But when he returned to the counter to ask Mrs. Cotter for suggestions, he spotted a magazine, The London Illustrated News, right next to the cashbox. It looked interesting, and better yet, he could afford it.

There were no park benches on Balesworth High Street in 1851, and so Brandon eventually settled down to read his magazine on the slightly damp grass of the village green. The front page story was an excited preview of the forthcoming Great Exhibition, and soon he was absorbed by its glowing descriptions of all the wonderful sights that visitors could expect. But how on earth would he afford the five shillings entrance fee?

When Brandon returned in the late afternoon, hungry and in time for tea, Mr. Veeriswamy informed him that Lady Chatsfield required his presence upstairs, immediately. Great, Brandon thought. Now he was in trouble. But why?

In the drawing room, Lady Chatsfield was seated on a large overstuffed sofa, and she invited Brandon to take a chair across from her. "I trust you are settling in," she said. He gave a wan smile that he hoped looked enthusiastic. Lady Chatsfield continued, "I am interested in learning of your experience of the evils of slavery."

Brandon was confused. "But, ma'am…"

"Your Ladyship."

"Okay, Your Ladyship. I've never been a slave."

If she was disconcerted by this revelation, she didn't show it. "Then you may tell me about your family's life in slavery."

Brandon sighed heavily. "My family aren't slaves. You have to go a long way back to my ancestors being slaves."

A look of irritation passed briefly across Lady Chatsfield's face, and then she said slowly, "Let me make myself clear. I am a patron of the anti-slavery cause, and I frequently entertain other ladies who share my convictions. I employed you as a footman principally because I thought that you might provide edification for the ladies who attend my salons. I'm sure that, as a Negro, you can at the very least imagine the predicament in which slaves find themselves, and that you can describe that predicament to my guests."

Brandon sighed inwardly. So Lady Chatsfield wanted to use him to impress her friends. He looked at her cynically. "You want me to make stuff up?"

Lady Chatsfield gave him an icy glare. "Certainly not. I was merely seeking your assistance in the fight against slavery. I expect to draw on your knowledge of that profane institution at the next discussion I shall hold. Kindly consider what I have said. That will be all."

Brandon took his cue, and without another word, stalked furiously from the room. So she had hired him only because he was black? That was almost as bad as not being hired only because he was black.

He was sitting on the grand staircase seething when Sarah Chatsfield came in through the front door, closely followed by Henry. They were both out of breath and laughing. No sooner was he inside, than Henry realized he had left the ball they had been playing with somewhere in the park, and he dashed back out. Sarah, left by herself, walked toward Brandon.

"You're not supposed to sit there, you know," she said, not unkindly. "If Mama or Mr. Veeriswamy should catch you, there would be a fearful row. What is troubling you?" To Brandon's surprise, she sat next to him on the stairs.

"I don't like to say," he mumbled, adding belatedly, "Miss Sarah." He hated being so polite to another kid.

"Very well, it is your business," Sarah said briskly, taking his answer as a rebuff. "Perhaps you had better return below stairs."

"Yeah, maybe I had better do that," Brandon said as he stood. "The company is better down there."

"What do you mean by that?" Sarah said sharply, rising to her feet.

Brandon considered explaining, but he realized that his remark might jeopardize his job. He thought quickly, and said, "I mean for me, Miss Sarah. I will be with the other servants, and I can relax."

"How odd that you should say such a thing to me," Sarah said. Her feelings were hurt, but Brandon thought he had merely offended her.

"Sorry, Miss Sarah," he said, gritting his teeth at having to apologize.

"You may go," Sarah said and, with that, she slowly started upstairs.

It did not occur to Brandon for quite some time that she had only been trying to be kind. Even then, he found the encounter frustrating. It was too weird to have to suck up to another kid, or else risk his job and his home. It wasn't Sarah's fault that she was rich and he was not, he knew, but he couldn't quite bring himself to admit it.

Chapter 12:
SIGHTSEEING

Alex was woken early the next morning by a footman carrying breakfast on a tray. Today was the day, the opening day of the Great Exhibition. Mr. Thornhill had ordered Jupe to remain behind at the hotel, and, after breakfast, he and Alex set off by hackney coach. The cabby and his horse struggled through the crowded streets, jostling among the carriages, horse-drawn buses, and pedestrians all surging toward Hyde Park, the site of the Crystal Palace, the home of the Exhibition. All along the route, food and souvenir stands lined the streets, as did people who had claimed spots to view the journey of Queen Victoria and Prince Albert to the opening ceremony. There was an excited atmosphere throughout London.

Alex gasped when he first glimpsed the Crystal Palace. It was the biggest greenhouse he had ever seen. It was cross-shaped, like a massive cathedral made entirely from glass and iron, and the glass sparkled as it caught the sunlight. Even in the twenty-first century, it would have been impressive, but in 1851, it seemed as unlikely as a spaceship landing in Hyde Park.

Stepping out of the taxi, Mr. Thornhill said to Alex, "They say that it has ten thousand windows. I shouldn't be surprised if that were true, would you?" He paid the cab driver, as Alex gaped at the thousands of people who were milling around outside the Palace. He and Mr. Thornhill had to push their way awkwardly through the crowd to reach the exhibitors' entrance. There, they stood in line for thirty minutes before the door opened promptly at eight o'clock. Mr. Thornhill showed the doorman a card, and they were in.

The early morning light poured onto the cross-shaped exhibition floor and the second-story balcony that ran around the building. Flags of all nations were strung from the rafters, and the very first that caught Alex's eye was the Stars and Stripes, which he excitedly pointed out to Mr. Thornhill. A red carpet led from the front entrance to the center of the building, where there was a gently bubbling fountain made from glittering crystal. A platform near the fountain awaited the arrival of speakers. And, unlikely though it seems, there was even a large mature tree at the center of the Palace.

"What's that?" asked Alex, pointing to a wooden object suspended by wires over the platform. It looked like an enormous ornately-painted lid.

"Oh, that's the sounding board," said Mr. Thornhill. "It will amplify Her

Majesty's voice when she declares the Exhibition open."

"Her Majesty? You mean Queen Victoria is gonna be here?" Alex was excited, and even Mr. Thornhill gave a slight smile.

At first glance, the United States section looked impressive. It was cheerfully decorated with American flags, and the names of all the states that existed in 1851. But on closer examination, it was pretty empty of exhibits, and the staff stood around forlornly. Mr. Thornhill warmly greeted one of the men, Mr. Meredith, and introduced Alex to him.

Mr. Meredith was clearly pleased to see Mr. Thornhill. "Glad you got my telegraph before you left the States, Thornhill," said the worried-looking American, "But we have something of a problem. Look around you, sir. At least one third of our exhibits haven't arrived. This is going to reflect badly on the United States."

Mr. Thornhill gave a small lopsided smile and reached into his jacket pocket. "Meredith, I have something for you to add to the Exhibit. It may help."

To Alex's horror, Mr. Thornhill produced the calculator. He switched it on, and demonstrated it.

"I'll be damned," said a delighted Mr. Meredith, turning the calculator over in his hands, and pushing at the buttons. "What the devil is this?"

Mr. Thornhill preened. "It's rather remarkable, is it not? I am glad to present it to you on loan. But I know nothing about it, neither who the manufacturer is, nor where it was made. However, it ought to be useful in attracting admiration for American manufactures."

Alex's stomach was churning at the thought of arguing with Mr. Thornhill, but he had to do it. "I'm sorry, Mr. Thornhill, but that's mine…"

Mr. Thornhill answered calmly, while giving Alex a keen look. "So it is, so it is," he said. "I merely intend you to continue the loan of it a little while longer."

"I'm sorry, sir," Alex said carefully, "but I really would prefer you not put it on display. It might… It might get stolen."

Mr. Thornhill scrutinized Alex's face. "Hmm, yes, I suppose it might… Meredith, what say you to the proposal that we only show it discreetly to choice patrons?"

Mr. Meredith shrugged with a smile. "Sure. That makes sense." He walked over with the calculator to a glass case, and tucked it inside.

Alex still wasn't happy, but he could tell there was no point in arguing further: His boss was too used to having people do as they were told without question. Instead, he waited until the two men were deep in conversation, reached inside the glass case, and quickly flipped the calculator onto its face, leaving only the back exposed. Hopefully, he thought, it looked so uninteresting that nobody would ask about it.

At nine o'clock, the Great Exhibition opened, and the crowds began to pour through the entrance. Ladies in their finery claimed the straight-backed chairs that lined the red carpet leading to the central platform, and their husbands took places standing behind them. Alex looked in vain for kids, but none had come to the opening ceremonies.

It was another hour before there was a great stir of excitement around the platform. Alex couldn't see what was going on, but he certainly heard the great round of applause and cheers. At that moment, a young man ran up to the American exhibitors, and cried, "It's the Duke! He's here!"

"Which duke?" called out Mr. Meredith.

The young Englishman stopped in his tracks, astonished by the question. "Wellington, of course. If you hurry, you may catch sight of him."

Mr. Meredith turned to Mr. Thornhill and joked, "You British have so many dukes and earls and whatnot, I can't tell them apart."

But Mr. Thornhill ignored his comment, put a hand on Alex's shoulder and said, "Come, Alexander, and let us lay our eyes upon the mighty victor of Waterloo, Napoleon's nemesis. Let us judge for ourselves whether Madame Tussaud's did him justice." Alex followed his boss, who was now walking briskly toward the center of the Crystal Palace.

When they caught sight of him, the elderly Duke, escorted by his daughter, was already halfway up the aisle toward the platform. He was easy to spot: Tall, with white hair and a huge nose, he was dressed in a bright red army uniform hung with medals. Alex and Mr. Thornhill watched in awe as the Duke acknowledged the cheers and applause of the crowd. He found his seat, and then, catching sight of an old friend in one of the balconies, he waved and said something to his daughter, before slowly making his way alone toward the staircase.

Before he could reach the stairs, Alex had dashed up to him. The Duke looked slightly annoyed at the interruption, and snapped, "Yes, boy, what is it?"

Alex was breathless with excitement. "Sir, I saw you in Madame Tussauds, I mean I saw the wax you, and it so looks like you. Mr. Thornhill, my boss, told me all about you in the Napoleon Room, and I'm a huge fan. Can I have your autograph?"

The Duke looked down imperiously at a hopeful Alex. "My autograph? Don't know what you're talking about, boy."

With that, he brushed past Alex, just before Mr. Thornhill caught up with him. "What are you doing?" Mr. Thornhill growled, jerking Alex backward by the collar. "One does not approach the Duke of Wellington unbidden!"

But the Duke, on hearing the commotion, slowly turned to look at Alex. "Must say, they did a fine job of Napoleon. Quite lifelike. Just like old times." He gave a short laugh at his own joke, and began to climb the stairs.

Mr. Thornhill tipped his hat to the Duke, and then, after waiting respectfully for the old man to reach the balcony, he quietly ushered Alex up the stairs. There, the two of them staked out spots to await the arrival of the Royal Family.

Massive explosions silenced the chattering in the Palace an hour later, and Alex panicked. "What was that?" he stammered.

"Cannon fire," said Mr. Thornhill, "to welcome Her Majesty and His Royal Highness."

Alex sighed with relief.

As Queen Victoria and Prince Albert walked slowly into the Crystal Palace, Alex couldn't help thinking that the Queen was a funny-looking little thing, just like her wax model. She was tiny and had a small head and a weak chin. But she certainly walked like a Queen, barely acknowledging the cheers of her subjects, except with a faint smile. Prince Albert walked stiffly upright, and Alex remarked to Mr. Thornhill that he looked very proud.

"And so he should," Mr. Thornhill replied. "The Exhibition was his idea. Anyhow, it is time for us to return to the American area."

"Now? Already?" exclaimed a dismayed Alex. "But they're just about to start the ceremony!"

"We must prepare for the arrival of the visitors," Mr. Thornhill said simply, as he led the way to the staircase. "Come along."

Back at the American section, workmen were installing a new exhibit in one of the empty spaces: It was a statue of a Native American man and woman, and unlike all the other statues in the building, which were made of white marble, it was brightly painted, and decorated with feathers and furs.

"What the devil is that?" laughed Mr. Thornhill.

"It is the best the commissioners could do," said Mr. Meredith stiffly. "We had to do something until the rest of the exhibits arrive."

"But that...that thing," Mr. Thornhill sputtered, "will only confirm the prejudices of Britons who think America is a savage land. That is hardly how we..."

"Indians aren't savages," interrupted Alex.

"I beg your pardon?" said Mr. Thornhill, in a tone that told Alex to shut up. Alex shut up.

Mr. Meredith said slyly, "It must be a while since you were last here, Thornhill. Nobody has asked me about the Indians since I landed in England. All they want to talk about is slavery. I'm from New York, I tell them, but they don't know the difference. They're quite insistent on taking up the matter with me, and some of them even tell me I should protest slavery to the President."

"How very awkward," said Mr. Thornhill, tutting.

Just then, they all turned at the sound of cheers echoing through the Crystal Palace. "Here comes the royal procession," said Mr. Meredith. "With luck, the Queen and Prince Albert should be here presently."

The American exhibitors straightened their ties. The two workmen installing the statue rubbed their hands on their aprons, and headed for the balcony. Mr. Thornhill and Alex took their places behind one of the glass display cases.

It wasn't long before the Royal couple and their entourage approached, and the exhibitors in the American section listened excitedly as the cheers grew closer and closer. To Alex's amazement, two men in fancy outfits were at the head of the procession, walking backward while facing Victoria and Albert. Even more astounding, they were walking quickly, and Alex wondered how on earth they didn't trip. He tried to make himself as tall as possible, hoping that the Queen would speak with him, but the Royals did not stop. However, he caught Victoria's eye, and she gave him a warm smile.

At one o'clock, trumpets sounded to announce that the Queen had declared the Exhibition open, and the Royals left the building. Now the flood of guests began: Women in huge dresses and men in top hats began arriving in the American section, eager to see the exhibits. And then an elderly gentleman with slightly messy hair introduced himself to Mr. Meredith.

"My name is Babbage," he said in a pompous voice. "You may have heard of me? I am the inventor of the Difference Engine, and I am currently devising an even more advanced machine for computation, which I have named the Analytical Engine. For some reason, political I fear, the Exhibition Committee declined to display my plans for the Difference Engine, but I would very much like to bring it to your attention, for I believe that Americans would appreciate the benefits of my work...."

The more Alex overheard, the more he became excited. It was Charles Babbage! The man who had invented the computer! The man whose pickled brain was in the Science Museum!

CHAPTER TWELVE

Alex couldn't help himself. "Sir, you gotta check this out!" he cried, leading the man to the display case, and pulling out the calculator. He began to punch the buttons. Wouldn't Babbage be thrilled, he thought, to find out that his inventions would lead to calculators and computers? But Babbage was looking at the calculator with a conflicted mix of wonder and horror across his face. By the time Alex had finished his impromptu demonstration, the inventor looked pale-faced and shaken.

"What is this contraption?" he managed to say. "Who is the inventor?"

Alex shrugged. "I don't know. We have loads of calculators like this in America. But you…"

Before he could say another word, a stunned Babbage had melted back into the crowd.

Seconds later, it occurred to Alex that there might be a reason why Charles Babbage had never gotten round to building his inventions.

By the afternoon, Alex was bored to death. There wasn't anything at all for him to do except to guard the calculator, and even that didn't seem important, because Mr. Thornhill and Mr. Meredith had shown no interest in showing it: They had found plenty to occupy them in talking business with visitors. Alex put his hands in his jacket pocket, his fingers wrapping around the original calculator cover. He pulled it out, and slipped it underneath the calculator in the glass case: He figured it was best to keep everything together.

Just then, Mr. Meredith greeted him cheerfully. "Come, Alex, let me explain the exhibits to you. Then you will be prepared to answer questions from the ladies and the old clergymen, while Mr. Thornhill and I attend to the gentle-men of business." He smiled pleasantly at Alex, who gamely agreed to help by chatting with the unimportant visitors.

****

Hannah scratched at a soup stain on the front of her pink dress. Standing by the Dundee, Perth and London Shipping Company's dock, she hoped that the dress and her bonnet were marks of respectability, even though the dress was seriously in need of a good cleaning. And, of course, she had money, but not enough that she could afford to blow it on more clothes.

Where would she go? Back in her cabin, she had panicked on realizing that the Professor had left her alone, but she had forced herself to calm down and think. There had to be a reason why she was on a package tour to the Great Exhibition, so it made sense to start there. Unfortunately, she learned from her cabin steward that tickets were not included in the vacation, and had to be purchased separately at the Crystal Palace.

Now, she was debating with herself how she should get there. She stopped an Asian man, one of the dozens of porters milling about, and asked him how she could get a cab. "You wait at rank, miss," he said in a Chinese-Cockney accent, pointing to the taxi stand. "And another cabriolet come along presently. It might take a time, though. The other passengers was out before you, and most of them had to wait long time. It's the Exhibition, miss. Ain't never been this much demand for cabs before." He shook his head, and went on his way.

Hannah sighed heavily, and prepared for a long wait. However, just then, she heard the clop of horses' hooves, and a taxi came racing up the road toward her. The driver was sitting on an elevated seat behind the tiny passenger compartment, flicking a long whip at his horse as it pulled his nimble two-wheeled black carriage. He brought the horse to a halt before jumping down, and opening the carriage door.

At once, Hannah made to enter, but the driver stopped her. "Excuse me, miss, but haven't you got a chaperone?"

Hannah stepped out again. "No. Why? I'm not going to a dance. I just want to go to the Crystal Palace."

The driver touched his cap in respect. "Begging your pardon, miss, it's just that a young lady like you shouldn't be out without a chaperone. London's not safe for you, Miss. But I can take you to the Crystal Palace. Got a ticket for opening day, have you?"

"No," said Hannah. "Do I need one?"

The cabbie looked very concerned. "Yes, miss. I'm afraid so. Today's opening costs a pound to get in, and everyone needs a…"

"HOW much?" Hannah screeched.

"A pound, miss. Goes down to five shillings tomorrow." The cabbie seemed amused by Hannah's horror. Now he looked at her sternly. "Come along, miss, I dunno what you're playing at, but London's no place for young ladies what takes it into their heads to run away. You tell me where we can find your mother."

"I'm not here with my mother," Hannah said resentfully. "I'm here with my governess, Miss Davies, and she took off and left me here at the boat."

The driver climbed aboard his cab. "Well, then, miss, you had best stay here until she comes back."

"So where is here, anyway?" Hannah said in her attitude voice.

"Here's Wapping, miss, and this is Hore's Wharf."

CHAPTER TWELVE

"Where?" Hannah asked incredulously.

"Hore's Wharf, miss, named for the late Mr. Hore. His widow lives over there." He pointed to a house with his whip, before waving it around to indicate the neighborhood. "And this is the borough of Wapping."

"Whopping?" Hannah was now convinced that the man was messing with her head.

But the driver was tired of repeating himself, and seeing no other customers, he cracked his whip and took off, leaving a very annoyed Hannah in his wake.

She decided to take matters into her own hands, and walk.

Hannah soon decided that she had made a major mistake. The docks were a nightmarish jumble of tall warehouses, some joined to each other by odd little overhead bridges. Wooden double doors hung open on even the highest stories, and from them extended drawbridges, just like on a castle, on which dockworkers stood precariously. They leaned over dangerously to grab at dangling bales of goods that hung from thick ropes. It gave Hannah vertigo just watching them.

She could barely walk through the warren of alleys for all the merchandise stacked everywhere, much of which, she couldn't help but notice, was packed in Dundee jute-wrapped bales. When she emerged from between two towering piles of goods, she was almost run down by an enormous blinkered draft horse, dragging a cart. She stepped back, and the driver swore at her as he passed.

More carefully now, Hannah entered the road, and looked about her. All she could see in the fog were warehouses, alleyways, and crowds of dockworkers and sailors. The men smoked short clay pipes, spat, and swore when she got in their way.

A grubby-looking man wearing a short cravat and dirty waistcoat turned to look at Hannah, then smiled broadly. "You look like a nice girl," he said. "Want to come with me?"

"You look like a creep," said Hannah. "Get lost."

But the man grabbed her by the arm, and tried to drag her down an alleyway. Suddenly, two huge dockworkers appeared, one of them seizing the man from behind, and the other punching him in the belly. They gave him a great shove, and he sprawled on the filthy ground. He scrambled to his feet and stumbled away, muttering curses.

The first of Hannah's rescuers, a huge bald guy wearing a broad hat, knee breeches, and a long jacket, brushed off his hands on his waistcoat. "Are you all right, miss?"

She finally caught her breath. "Yeah, awesome. Thanks, you guys."

"You oughtn't to be here, miss," said the smaller man, who had only a few teeth.

"Yeah, this ain't no place for a young lady," said the large docker. "Come on, Bob and me will see you where you need to go. The name's Charlie, by the by."

Hannah sighed. "Look, could you just show me to where I could catch a bus, or something? I just want to go sightseeing."

The two men looked doubtfully at her, at each other, and then at her again. "Honestly, miss," said Bob, "Don't you know where you are? You're in the East End of London, and that's no place for the likes of you. Come on."

Where had Hannah heard of the East End before? Then she remembered: This was where Jack the Ripper committed his dastardly crimes, or would commit them in the future. She hesitated only briefly before following the two men down the street.

As they emerged onto the main road, Hannah pointed to a huge octagonal pavilion ahead of them. It was made from shining marble, and adorned with flags. "What's that?"

"The entrance to the Thames Tunnel, that is," said Charlie. "Ain't never been down there, I ain't, on account of I haven't got no business across the River. Still, it attracts all the ladies and gentlemen…"

Hannah looked more closely. People were queuing to enter, and they did indeed look like ladies and gentlemen. There was a line of cabs waiting, too, and surely one of them would give her a ride back to the steamer?

"Thanks, you guys," she said to the two dockers. "This'll do."

She was about to walk away when she saw that Bob had extended a hand.

"Yeah?" Hannah stared blankly at his outstretched palm.

"A little gratuity wouldn't be remiss, begging your pardon, miss," he said. "Me and Charlie here, we're getting on in years, and we present ourselves every day down at the pub, when the foreman comes and picks out the blokes who he'll give work for the day. Only, we don't get picked as often as we used to, and we both still got families to feed…" Charlie nodded frantically in agreement.

Now Hannah knew why the two dockers had been so eager to help. Like most poor people, they weren't criminals, but they knew that middle-class folks had enough money to tip every poor person who helped them out. Hannah reached into her purse, and, without thinking, handed Bob a one-pound note. His eyes widened when he saw what she had given him. He nudged his companion, and they beat a hasty retreat.

Shell-shocked, Hannah watched them take off. By the time she thought to call after them, to tell them she had made a mistake by giving them such a large tip, it was too late. They had vanished into the docklands. Now she had even less money to spend. Sighing heavily, she walked the last few yards to the entrance of the Thames Tunnel.

The marble octagonal building was not quite as elegant inside as out. Shoved up against the walls were kiosks selling candies, newspapers, and even beer. Hannah joined the line of people waiting to get in at the brass turnstile, which was staffed by a fat man on a stool. As she neared the front of the queue, she turned to the short middle-aged man with bushy eyebrows who was standing behind her.

"So where does this thing go?" she asked, jerking her head at the tunnel entrance.

"It goes, young lady, under the River Thames to the South Bank. But where precisely it ends, I cannot tell you, and it matters not to me. I have no intention of traversing it, but wish merely to cast my eye upon it. After all, one cannot fairly claim to have visited London without having visited the Thames Tunnel."

Hannah shrugged, returning her attention to the man on the stool, who was extending his chubby hand and asking her for a penny.

Pushing through the turnstile, Hannah found herself in a slow-moving queue of people waiting to take the gas-lit stairs. Organ music wafted up from below, and she instinctively peered over the handrail to see where it came from. She got a shock: It was a very long way down, and the line of people zigzagged from flight to flight of stairs. Still, she was stuck now, with more people lined up behind her. And what else was she going to do with her time?

When Hannah used to visit Disneyland in California, the waiting areas were decorated with little features, like silly pictures and signs, to help people pass the time. Apparently, that idea wasn't new: The plaster walls of the Thames Tunnel staircase were hung with paintings and statues. On the first landing, Hannah discovered the source of the music: A skinny young man was playing an organ.

It took a long time to descend the staircase. When Hannah reached the bottom, she found herself in a brightly-lit room that looked almost exactly like the one at the top, lined with small shops. A man in exotic dress held a tiny monkey in suit and cap, and he invited people to watch it play tricks in exchange for tips.

The entrance to the tunnel itself was two large archways, each leading to an underground road. Shops lined the wall that divided the two sides of the tunnel from each other. Hannah could see all the way to the other end of the tunnel, and so far as she could see, there was a shop under every arch, maybe fifty of them. She smiled to herself: She knew a mall when she saw one. Eagerly, she approached a booth selling souvenirs. She picked up a little china telescope on which was printed *A Present from the Thames Tunnel*, and peeped through it. Inside was a 3-D drawing of the tunnel's inside. Alex would love this, she thought, before realizing with a pang of guilt that she hadn't thought much about her brother lately. She decided to buy the peepshow for him. She also picked out an ink stand (labeled *Bought in the Thames Tunnel*) for Brandon, and a souvenir for herself, a tiny shoe made of clay dug from the Tunnel during its construction. The woman behind the counter looked very pleased with Hannah's purchases, and complimented her on her good taste. Hannah congratulated herself for being a great shopper as she handed the shopkeeper six shillings.

Not bad, she thought, as she walked away. Then she remembered that six shillings was two weeks' wages in Dundee, and that there was no way to get the souvenirs back to the twenty-first century. She thought about trying to return her purchases, but she didn't want to admit to the saleswoman that she couldn't afford them.

Sighing heavily again, Hannah returned to the rotunda, where she realized with dismay that she would now have to climb back up the staircase. At that moment, a man standing with a notebook in front of a booth caught Hannah's eye, and called over to her, "Come inside, young lady, and have your fortune told!"

Why not, Hannah asked herself? It would make for a nice break before she had to tackle the stairs again. As the man held back the curtain, she entered the small, musty booth, and sat down on a rickety chair across from the fortune-teller. The booth was so dimly-lit that it was practically dark. The fortune-teller wore a veil, making her look very spooky. "First," she said in a hushed crackly voice, "You must cross my palm with silver."

Hannah stared at her. "What?"

The fortune-teller looked irritated. "That'll be sixpence," she said, extending her hand.

It seemed like a lot of money to Hannah the former Dundee jute worker, but to Hannah the Victorian young lady in London, it seemed like a pretty reasonable price. She dropped a silver sixpence into the waiting fingers.

The woman took Hannah's hand, and she looked at it for quite some time. Then, with an air of great importance, she said, "You have been on a long journey."

CHAPTER TWELVE

Hannah looked at her skeptically. "Well, that's kind of obvious. "

The woman paused in an annoyed sort of way, and then continued. "I see that you have had companions, but now are all alone."

Hannah was impressed for a moment, but then it occurred to her that this would be true of anyone. What she said was, "Duh."

The fortune teller examined her palm a third time. "I can tell that you are a girl who wastes money on any old rubbish that comes her way."

"What?" Hannah was startled and offended, all at once. The fortune-teller threw off her veil, and the Professor revealed herself. "So why have you been wasting all the money I left with you? Oh, and here's your tanner back." She threw a sixpence on the table.

"What do you mean wasting money?" Hannah said defensively, picking up the sixpence coin. "You dumped me, remember? You left me all by myself so you could go off and…and… And what are you doing telling fortunes underground? Oh my God, you are so weird…"

"It's research," the Professor said. "I want to know what sort of people consulted fortune tellers in London in 1851, and Tom out there is keeping a record of who visits me. Congratulations. Your visit has been noted."

Hannah snorted. "Whatever, but… Hey, why did you steal my dresses?"

"I didn't steal them," the Professor said. "I confiscated them. Turns out you won't be needing them anyway. Haven't you noticed how hard it is for you to go around alone when you're dressed like a lady?"

Hannah had noticed. In Dundee, nobody had ever asked her why she didn't have a chaperone. Here, everyone looked at her with concern.

The Professor stood up, and dusted off her own rather drab clothing. "There are very few advantages in 1851 to being a woman but not a lady," she said. "But one of them is freedom of movement. I have to watch myself a bit more carefully, but one reason I hired Tom was so I could have protection in the scary parts of London. You, on the other hand, have been harassed, I imagine, yes?"

It was true, of course. Hannah scowled.

"Come on," the Professor said, getting to her feet. "I could use a break."

At the tea stall, the Professor bought herself a cup of tea in a china mug, and a cup of hot chocolate for Hannah. "Pretty useless tunnel, isn't it?" she said, handing Hannah her steaming cocoa.

"I guess," Hannah said. "I mean, not many people seem to go all the way to the other side."

"That's because there's no point," the Professor said. "There's not much to

see in Rotherhithe, and it's a bit of a rough neighborhood. Plus who wants to traipse up and down an eighty-foot staircase when you can cross the river on a bridge? The tunnel is only a tourist attraction, really, and the novelty will wear off soon. Mind you, it's a spectacular accomplishment: The world's very first tunnel under a river. Too bad that the roads aren't wide enough for carriages, and Lord knows how they thought they could get horses down here. About ten years from now, this will be turned into part of the London Underground, the subway system."

The Professor drained her tea, and returned the cup to the tea stall. "Tom and I will escort you back to the ship," she told Hannah. "Tomorrow, you're going to the Great Exhibition. I'll see you onto the bus."

"Bus?" exclaimed Hannah.

"Yes, bus. You, my dear, have spent far too much money to take a taxi."

****

Lady Chatsfield's visitors were arriving, and Mr. Veeriswamy greeted them, taking their coats while Brandon, now dressed in his servant's livery, directed the carriage drivers to the back of Balesworth Hall. As the last guest arrived, Mr. Veeriswamy and Brandon followed her in.

"I travelled on a railway train!" she announced. She was a twittery little lady who introduced herself as Mrs. Baston-Hume, while her maid hovered nearby. "The journey was not in the least unpleasant. Have you ever travelled on a railway train, Veeris…Veer…I'm sorry, I cannot say your name."

Mr. Veeriswamy replied smoothly. "I have not yet had that pleasure, madam. Please address me as Vereham should you find it easier to do so."

"Well, Vereham," said Mrs. Baston-Hume, as her maid removed her coat, "I recommend a railway journey as altogether most satisfactory."

"Indeed, madam." Mr. Veeriswamy nodded as he took the coat from the maid, to whom he said quietly, "Please go downstairs to the servants' hall, and Mrs. Watson will serve you your tea." The maid gratefully followed the direction pointed by his outstretched gloved hand. Brandon was about to follow her, but Mr. Veeriswamy stopped him. "Brandon, remain here until you are sent for. There may be other guests to follow."

Brandon had been looking forward to the freshly-baked scones he had seen cooling in the kitchen, and he hoped Mrs. Watson would save one or two for him. He sighed, and, checking that the butler was out of sight, sank into one of the hall chairs.

Less than a minute later, he jumped up hastily as he heard Mr. Veeriswamy's feet descending the grand staircase. Brandon was also surprised because, usually, the butler used the servants' narrow dark stairway.

Mr. Veeriswamy had spotted Brandon rising from the chair, and he opened his mouth to rebuke him, but at that moment, Lady Chatsfield appeared on the landing, and called out, "Sanjeev!" When she saw Brandon, she exclaimed, "Oh!" Brandon was fascinated to hear that Lady Chatsfield apparently knew at least one word in her butler's native language.

Mr. Veeriswamy took a deep bow. Brandon shuffled awkwardly. Lady Chatsfield quickly gathered her senses. "Veeriswamy, the bell in the drawing room is broken. I shall ring for the servants from the Blue Room this afternoon, but please see that the bell is mended as soon as possible. Brandon, you will return to the drawing room with me."

Brandon assumed that he was wanted to serve tea to the ladies, and so he was a little surprised to be asked to sit down in front of an audience of assembled guests. That was when he realized with dismay that it was time to do his performing trick. He slumped in his seat under the expectant gaze of seven pairs of eyes.

Lady Chatsfield cleared her throat and introduced him. "This is my footman Brandon, whom I have asked to address you on the subject of slavery, and who will entertain your questions." With that, she sat down. All eyes snapped back to Brandon. There was an awkward silence, and Brandon could feel the tension radiating from Lady Chatsfield. If he didn't want to be thrown out of a job, he realized, he had better say something.

He cleared his throat, and began. "Slavery was… I mean… slavery is a bad thing." He struggled to remember his school textbook, and wished that he was as interested in American history as he was in European history. "Slaves got… get…whipped. All the time. And…shackles are put on them, on their legs… and stuff. And they have to work all day, picking cotton. Sometimes they run away…and…" Suddenly his eyes lit up as he remembered getting an answer right on a test. "And the Underground Railroad helps them!"

There was a polite silence. Evidently, the ladies were expecting more. But Brandon didn't have more. He turned round and looked pleadingly at Lady Chatsfield, who gave him only a cold hard stare, and a nod to go on.

Brandon exhaled sharply. Then he said, "Any questions?"

An elderly woman raised a slightly trembling hand. "Yes. Have you been free for very long?"

Brandon glanced again at Lady Chatsfield, whose stony face spoke volumes. "Yes," he said carefully. "A long time."

The elderly woman looked curiously at him. "Surely you have been free for only a few years, for you are very young, I believe."

"Yes," said Brandon guardedly. "Only a few years."

"Was it dreadful being a slave?" asked another lady from the back.

"Oh, yes," said Brandon eagerly. "Horrible. Terrible. I was whipped. Lots of times."

The group looked uncertainly at him. One rather skeptical-looking old lady sitting by the window said, "Well, surely you can tell us more than that. Where were you enslaved?"

"In Georgia," said Brandon. "Snipesville."

"Never heard of it," snorted the woman. "And why do you not have an American accent? You sound as English as I do."

Lady Chatsfield hurriedly explained. "Brandon has lived in England for several years."

"How long exactly?" asked the sharp-eyed old woman.

"I don't remember," Brandon replied lamely.

"Well, it does rather seem to me that you have forgotten a great many things," said the old lady, or, as Brandon now thought of her, the old dragon. She looked piercingly at Brandon, who avoided her gaze.

"I have a question," Mrs. Baston-Hume said timorously. "May I touch your hair?"

Brandon now felt like a performing poodle, but he obligingly went up to the lady and leaned down. She grasped his hair, and immediately let go. "It looks like lambs' wool," she said, giggling to the ladies on either side of her, "but it certainly doesn't feel like it."

Lady Chatsfield now got to her feet. "If there are no further questions, Brandon will return to his duties below stairs. Ladies, may I offer you more tea? " There was a buzz of happy agreement, and Lady Chatsfield quietly told Brandon to ask Mrs. Watson to send up refreshments.

As Brandon slowly walked away, he overheard Mrs. Baston-Hume mutter to her neighbor, "I'm afraid he was not nearly as entertaining as that nice Mr. Douglass." Just before he reached the door, another woman grabbed his hand, and put a shilling into it. He gazed at it blankly, before realizing it was a tip.

Brandon returned to the kitchen feeling more embarrassed than he had ever done in his life. No, it was worse than embarrassment. It was humiliation. Lady Chatsfield had humiliated him, had forced him to pretend he was a former slave when he was nothing of the kind. If anything, he felt more like a slave now than at any other time in his life, for he knew that his job, his living, depended on his willingness to degrade himself. It was awful. He wondered if that was how slaves felt, too. Maybe he should have talked to the ladies about that. Too late now.

That evening, Brandon was slumped in a chair in the servants' hall, feeling depressed, and trying to read a book that Henry had brought him from the library, much to his surprise. Unfortunately, it was a staggeringly dull old history of Hertfordshire. The best that could be said of it was that it made Brandon long for sleep. He couldn't help obsessing over the events of that afternoon, and wondered if he should quit his job in protest at Lady Chatsfield's treatment of him. But where would he go?

Unexpectedly, Mr. Veeriswamy approached him and said gently, "That was a very good deed you performed this afternoon, Brandon. I am well aware that you were never a slave, but the ladies were not, and Her Ladyship informs me that your talk helped her to raise the considerable sum of twenty pounds for the Anti-Slavery Society."

Brandon brushed off the compliment. He still felt gross about the whole thing.

Mr. Veeriswamy smiled, and his eyes crinkled as he lowered his voice, so as not to be heard by the other servants. "I am about to tell you something that I forbid you to repeat to anyone, you understand?"

Brandon nodded, and Mr. Veeriswamy continued. "You may be interested to know that Her Ladyship's mother was among those present. That esteemed lady is well known as an attentive observer and listener, and I assure you that her reputation is well earned. She quickly discerned that it was Her Ladyship and not you who conceived the idea of presenting you as a former slave. She roundly scolded her daughter for the deception, and obtained a promise from her that you will not be punished for your unconvincing performance."

A light went on in Brandon's head, and he said, "Wait...Was she the tall old lady who sat next to the window?" The dragon, he thought to himself.

Mr. Veeriswamy nodded, and Brandon knew now why the old woman had seemed so familiar. She was Verity's great-great-great... Oh, never mind. He got it. Wow, that made sense. He smiled to himself.

Mr. Veeriswamy was holding a magnifying glass to a newspaper as it lay on the table, reading the tiny print. Suddenly, he asked everyone in the servants' hall to be quiet so that he could speak. Mrs. Watson laid down her sewing in her lap, and prepared to listen attentively. Mr. Veeriswamy often liked to read aloud from the newspaper, but Brandon zoned out when he did. Victorian British writing went on and on, and Brandon had never heard of most of the people and places described.

But what Mr. Veeriswamy read today had Brandon's ears perking up. It was all about the Great Exhibition.

"I want to go to that!" Brandon exclaimed.

Mr. Veeriswamy peered at him. "Oh, I doubt you may, Brandon. True, there is a debate raging about whether the working classes ought to be allowed into the Crystal Palace, and gentlemen have proposed that there should be special days when the price of admission is only one shilling, to permit the common people to visit. But the Palace is closed on Sundays, and the shilling days will not include Saturdays, when most common people have time to attend."

Mrs. Watson protested. "Well, I don't think that's fair. I've heard so much about the Exhibition from you, Mr. Veeriswamy, and I hoped to see it. Do you think Her Ladyship would allow us time away to go up to London?"

"I have no idea," said Mr. Veeriswamy, "but I shall approach her on the subject. For myself, I am very keen to see the curiosities from India." He smiled.

The answer came the very next day. Mr. Veeriswamy announced that Lady Chatsfield wished to speak with everyone in the servants' hall.

The servants rose to their feet respectfully when she entered the room. She paused in the doorway, looking awkward, and cleared her throat. "I understand from Mr. Veeriswamy that several of you have expressed an interest in paying a visit to the Exhibition of the Industry of All Nations. I regret that I cannot be inconvenienced by the frequent absences of my servants, particularly when Balesworth Hall is understaffed."

Faces fell, and she hurried to add, "However, I may have arrived at a solution to this particular difficulty. Provided that you pay for your own tickets and railway fare, I am prepared to permit those of you who wish to attend to accompany me when I visit on Wednesday. "

Mrs. Watson raised her hand, and Lady Chatsfield acknowledged her.

"Begging your pardon, Your Ladyship, but that would mean we would have to pay the five shillings admission price, and the cost of the railway ticket."

Lady Chatsfield looked sympathetic. "I appreciate that this may present some difficulties. However, I am offering to allow the time to those of you who have diligently saved money. Those of you who are able may attend. The finances of the estate simply do not permit me to present you with a more generous offer."

CHAPTER TWELVE

There was some shuffling and Brandon suspected that everyone would have grumbled if they could.

"I do intend to make an exception for Brandon," said Lady Chatsfield.

What? Wasn't he allowed to go at all? Had his performance for the ladies really ticked her off that much?

But Lady Chatsfield continued: "I have already decided to make a charitable gesture to pay for Henry to visit the Exhibition and thus further his education. Brandon may accompany us, as Henry's companion."

Great, an unpaid babysitter, thought Brandon. Still, at least he could go. Meanwhile, judging from the murderous looks on the faces of some of the junior staff, this decision would not make him popular.

When Lady Chatsfield and Mr. Veeriswamy left the room, the servants vented their anger. "I haven't had more than a half day off since last year," complained Jane, the senior housemaid. "I got my heart set on seeing the Exhibition. And I'm tired of being passed over. You know, I think I'm going to ask Lady Chatsfield for a reference. I've heard tell that there's a senior housemaid's post at Benton Manor, and I might just apply for that."

"Ooh, do you think they might have a place for me, too?" asked Flora, the junior housemaid.

"Now don't be hasty, you two," said Mrs. Watson.

"I don't mean no disrespect," said Jane, "but you and Mr. Veeriswamy can afford to go, can't you? I can't. And anyway, it hasn't been the same at Balesworth Hall since old Lord Chatsfield died. I'm doing the work of three housemaids, and now Her Ladyship wants me and Flora to help her with dressing in the morning, and undressing last thing. I'm sick to death of it. Every landed family around here is prospering, except this one. I can't understand it."

Then Roberts, the quiet carriage driver, spoke. "It's because of the money being tied up. The last young Lord Chatsfield didn't leave a will, and his money's all tied up in court, with the lawyers arguing over who gets what. And Lady Chatsfield can't do nothing about it, certainly not until His Lordship, her husband, comes back. If he comes back."

Brandon was amazed by how much these people knew about their employer's business. Then again, considering that they lived with their employer, and that she controlled their lives but had very little contact with them, perhaps their gossip and curiosity wasn't such a surprise.

Mrs. Watson tutted. "And he's only a Viscount, and that's practically the lowest rank of aristocracy." While this was true, it had nothing to do with the conversation, and so everyone fell into silence just as Mr. Veeriswamy returned.

He looked at all of them with suspicion. Brandon, however, was not paying attention. He was thinking about the fact that he, Brandon, would be the only kid from the twenty-first century ever to visit the Great Exhibition. How cool was that? Mr. Veeriswamy saw him daydreaming, and sent him upstairs to dust the library.

When he entered the library Brandon groaned inwardly. Henry and Sarah were already there. Henry was reading, as usual, but Sarah was sitting in the window seat, forlornly gazing outside. Brandon hoped that they would tell him to come back later, but no such luck: Henry liked to taunt Brandon with the fact that he was uniquely privileged, and he was happy to have him working in the same room. Sarah barely noticed him at all.

"This is a fascinating book, Brandon," Henry said. "It is Charles Darwin's account of the voyage of the Beagle."

Brandon refused to take the bait. Anyway, he didn't know much about Darwin, except that a lot of people in Snipesville were offended by his theory of evolution. Brandon suddenly wished he had Alex's interest in science. He made a note to ask Alex about Darwin when he saw him again. If he ever saw him again.

Undaunted, Henry kept on "oohing" and "aahing" as he turned the pages, trying (rather successfully) to make Brandon jealous. After a few minutes of this, Sarah unexpectedly turned around and ordered Henry out of the room. Henry, taken aback, was instantly humbled, and, apologizing to Sarah, made a swift departure with his book.

Brandon carried on dusting, pretending that nothing had happened, but the silence in the room hung heavy.

"Are you settling in well?" Sarah asked him.

It was an awkward, formal question, but Brandon answered honestly. He sighed heavily, and put down his duster. "I guess. It's really hard work, and the pay is lousy, plus I hate working all the time. I wouldn't mind some time off."

Sarah was astounded by his reply. Servants normally answered politely, and smiled at her. But she was also intrigued. "You don't sound much like a servant," she said. "You haven't always been a servant, have you? Mama said that formerly you were an undertaker's mute."

"That's right," Brandon said. "And before that, I was in a coal mine."

"Really?" Sarah exclaimed, sitting up eagerly. "What was that like?"

"Awful," Brandon said, and he described it to her. She was fascinated, and asked all sorts of questions about coal mining, many of which he could not

CHAPTER TWELVE

answer. Finally, he suggested that she read about the subject if she was so interested in it. But Sarah looked away, and pretended that he had not spoken.

In the silence, Brandon plucked up the courage to turn the tables, and ask her a question. "Miss Sarah, why do you put up with Henry? He's such an annoying kid."

She looked waveringly at him, trying to decide whether the question was too disrespectful. But she wanted to answer it, and so she did. "He is my best friend," she said. "Actually, since we removed to Balesworth Hall, he is my only friend. I still write to my old friends, but Henry is the only friend I see." She looked very wistful, and then, suddenly, she straightened up, and said, "Perhaps we ought not to talk about this. It is a private matter." With that, she turned back to look out of the window, at the huge private park for which she had no other playmates, except the irritating Henry.

Brandon knew he had been dismissed, and he resented Sarah for it.

Chapter 13:
TEN THOUSAND WINDOWS

The Professor showed up the next day, with her assistant Tom, to see Hannah to the bus stop. But as the bus approached, they said goodbye to her and walked away, which was fine with Hannah.

The bus was a horse-drawn carriage, along which ran a thin painted stripe on which were listed its destinations: Strand, Exhibition, Bank... and many more. Another small sign helpfully explained that the bus would also stop at the Great Exhibition. Advertisements covered almost all other space on the outside of the bus, except the windows. Passengers were already crowded onto the outside top deck, and Hannah wondered how they had managed to get up there.

"Going to the Crystal Palace, Miss?" the conductor called from his perch. Like the driver and many of the passengers, he was wearing a tall hat and a long black coat.

"What, are you psychic or something?" Hannah called back.

"Just looking for business, Miss," the conductor said apologetically. He stepped down from the running board and helped her on, before taking Hannah's three pennies, and closing the door behind her. Her head lowered, she squeezed into the last available seat, next to the door. Her knees were pressed uncomfortably against those of the woman sitting next to her. Now the bus resumed its journey, and lurched along uncomfortably and slowly, through the London traffic.

Hannah's mood improved dramatically as she waited in line outside the Crystal Palace. Now this is a mall, she thought. A giant shopping mall! Maybe this wouldn't be such a huge bore after all. She didn't have much money left, only a pound, but that would surely buy her a souvenir or two... or three.

At the entrance turnstile, a man in a cap asked her for five shillings entrance fee.

"Five shillings? Wow, that's expensive!" Hannah blurted out.

He shrugged. "Maybe, Miss, but that's the only way to assure the respectability of our patrons. Count your blessings, Miss, because this is the first day the price has come down from a pound."

As Hannah took her ticket, she tried to remember how many shillings made a pound. Twenty shillings, that was it. Nearly two months wages in Dundee. That makes Disneyland tickets seem cheap, she thought. And the ticket collector was right: The high prices certainly kept out the riff-raff. Everyone around her, judging from the clothes and atmosphere, was solidly middle- or upper-class. When, Hannah wondered, had she started thinking about what class people were? Weird.

Inside the Crystal Palace, Hannah followed the crowd to the crystal fountain at the center of the building, where the transept (the short part of the cross-shaped building) met the nave (the long part), giving a view of the Palace in every direction. The fountain itself was like a transparent, watery, towering wedding cake, and it was surrounded by palm trees in pots, and enormous elm trees that reached up to the iron rafters.

Glass… potted palms…indoor trees… It was all incredibly familiar. This has got to be, Hannah decided, the very first shopping mall! But what was she supposed to be doing here? The Professor had never said. So maybe the best thing was just to do what came naturally, and go shop. Clutching her purse tightly, she headed westward down the nave.

On her left, a large section was helpfully labeled *INDIA* by a small sign hanging from the balcony above it. An Indian man in traditional dress, with a sash and turban, was chatting animatedly in Hindi with another Indian man, who was in Western clothing. Visitors stared even more at them than they did at the huge stuffed elephant wearing a golden dress and a canopied passenger seat on its back.

A mother and daughter, their backs to Hannah, were admiring the elephant. "I wonder how it died, Mama?" said the girl, who was wearing a frilly white dress with white, equally frilly bloomers, and a huge beribboned sun-hat.

"Never mind that, Sarah," said her mother, who wore a bonnet and a dress in bright blue satin. "Let us hear what Veeriswamy and his new acquaintance can tell us about this method of conveyance."

Having no interest in mother, daughter, or elephant, Hannah continued on her wandering tour. Her next stop was a court labeled *BIRMINGHAM*, where a young exhibitor mistook her entrance for enthusiasm. "Good morning, Miss," he said. "I trust you are enjoying your day?"

"I just got here," said Hannah without returning his smile.

He was baffled by her rudeness, but tried again. "Perhaps, if I may, I might interest you in the manufactures of my home city, Birmingham?"

Hannah looked coldly at him. But he was persistent, and shepherded her through the exhibit area. "Kindly allow me to show you some of the objects that might be of interest to a young lady such as yourself."

She followed him to a glass counter, which she hoped would be full of jewelry. But he pulled out a display case of buttons and needles.

"I don't sew," said Hannah bluntly. "Don't you have earrings or anything?"

He looked at her uncertainly, and she could swear he was staring at the stains on her dress as he tried to figure out what class she belonged to.

"No, alas, I regret that I do not," he said hurriedly, reaching for another item. "Aha! Here is the latest in writing implements, the modern replacement for the trusty quill." He brought out a metal ink pen. "This, for example, is manufactured in Birmingham, using Sheffield steel..." He handed it to Hannah, who examined it closely.

"Where's the ink go?" she asked.

"The ink?" The man blinked. "I regret that this is not a fountain pen, for those clever new inventions are still not quite designed to my company's standards, and so it may be some time before we manufacture them..."

"So you kind of have to dip this in ink?" Hannah asked skeptically.

The man looked awkward. "Well, yes..."

Hannah put it down again. "Big whoop. Look, I gotta go."

As she swept away, the young man thought to himself that it was going to be a very long day.

****

Brandon was stuck with Henry, but he was determined, all the same, to have a good time at the Great Exhibition. "Hey, Birmingham," he said eagerly, pointing to the city's exhibit sign. "I used to live near there, in the Black Country!"

"How appropriate," said Henry sarcastically. "Come along, I want to see the Medieval Court, don't you?"

Brandon was baffled. Medieval? The Middle Ages? Like knights and castles? What does that have to do with an exhibition about modern industry? And why did they put it between Birmingham and Australia? How did anyone put all those together?

But Henry was already admiring a collection of silver chalices, cups used for church communions. Brandon surveyed the Medieval Court: There was a statue of the Virgin Mary, and various bits of furniture that reminded him of church spires. In fact, wasn't that an actual church spire over there?

A young exhibitor approached them. "These objects are all made in Birmingham, young sirs. As I was just explaining to a young lady of about your age a few minutes ago, the variety of manufactures in Birmingham is truly astonishing."

Brandon couldn't see the point. "But why do you use all this new technology to make stuff that looks old?"

The man wondered why there were so many difficult children among the visitors that morning, but he explained patiently, "It is the fashion, you see, the Gothic style. Manufacturing merely allows more people to own these objects of fashion and beauty."

Brandon didn't know what to say to that, so he thanked the exhibitor, who seemed relieved to see the back of him, and who went off to chat with some nice adult customers.

Brandon was just about to follow Henry to the next exhibit when someone caught him by the arm. "'Ere, it's Brandon, in't it? Brandon, don't you recognize me? It's me, Ben, from the mine in Hitherton."

Brandon was amazed and delighted, and he greeted Ben warmly.

Ben, meanwhile, admired Brandon's smart clothing. "Look at you! Looks like you went to London and made something of yourself, after all."

"Well, you too," Brandon said. "I mean, it costs a fortune to get into the Great Exhibition."

"Nah, I only paid a shilling," Ben said. "I'm here with a group of us who are emigrating to Australia tomorrow, and some kind gentleman persuaded the organizers to allow us in for only a shilling, since we won't have another chance to come to the Exhibition."

"You're going to Australia?" Brandon said, astonished. "But why?"

Ben smiled. "I reckon I'll have a chance for a better life out there. No more mines for me, Brandon. I'll be a sheep farmer, I reckon. It can't be worse than my life in Hitherton. Mind you, I'll miss the Black Country. But I have to take my chances while I get them, 'aven't I? Just like you."

"Yeah," Brandon said. "Just like me."

****

Alex had given Jupe money to pay for an omnibus, but after Jupe watched a horse-drawn bus careen down the street, he had decided to walk. It was a windy day, but there were very few clouds in the sky, and while he was nervous about walking through London by himself, he wanted to see something of the city. He had been suffering from cabin fever in Carhart's Hotel, so when Alex had proposed to him that he visit the Exhibition, he had jumped at the chance.

And, anyway, the walk wasn't too far.

Mr. Thornhill had forbidden him to leave the hotel, but Alex had assured him that he wouldn't get in trouble. "Mr. Thornhill never leaves the American section, even for lunch. He's always busy. So long as you stay well away from there, it's guaranteed you won't be spotted."

Now, as Jupe approached the Crystal Palace on his walk through Hyde Park, he was amazed at the sight. The Palace was the most magnificent thing he had ever seen, greater than any building in Savannah, even greater than the buildings he had seen on his carriage ride through London. Hesitantly, he paid his money at the south entrance, as Alex had instructed, and walked inside. At that moment, a toddler dashed in front of him, and Jupe almost tripped over the kid. The little boy's mother scolded him, and then apologized to Jupe.

No white person had ever apologized to Jupe. "Thank you, ma'am," he said with a smile.

The woman's older son looked at him wonderingly. "Are you an American?"

Jupe had never been asked that question before. "Yes, I guess I am. Yes, sir."

The boy turned excitedly to his mother, and said, "Mama, this is a real American slave!"

But Jupe was quick to disagree. "No, I ain't a slave no more," he rushed to assure them. "I'm free."

The mother looked at him curiously. "But, if I may be so bold to ask, were you a slave when you lived in America?"

Jupe nodded. "Yes, ma'am. In Georgia."

"How dreadful for you," she said, a hand to her chest. "You must be so pleased to be here in the land of the free."

"I reckon so, ma'am," said Jupe with an obliging smile. It was nice to be the center of attention, and even nicer to have white people speak to him like he was a real human being.

"I wish you well," said the woman admiringly, as she gathered up her sons and went to look for her husband. Jupe, a new spring in his step, walked into the magical world laid out before him.

****

"But I don't understand," said the elderly clergyman to Alex as they stood before the McCormick Reaper, a state-of-the-art American farming machine. "This reaping machine looks thoroughly flimsy to me, and I cannot believe that it is any sort of improvement on British manufactures."

Alex, for the umpteenth time, repeated the pitch he had learned from Mr.

Meredith. "No sir, it's stronger than it looks, and its light weight helps farmers to reap more efficiently. In fact, with this, you can clear up to twenty acres of land a day."

"I'm not sure I believe it," sniffed the old man, tugging at his clerical collar.

"There are plans for a demonstration in England soon, sir," Alex said wearily. "This McCormick reaper will compete in a trial with another American machine."

The old man raised an eyebrow. "Well, I shall look forward to reading about it in the newspapers. I've come all the way from Hastings, you see, so I doubt I shall return for a demonstration. And you are from America, are you, young man?"

Alex nodded. "Yes, sir. I live in Georgia."

"I see," said the old vicar. "You are aware, I suppose, that slavery was ended in the British colonies in 1833? When do you think that the wicked practice of slavery will be ended in the United States of America?"

"Eighteen sixty-five," Alex said bluntly. He was fed up with having to defend slavery. It was all the Brits wanted to talk about.

"Good Lord," said the vicar, brightening. "Have proposals been made to that effect? I had no idea. How splendid."

And with that, he wandered off before Alex had a chance to tell him that it was not political debate but the Civil War that would end slavery. Probably just as well, he thought. It was best not to confuse the man any more than he already had.

Now Mr. Meredith approached. "Look, Day, Mr. Thornhill and I were just thinking, why don't you take a couple of hours to inspect the other exhibits? There are some mighty impressive sights. Now, don't be late back, because we need you here."

Alex was delighted by the offer, and not only because he wanted a break from discussing agricultural equipment. Perhaps he might find Jupe, and then they could enjoy the Exhibition together.

He did not get far. In the American section, beneath the sign for New York, his attention was caught by a man with unruly hair, a full beard, and a New England accent, who was standing in front of a glass case full of handguns, brandishing a revolver before an impressed crowd of onlookers

"Now, ladies and gentlemen, you will see here how smoothly this revolving barrel operates. I, Colonel Samuel Colt, guarantee to you that this is the finest New World craftsmanship, the inferior of none that you will find, even here in London. See how my revolver's barrel does not interfere with the line of sight, for it falls below it at full-cock. You just cock the hammer as with any pistol, and then fire up to six shots without reloading, in rapid succession if you wish. Let me show you the ease of loading. Why, even a child could do it. You there, young man, step up, if you would…"

Alex suddenly realized that Colt was pointing to him. Hesitantly, he stepped forward, and Colt carefully handed him the revolver. "Now, young sir, this revolver is not yet loaded, but you are wise to handle every firearm with care. Note its exquisite appearance. Yet it is affordable to purchase and repair, should repair ever be needed, for it is mass-produced by my patented system of manufacture of interchangeable parts."

Actually, the first thing Alex noted about the gun was how heavy it was. He had never held a gun before, not even a BB gun. This revolver was a foot long, and his hand shook as he struggled to keep it upright. He could see a drawing of sailing ships engraved on the revolving chamber. Colt stood to one side of Alex, and carefully loaded the gun for him. He took almost a minute to finish, and when he was done, Alex found himself holding a loaded pistol. He didn't like it.

Colt, meanwhile, was once again extolling the virtues of his amazing invention. Alex coughed, desperately wanting him to take away the loaded gun. Finally, Colt reached over and reclaimed his invention from Alex. "Thank you for your assistance…"

"Um, sure, but don't you think these are dangerous?" Alex said, shaking his hand to ease the cramp.

Colonel Colt laughed, along with some in the crowd. "Why, of course it's dangerous! That's the general idea."

"Little chap has a point, mind you," boomed a tall man in a moustache. "I can hardly see the sense of owning one of your guns in England. It's not as though I have to defend my gold mine from Indian attack, or whatnot."

The crowd laughed again: It was very fashionable to laugh at Americans and their wild country.

If Colonel Colt was put out, he didn't show it. He smiled and said, "I do believe that my weapons are of value to the British gentleman who seeks to defend his home. I know for certain that these weapons are important to the British Army, for I have this very day demonstrated this same revolver to senior officers, who are most interested in purchasing my wares. You, sir, what is your name, may I ask?"

"Standford," said the loud man. "Sir Henry Standford."

"In that case," said Colt, hurriedly emptying the chamber of bullets, "allow me, sir, to make a present of my revolver to you, Sir Henry, with my compliments."

Sir Henry was astonished and flattered, and he accepted the gun from Colt, as an excited buzz passed through the crowd. Wow, Alex thought, this guy is quite a salesman.

Alex's next stop was to gawp at several gigantic statues of naked angels carrying swords. What caught his attention after that was an exhibit in the India section: A stuffed elephant in magnificent costume.

But Alex grew puzzled as he approached the elephant. For an Asian elephant, it was very large. Standing close to the creature's head, he peered under its head covering. If he could just see its ears, he could confirm his hunch that this was actually an African elephant masquerading as an Asian elephant...

He suddenly became aware that someone was watching him, and turned to see an Indian man with an amused smile.

"So you have discovered that this Indian is an imposter?" he said to Alex. "I noticed it also. I have learned that it belongs to a museum in Essex. The Indian exhibitor told me that this howdah, the covering, arrived without an elephant on which to display it. Fortunately, he was able to arrange to borrow this animal. Then, to his horror, he finds it is an African elephant. This is why he hastily added material to the headdress to disguise the ears. So this is a British elephant, pretending to be an African elephant, pretending to be an Indian elephant!"

Alex laughed, but the man now looked thoughtful. "I suppose that we all, at some time or other, pretend to be something we are not. We are all imposters. Do you not agree?"

Alex was about to say "Not really," but Mr. Veeriswamy was walking away, for Lady Chatsfield had called him over.

****

Soon after Hannah left the Birmingham exhibit, she was excited to spot a small booth displaying handbags from Morocco, and she picked out one she liked. But the exhibitor, a Moroccan man in a turban, told her that the exhibits were not for sale.

Now that she knew the Great Exhibition was not a mall after all, she was in a lousy mood. It wasn't helped by her growing fear that her visit to the Exhibition was one of the Professor's wild goose chases, and that she would return to the steamer that night no closer to finding a way home. She was bored, antsy, and, most of all, hungry. She followed a sign that said *REFRESHMENTS*, illustrated by a drawing of a human hand, its index finger pointing to the Palace's transept.

The refreshment area was crowded. The large dresses of the women customers practically filled the room, and the best anyone could do was to sit within reaching distance of a table, while balancing a teacup and saucer in their lap. Hannah found a seat by a family composed of a husband with mutton-chop whiskers, his wife, and their two sons. A harried-looking young waitress in a dirty dress appeared to take their orders.

The young mother ordered sandwiches, cakes, coffee, and for the children, soda water. "May I have an ice, please, Mama?" asked the older boy, pointing to a freezer full of ice-creams, which was powered by a noisy steam-engine.

"Not for a shilling you won't," declared his father. "It's sheer robbery. We'll have ices after we leave, Edward."

"And for you, madam?" The grim-faced waitress didn't even look at Hannah as she asked, but stared at her notebook instead, pencil poised.

Hannah hesitated. "I guess I'll have a tea and… How much are the pork pies?"

"Sixpence."

"Wow, that is expensive," said Hannah. "But okay, I guess."

The young mother turned to Hannah. "I'm afraid the prices are very high. We considered taking the children elsewhere to eat, but once one has left the Crystal Palace, I understand, one cannot return, except upon payment of another admission fee."

"That's a total rip-off," exclaimed Hannah.

The lady nodded. "Yes, my husband rather thinks so, too… Still, we are enjoying the most wonderful time here, and it is so instructive for the boys. They have learned so much that is edifying."

"I can't say I'm enjoying it," Hannah said gloomily. "It's so random. And what's the point, when we can't even buy any of the stuff on show?"

"Oh, but one day we shall!" the mother replied gleefully. "What promise this new industrial age holds! Each gentleman shall own a mansion, and each lady shall be surrounded by furnishings fit for a queen. Do you not believe that is true?"

"Um," Hannah grunted, looking at her fingernails. But she did think about her own large house and the Johnsons' enormous home, back in modern Snipesville.

As they waited for their refreshments, Hannah became uncomfortably aware that she needed to use the bathroom. But where were the restrooms? She asked the lady next to her, who immediately looked embarrassed that Hannah had brought up the indelicate subject of toilets. Lowering her voice so that her husband could not hear, she said, "I have heard that there are water closets in the retiring room."

Hannah looked at her blankly. Water closets? Surely she could not mean flushing toilets? With a huge smile, Hannah called over one of the waitresses to ask for directions.

She found the "retiring room," and it was, indeed, a real restroom. The regular sound of flushing was music to her ears. An old lady standing in line with her said giddily, "Isn't this splendid? What a wonder of the modern age." She held up a huge bronze coin. "Look, I have my penny ready!"

"What for?" Hannah asked. The answer came as they watched another lady fiddle with placing a penny in a slot on the door.

"We have to pay to pee?" Hannah exclaimed. The old lady tutted and looked away, offended by Hannah's coarseness.

Grudgingly, Hannah pulled a penny from her purse. It was worth the expense to use a flushing toilet. And judging from the long lines, lots of people felt the same way.

By the time Hannah returned to the refreshment area, the food, if it could be called that, had arrived. The thin sandwiches were so old, they were curling at the edges. The coffee and tea were not steaming at all. Only the soda water looked fresh and appealing.

Hannah contemplated her sad little pork pie, and then took a bite of gristly pork and dry pastry. She washed it down with tea. The tea wasn't just unsweetened, it was cold, and possibly, it was not even tea. The family next to her looked unhappy with their food, too.

"The company has a deuced monopoly of the catering," said the outraged father. "I read about it in *The Times*. This company, Schweppes, was awarded the contract, and now they do as they please. I shall write a letter of a complaint."

Hannah wondered if this was the same Schweppes that made the Ginger Ale her mother had liked? Surely not.

The Victorian mother next to Hannah returned to explaining the educational benefits of bringing her sons to the Exhibition. "We saw a knife with no fewer than eighty blades, and an astonishing bed, which tips out the occupant when it is time to rise. And my sons and I have met a real American slave!"

Hannah wasn't really listening, and she took another tentative nibble from her dreadful pork pie. Suddenly, an excited thought struck her. "Did you say an American slave?"

"Yes," said the mother, as she held up a sandwich to her younger son to encourage the reluctant little boy to eat it. "Of course, he is no longer a slave, since he lives in England, but he is certainly a Negro, and he said he was from the state of Georgia."

Brandon! It had to be Brandon! "Where did you see him?" Hannah asked excitedly.

The lady gave Hannah a look of surprised delight. "Why, are you acquainted with him?"

Hannah spoke quickly, the words tumbling out. "Yes, he's a friend of mine, and I've been looking for him for, like, forever. Please, where did you see him?"

The lady nodded across the nave of the Exhibition, to the other side of the transept. "We met just inside the entrance over there. However, I rather doubt that he's still…"

But Hannah was already gone, moving as fast as she could in her heavy clothes.

Within ten minutes, Hannah was starting to despair of ever finding Brandon in the crowds that thronged the Crystal Palace. She had asked people if they had seen a black boy, only to be directed back to the Indian section, where an Indian man in a blue outfit with a pink sash and gold turban was among the exhibitors.

Turning back to the nave, Hannah wondered if she could hang around the exit to spot Brandon as he was leaving. But there were four exits. The situation seemed hopeless.

Just then, her heart leaped as she caught a momentary glimpse of dark, curly hair. She dashed through the crowd, which immediately cleared a way for the running girl in a large dress, and she almost collided with the boy before tapping him on the shoulder.

As he whirled around, she saw that he was not Brandon. "Uh, I'm sorry. I was looking for a friend who kind of looks like you."

"You have a friend here who looks like me?" asked Jupe excitedly. He was thrilled by the idea of meeting a black Englishman.

Now it was Hannah's turn to be surprised. "You're an American!" she said in wonderment.

"Yes, miss. I'm a free American," said Jupe proudly. "From Georgia."

Hannah was about to tell him that she lived in Georgia, too, when she felt a heavy hand on her own shoulder. She spun around in alarm.

CHAPTER THIRTEEN

"Looking for me?" asked Brandon with a grin. "And what's with the dress? You look like the Barbie doll my grandma uses for storing toilet rolls."

With a great and very unVictorian whoop, Hannah threw her arms around him.

They both talked over each other's sentences at first, until Hannah said, "Do you think Alex is here?"

"I don't know," said Brandon, "but it's going to be hard to find him among all these white people, especially with everyone dressed the same."

Henry and Jupe, meanwhile, stood by awkwardly, wondering if they were supposed to be part of the conversation. They eyed each other shyly.

"Excuse me," Henry asked Brandon, "but who are these people?" He indicated Hannah and Jupe.

"Sorry, Henry," said Brandon, reluctantly. "Um, this is my friend Hannah, and…" He looked at Jupe. "Sorry, but who are you?"

"My name's Jupe, sir."

Brandon looked curiously at him. "And you said you're from Georgia, right? Where do you stay?"

"I don't rightly know," said Jupe, "because I'm free now, but I was born at Kintyre Plantation, near Savannah."

"Where near Savannah?" Brandon asked urgently.

"Snipes County. You hear of it?"

Brandon's eyes widened, and so did Hannah's.

"Do you think that's a coincidence?" Hannah asked Brandon.

Brandon shook his head.

Henry was getting really fed up with not being the center of attention. "I say, what is going on?"

"Shut up, Henry," said Brandon. Henry was speechless at being spoken to like that. Brandon, meanwhile, had turned back to Jupe. "We're looking for another kid from Snipes County, a white guy called Alex."

Now Jupe was surprised. "Why, sir, I'm with a young gentleman from Georgia called Alex. Y'all might could find him in the United States exhibit. His name is Alexander Day."

"That's him!" Hannah and Brandon yelled simultaneously, and high-fived.

Hannah and Brandon asked Jupe and Henry to wait for them at the refreshment area. Hannah bribed Henry with two shillings for ice creams, before she and Brandon took off.

They explored what felt like every inch of the American section, but Alex was nowhere to be found. Finally, Hannah bent down and peered into a glass display case, as if her brother were invisibly hiding in it. She drew the attention of Mr. Meredith, who asked, "You looking for something, miss?"

Hannah had pulled out the calculator, and was now looking wonderingly at the little wooden box in her hands. "What is this doing here?" she gasped.

Mr. Meredith thought she was impressed. "Oh, that's the calculating engine. Yes, it's another fine example of American manufacture."

Hannah punched the buttons as he spoke and thought carefully about what to do next. "Well, it's pretty impressive," she said brightly as she put it back in the case. "Okay, I'm looking for… ALEX!"

She ran to her brother, and they fell into an ecstatic hug.

"Alex, is everything all right?" asked a voice from behind them.

Hannah looked up and saw the speaker, a well-dressed Englishman who was watching them with concern.

Alex reassured him. "Yes, Mr. Thornhill. This is my sister, Hannah. Hannah, this is my boss, Mr. Thornhill. He's a lawyer in Savannah, and we're here for the Exhibition."

"Hi, pleased to meet you," said Hannah, putting out a hand, which Mr. Thornhill observed with astonishment. He was almost as surprised by her English accent.

"You're English," he said. "How strange, when Alexander is American."

"Oh, we're both American," said Alex, "but we were, uh, separated at birth, and I came to England with my, uh, our mother. After the divorce."

Mr. Thornhill wasn't buying it. "But how did you recognize each other if you were separated at birth?"

Hannah thought quickly. "Alex, did you say we were separated at birth? You idiot. You meant we were separated from each other three years ago, didn't you? Anyway, great to meet you, Mr. Toadhall, but we…"

Just then, Mr. Meredith interrupted and saved the day. "Excuse me, Thornhill, but there's a gentleman over there who has some questions about the plough, and I'm in the middle of negotiations with a fellow from Manchester. Could you kindly help me out?"

Mr. Thornhill nodded, before turning back to Hannah. "It was a pleasure to meet you, Miss Day." He bowed.

As he left, Hannah grabbed Alex by the shoulders. "Who is that guy? Never mind, tell me later. Now let's go."

But Alex hissed at his sister, "I can't just leave…."

Now Brandon intervened. "Hannah, what are you doing for a living?"

"I'm kind of…" She tried to bluff, and immediately gave up. "Okay, I haven't got a job right now."

Brandon made up his mind what to do. "I've got to figure out how to get you two to Balesworth Hall with me. Hannah, stick with me. Alex, you have a steady job here, right?"

"Yes, I think so," Alex said uncertainly. He supposed it was a job, although he never seemed to do very much that was very useful.

Brandon pulled out a pencil and scrap of paper. "Okay, wait until I get in touch. Where do you live? What's your boss's full name? "

Quickly, Alex told Brandon, and Brandon wrote down the particulars of Carhart's Hotel.

"So what do you want me to do?" asked Hannah.

Brandon had an answer. "Balesworth Hall needs a new housemaid, and I think I can talk Mr. Veeriswamy into hiring you to replace Jane. You have experience as a housemaid, right?"

"No, of course I don't," Hannah said sourly.

"Yes, you do," Brandon insisted. "You're experienced. And you're very affordable. You will work for room, board, and a shilling a week. Got that?" Then he looked at Hannah's clothes. "But you're too posh… Look, can you dress kind of poor, and come to Balesworth tomorrow? You can take a train from…'

"Let me guess," Hannah interrupted, "Kings Cross Station?"

"No," Brandon shook his head. "They haven't finished building it. You need to depart from the temporary station at Maiden Lane, get off at Balesworth, and then walk. Just ask someone to give you directions to Balesworth Hall."

"Okay, I guess," Hannah said reluctantly. Thinking about the clothes in the travel trunk back at the steamer, she had an uncomfortable feeling that the Professor had known all along what was going to happen.

At that moment, Henry ran up, breathless. "Brandon… Mr. Veeriswamy… has been looking all over for you! Lady Chatsfield… has a headache… we must leave now."

Hannah asked Henry, "Where's that kid Julep, or whatever his name was?"

"Jupe?" asked Alex. "You met Jupe?"

"Yeah," said Hannah. "What's with that kid? How did he wind up here?"

But Mr. Thornhill's conversation with his customer was clearly coming to an end, and Alex thought it best for Hannah and Brandon to take off before there were more awkward questions.

Hurriedly, Brandon said, "Hannah, I'll expect you tomorrow sometime. Alex, we'll be in touch. Come on, Henry."

But Hannah suddenly remembered something. "Hey, Alex, is that the Professor's calculator over there in that glass case?"

"Yeah, it is, but it's…" Alex hesitated when he saw that Mr. Thornhill was frantically beckoning to him. He whispered to Hannah and Brandon, "Go, I'll catch up with you guys somehow!"

As Alex rushed to find out what Mr. Thornhill wanted, Hannah quickly slipped over to the display case, retrieved the calculator, and shoved it into her purse. Her hands shaking, she hurried toward the nearest exit as fast as her enormous skirts would allow.

Mr. Thornhill was not happy. "I heard your sister say that Jupe is here," he hissed at Alex. "Why is he here, against my express instructions? Do you know?"

Alex was nervous, but he decided to tell the truth. "He wanted to come, and I gave him the money. It didn't seem like a big deal…"

Mr. Thornhill scowled. "Oh, did you not? Well, allow me to explain. Jupe's presence is a distraction. The British have a bee in their bonnet about American slavery, and I have no desire to entertain endless debates on the subject with ladies, while I am attempting to do business with their husbands."

This made no sense to Alex. "I don't understand what that's got to do with Jupe. He doesn't even have to say he's with us. In fact, I told him to stay clear of the American section."

Mr. Thornhill looked over Alex's shoulder. "Obviously, he did not pay attention, because he is right behind you."

Jupe coughed nervously, afraid of what he was about to say next. "I was just wondering, sir, why did you want me not to come here? I've had fine conversations with English people, sir."

Mr. Meredith had appeared next to Mr. Thornhill, and he jerked his head at Jupe. "Who have we here?"

"This is Jupe," said Alex. "Mr. Thornhill set him free, and he doesn't want anyone to know about it."

Mr. Thornhill groaned, and Mr. Meredith smiled with amusement. "Well, Thornhill, you old rascal! I never knew you had abolitionist leanings."

"Shhh!" said a stony-faced Mr. Thornhill to Mr. Meredith. "Have you any idea what this would do to my business in Savannah if word got back to Georgia? Alexander, escort Jupe back to Carhart's."

Now Alex understood. He grabbed Jupe's arm, and turned up the aisle of the Crystal Palace, only to see Brandon headed in his direction with a small group of people. At the head of this group was the Indian man whom Alex had met earlier, and a finely-dressed lady wearing a pained expression.

Alex wondered who Brandon was with. But Mr. Thornhill was staring in shock at the lady. At that moment, she caught Mr. Thornhill's eye, and froze.

Collecting herself, Lady Chatsfield approached Mr. Thornhill. "What brings you here?"

"My business," said Mr. Thornhill, when he had recovered his voice. "Do not worry. I am not here to interfere where I am neither wanted nor needed. Are you well?"

She gave him a hard look of distaste. "As well as I can ever hope to be, thank you," she said icily. "I have made every effort to trace you during the past year. I regret to inform you that both of your brothers have died."

"Both?" Mr. Thornhill looked shocked and saddened. "But how?"

"Alfred was killed in a hunting accident," Lady Chatsfield said, "and you know that Charles was never a well man. He finally succumbed to consumption."

"But surely," Mr. Thornhill said desperately, "One of them had a son…"

"No, neither produced an heir," Lady Chatsfield said. "You must contact our solicitor, for you are now the Viscount Chatsfield, and you will need to decide what is to be done with the estate. In your absence, I have taken charge and occupancy of Balesworth Hall until I learn what it pleases you to do. But first, contact our solicitor. Come along, Veeriswamy."

As Lady Chatsfield and her butler walked away, Mr. Thornhill called after them, "Look after her, Veeriswamy."

Neither Mr. Veeriswamy or Lady Chatsfield turned around. But Sarah Chatsfield and Henry were now staring back at Mr. Thornhill. Suddenly, Sarah broke from the group, and ran to him. "Papa," she said pleadingly, "You are my Papa, aren't you? Won't you come home to Balesworth Hall with Mama and me?"

Meanwhile, Brandon had quietly sidled over to Alex. "Don't look now," said Brandon, "but I think Mr. Thornhill just ran into his wife. And that means that we're looking at Verity's great-great-grandparents."

Alex gaped in astonishment. Mr. Thornhill was Verity's ancestor? Wow.

Meanwhile, Mr. Thornhill had leaned down and kissed Sarah on the cheek, and put a hand on her shoulder. "One day," he said, "You will be old enough to understand. Now go, for your mother is waiting."

Chapter 14:
A DiFFERENT DAY

Hannah smoothed down her rough skirt as she sat alone in the open third-class carriage of the train to Balesworth, and sighed at the bittersweet memory of her pink dress. It had been so nice to be well-dressed, if only for a short time.

Entering a tunnel, the steam engine belched out smoke, and Hannah coughed hard as the train moved through the pitch blackness. As she emerged into the light, the train slowed on its approach to Welwyn station. As soon as the engine hissed to a halt, someone jumped out of the carriage behind, and ran up to her.

It was Jupe. He cried, "You're Miss Hannah!"

She was astonished to see him. "Julep! What are you doing here?"

"Jupe. My name's Jupe," he said, opening the gate and climbing up.

Hannah patted the seat next to her, inviting him to sit down. "Okay. In that case, my name's Hannah, not Miss Hannah. You make me sound like some old Southern biddy. Where are you headed?"

Jupe seemed troubled. "Mr. Thornhill sure was angry that I went to the Exhibition. He's sending me to where he found me a job, and he told me I had better not leave there."

"Yeah? What kind of job?"

"I don't rightly know, but he gave me this." He handed her a sealed envelope.

She took it from him, and turned it over. "But why haven't you opened it?"

Shaking his head, he said, "'T'ain't addressed to me."

Hannah closely examined the back of the envelope. "Look, the seal is almost broken, so why don't we open it? This is, like, your future. You've got a right to know what's up."

Jupe didn't look convinced, but when she gave the envelope back to him, he carefully peeled it open, pulled out the letter, and began to read the spidery writing, his brow furrowed.

Finally, he said, "I sure don't know what to make of this. What do you think?" He handed it back to her with a perplexed look.

Hannah read over the letter, and raised her eyebrows. "I have no clue, but this is really interesting. And it's bizarre that we're headed to the same place. Who is this Thornhill guy, anyway?"

CHAPTER FOURTEEN

****

That evening at Balesworth Hall, Brandon found himself alone in the kitchen with Henry and Mrs. Watson. "So, Henry," Brandon asked as casually as he could, "Where were you born?"

Not for the first time, Henry looked at him as though he were an idiot. "Here," he said abruptly, immediately returning his attention to the carrots he was slicing.

"Where's here?" Brandon persisted. "At your house, right?"

"Oh, now, there's a story," chimed in Mrs. Watson. She stopped beating a cake batter, put down her a wooden spoon, and wiped her brow with her apron. "In those days, I helped out at Balesworth Hall only from time to time, like, and I was helping to prepare a big dinner for old Lord Chatsfield's visitors, when I could tell it was time for the baby to come. Well, I couldn't just stop work, could I? So I carried on pulling the leaves off the cabbage. Next thing I knew, the baby was on the way. I wanted to lie down right here in the kitchen, but the old cook, Mr. Baylis, he wouldn't hear of such a thing. There wasn't time for nothing else, so they heaved me into an old wheelbarrow and the gardening boy ran with me all the way home! Henry was born right there in the front room of my house, and hardly a moment to spare."

"But Mother," protested Henry, "You always said I was born in Balesworth Hall!"

Mrs. Watson gave her son an indulgent look. "No, dear, you're just confused. I told you I started labor here, but you were born at our house. The gardener's boy fetched Granny to help."

"Yeah, I could see how that story could get confused," said Brandon. "By the way, where is your house?" He tried to ask as casually as he could.

Mrs. Watson threw some flour into the cake batter. "Quite a ways from here" she said, "which is why Henry and me lodge in the housekeepers' quarters these days."

Henry explained. "It's about a quarter mile past the grammar school at the end of the High Street, on the left."

Brandon knew the only time he could check out the house was during his half-days off. Otherwise, his time belonged to Lady Chatsfield, just like that of all the servants. Fortunately, he thought, his next half-day was tomorrow.

Loud knocking at the back door startled everyone. Henry dropped his knife and carrot on the table, and rushed to answer. When he opened the door, standing there, dripping wet, were Jupe and Hannah.

"Can I help you?" asked Henry, astonished by the sight. At first, he didn't recognize Hannah from the Exhibition, although he certainly recognized Jupe, who was running his fingers through his hair to shake loose the glistening droplets of water.

"Yeah," said Hannah. "I'm your new housemaid, and this here's your new junior footman." She jerked her thumb at Jupe.

Mr. Veeriswamy arrived from upstairs just in time to catch the introduction. He looked skeptically at the two youngsters standing in the doorway. "It is true that we require a new housemaid," he said, "but I shall need a character from your former employer before I can consider you for the position. And we do not require another footman."

Hannah was unfazed. She walked inside, reluctantly followed by Jupe, and took off her shawl. "Don't worry, it's cool," she said to Mr. Veeriswamy. "Jupe here has a letter for Lady Chatsfield. It explains everything. I lost my reference letter somewhere, but Brandon here can vouch for me. Right, Brandon?"

'Shut up, Hannah' was written across Brandon's face, but after only a moment's pause to gather his wits, he stepped up to the task. He took a deep breath, and said, "Yes, sir, Mr. Veeriswamy. This is Hannah Day, and she's an excellent housemaid. Let me tell you, she just loves doing housework. You won't get a more enthusiastic girl when it comes to scrubbing floors, blackleading fireplaces, beating rugs, or emptying chamberpots. And she never complains. She has such a positive attitude." Hannah was staring daggers at him, but Brandon carried on, enjoying himself now. "She worked with me at... er...Devenish House in...er...Yorkshire, and she was excellent. Just excellent. That's why I asked her to apply for this job."

Mr. Veeriswamy gave Hannah a sweeping look, and sighed. "I suppose a bird in the hand... Very well, Hannah, you may start on trial. If your work is satisfactory, we shall see. And if it is not, then you and Brandon will be discharged from our employment."

Hannah gave a small smile of revenge at Brandon, and said to Mr. Veeriswamy, "Oh, don't worry. I'm sure I have Brandon's full support, and we won't disappoint you. By the way, what did you say your name was?"

Mr. Veeriswamy was taken aback by her disrespectful tone. He drew himself up. "I am the butler of Balesworth Hall, and my name is Mr. Veeriswamy."

Hannah wasn't impressed. "Wow, I'm sorry, but I can't pronounce that," she said dismissively. "Can I call you Mr. V.?"

"No," he said, "You may not call me that."

Hannah shrugged. "Fine, whatever, I'll just do my best to say Veeriswhatyousaid. Brandon, show me where I sleep."

CHAPTER FOURTEEN

Shortly after Mr. Veeriswamy took the letter up to Lady Chatsfield, word came down that Jupe, too, was hired. But Brandon couldn't help noticing the troubled look on the butler's face as he communicated the news.

At noon the next day, an exhausted Hannah arrived in the kitchen for the servants' midday dinner. She looked dreadful. She slumped into a chair with dirt on her hands and face, but Mr. Veeriswamy immediately sent her off to wash. By the time she returned, everyone else had served themselves, and she gazed forlornly at the scanty thin remains of the soup in the bottom of the tureen. Carefully, she ladled what she could into her bowl, before giving up and lifting up the tureen to pour the rest. But Mr. Veeriswamy snapped at her to put it down, and so she did. She was just starting to slurp from her spoon, when she realized that everybody was staring at her.

"I have not yet said grace," Mr. Veeriswamy said reproachfully. Then he closed his eyes, clasped his hands, bowed his head, and intoned, "For what we are about to receive, may the Good Lord make us truly thankful."

Hannah immediately took a great spoonful of soup, and swallowed it. Everybody ate silently for the next few minutes. Finally, Hannah, who had finished the meal first, could stand the silence no longer, and began, "So, Mr. Veerisrunny…"

Mr. Veeriswamy looked pained, and briefly closed his eyes before correcting her. "Hannah, my name is Mr. Veeriswamy."

Hannah waved aside his complaint. "Whatever… That was an interesting grace you said. But aren't you, like a Muslim? Or one of those Indian people that worships gods with elephant heads, or the god with, like, fifteen arms?"

Mr. Veeriswamy was glowering at Hannah now. "I am not a Mahometan," he said sharply. "I was raised as a Hindu, certainly, but I am now a baptized Christian of the Church of England."

Brandon was so embarrassed, he put his head in his hands. Hannah turned to look at him.

"What's with you?" she said in an aggrieved tone. "I was just asking."

Brandon slowly shook his head in despair.

Mr. Veeriswamy gave up on Hannah, and addressed the other maid. "Flora, did you finish blackleading the fireplace in the Library?"

"Yes, sir," Flora said meekly.

"In that case, this afternoon, you and Hannah will commence cleaning the rugs in the Rose and Lilac bedrooms."

"Have fun," said Brandon with a wink to Hannah, as he folded his cloth napkin. She scowled back at him.

But as she and Brandon took the dishes back to the kitchen, he whispered, "There's something I gotta tell you." He broke the news to her that Lady Chatsfield was Verity's great-great-grandmother. Hannah was so surprised, she dropped and broke her plate, and Mrs. Watson scolded her.

The Rose bedroom was, as its name suggested, decorated with roses, most of them deep red. There was a leak in the ceiling, and a chamber pot had been placed below it to catch the rainwater.

Hannah followed Flora into the room with a new spring in her step. She had counted the generations on her fingers, and realized that Lady Chatsfield must be Mrs. Devenish's grandmother, and Sarah, her mother. How exciting was that? Maybe they would be just like Mrs. D. and Verity. It was an amazing thought, and Hannah was dying to meet them. No wonder Lady Chatsfield had sounded like a familiar name: Hannah could swear she had heard the name before, but she couldn't think where.

Flora, meanwhile, was talking. She spoke in a slow, monotonous voice, and her usual subject of conversation was her large family. She was in mid-drone. "My Uncle Davy, he's the one I told you about who's married to my ma's sister, well, he tripped on a haystack and twisted his ankle last week. Imagine, twisting your ankle on a haystack! Well, I never, I said to Ma when she told me. I heard of some funny things, but that do take all. Mind you, there's some as say that field is haunted by a ghost what's full of mischief."

"Fascinating," said Hannah in a bored voice.

Flora, however, was not to be deterred. "My little brother saw it once."

"What?" said Hannah without enthusiasm as she looked anxiously at the carpet.

"The ghost! And do you know, it was a little…"

"Flora, be quiet, okay?" Hannah said huffily.

Flora was deeply offended. "You are so rude, Hannah Day! And don't forget that I was housemaid here first!"

There was an awkward silence as they got to work. As Hannah helped Flora to roll up the carpet, she asked, "Who sleeps in this room?"

"Nobody," Flora said, puffing slightly. "It's for visitors."

"So do a lot of people stay at the house?" Hannah asked, picking up the other end.

"They used to, in old Lord Chatsfield's time, but…" and here Flora looked around to make sure nobody was listening, "but this new Lady Chatsfield don't have many visitors, except her mother. Mrs. Watson thinks it's on account of her not having much money, like. Here, what do you think of that Mr. Veeriswamy?"

Hannah stood up, and wiped dust from her eyes with the back of her hand. "I don't know. He's all right, I guess. Why?"

"Here, help me," Flora said, as she picked up one end of the rug. "Take the other end, and we'll heave it down to the courtyard to beat it."

As Hannah did so, Flora continued in a hushed voice, "I didn't know what to think when Lady Chatsfield brought an Indian gentleman as her butler. Old Mr. Wagstaff, our old butler, retired to the Earl of Chatsfield's estate at Rantham, which is a long way from here, and Mrs. Watson reckons that Lady Chatsfield forced him out so she could bring Mr. Veeriswamy in his place. What do you reckon to that, then?"

"Not much," gasped Hannah, as she staggered under the weight of the rug. "Come on, let's get this downstairs before I drop it. Man, this thing weighs a ton!"

The two girls maneuvered the rug through the door, and tottered down the hallway toward the grand staircase, Hannah taking the back.

"We can't take this down the servants' staircase," Flora explained breathlessly. "We'll never manage. It's too big. Just be careful going down the mistress's stairs."

"Okay," Hannah grunted. They made it halfway down to the first landing, when the sound of footsteps approached. Flora gasped, and awkwardly moved to face the wall.

"What are you doing?" Hannah hissed.

"Someone's coming!" Flora whispered back. "I'm facing the wall, same as you ought! Hurry!"

Hannah had no idea what this was about. Was there a gorgon approaching? Should she shut her eyes or else turn to stone? Whoever it was had now reached the top of the stairs. As Hannah quickly turned herself around, she wrestled with the rug, and dropped it. Flora then lost her end, and the rug fell open across the stairs in an explosion of dust.

"Sorry, Your Ladyship," Flora gabbled. "We couldn't take it down the servants' stairs, see, because…"

Lady Chatsfield held up a hand to silence her. "Enough. I am not in the least interested. Clean up this mess at once." For the first time, Lady Chatsfield looked at Hannah's face and stared. "If I knew no better, I would be absolutely certain we had met before…"

Hannah recognized her now, and not just because she looked vaguely like

Verity. Lady Chatsfield was the woman she had led astray in the slums of Dundee. No wonder the name had seemed familiar. She remained silent, desperately willing Lady Chatsfield not to identify her.

Lady Chatsfield looked at Hannah's face, all clean and scrubbed, unlike the dirty urchin Hannah had been in Dundee, and under her breath said with a peculiar smile, "Extraordinary," before making her way as best she could past the dropped rug.

This wasn't Hannah's only encounter that day with the Chatsfield family. When she and Flora had finished beating rugs, she had her usual duty of dusting the morning room, one of many living rooms in the house. Hannah was already exhausted as she set to work with her damp dusting cloth, but she knew that if she missed even the smallest speck of dirt, Mr. Veeriswamy was likely to spot it and blame her.

Hannah had just lifted a china knick-knack, a model of a spaniel, when the door slammed behind her. Startled, she dropped the ornament, and it smashed into tiny pieces, flying all over the floor. "Oh, you idiot," she said, "look what you made me do!" She whirled around to see who she was speaking to, only to find herself face to face with a dark-haired young girl wearing a fancy white dress with bloomers. This, Hannah realized, had to be Sarah Chatsfield. For one crazy moment she considered curtseying, before deciding that there was no way she was going to curtsey to a kid who was younger than her.

"Why are you looking at me?" Sarah snapped, and she instantly reminded Hannah of Verity.

"You're Sarah, right? I'm Hannah. I've heard all about…"

"How dare you speak to me with such familiarity?" Sarah said sharply.

"Well, excuuuuuse me," Hannah sputtered, one hand on her hip. "I was just being, like, friendly, which I thought was kind of nice of me, after you made me drop that doggy thing. I mean, what's with the door slamming? Are you throwing a hissy fit, or what?"

Sarah looked crossly at her, but suddenly, the corners of her mouth began to turn up, and she put a hand to her face, and closed her eyes. Was she going to barf, Hannah wondered with alarm? No, she was giggling. When she caught her breath, she said, "I ought to be offended, but you are a rather amusing creature."

Hannah didn't know what to say. Nobody had ever called her a creature before. She threw down her duster on a nearby table. "So don't you go to school?" she asked Sarah.

"No, of course not. I had a governess until last year, but Mama says that I need no more schooling, except perhaps lessons from a dancing master. Mama teaches me all that I need know."

"Lucky you," Hannah said. "It would be so cool not to work or go to school."

"Perhaps," said Sarah, looking sad, "but it can be rather dull at times. However, Mama says that in a few years I shall attend all manner of balls and parties and make my debut in society. She already has a list of suitors for me, so I am very confident of making a good match."

"Hang on," Hannah said, aghast. "You're how old? Ten? And your mom is already picking out boyfriends for you? That's kind of weird."

Sarah raised her eyebrows. "Not at all. I can hardly expect a lowly housemaid to understand matters such as these. Mama has my best interests at heart, and I am sure she will help me to find a good husband."

Hannah looked at Sarah pityingly. "That sounds kind of boring. Don't you want to do anything else apart from get married?"

Now Sarah paused, and, biting her lip, appeared doubtful. "How odd you should say that. That is what our footman also asked me."

"Brandon, right?" Hannah said. "Figures. He's big on telling people to read books, and stuff like that. So what do you like to do for fun?" Without asking for permission, she perched on the arm of a chair.

Sarah found herself intrigued and impressed by the impertinence of this young maid. She also found her likeable. She ignored Hannah's sitting down in her presence. "I suppose I like to play in the gardens, although it's more pleasant to do so when we have visitors. Henry is not always the best company, and playing by oneself can be... well..."

"Lonely?" Hannah offered.

"Yes, I suppose one could say that," Sarah said hesitantly.

"So what's with the door slamming?"

To Hannah's surprise, Sarah's eyes welled up with tears. "Perhaps I ought not to tell," she said, her chin trembling. "But I was angry. Mama will not invite Papa to Balesworth."

Hannah smoothed down her apron, and said, "Have you asked her why?"

"Oh, no," Sarah exclaimed. "I could hardly be so insolent."

"What's rude about asking?" Hannah said. "This is your dad we're talking about. You've got a right to know why your mom won't let you see him."

"I do?" Sarah asked uncertainly.

"Of course you do," Hannah said. "You gotta tell her she has to let you see him."

Suddenly, Sarah's face became set. "No, I could not possibly do that."

"Okay," Hannah said, picking up her duster. "Suit yourself. Your funeral."

"And you ought not to speak to me like this," Sarah said, angry that she had allowed herself to be drawn into telling family stories to the new housemaid. "It is not your place. Now return to your work."

Thinking later about this encounter, and her reunion with Lady Chatsfield, Hannah wondered nervously if her days at Balesworth Hall were numbered.

For England in early May, Thursday evening's weather was unusually good. Lady Chatsfield had left the estate to visit her mother, along with Sarah, and Mr. Veeriswamy had gone with them, leaving Mrs. Watson in charge. She promptly gave the junior staff permission to spend the evening as they pleased.

Hannah and Brandon decided to take a walk. As they pulled on their outdoor shoes, Hannah told Brandon of her encounter with Lady Chatsfield, but he insisted that she had nothing to worry about. "And she acted like she recognized you, but couldn't quite place you, right?"

"That's right," Hannah said, tapping her heel on the ground to push her foot into her shoe. "But she smiled at me, like I was someone she knew and liked, not the girl who almost got her killed in Dundee. It was very weird."

"Ah, I wouldn't stress about it," Brandon said. "Let it go."

When they stepped outside, they saw Jupe hanging around in the rose garden, and Brandon invited him to join them on their walk.

Jupe happily accepted the invitation, but Hannah was annoyed. She had wanted to talk alone to somebody from the twenty-first century, even if it had to be Brandon. To show her displeasure, she walked ahead of the boys. But Brandon soon caught up with her. "Wait up, Hannah!" he puffed. "You have to hear what Jupe is telling me."

Hannah rolled her eyes and tutted. "How come we couldn't go without him? I wanted to talk to you about what I've been doing without having to explain everything to him."

"Never mind about that," Brandon said, frowning. "This is important. And it's about your brother, too."

That got Hannah's attention. "What? Is something wrong?"

"Not exactly," Brandon said. "But... Look, I'll let Jupe explain."

Jupe was sitting by the side of a field with his knees drawn up to his chin, watching two black and white dairy cattle graze. "I never saw this color of cows in Georgia," he said to Brandon and Hannah as they sat down facing him.

"Never mind that," snapped Hannah. "What's wrong with Alex?"

Jupe's face fell, and he looked away from Hannah.

Brandon gave Hannah an angry glare. "Hannah, nothing's wrong with Alex… Jupe, please tell Hannah what you told me. It's okay. She's kind of a pain, but you can trust her."

Slowly, Jupe told his story, and it was a disturbing one. Mr. Thornhill had come to him on the ship to tell him that he was free, and that he had a job waiting for him in England. At first, Jupe was ecstatic. But then Mr. Thornhill went on to say that there were conditions attached to his offer.

When Jupe told Hannah about the conditions, she gasped. "Are you telling me that Thornhill told you that you can't leave this job?"

"Yes, he did," Jupe said. "And if I ever do leave here, he'll sell my mama and daddy away from Kintyre, and from each other."

"But why?" Hannah asked.

"That's the part I can't figure out," Brandon said. "There has to be some reason. Jupe, did he say anything else?"

Jupe hesitated. "Well, he did say that I must not tell Lady Chatsfield of my circumstances. So, please, I'm begging you, don't tell her nothing about this."

Hannah looked thoughtful. "Jupe, that letter you brought with you, the one addressed to Lady Chatsfield, said that Mr. Thornhill or Lord Chatsfield or whatever he's called, would pay for you to work here. That's kind of weird, isn't it? I mean, who else would pay? It's his house."

Brandon looked askance at her. "Hannah, this Thornhill is obviously a sleazebag playing some kind of sick game, and your brother is hanging out with him. Doesn't that worry you?"

"Maybe," Hannah said doubtfully. "But Thornhill's his boss, right? A lot of people have mean bosses."

Brandon gave her a hard stare. "I don't like to think of Alex hanging out with a guy who's so totally manipulative. Do you?"

"No," Hannah said quietly. "I guess not."

"We have to get Alex to Balesworth , and figure out what the deal is with this Thornhill character. And I have to check out Mrs. Watson's old house, to make sure it's Verity and Eric's."

"But we have to get home," Hannah reminded him.

"Oh, yeah," Brandon said wistfully. "That too. But first of all, we gotta send Mr. Thornhill a telegram."

"What's that?" Hannah asked.

"Kind of like a Victorian email," Brandon said. "It's better than a letter, because we won't have to worry about people seeing our handwriting."

"Why would we worry about that?"

"Because, officially, the telegram won't be from us. It will be from Lady Chatsfield."

Hannah smiled. "Sweet."

The very next day, Brandon rose early, and hurriedly pulled on his shoes. He knew he would have to be quick if he was to be back at Balesworth Hall before Lady Chatsfield and Mr. Veeriswamy returned.

Walking briskly through the huge park, he once again thought how bizarre it was that it was intended for the exclusive enjoyment of a family of three. He had not seen a single public park in all of England in 1851 until he had visited Hyde Park for the Great Exhibition. Not that he had much of a chance to enjoy walking through Balesworth Park now: He was too busy trying to stick closely to the trees to avoid being seen from the house.

When he reached Balesworth, the cattle market was in progress, but there were even fewer cattle for sale than before. The old man Brandon had chatted with on his last visit was standing with a gaggle of farmers who were dickering over prices, and Brandon approached him.

"Hi, sir, do you remember me?"

The old man smiled at him. "Of course I remember you! I hain't seen a lad of your complexion elsewise. Come looking for more books, have you?"

But Brandon didn't have time for chitchat. "Sir, do you know where there's a post office? I need to send a telegram."

"What's that now?" said the old farmer, wrinkling his nose. "That another of them new inventions, is it? Can't say as I've ever seen one, nor as likely to. I been in our post office often enough, but I never saw such a thing as a terror grum."

"Telegram," Brandon corrected him. "It's called a telegram."

A younger farmer had overheard part of the conversation, and he stepped in to help. "What's that he's asking about?"

"Something called a tully grain," the old farmer said.

The younger farmer asked Brandon, "Here, do you mean a telegraphic despatch? You'll have to go to the railway station for that, to the Electric Telegraph Company office."

Brandon decided that if he had to walk all the way to the station, he might as well make a detour to Mrs. Watson's house. As he reached the end of the High Street, he saw the only house it could possibly be. But Brandon's heart sank. It was on the exact same spot as Verity and Eric's house, but it wasn't theirs. As he got closer, he examined the building carefully, and, to his relief, he began to recognize parts of it. Of course! It was the same house, but the paint was different, and the roof was thatched. Over the door was carved *DG 1734*. He didn't remember that inscription being there, but in 1940, Mrs. Devenish had told him that most of the house had been built in the eighteenth century, so it made sense. He touched the door, and to his surprise, it swung open.

Tentatively, Brandon walked in, calling "Hello?" There was only silence. He recognized the inside of the house at once, despite its very different décor. He crept down the hall into the kitchen, which was practically empty. The fireplace was much larger than he remembered, but he was most surprised to recognize the huge kitchen table: He was beginning to suspect that the house had been built around it.

Just then, he heard the front door creak open behind him, and he whirled around. The old farmer from the High Street was standing in the doorway. "What are you doing in here, then?" he asked Brandon sharply.

"Nothing, sorry...," Brandon stammered in alarm. "I just wanted to see Mrs. Watson's house, and I thought..."

"You know my daughter, do you? I'm Mr. Letchmore. Well, you got no business in here, anyhow."

Then he stopped. "Mind you," he said, "I don't suppose there's nothing to steal, even if that was what you was up to."

"Oh, no, I'm really not..." stammered Brandon.

But the old man waved him quiet. "She and that son of hers, that grandson of mine, Henry, they live in the big house now. Waste of a good house this is, if you ask me, but I don't own it, and neither does my daughter. Belongs to the estate, it does."

"It belongs to Lord Chatsfield?" Brandon asked.

But Mr. Letchmore shook his head impatiently. "It's a grace and favor place, isn't it? His Lordship, that is, the old Lord, he give it to my daughter when she married, as a place to live, like. I just hope this new Lordship will let her keep it for her old age. If they ever find His Lordship, that is."

"Oh, we've found him," Brandon blurted out.

"Well, I never," the farmer said, holding open the door for Brandon. "I never heard nothing about that."

Brandon regretted being so indiscreet. He had lived in Snipesville his whole life, long enough to know how fast rumors spread in a small town. "It's just something I overheard," he added unconvincingly. "Might not be true."

"Well then," said the old man, jerking his head toward the door, "you had better look sharp and be on your way." But he stopped Brandon on his way out, and said, "I've only met two blacks in my life, and you're the second of them. You all look the same, don't you?"

Brandon was offended now. "Excuse me? That's kind of rude, you know?"

"Begging your pardon," Mr. Letchmore said. "But I reckon it's true. You know, I'm 88 years old, and maybe my memory is playing tricks, but to me you look a lot like a young lad I knew some seventy years ago. Maybe he were your old granddad? His name was Brandon Clark."

Brandon gasped.

The train station was much as Brandon remembered it from 1915, plastered with advertisements, although these, unlike the colorful ads of the twentieth century, were black and white posters with large headlines, lots of text, and no pictures. It was good to stand on the platform once again, and sad to know that the pretty old station would be no more than a distant memory by the twenty-first century.

Brandon could not stop thinking about Mr. Letchmore, and what he said. He could not escape the only possible conclusion, which was that he had yet to meet Mr. Letchmore as a young man. He was afraid to think that another journey in time might lie in his future.

For now, however, he had something important to do. Inside the telegraph office, a clerk was sitting before a wooden machine that looked like a cross between a wardrobe and a grandfather clock. He was scribbling away on a sheet of paper, translating messages into the rapid dots and dashes of Morse code.

After Brandon wrote out his message on a special form, he handed it to the clerk, who said, "That will be four shillings and sixpence, sir."

Brandon was floored. "How much?"

The clerk repeated, "Four shillings and sixpence. There's also extra charges if you wish me to repeat the message, or to insure its accuracy, both of which we do recommend."

Brandon thought about instead sending a letter, which would only cost a few pennies, but he realized that his handwriting might give the game away, so he said, "I'll think about it. Give me back my message."

There was nothing for it but to return to Balesworth Hall and hit up Hannah for the money.

Brandon found Hannah working alone in the servants' hall, scrubbing the floor. When he explained his problem, she got off her knees, wiped her hands on her apron, and smirked at him triumphantly.

"I'll give you the money," she said. "But on one condition: You gotta get back here in one hour."

"Why? Is Mrs. Watson getting suspicious?"

"No, it's not that. You have the afternoon off, right? Well, guess who's gonna finish washing the floors for me?"

Brandon was not amused. "Wrong. First, it's not my job, and Mr. Veeriswamy won't let you palm it off on me. And, second, this is your brother we're rescuing, remember?"

Hannah was seriously disappointed. "Oh, yeah. Rats… Hold on, I'll go get my cash."

****

A knock at the door of the suite in Carhart's Hotel announced the arrival of the telegram. Mr. Thornhill opened the envelope, glanced over the contents and frowned. "Alex, I must go to Hertfordshire tomorrow. For some reason, your presence is also required."

Alex had been expecting to hear from Hannah and Brandon, and he tried to look surprised rather than excited. He thought it would look less fishy if he asked questions, so he asked Mr. Thornhill why he had been invited.

"I don't know," said Mr. Thornhill, his brow furrowed, as he dropped the telegram onto a table. "I expect we will find out. I have some serious business to conclude with the sender, and it would be as well to do so in person. Indeed, it would give me great satisfaction. Make haste, Alexander, for we must take a coach. Or, I suppose, catch a train. That is what people do these days, is it not?"

Alex assumed that it was. But his thoughts were elsewhere: While he was looking forward to seeing his sister and Brandon, how on earth was he going to explain to them that the calculator had disappeared?

Brandon had arrived back at Balesworth Hall in the nick of time, only thirty seconds before Lady Chatsfield's carriage pulled up at the front entrance. He spent the rest of the morning at his usual task, polishing silver. After the noontime dinner, he was relaxing in the servants' hall with a book that he had persuaded Henry to bring him from the library, when Mr. Veeriswamy entered.

The butler took a chair by the fire, across from Brandon. "It is a pity that the weather is so poor on your free afternoon," he said kindly. "You could have taken a walk in the fresh air."

Brandon smiled to himself at the thought of his strenuous trek into Bales-worth earlier that day. "Oh, that's all right. I'm sure I get plenty of exercise."

Mrs. Watson appeared from the kitchen. "I never asked, Brandon, whether you ever had a look at my house?"

"I did," said Brandon. "It was very nice. Oh, and I met your father." He paused, suddenly fearful that he might say too much about his secret expedition to town, but Mrs. Watson's suspicions were not alerted.

Brandon told an edited version of the story of meeting Mr. Letchmore, and he mentioned casually that he was surprised to learn that the house belonged to the estate. Henry immediately chimed in: "I've read about that. Hundreds of years ago, Balesworth was just a tiny village, and it belonged to the Balesworth Hall estate, until it broke away as an independent borough. Now the estate is much smaller, just the land around the house, and a few farms, including my grandfather's."

In a worried tone Mr. Veeriswamy added, "And it is unlikely to thrive more than it does. Many of the tenant farmers in Hertfordshire are keen to learn new agriculture, but ours, alas, are not."

"Yeah," Brandon said in a deadpan voice, "I could see where Mr. Letchmore might not be so interested in progress."

A bell rang in the servants' hall, telling the staff that Lady Chatsfield was in the Morning Room, and that Mr. Veeriswamy's presence was required. After the butler went to answer the call, Mrs. Watson turned to Brandon. "Listen, lad, I'll tell you why we don't prosper, and it isn't just my father's fault for being an old fuddy-duddy. Old Lord Chatsfield became too old to manage things, and he was too miserly to employ an estate manager. My old father says this new Lady Chatsfield doesn't know the first thing about managing the estate. I hope the new Lord Chatsfield comes soon."

Sooner, than you might imagine, Brandon thought.

The bell rang in the servants' hall, and Mr. Veeriswamy moved swiftly to answer it. As soon as he had disappeared up the servants' staircase, Brandon leaped up from his polishing, and followed. At the first landing, he peeked out of the window in time to see Mr. Thornhill and Alex leave their carriage in the pouring rain, as Mr. Veeriswamy held an umbrella over their heads. Brandon felt his heart start to pound.

They were here. So far, so good.

He tore upstairs, two steps at a time, and found Hannah dusting the dining room. Together, they ran down to the main hall. But they were too late: Alex and Mr. Thornhill had already been summoned into Lady Chatsfield's presence.

****

Mr. Thornhill removed his gloves. He gestured vaguely to Alex, and said, "This is my assistant, Alexander Day, whom I brought with me from Georgia." Lady Chatsfield looked apprehensive. Only Alex knew that it was Brandon's telegram that had brought them together, and it was nerve-racking to watch their confusion.

Fortunately, Lady Chatsfield had plans for Alex. "Master Day, if you will kindly wait in the library, I shall have Veeriswamy bring you tea."

There was an awkward silence as she rang for the butler. Alex couldn't wait to get out of the room.

Soon afterward, Brandon dashed into the library, followed by Hannah, who quietly closed the door behind them. Alex, wearing a huge grin, was seated at a low tea table, on which were arranged a silver teapot, sugar bowl, and milk jug, along with a plate of cakes and another of sandwiches.

"Guys!" Alex exclaimed, as Brandon immediately helped himself to a sweet bun.

Through a mouthful of crumbs, Brandon said, "Hey, when you pour out that tea, just remember who polished that teapot."

Hannah reached around her brother's shoulders and gave him a quick hug. "So," she said, grabbing a small ham sandwich and pulling up a chair. "Who wants to tell their story?"

Alex went first, describing his travels since the day he woke up in a cotton field in Snipes County. Before he had finished, Hannah jumped in. "Okay," she said, "now, about Scotland…"

But Alex interrupted her, looking very guilty. "I have to tell you something," he said hesitantly. "Somebody stole the calculator from the Crystal Palace."

"Oh, don't worry about that," Hannah said breezily. She reached into her pocket, and pulled out the calculator. "This it?"

Alex gasped with relief. "Yes! How did you find it?"

Hannah preened. "Oh, you know, I have my ways…"

"She stole it," Brandon said.

"Hey, there was a reason," Hannah protested. "I figured we needed to give it to That Woman. Now we just have to wait for her to show up."

Alex looked uncomfortable. "I keep trying to give it to her, but she won't take it from me. She keeps saying the time isn't right, or something like that…"

Brandon exhaled noisily. "You know what I think? I think that finding the calculator is only one of the things we're supposed to do. Trouble is, I don't think even she knows what they are. Oh, hey, wait a minute… I did find out that Henry Watson was born in Verity and Eric's house!"

"Uh-huh," Hannah said skeptically. "But like I told you, how are you going to prove it?"

Brandon looked worried. "Maybe that's what we have to do before we can go home. We have to find some way to prove where Henry was really born."

But Alex, staring into space, had his mind elsewhere. "It would help," he said quietly, "if I knew what was up between Mr. Thornhill and Lady Chatsfield. It's weird that she's still alive. Everyone in Savannah thinks he's a widower. Are they divorced?"

Brandon sat up straight and pointed at Alex. "That's it! No, they're not divorced. But I read how divorces are hard to get in Victorian England. Even if you're rich and can afford it, it's a big scandal, and the husbands get custody of the kids, no matter what. So a lot of people just quietly split up, you know, separate, because it's less hassle than a divorce. I'm guessing that's what those two did. But now they have a problem: Now Mr. Thornhill is Lord Chatsfield, it's like he's won the lottery. Do you guys think they'll get back together?"

Alex looked pained. "I don't know… He hasn't talked about it. Did you guys know that they had two sons who moved to Georgia with him, and that they both died?"

Hannah and Brandon exchanged shocked looks. "No way," Hannah said. "But why did he leave Sarah here?"

"Who's Sarah?" Alex asked. "Is she that girl who came up to him at the Exhibition?"

"That's her," Brandon said. "She's his daughter."

"That's even more weird," Alex said slowly. "And get this. His house slaves in Georgia said he's remarried, and he has a new family in a plantation way south of Savannah. But he never mentions them to me, either…" His voice trailed off, and he slumped in his chair, looking miserable. "I wish I knew what they were saying to each other, Mr. Thornhill and his wife."

Then suddenly, he had a moment of inspiration. He jumped to his feet, ran to the fireplace, and to the surprise of the others, stepped inside, sticking his head up the chimney. Seconds later, he ducked down, and hissed to Brandon and Hannah, "Come on, we can hear!"

Hannah was unimpressed. "What? I'm so not going in a dirty chimney."

"After everything you've been through," Brandon said to her skeptically, "I'm surprised you care about a bit of soot."

CHAPTER FOURTEEN

"Shush!" whispered Alex as they joined him. And then they could hear the voices, unclearly at first, but soon, with a little concentration, they could make out all the words. Mr. Thornhill was speaking.

Mr. Thornhill was pacing around the room, while Lady Chatsfield sat anxiously wringing out a handkerchief. "I have told you a thousand times," he said, "and yet apparently I do not make myself plain. I intend to sell this estate."

She spoke to him in a frightened voice, to Hannah and Brandon's surprise: This was not the self-confident Lady Chatsfield they knew. "But surely the estate is entailed. It cannot be sold, but must remain within the family."

"You are mistaken, Emma. The estate belongs to my cousin, the Earl, and he has his own lands in the Midlands. He has agreed to my selling this property for my own profit and, in return, his son will assume the title as Viscount Chatsfield. He already has an estate for his son, and so has no need of Balesworth Hall. We have no sons, so who would inherit the title after me, eh? Moreover, I have no interest in managing farmland or sitting in the House of Lords. Manufacturing, exporting and importing, that's Britain's future, and that is what interests me. Being Lord Chatsfield does not provide me with cash, but the sale of Balesworth Hall will provide me with all the capital I need to expand my business as a merchant. And it will allow me to afford a divorce, so that you will be free to remarry if you wish…"

"But what of me… and of Sarah?" Lady Chatsfield pleaded.

Mr. Thornhill's voice was firm. "I shall make provision for you. There is a cottage in Balesworth that belongs to the estate. You and Sarah…"

"No!" cried Lady Chatsfield, putting her handkerchief to her mouth. "I couldn't bear it. It is but a mean little place, fit only for servants. I would be excluded from society if I lived in such a place. How could you possibly consider it?"

His voice grew hard. "It does not matter to me where you live. Your position in society, and that of your daughter, is worse than precarious. But you will not be poor, so count your blessings. Understand that the money from the sale of Balesworth Hall is mine, and that I will not be told what to do with it."

The kids could hear Lady Chatsfield weeping bitterly, and they exchanged uncomfortable looks. "I dunno, you guys, this is kind of embarrassing…" whispered Hannah.

"No, listen…" said Brandon.

Mr. Thornhill was continuing in a quiet but steely voice. "I have not forsaken you. Not only will I provide you with the house in Balesworth, but I have purchased an estate in America, and you may live on its proceeds."

"He won the plantation in a poker game," Alex whispered.

"This estate," Mr. Thornhill was explaining, "will afford you a greater quality of life than has been possible on the slim allowance that I have sent you in the past. I have also provided you with a servant. Young Jupiter will remain my property... Er, that is, he will remain in my employ..."

But Lady Chatsfield had not missed his stumble. "He's your slave?" she asked, shocked.

"Sounds like it to me," Hannah whispered to Brandon, "From what Jupe told you, he might as well be a slave."

But Mr. Thornhill was trying to backtrack. "No, he is not a slave. I have freed him. Jupiter is now your servant, and I shall pay his expenses. You will need fewer servants in your new home. You may retain one of your maids and your cook, but you must discharge the rest of the household staff."

"Your arrogance, sir, is beyond measure," said Lady Chatsfield. "America has changed you for the worse."

"Silence," roared Mr. Thornhill. Alex jumped. He had never heard Mr. Thornhill so angry.

"I have one further question," Lady Chatsfield said, sounding quite defeated. "What is this place in America on which you say my future fortune will depend?"

"Are you quite sure that you wish to know?" Mr. Thornhill said quietly. "Very well, I shall tell you. It is a small plantation near Savannah. It is not terribly profitable, but it is, nonetheless, profitable. I will draw up papers transferring its ownership to you."

"Knowing how deeply I oppose slavery, you insist upon me accepting a slave-run plantation for my income?"

There was a silence, and Alex imagined Mr. Thornhill nodding. In fact, he was simply gazing at his wife, watching her reaction. Satisfied, he said, "Yes. It is time that you understood the ways of the world. What, you think your riches come from Chatsfield's puny estate? Of course not. I have seen men work as machines, Emma. Whether they work in factories or in fields, their labor makes our wealth possible. It is a pity, perhaps. But there it is."

"Very well," said Lady Chatsfield. "But I will grant my slaves their freedom, as you have done for young Jupiter."

"Oh, you cannot do that," Mr. Thornhill said calmly. "It is now illegal for a plantation owner to free his slaves in Georgia. Even if it were not, the plantation has no value without slaves, you see. You do not understand America,

Emma. There are precious few free workers in Georgia, and there is abundant land for all free men who desire to own it and work it themselves. They cannot and will not work my land for wages. Slaves are all we have. And if you decide to sell the land, I promise you that its next owners would not have the same scruples about slavery as you do. They would buy more slaves to work on it. In any event, the point is moot: I will retain ownership of the slaves."

"You are a cruel, wicked man," sobbed Lady Chatsfield.

Mr. Thornhill sighed heavily. "No, Emma, I am not. I am merely a man of the world."

Hannah muttered to Brandon, "I vote for 'cruel and wicked.' He's charming and all, but he's such a sleazy character."

In the darkened fireplace, Hannah did not see that her brother was standing wide-eyed in disbelief.

Now the three of them were all ears as they heard Lady Chatsfield ask about Alex. "Who is that boy with you?" she said suddenly. "Is he your son by another woman?'"

Mr. Thornhill paused for a second, almost as though he was taunting her. Then he said, "Alexander? Oh, he's my protégé, if you will. I intend to remarry, but I already know that my future wife is unable to bear me sons. At least I shall have Alex to train up as my successor, to take over my business from me."

Hannah glanced at Alex, who continued to look stunned.

Suddenly, the sounds of skirts rustling and feet moving announced that the meeting was coming to an end. The kids quickly ducked out of the fireplace.

"Let's get out of here," Brandon said to Hannah. "If Mr. Veeriswamy catches us in the library, we'll be in deep trouble. Alex, look, I know you have to go with Thornhill, but we'll be in touch. We'll send a letter, though, because those telegrams cost a ton."

Alex was left alone, feeling very empty. He had liked Mr. Thornhill. He had ignored the warning signs that this man, while pleasant and kind, was not someone to be trusted. Thornhill was no better than MacGregor the slave trader. How could he not have seen what kind of man he was? And how was he going to get away from him?

A few minutes later, Mr. Thornhill opened the door to the library, and said abruptly, "Come along, Alexander, we must leave."

But Alex didn't move. "Sir, I don't feel too good. I have a really bad headache. I think it's a migraine. Can I stay behind?"

Mr. Thornhill looked concerned. "Yes, of course. I will tell the servants to make up a bed for you."

Then he reached into his inner coat pocket, and pulled out a small bundle of papers tied with a white cloth ribbon. "Alexander, once you feel better, copy out these papers for me. Send the originals to Baird in Savannah, so that he can set to work while we remain in England."

"Yes, sir," Alex said, taking the papers from Mr. Thornhill. "I'll see to it."

But Alex knew the chances were good he would never see Mr. Thornhill again. And, despite everything, that made him sad. Despite everything, he would miss him.

Alex had just settled into a huge comfortable curtained four-poster bed when he heard a knock at the door. It was Hannah, bringing his supper on a tray.

"I don't know why you get to lounge around in bed stuffing your face," she grumbled as she dumped the tray in her brother's lap. "You never have migraines. That was Mom's thing."

"Of course I don't have a headache," said Alex as he rearranged his pillows and tray to get comfortable. "I was just trying to buy time, and it was the only thing I could think of. I thought it was pretty quick thinking."

"Uh-huh," said Hannah, sitting down on the bed. "Listen, I gotta talk to you about this Julep kid…"

"Jupe," Alex corrected her, before slurping a spoonful of beef broth.

"Whatever. Do you know what Thornhill told him?"

Alex shook his head, and spooned another load of soup in his mouth.

"He told Jupe that he would earn room, board, and one shilling a week…."

"Wow, that's not good," Alex interjected.

"No, no, wait, that's not my point…. Actually, that's what I get paid, too… No, here's the weird part. Thornhill told Jupe that if he ever left Balesworth Hall without permission, he would sell his parents."

Now she had Alex's full attention. He put down his spoon. "Whoa, he said he would sell Jupe's parents?"

"That's what I just said," said Hannah crossly. "Man, he's totally sleazy. How did you manage to put up with him for so long?"

Alex considered this. It all, horribly, made sense. Mr. Thornhill had only freed Jupe as a sick joke, to taunt his wife about her anti-slavery beliefs. In fact, he hadn't really freed Jupe at all, but was keeping him enslaved by blackmail. It was evil.

To his sister, Alex said simply, "He seemed nice, but he wasn't. Look, I don't want to talk about it anymore, okay?"

He took a bite of chicken pie and chewed slowly. The pie was delicious, but suddenly he wasn't very hungry. He wiped his mouth and sighed. "I dunno, sis, I just feel really stupid. Why the heck did I trust him? What was I thinking?"

"You're a good person," Hannah said, stealing a bit of pastry from the pie. "You wanted to think he was cool and, anyway, like you said, he was nice to you. Don't be so hard on yourself."

Just then, there was another knock on the door. Hannah jumped up, but it was only Brandon. "Hi, I guessed I would find Hannah in here," he said, as he sat down on the other side of the bed.

Alex cleared his throat. "Brandon, I think I have the perfect idea for an official-looking document that says Henry was born in Verity's house. I got the idea from some legal papers that Mr. Thornhill gave me to copy out. And I think I can help Jupe, too."

"You're like the Wizard of Oz, aren't you?" said Hannah. "What you gonna do, give Jupe some courage?"

Alex smiled. "Oh, he already has that, and a brain, and a heart. No, I have another idea. What Jupe needs is just a little prod in the right direction… and a lot of money. That's the hard part."

Now Alex explained his second idea. By the time he finished, Brandon and Hannah were gazing at him with new respect. "Wow," said Hannah, "You're not as stupid as you look."

"Thanks a lot," said Alex sarcastically.

"I hope you're right about all this," Brandon said with a grin. "Otherwise, you're not the Wizard of Oz, you're just a little guy behind a curtain." He yanked on one of the bed drapes and laughed. "Oh, and by the way, did you know that Jupe has an auntie in Massachusetts?"

"He never told me that," said Alex, his eyes widening. "How come he's telling you all this stuff, Brandon? He just met you."

Brandon looked embarrassed, and shrugged his shoulders.

"It's because you're black, isn't it?" Hannah said matter-of-factly.

"For once, Hannah's right," Brandon said. "Look, Alex, think about it. Do you think Jupe knows any white people? I mean, really knows them? In 1851?"

"He knows me," Alex said stubbornly.

Brandon sighed. "Man, this is kind of awkward… Listen, before he met you, Jupe had never met a white person who wasn't mean, and who didn't think that black people were dumb animals. He trusted your Mr. Thornhill, and look where that got him. He's basically still a slave, only now he's three thousand miles from his folks, too. He doesn't trust you much, either. Never did. It's not personal, Alex. It's just the way it is. Hey, even now, there are plenty of really racist white people in Snipesville. I made friends with this white kid in second grade, but our friendship kind of died because his mom always sort of 'forgot' to invite me to his parties and sleepovers. Whenever I invited him to my house, there was always some reason why he couldn't come. Then he transferred to Snipesville Academy, so there wasn't any more danger of him making a black friend. "

Brandon looked sad for a moment, and Hannah unexpectedly patted him on the back. "His loss, Brandon. What do you care? I bet you have tons of friends…"

"Is that what you guys think?" Brandon said. "Man, you don't know me as well as you think you do… Anyway, this isn't about me. This is about Jupe. We have to get him out of here before he spends his life as Lady Chatsfield's slave."

Chapter 15

LAND, LANDED, AND LANDING

The following morning, Brandon stole into Alex's room, and found him sitting in bed with a large wooden box across his lap.

"Check out my new laptop!" laughed Alex, opening it up to reveal a flat writing surface covered in green felt and topped with a sheet of blotting paper, along with compartments for pens and an ink bottle.

Alex lifted the writing surface, and pulled out from underneath it the packet of papers that Mr. Thornhill had given him. "This is what he asked me to copy, the documents that give Kintyre Plantation to Lady Chatsfield... Mrs. Thornhill. "

Brandon was confused. "How can you copy these? It's not like we have copier machines in 1851."

"No, of course not," said Alex, "That's why Mr. Baird and I always copy out documents by hand. Anyway, I did it last night. All we have to do now is make some changes to the originals."

Brandon looked worried. "I've been thinking about that part of your plan, and I have a question for you. Won't Lady Chatsfield get half of all his money if they get divorced?"

"No," Alex said. "In England, even if a lady owned money or land before she got married, it doesn't belong to her. It belongs to her husband. In Georgia, she would at least be allowed to keep the property that she had when she got married, but not here. I didn't spend all my time with Mr. Baird doing errands, you know. He taught me stuff about law, and we even handled a divorce. Mr. Baird said that, even in Georgia, a woman can't keep anything after a divorce unless her husband gives it to her, except what she owned when they got married."

"Wow, that's tough," Brandon said. "I guess Lady C. is lucky that Thornhill will let her have anything, huh?"

Alex handed Brandon his pen and ink bottle, together with one page of the original document. "Yes, she is, but he didn't give her the slaves at Kintyre. That's where we come in. See Mr. Thornhill's initials at the end of the page? I want you to practice copying those until nobody can tell the difference."

Brandon was shocked. "You want me to forge this guy's signature?"

"Yes, I do," said Alex. "But first, here's a sheet of paper. Write to Mr. Thornhill, and tell him that I have flu, and won't be back in London for a while. I don't want him to get suspicious."

"Okay," said Brandon doubtfully. "I hope you're right, because I don't want Jupe's life messed up any more than it already is… Alex, you know this Thornhill guy. Why is he being so nasty to Lady Chatsfield? What's his problem?"

"Beats me," Alex said. "Grown-ups can be weird like that."

"You know what," Brandon said, "Maybe he blames his wife because she wouldn't come with him to Georgia."

There was a pause while Alex looked over the papers once more. "Okay, so Mr. Thornhill wants to get back at his wife, but he's not totally evil, and he knows he has to support her, because it's not like Lady Chatsfield can work in WalMart, right? So he gives her Kintyre Plantation as a gift, but kind of a mean one, because he knows she hates slavery, but he doesn't give her the slaves, so she can't free any of them, including Jupe's parents."

He read aloud from a document, 'I give to my former wife the estate of Kintyre Plantation and all chattel except slaves.' Then, dipping his pen in ink, he wrote something, and carefully handed the document to Brandon. "Watch out, the ink's wet."

Brandon blinked when he saw what Alex done. He had heavily crossed out the words *except slaves*. Brandon sighed heavily. "Alex, that's so not going to fly."

"Yes, it is. You're going to initial it, after you practice Mr. Thornhill's initials."

"Are you sure about this?" asked Brandon. "I mean, won't he find out? Who are you sending this to?"

Alex shrugged. "I'm not one hundred percent sure, but I think it might work. I'm sending it to Mr. Baird. He's loyal to Mr. Thornhill, and Mr. Thornhill just trusts him to get things done. Plus, Mr. Baird doesn't work too hard. I mean, if we had computer solitaire in 1851, he's the kind of guy who would play it all day. He won't look at this too closely or think too hard about it, especially if I send him a letter telling him to put it in the files. I'll send copies directly to the city government in Savannah, and to Lady Chatsfield's lawyer. But we will need to tell Lady Chatsfield about all this."

Lady Chatsfield put down her needlepoint to wring her hands. She was very worried. Soon, she would once again be just plain Emma Thornhill, now a divorced woman living on the proceeds of slavery, and excluded from polite society. The humiliation was almost more than she could bear. She was startled by the knock at the drawing-room door, and even more surprised by the appearance of Alex.

He cleared his throat. "Sorry to disturb you, ma'am, but may I speak with you? It's important."

She rubbed her forehead, sighed heavily, and told him not to take long.

Alex looked at her closely, and he could see echoes of Verity and Mrs. Devenish in her long face and tall figure. He took a seat on an uncomfortable sofa. "I know you're upset about owning a plantation…" he began.

Lady Chatsfield flinched: She was not used to discussing her feelings with strange little boys.

But Alex persevered. "You know, slavery will be over in a few years…."

She was agog. "How, pray tell, could you possibly know that?"

"Um… Ah," Alex sputtered. And then he thought of something. "There's rumors in America about slavery ending. They say there might even be a war, you know, a civil war, when Americans fight each other over slavery. Might be a good idea for you to save as much money as you can from the plantation income, you know, just in case. Anyway, I've visited that plantation…"

Lady Chatsfield looked at him eagerly. "Oh, you have? What do you suggest?"

Alex was pleased. Grown-ups weren't usually interested in his suggestions. He sat up proudly. "I suggest you let Jupe's dad run it. He's the slave driver, and his name's Jupiter, too. He's pretty much already running the place as it is. He's a great guy. Just put down my name as the overseer, because you're supposed to have a white person in charge, but Jupiter can actually run the plantation. You can trust him."

Lady Chatsfield looked confused. "But you don't understand. My husband will continue to own the slaves."

"No, he won't," Alex said. "I've come to tell you a secret. I've arranged it so the slaves will belong to you. Mr. Thornhill doesn't know, and I hope you don't mind. I know you don't want to be a slaveowner, but you're the slaves' best chance to have a good life, and maybe become free one day."

Lady Chatsfield nodded crisply. She understood.

"There's one more thing," Alex said hesitantly. "Jupe wants to go back to America, but, obviously, he can't go back to Georgia. He's got an aunt in Massachusetts, but he can't afford to take a ship there."

"I will pay his passage, gladly," said Lady Chatsfield. "And I thank you from the bottom of my heart for your kind intervention. But is there nothing more I can do for the unfortunate slaves of Kintyre Plantation? Can I not free them?"

Alex said, "No, I don't think so. It's not legal to free your slaves."

LAND, LANDED, LANDING

Lady Chatsfield paused momentarily, and then she said, "I shall bear your advice in mind. I appreciate your kind assistance, Master Day, and I take it that our conversation will remain in confidence."

"Yes, of course," Alex said, and he gave a short bow. "I've got one more favor to ask you. Please could I stay on at Balesworth Hall for a while?"

"You wish to remain for your health, I presume? You are most welcome to stay, but only for a few days, because I am preparing to leave. I will announce my imminent departure to the servants this afternoon. They will remain here, with the exception of Flora and my butler, who will accompany me."

Alex blurted out, "But wouldn't it make more sense to keep Mrs. Watson with you, and leave Mr. Veeriswamy? I mean, it's her house you're moving to, and she can cook for you…"

Lady Chatsfield looked icily at him. "That is not your business. I am grateful for your assistance. You may go now."

Nobody, Hannah thought, would notice if a room wasn't dusted today. Now that Lady Chatsfield had announced that she was leaving, the servants had been slacking off whenever they got the chance. Roberts the carriage driver had slipped off to Balesworth, to look for a new position (he said), although Mrs. Watson grumbled that it was more likely he was going to the pub. Since the furniture belonged with the house, only Flora and Mr. Veeriswamy were needed to help Lady Chatsfield and Sarah to pack their few belongings.

Hannah took full advantage of the stupor that had settled over the household. She found a sunny corner of the large formal garden that could not be seen from the house. There, she pulled off her apron and dress, and lay down to enjoy the spring sunshine, wearing only her shift. She couldn't believe how much lighter she felt without her heavy clothes. Blissfully, she drifted into sleep.

She was rudely awoken by a sharp light kick to the ankle. Struggling upright, she found Brandon standing over her, glowering.

"You are so lazy," he said. "Come on, get up and come help me."

"Help you do what?" exclaimed Hannah.

"Our jobs!" Brandon said. "Unless you want to be fired?"

"Sure," Hannah said. "Why not? Lady Chatsfield is leaving, so we're getting canned anyway."

Brandon sighed heavily. "No, we're not. The servants stay with the estate even when it changes hands, and the chances are excellent that the new Lord Chatsfield will keep us on. But, yeah, you will get fired if Mr. V. catches you out here tanning yourself. Oh, and by the way, he's sent Jupe to ask Mr. Letchmore to send a wagon to remove Mrs. Watson's stuff from the cottage in Balesworth. He wants you and me to go to Mrs. Watson's house and get her stuff ready to be moved this afternoon."

"Oh, great," Hannah groaned.

"No, it really is great," Brandon said. "It gives us an excuse to plant some proof of Henry's birthplace at the house."

Just then, they were both startled by a shriek of indignation. Sarah was standing behind them with a hand over her mouth. Hannah clambered to her feet, and brushed the grass off her shift. It was then that she realized she was standing in the Victorian version of underwear. No wonder Sarah was shocked.

"How…How dare you…" she spluttered, growing red in the face.

For once, Hannah looked chagrined. Brandon leaped to her defense as Hannah hastily dressed. "Hey, Miss Sarah, it's no big deal," he said. "You and your mother are leaving, and Hannah's been working her brains out at Balesworth Hall. We all have. Does it really matter if she takes a break?"

At that moment, Henry ran up, coming to a screeching halt when he saw that Hannah was dressing. He looked agog for a second, and then said pompously, "You two ought to be attending to your duties. Servants are not permitted to roam in the gardens."

Now Brandon felt his temper rising to the boil. "We're at least as smart as the both of you, but you get to hang out in nice rooms…and libraries…and stuff, while all we do is work… How come? Who made you the boss of us?"

Hannah stood stock still. She had never seen Brandon so angry. Sarah looked askance at him, blinking slowly, while Henry watched, fascinated. This was clearly not a conversation that anyone had expected.

Truthfully, Brandon didn't care. He was tired of being in the nineteenth century, tired of doing work that was hard, boring, and earned him no respect. He was tired of feeling as though he was unimportant. He had had enough. "Why should you guys have a fun life, and us not? Huh? Hannah and me, we're kids, too."

Sarah looked levelly at him, and finally, she spoke calmly. "You are servants, and your place is below stairs. I was born to the upper class, and Henry has been fortunate to receive my mother's patronage, for which he is grateful. Aren't you, Henry?"

Henry nodded frantically. "Oh, yes, Miss Sarah. Very grateful indeed."

What a suck-up, Brandon thought. Instantly, he was horrified to realize that he had said that out loud.

"Be quiet, Brandon," snapped Sarah. "I will allow your remarks to go unreported and unpunished, provided you…"

"Oh, shut up," yelled Hannah. "You just go on and on and on, like you're the queen, or something. You aren't all that. You won't even be living here soon."

Sarah Chatsfield was amazed to be spoken to like this by anyone, least of all by servants. But she also saw how distressed Brandon and Hannah were. She wasn't an unkind girl, but she was very serious, more so than her mother thought proper for a young lady. She was embarrassed by her part in creating a scene, and knowing that Brandon and Hannah were touchier than any servants she had ever met before, she felt responsible for having upset them. When she spoke again, she said quietly, "I'm sorry I upset you both. It's not personal, you see… But, surely, you must understand that you are both servants?"

Brandon rolled his eyes. "We're servants right now, but we won't be in the future. We'll have the chance to do something with our lives, and not just work for rich people. In fact, we'll have more of a chance at a life than you will, Sarah. I mean, don't you want to be somebody?"

She raised an eyebrow at him. "What do you mean?"

Brandon knew what her answer would be, but he was in a lousy mood, and he wanted to force Sarah to admit that, for all her wealth, she had no ambition. "What I mean is, what do you want to do with your life when you grow up?"

Sarah looked at him as though he were incredibly stupid. "I have told you before. I shall marry, of course. I shall marry a gentleman and live as a lady."

Hannah glanced at Brandon, and said, "So, really, that's it? You don't want to travel, or anything like that? That sounds kind of boring."

Sarah hesitated, and Henry interrupted. "I shall tell Mr. Veeriswamy that you were rude to Miss Sarah…"

At once, Sarah told Henry to be quiet; Hannah and Brandon told him to shut up.

"Hannah, Brandon," Sarah said cautiously, "Both of you have urged me repeatedly to have ambition, and I don't understand. Please explain. What do you mean?"

Hannah said, "I guess I mean you need to get a life. Have some fun. Go shopping…"

"That's fun?" Brandon said skeptically, as he turned to Hannah. "I was thinking more like she should read some books, get out more…"

Sarah was even more baffled by their exchange. "But I'm a girl," she said weakly. "And I don't want to be thought of as a bluestocking. If gentlemen think me too clever, I shall never marry."

"But that's crazy," Hannah exclaimed. "Why would anyone want a stupid wife?"

Sarah didn't know how to answer, but she thought to herself that it was a very interesting question.

Now, quite unexpectedly, Henry said solemnly, "I, too, should like to become a person of some importance when I grow up. But I doubt that it will ever happen, now that Lady Chatsfield is leaving Balesworth Hall. She has told me that she no longer plans to send me to the East India College. However, I am glad to have had so many books to read, and perhaps the new Lord Chatsfield will allow me to continue to borrow from his library."

Brandon looked at Henry with new compassion. "Look, Henry, we're going on a secret adventure in Balesworth this afternoon, Alex, Hannah, and me, and we need you to come along."

"You do?" Henry squeaked. He was flattered.

"I... I would like to join you, also," Sarah said timidly.

Brandon gave her a delighted smile.

Early that afternoon, Hannah and Brandon rounded up Henry, Alex, and Sarah, and the four of them set off. On the way, Alex begged two large scraps of parchment from a lawyer's office on Balesworth High Street, claiming that they were needed for important business at Balesworth Hall. When he returned outside, he held up the parchment proudly.

Hannah looked at it without interest. "It's paper," she said. "So what?"

"No, it's not paper," said Alex. "It's much tougher. It's scraped animal hide, and it stands a chance of surviving to the twenty-first century. Just to make sure, though, we're going to plant two copies."

"What are you doing?" Henry asked, feeling the parchment.

Brandon turned to him. "Henry? We want you to write out something for us, okay? Have you ever heard of time capsules?"

"No, I have not," Henry said sourly.

Brandon explained. "A time capsule is like a collection of stuff from the present that you bury somewhere so that people in the future can dig it up."

Henry looked baffled. "I still don't... Oh. Do you mean something like a message in a bottle?"

"That's right!" Alex said cheerfully. "A message in a bottle, sent from 1851 to the future. And we would like you to write it." He handed Henry the parchment, a pen, and an ink bottle.

"But why must I do it?" asked Henry suspiciously.

Brandon had an answer for him. "Because we think you're going to be very famous, and we want people in the future to know where you were born."

Henry was thrilled. "I have always thought that it is my destiny to become something greater than a cook's son! Very well, then. What is it that you wish me to write?"

"Easy," said Alex, and he began to dictate: "I, Henry Watson, was born in this house at... Wait, what's your address?"

Henry said, "Weston Cottage, Balesworth, Hertfordshire."

"Your little house has a name?" giggled Hannah.

"Of course, why not?" said Brandon. "Lots of English houses have names. I think Mrs. D. even had a name for her house... What was it?

Alex looked at them and then burst out laughing. "Weston Cottage! Don't you remember, Hannah?"

Sarah was watching them, fascinated. She had never done anything quite so out of the ordinary as this small adventure, and she was enjoying every minute of it, however baffling she found it. "Who is this 'Mrs. Dee' of whom you speak?" she asked.

"Oh, you would never believe us if we told you," Alex said simply. "She's a lady we once knew. Or will know. Depends on how you look at it."

Hannah muttered in an aside to Brandon, "And she's also Sarah's daughter, but I don't think I'm gonna mention that."

"Don't," warned Brandon.

After they bought a small tin box in which to store the letter, they walked to Weston Cottage, and, taking a shovel from the garden shed, they took turns digging the ground. Two hours later, a tired and grubby Alex piled on the last shovelful of earth and said, "I hope Mrs. D. doesn't dig it up, planting cabbages or something."

"No, I don't think so," said Brandon, who was equally tired and grubby. "We put it six feet under, just like a dead body."

Hannah was picking at a broken fingernail that she had used as an excuse to hand over the digging job to the others. "It's all dead bodies with you, isn't it, Brandon?"

Brandon gave Hannah a pointed look. "Yeah, that's right. Are you volunteering to be the next one?"

"Ha. Ha. Ha," Hannah said mirthlessly.

Sarah was slumped against a tree, dirty and exhausted, but happy. She was part of something important, she knew that, and she had done something useful, helping with the digging. She seldom did anything useful.

Brandon wiped his brow, and muttered to Hannah and Alex, "Okay, so now where do we put the other copy of Henry's document?"

"Somewhere in the house, I guess," Hannah suggested. "How about underneath a loose floorboard or something?"

"Okay," Alex said, "but we should leave Henry and Sarah out of this, in case they decide to tell someone and give the game away. Leave it to me."

While Brandon and Hannah distracted the others, Alex slipped to the front of the house, and ran upstairs. In what would become his and Eric's bedroom in 1940, he got on his knees, then pressed, pulled, pushed, and finally yanked out a short floorboard near the wall.

"Well, if it wasn't loose before, it is now," he muttered to himself. He slipped the letter into the small hole, and replaced the floorboard, pushing it down hard to make it stick. As he did so, he heard a horse and cart pull up outside. Mr. Letchmore and Jupe had come to fetch Mrs. Watson's belongings.

All the kids helped old Mr. Letchmore to load up the furniture to be moved. Sarah, who rarely exercised her arm muscles, found lifting difficult, and she hesitated, until Hannah teased her about being weak and helpless. She tried to tell herself that Hannah, being a servant, was somehow more suited to grunt work, but the more she spoke with Hannah, the more she realized that this maid wasn't at all stupid, unlike poor Flora. Sarah couldn't stop thinking about what Brandon and Hannah had said to her earlier. She also wondered what her future would be, now that she was leaving Balesworth Hall.

Jupe loaded a chair onto the back of the wagon, wiped off his hands, and smiled at Alex. "Lady Chatsfield told me this morning that she's going to send me to my auntie in Massachusetts, and that I should thank you. So I thank you kindly, Alex, with all my heart."

Alex was genuinely happy for him. "That's awesome! So you really will be free. But I'm sorry you can't go home to Kintyre."

"I'll get home again, don't you fret," Jupe said, as they walked back into the cottage. "I promised my momma I would. I can't stay away from Georgia forever. It's my home."

Alex hoped that Jupe would make good on his promise, but not until slavery had ended.

****

Two days later, Alex, Brandon and Hannah were sitting at the table in the servants' hall, going over what they had accomplished. But Brandon was stressed out. Everything seemed to be done, yet they were still stuck in England in 1851. What had they missed?

"Maybe we're supposed to save the park next to your house?" Alex said to Brandon.

Hannah was not impressed. "Now you're making stuff up. Like, what does that have to do with anything? It's in Snipesville."

But Alex was insistent. "I think it might. But we have to figure out how."

He thought again, and asked Brandon and Hannah to think, too. Nobody could think of anything.

Just then, a voice behind them said, "Sorry I'm late. I forgot how long it takes to walk from the station, and it was raining rather heavily."

Hannah jumped up, but she wasn't exactly welcoming. "Well, it's about time! Where have you been? I was starting to think I was stuck being a house-maid until I died."

Brandon had also leapt to his feet. "Professor! Man, am I glad to see you! But what are you late for?"

The Professor shook the rain off her coat. "To take you home, of course. I suppose you will all be weepy, like last time…"

"No," said Brandon. "Definitely not. I don't think any of us have any regrets about leaving 1851. I mean, maybe I shouldn't speak for Hannah and Alex, but I'm pretty sure you guys feel the same way, right?"

"You think?" Hannah said with a groan.

The Professor held up a hand. "Well done, everyone. Hannah, have you got the calculator?"

Hannah reached into her apron pocket, and handed over the calculator to the Professor, who had already opened the door.

But Hannah wasn't budging. "It's freezing out there! And it's already dark. I hope you have a coach or something."

The Professor smiled and said, "No, I don't. But it doesn't matter. It'll be light soon. Come on."

Following her, the three kids stepped uncertainly into the night. It was cold, even for May in England, and it was dark. The wind was blowing, and the freezing air stung their ears.

"Please tell me we're not walking," Hannah protested.

"It's not far to Balesworth," said the Professor firmly, crunching her way briskly down the gravel driveway.

As the boys trudged behind, Hannah caught up with her. "Are you mad? Yes, it is a long way to walk in the freezing cold at night."

"Look, the sun's coming up," said the Professor calmly.

And it was. There was the beginning of a dawn. As the kids watched in amazement, the sun rose as though in fast-forward. It was light, it was sunny, it was warm, and small puffy clouds were scudding across the blue sky. They were still walking through the grounds of Balesworth Hall, but ahead of them was the freeway buzzing with traffic, and the squat skyline of New Balesworth. On impulse, the kids turned around and looked back. Balesworth Hall was still there, but very much changed. It was larger than before, and it now looked like a medieval castle.

"A later owner decided it needed updating," explained the Professor. "After the Great Exhibition, Gothic architecture became very popular. That's the sort of churchy style you saw in the Medieval Court at the Crystal Palace." She pointed to an empty parking lot, and a sign showing the way to a tea room. "It's open to the public these days. It costs a lot to run a house this large, and not everybody who inherits one can afford to keep it," she said. "The last owner gave the estate to the National Trust. Now anyone can enjoy visiting the house and playing in the park. But let's hurry. People are waiting for you."

It was quite a different walk into Balesworth in the twenty-first century than it had been in the nineteenth. At the end of the gravel driveway, there was a gate, a ticket booth, and a sign reading, Welcome to Balesworth Hall. Then the small group crossed a bridge over the busy freeway, and walked through an area of office buildings and traffic circles.

"I still don't like New Balesworth," Alex said.

"Me neither," Brandon agreed, "but I'd rather work in one of those," he pointed to a tall glass building, "than down a coal mine."

Alex still wasn't impressed. "I worked in an office, and it was really boring. That's what my dad does too, but I hope I don't have to work in one when I grow up."

"Oh, hey," Hannah said, "Anything would be better than working in a factory. At least you guys got to sit on your butts and stare into space. I was on my feet all day, and I had to totally concentrate the whole time."

As the group neared Verity and Eric's house, the kids grew nervous and excited. But the Professor stopped about a hundred yards away. "Okay, here's where I leave you for now. Go ahead and knock. But don't worry, I'll be back very shortly. I promise."

Hannah cried, "Don't you leave us now! Wait..." But the Professor ignored her. She dashed across the road, turned a corner behind a hedge, and disappeared from view.

Alex said what Hannah was thinking. "How are we going to explain to Grandma how we vanished, and then reappeared? What happens if it turns out we've been gone for months?"

"Face it, it's going to be weird," said Brandon. "Our lives are now officially weird."

Reluctantly, the three of them walked through the front garden and knocked on the door. They waited anxiously, shifting from foot to foot. When the door opened, Eric greeted them impatiently, as though they were strangers. "Yes, can I help you? I've already given money for the school charity appeal, if that's what you're here for."

The kids looked at him. He looked back at them with a remote stare. Something had clearly happened. He didn't recognize them. Finally, Hannah broke the silence. "Is our grandma here?"

"No, love, I'm sorry, you have the wrong house."

He was about to close the door, when Hannah took a deep breath. "Eric, it's me, Hannah. This is Alex, and that's Brandon. From 1940. The evacuees? George Braithwaite? Mrs. D. looked after us?"

Eric staggered backward, and the kids were afraid he was having a heart attack. He sputtered, "Is this a joke?"

"No," sighed Hannah, "It's not a joke. Do I look like I'm joking? Let us in and we'll prove it."

Hannah was freaked out to realize that the trip to England with Grandma and Grandpa had ceased to exist: Time had wiped it away. But at least, she reflected, it had given them practice in persuading Eric that they were who they said they were. It took much less time to convince him the second time around.

Eric and the kids were all talking excitedly in the living room, when the back door slammed shut.

"That'll be Verity," said Eric, slowly getting to his feet. He wagged a finger at the kids. "Now don't start in on her, you three. Give her time, all right?"

At that moment, a tired-looking man with a suitcase appeared in the doorway of the living room.

"Mark?" said Eric in surprise. "What are you doing here?"

"Hello, Dad," said Mark Powell. "I've come to stay for a bit, just to get myself sorted out. Mum will explain. I'm going upstairs for a lie-down, okay?"

Verity was standing behind him, clutching her car keys. "You do that, dear," she said acidly. "Eric, Mark has lost his job at the bank, he's been evicted from his flat…"

"Apartment," corrected Mark wearily.

"It's a flat," Verity said firmly. "I speak English, not American. Now, as I was saying before I was so rudely interrupted, our son has lost his job, flat, and car, none of which are his fault, I suppose. But it's worse than that. He's up to his ears in credit card debt. So he's coming home…"

"It'll just be a couple of days, Mum," Mark protested, "Just until I can get back on my feet."

"Mark, don't interrupt," said Verity, who didn't notice her husband desperately trying to hint that they had company. "He's moving home until he gets it through his thick skull that his job is gone, it's not coming back, and he's going to have to rethink his future."

Mark groaned and muttered before carrying his suitcase upstairs.

Now Verity walked into the living room, and she saw the kids for the first time. She frowned at her husband. "Eric, you could have told me someone was here. Who's this?"

Then she looked at the three kids' faces, and her hand flew to her mouth in shock. "Impossible! It can't be…" she stammered.

With a sly smile, Brandon muttered, "Here we go again."

An hour later, the kids were tucking into home-made scones and jam. "These taste just like Mrs. D.'s!" Alex said happily through a mouthful of crumbs.

"They ought to, dear," said Verity, offering him the plate. "It's Granny's recipe. She was famous for her scones. Here, have some more tea, Hannah. You know, it must be very strange for you to meet me as an old lady."

"It's okay," said Hannah politely. "I've had months to get used to it."

"You have?" said Verity in surprise.

Hannah sighed. "I guess I'm gonna have to explain that."

And so, Eric and Verity sat spellbound as Hannah and Brandon told their stories of the visit with their grandparents, and of life in 1851, while Alex remained quiet, looking very uncomfortable. It was Brandon who told the story of Mr. Thornhill and Lady Chatsfield.

When Brandon had finished his tale, Verity said thoughtfully, "You know, Granny once or twice made a dark reference to some wicked ancestor and a scandal involving her own grandmother. I wasn't really listening, more's the pity. But I had no idea that our family ever had a claim to Balesworth Hall. Just think, Eric, I could have been lady of the manor!"

Eric shook his head. "Not through your mother and grandmother, you couldn't. You can't inherit one of those aristocratic titles through the female line. And quite right, too," he said with a wink to Brandon and Alex.

"You old sexist," said Verity, digging him gently in the ribs. "I have to say, though, it's very odd that you kids would encounter other members of our family in your latest adventure. I've never thought of us as being especially interesting, or prone to time travel, come to that."

Brandon suddenly sat up. "Oh, that reminds me…We have good news. That writer you guys told us about, Henry Watson? We can prove he was born in this house."

Eric and Verity looked at each other in puzzlement. "But we know that," said Eric slowly. "We've always known that."

"How?" sputtered Hannah. The three kids exchanged confused glances.

Alex was most disappointed. "Man, after we went to all that trouble burying that box in the garden…"

Eric held up a finger and said, "Here, let me show you." He stepped over to the old writing desk, opened a drawer, and pulled out a crumpled yellowed document, then handed it to Brandon.

Brandon took one look at it, and said excitedly, "No, guys, it was all worthwhile."

Alex looked. The ink had faded a little, but it was unmistakably the note that Henry had written out for them. "Eric, where did you get this?"

Eric furrowed his brow as he reached back in time for a distant memory. "When I was a teenager, just after the Second World War, I was looking for a loose floorboard to hide a few cigarettes where Granny wouldn't find them."

Hannah interrupted him, "Hey, when did you start calling Mrs. D. 'Granny'? You always called her Mrs. D. when we knew you."

He smiled. "Oh, when she decided to adopt me…"

Brandon turned to Hannah. "Come on, let Eric tell his story!"

Irked, Hannah slumped on the sofa, her arms clasped across her chest. Eric continued. "Anyway, it took me a while to pry open the most likely floorboard in my room, the one that always creaked when I stepped on it. When I finally managed to open it, I found this document. I got so excited, I rushed downstairs to tell her, only I'd completely forgot I was holding the ciggies in the other hand. What's worse, I'd pinched them from her handbag. She recognized the type."

Verity laughed. "I'm surprised she didn't kill you."

"She very nearly did," said Eric with a grimace. "But this bit of paper here saved my bacon. She was fascinated, even though she had always said that Henry Watson was the most boring writer ever."

Alex was delighted. "We planted this letter," he said proudly. "And we planted a second copy in a box in the garden."

"Getaway!" laughed Eric. "That's extraordinary."

Verity turned to the kids. "You know, it's been very helpful, us knowing about old Henry. Since the War, Balesworth New Town has been growing and growing. There have been various efforts to build on the land around us, and Granny was once even threatened with compulsory purchase…"

Eric explained: "That means the council was going to make her sell the house to the government, and then knock it down."

Verity took up the story again. "But the Henry Watson connection has always helped us. You didn't notice the little blue plaque next to the front door, did you? It says that this house was his birthplace. We have supporters called the Friends of the Henry Watson Country, who have helped us time and time again to stop the land being built on. This year, the council finally approved plans for Henry Watson Country Park, to include all the land around us, so we can relax a bit."

Eric was curious. "So you three met Henry Watson, then? What was he like?"

Brandon minced no words. "He was a jerk. Full of himself."

"That makes sense," muttered Verity. "Now, to change the subject, how are you three getting home to America?"

Hannah raised an eyebrow. "I have no idea," she said. "The Professor is going to take us, I guess."

"The Professor? Who's that?"

Hannah sighed. "You might remember her, but probably not. She was the WVS lady who came to take us home in 1940. She took that picture of all of us in the back garden."

Verity looked doubtful. "Well, I remember somebody took you away, but I don't remember her."

Hannah said, "She wasn't really with the WVS. She's an evil time-traveling witch, and she's responsible for dragging us all over the place, and all over time."

"Witch or not, I'd very much like to meet her," said Verity. "And she can't be that bad, Hannah. It sounds as though you three have been doing some good on your travels, and you're having an adventure that the rest of us can only dream of."

Hannah pouted, but Brandon, nodding enthusiastically, agreed with Verity. "Yeah, I mean it's way more interesting than hanging out in Snipesville for the summer."

Hannah looked dubiously at Brandon. "Oh, yeah, like you had tons of fun down that coal mine…"

"I didn't say fun," Brandon shot back. "I said it was interesting. That's not the same thing, is it?"

Suddenly, Alex said very quietly, "I hated it."

There was a silence. Then Alex said in the same small voice. "1851 was awful. I don't want to go through this again."

The doorbell rang, and when Verity opened the door, the Professor introduced herself. "Hello, Verity. Lovely to see you again. I've come to take these three home."

As the Professor entered, Verity, following her, said, "Yes, I want to talk to you about that. Who are you, exactly? Do I know you?"

The Professor seemed surprised to be asked. "Me? Oh, I'm Kate Harrower. I teach history at Snipesville State College in America."

"No, that's not good enough," said Verity, perching on the edge of the sofa and folding her arms. "I'm talking about this time travel business, about three kids, and they are just kids, being involved in it. Please take a seat, because I want to talk with you."

"I don't know what you mean," the Professor said, glancing at her watch. "Good Lord, is that the time? Come on, kids, we have to go. Say your good-byes."

But Verity wasn't giving up so easily, and she swiftly blocked the door. "I think the children and Eric and I deserve an explanation, don't you? Who are you really? How do you have the power to travel through time?"

The Professor spoke breezily while trying to inch her way past Verity. "Oh, I'm an historian, and we all have the power to travel through time. It's the documents, you see, they're absolutely transporting."

Verity would have none of it. "Nonsense. Now why don't you… Wait, have we met before?" She peered closely at the Professor's face.

"She's the WVS lady," said Hannah. "Remember I told you?"

"Yes, of course I remember you telling me," said Verity, "But it's not that…"

The Professor was quite a bit shorter than Verity, and she suddenly ducked under her arm, pulling Alex behind her. Brandon and Hannah gave apologetic shrugs, and followed the Professor as she trotted up the garden path. "I'll write, Verity," Hannah called back. "Maybe I can convince my Grandma to bring us here next summer."

"If we're still here," Eric replied glumly. "We're both knocking on a bit, you know. We're not as young as we used to be."

"He's right," said Verity. "And so long as this Harrower woman is dragging the three of you around, perhaps you could persuade her to let you visit us thirty years ago? Or fifty? When we were younger? Granny would have loved to have seen you again, although I doubt she would have believed this time travel malarkey."

But the children and the Professor were gone.

Verity turned to Eric. "Of course, it might mess up something in time if they visited us again in the past, wouldn't it?"

"We wouldn't know," said Eric, shepherding her back into the living room. "Rather like we have no memory of the kids coming to England with their grandparents. It would just be how things had always been."

"That's a very strange thought, Eric," said Verity. "Look, shouldn't we at least ring George Braithwaite and ask him to keep an eye on the kids for us?"

"From the sound of it, he already is," said Eric.

"All the same," Verity said, "I'd like to be sure. I don't like the look of that Harrower woman."

The kids sat in a first class carriage, and it was their best train journey ever: The seats were comfortable, and a steward served tea for them all in real china tea cups, which he presented along with shortbread cookies.

"This is way nicer than the first class carriage we took with my grandparents," Hannah said to the Professor. "Did it change because we messed with Time?"

The Professor shook her head and smiled. "No, this is just proof that seeing is not believing. It's nothing to do with that. When you were with your grandparents, you took one of the local commuter trains, and first class compartments on those are always a bit grim. This is a long-distance train, and their first class compartments are always much nicer. We were just lucky that Balesworth is the last major train station before London, so lots of long-distance trains stop there."

As the train began to pull smoothly out of Vauxhall Station, the very last stop before Kings Cross, a blond man in uniform entered the carriage, calling out, "Tickets, please!"

"It's Mr. Veeriswhat'shisname !" cried Hannah, jumping in her seat.

"I beg your pardon, love?" said the startled ticket inspector. "Have we met before?"

"Yes, when we were…" said Hannah, but Brandon elbowed her in the ribs.

"Ow... No. I guess not. I saw your nametag."

"What about it?" said Mr. Veeriswamy, looking as though he dared her to make a joke of his name.

Brandon intervened. "We've been researching the history of Balesworth Hall, and you have the same name as a butler who worked there."

"That's right," said Mr. Veeriswamy in surprise. "Well, well, well... how about that... You know, my great-great-great-grandad, he was the first Indian butler in England. He came from the Punjab, you know. Later on, he married some lady who'd lost her title, or so the family story goes. All very scandalous, I'm sure."

"Lady Chatsfield!" exclaimed Brandon. "He married Lady Chatsfield!"

Now all the kids were agog. Lady Chatsfield had married her butler?

"Might have been the name," said Mr. Veeriswamy, pointing his ballpoint pen at Brandon. "Very well might be. Imagine, me, descended from aristocracy. That's a laugh, that is!"

Brandon said excitedly, "But that means you're, like, related to some people we know."

About this, Mr. Veeriswamy seemed less surprised. "I don't doubt it. I mean, some cousins of mine call themselves Vereham. They didn't like people making fun of the name, so they changed it. Some of my Vereham cousins are very prejudiced against Indian people. Would you credit it, eh?" He rolled his eyes and tutted. "Mind you, even my part of the family called ourselves Vereham for a long time, until my old great-grandad got involved in Theosophy, this funny religion back in the 1920s, which made it very fashionable to be Indian. So he changed our name back to Veeriswamy, and we've been Veeriswamy ever since. Of course, at school, I did take a bit of teasing off the other kids, English and Indian."

Quietly, the Professor leaned over and whispered to Hannah, "Go into the restroom over there."

"Why?" whispered Hannah.

"Just do it," said the Professor.

As Hannah got up, Mr. Veeriswamy put out a hand. "Hang on a sec. I need to see your ticket, if you don't mind."

The Professor intervened. "Hannah thinks she dropped her ticket in the loo," she said. "I'm going to help her look. We'll be right back."

"Don't be long, please, Mr. Veeriswamy said warningly. "I've got this whole train to inspect. Now, then, where was I... Oh, yes. My grandmother always said..."

Brandon and Alex were nodding politely at Mr. Veeriswamy's recitation of his family history, when Brandon spied the Professor frantically signaling to them over the ticket inspector's shoulder. "Excuse me, I gotta throw up," said Brandon, leaping out of his seat. Now Alex saw her too. "Me, too," he squeaked, dashing after Brandon.

"Hey, wait a minute!" yelled Mr. Veeriswamy. But the kids were already in the bathroom, and the Professor had locked the electronic door behind them.

As Mr. Veeriswamy banged on the door, Hannah was holding onto the restroom wall to steady herself. "Your time machine is a toilet?" she asked the Professor in disbelief. "Wow, that makes sense. What do we do, jump in the bowl while you flush?"

"No, this isn't a time machine," said the Professor. "I just forgot to buy train tickets. Hang on, it won't be long until our stop."

Hannah was about to point out that Mr. Veeriswamy would be waiting for them outside the restroom when they arrived at Kings Cross. But at that moment, the train entered a tunnel, and the lights flickered out. They were plunged into pitch darkness.

In an instant, the light flickered on again: The kids were in Alex and Hannah's living room in Snipesville. The Professor had vanished.

Alex sighed with relief. But Hannah, holding her breath, frantically rushed over to the table where her cellphone was recharging, snatched it up, and flipped it open. She peered at the date, and there it was: August 17, 11 a.m. They were home.

Chapter 16
A DiFFERENT DESTiNY

On the evening of August 17, the smoky, meaty smell of barbecuing ribs hung deliciously over the park in Snipesville, Georgia. Church ladies toted grocery bags filled with paper plates, side dishes packed in plastic boxes and aluminum foil containers, pie plates, and jugs of punch. They laid out the food on the picnic tables, which they had covered in plastic tablecloths. A colorful home-made banner strung between two pecan trees announced the occasion: Dr. George Braithwaite Park Dedication Celebration.

Hannah and Alex were among a handful of white guests at the party, and Brandon soon spotted them. The three kids gazed at the banner.

"Man, that's weird," Alex said. "When we left, the city council had said the park wasn't even a park, and they were gonna build on it. Now we're back, and they're naming it after Doctor B. We must have changed something else when we travelled in time."

Just then, Dr. Braithwaite himself approached and hugged the kids. "Thank you for coming, all of you!"

Hannah sniffed. "It was just lucky that we found the invite Scotch-taped to the mailbox when we got home this afternoon."

"Wait until you hear what we've been up to," Alex said.

"I dread to think," laughed Dr. Braithwaite. "But you couldn't possibly have done much damage since last night's meeting, surely?"

"What exactly happened at the meeting?" Hannah asked cautiously.

Dr. Braithwaite looked puzzled. "But you were there…"

"Dr. B., we've been time-travelling again," said Alex. "You know? Balesworth? Please, just tell us."

Dr. Braithwaite was looking at them very seriously now. He cleared his throat. "The city council voted down the Renaissance Project. Instead, they decided to name the park in my honor."

"But I don't understand, sir," Brandon said. "We went to that same meeting, and the council voted to approve the development."

Dr. Braithwaite looked baffled. "Brandon, I don't know what you're talking about. You three know the economy is pretty rough right now, and the market for houses in Snipesville is terrible. Turns out, the bank's main office in New York was considering withdrawing the proposal. But don't you remember? We reminded the councilmen that the park is a traditional gathering space for black people in Snipesville. This isn't a fancy park, but it's what the English would call a common, or common land. That means that nobody really owns it: Everybody does, which is why the city has a responsibility to preserve it. Fortunately, they agreed to do so."

So Alex had been right: The outcome of the meeting had changed while they were away. And it wasn't the only thing.

"Where did all these pecan trees come from?" Brandon asked. When the kids had left on their latest adventure, there were almost no trees of any kind in the park.

"Oh, it's really very interesting," answered Dr. Braithwaite. "You know, I learned that there have been pecan trees here for longer than anyone can remember, from back when this was part of Kintyre Plantation. Brandon, it is said that one of your ancestors, a slave named Jupiter, planted the first pecan trees here so all the Kintyre slaves could gather them. I don't know if that's true, mind you, but it's a nice story."

Brandon was astonished. He excused himself to go and look for his father. Minutes later, he found his dad skulking behind a tree, sinking his teeth into an enormous barbecue pork sandwich. "Don't you tell your mom," Mr. Clark hissed, through a mouthful of shredded pork and bread. "Mmm, this is so good. Boy, I miss real food."

Brandon asked his dad about the story of Jupiter and the pecan trees, and to his amazement, Mr. Clark was not surprised. "Oh, sure," he said. "That was one of those stories my Great-Aunt Constance was always going on about. She used to sit on our porch with all the other old ladies, and they'd tell stories about slavery times. I didn't pay too much attention, to be honest with you."

"Can you remember that story?" Brandon asked urgently.

Mr. Clark inhaled another mouthful of sandwich, and chewed thoughtfully for a while. "Um, let's see… Jupiter was your several times great-grandfather. He was the slave driver, which made him pretty unpopular, because he punished other slaves. His master ran off, and Jupiter found himself in charge, although that's the part of the story that I don't buy. Anyhow, I guess he decided one day to plant some pecan trees, so folks would have some to eat, and so they could sell some to raise cash. The trees didn't actually produce nuts until after the end of the Civil War, but folks have been picking them ever since."

"Are those the same trees?" Brandon was amazed.

"Oh, sure. Pecan trees can live for hundreds of years."

Brandon was pretty annoyed with his father. "Dad, how come you never told me this before?"

His dad shrugged. "It never seemed that big of a deal. I think I told your brother Jonathan once or twice, but he's not much interested in family history. I'm glad to know you are, though. You know, now that I think about it, the old ladies used to say something else about Jupiter… He had a son, whose name was also Jupiter, and he ran off. Aunt Constance said he made it all the way to England, but I definitely don't buy that. I think that was just the old ladies' wishful thinking."

"No, it's true," interrupted Brandon excitedly. His father gave him a puzzled look.

"Um," he added lamely, "It's true. It's gotta be. It's a family story."

His dad laughed. "In my experience, son, you have to take most family stories with a grain of salt. So I doubt young Jupiter ever made it to London. Wherever he went, though, he did come back to Georgia, I know that much. But that's as much as I do know about him. Young Jupiter was kin to us, but he's not directly related. He'd be like your several-times great-uncle."

Brandon had another question. "Dad, why is your first name Gordon? I mean, were you named after anyone?"

"I have no idea. Maybe it's an old family name. Or maybe my mama just liked it. Why do you ask?"

"Just wondered, that's all," Brandon said. "It doesn't matter."

Alex and Hannah, meanwhile, had spotted someone familiar. "Excuse me," said Hannah, nudging Alex, "but look who just crashed the party."

The Professor was helping herself to thickly-shredded pork in a creamy mustard barbecue sauce, heaping it onto a bun next to a pile of coleslaw. "Hi, Hannah. Great food, isn't it? One of the best things about the South, I reckon, is Southern food."

Hannah looked skeptically at her. "Uh, huh. Whatever. I have questions, so don't take off, okay?"

"I won't," said the Professor, settling down into a folding chair with her plate and a cup of sweet iced tea. She invited Hannah to sit next to her.

Hannah sat down, leaned forward, and said, "First question: Why do you keep doing this to us?"

The Professor sighed. "I don't do anything to you, and I do wish you wouldn't keep on about it. You can be very tiresome, Hannah."

Hannah sat up straight. "Okay, still not answering, no surprise there. Second, why did I end up in Dundee? What did that have to do with anything?"

CHAPTER SIXTEEN

The Professor took a forkful of food. "Why not end up in Dundee?"

Hannah started to lose her temper, but caught herself in time. "Okay, let me try asking you about Dundee another way. The people I stayed with were called Gordon, and Brandon's dentist boss in 1915 was called Gordon…"

"…And my dad's first name is Gordon," said Brandon, who had just arrived with Alex.

"Goodness, is this an ambush?" said the Professor. "Gordon is a very common Scottish name, kids. I wouldn't worry about it."

Hannah jabbed a finger at her. "Yeah, okay, whatever, but help me out here, okay? We three kids all end up in Balesworth, so I have to think that Balesworth is somehow connected to why this stuff keeps happening to us. And Alex was with Mr. Thornhill, which explains some sort of weird connection between Snipesville and Balesworth. But I totally don't understand what Dundee has to do with anything…"

"…Or Hitherton…." said Brandon.

"Six degrees of separation," the Professor said suddenly.

"What?" Hannah said.

"It's a saying. It means, in short, that everyone on Earth is connected somehow. Everything you guys were doing had something to do with the Industrial Revolution, which is the big shift in the way that people live that began in England. Instead of most people farming the land and making the things they need for themselves, people started working in factories."

"More and more people in the nineteenth century began to think that they really deserved a share of the money they were creating with their work. Then they saw the Great Exhibition, and it said to them: One day, you, too, will be able to afford stuff like flushing toilets and hideous ornaments."

"But if the slaves and the factory workers didn't get the money that was being made," Brandon asked, "who did?"

The Professor said carefully, "Well, I think you know the answer to that, if you think about it. People like Mr. Thornhill and Lady Chatsfield, and the mill owners, like Mr. Sutherland, who…"

"But where did he get the money from to start a factory?" Hannah suddenly asked.

The Professor was taken aback by Hannah's question. Then she smiled. "That, Hannah, is the best question you have ever asked. Since you ask, I shall tell you. Mr. Sutherland wasn't born rich. Along with a couple of rather richer friends from his church, he got the money as a bank loan to start a jute mill. It turned out to be the best decision of his life: Jute wasn't glamorous, but it was made into sacks, as you know, and sacks were like the brown cardboard boxes of the nineteenth century, used to transport all sorts of things, including cotton. He made a fortune. Now what's the next obvious question, Hannah?"

Hannah looked blank and shrugged her shoulders.

The Professor sighed. "Well, I suppose it was too much to ask... Where did the banks get the money from, to loan to Mr. Sutherland and his partners?"

"Okay then," said Brandon. "Tell us. Where?"

The Professor smiled. "That's a story for yet another day."

"My brain hurts," Hannah groaned. "And don't think I haven't noticed that you never answered my question about Dundee."

"No, wait, I get it!" Brandon said. "Okay, so Mr. Sutherland was like Mr. Spencer. They made money because they figured out what was a good idea at the right time, yeah? And so did the Earl who owned the mine I worked in, in Hitherton..."

"The Earl of Chatsfield," said the Professor, "He was the cousin of Viscount Chatsfield, who is better known to you guys as Mr. Thornhill."

"But," Brandon yelled, "the Earl had money to start with! The Earl owned the land where the coal was found."

"That's right. The land was his capital. Now I should add that Mr. Sutherland also had another kind of capital: He was the son of a minister, and had had a good education. If he had been an illiterate Irish laborer or a jute spinner, the bank would not have loaned him a penny. Not everybody has the same chances today, and in the nineteenth century, most people had very few chances at all. That's why Mina went to America: People saw it as a land of opportunity, where land was free, and so were people."

"Except for slaves," said Brandon quietly.

Alex had a question now. "Why didn't Mr. Thornhill want to be a lord? I heard what he said, about not being interested in running an estate and stuff, but I don't get it. Why sell Balesworth Hall and give up a fancy title unless you have to?"

"Oh, but he did have to. At least the way he saw it," said the Professor. "You see, Mr. Thornhill needed to go home to his family in Georgia."

Hannah's eyes got big. "I knew it! He was a biggie...a bigga... What's that word?"

"Bigamist," supplied Brandon.

"Thanks," said Hannah, "He was one of those! He had two wives!"

"Not exactly," the Professor said. "He could not marry his second wife. Indeed, her very existence was a closely-guarded secret in 1851. You need to know a few things about Mr. Thornhill. He emigrated to America because he was failing in England. He liked gambling a little too much, and he lost the money he had inherited from his father, the old Earl of Chatsfield. Then he heard that it was easy to make a fortune in Georgia, and decided to set up his law practice in Savannah. But his wife did not come with him, and Mr. Thornhill was lonely, you see."

"That makes sense," Brandon said. "But if he was lonely, why didn't he take his wife?"

"Aha," the Professor said. "Lady Chatsfield, or Mrs. Thornhill as she was then, refused to come to America with him, and I can hardly blame her. Savannah was prone to malaria and yellow fever. So young Mr. Thornhill decided to cross the Atlantic alone. He could have got a divorce, but divorce in the 1830s was very expensive, so like most couples at the time who had problems, Mr. and Mrs. Thornhill simply split up."

"I knew it!" Brandon exclaimed.

The Professor continued. "As the husband, Mr. Thornhill was given custody of the children. That's how it was in the 1830s, and that's why he took the boys. And then, of course, years later, the boys died."

"Wow, that's sad," Brandon said.

The Professor nodded. "Later, Mr. Thornhill entered a relationship with another woman in Savannah. Then, after her master died, he bought her."

"He bought her? His girlfriend was a slave? That's disgusting," Hannah said.

"I would tend to agree with you," the Professor said. "But I cannot say for certain that I know what she thought of it. Perhaps she had no choice. She may have preferred being his companion to working in the fields, for all I know. He, however, genuinely fell in love with her, and that was where the trouble started. She looked as white as, well, any white person, but because some of her ancestors were African, the law said she was black, and it was illegal for a white person to marry a black person. A person could be blonde, blue-eyed, and still be considered black. In any case, after he freed her, Mr. Thornhill quietly gave her a house on a plantation he owned near the Florida border. There, she bore him six children, five of whom lived to adulthood."

Hannah said, "Hang on a second. You said that he took his sons to Georgia. Why didn't he take Sarah, then?"

"Because Sarah had not yet been born when he left for Georgia," said the Professor. "And she wasn't his child, anyway. She was Mr. Veeriswamy's daughter. With Lady Chatsfield."

The three kids' mouths were now hanging open.

Brandon was first to say something. "You mean Lady Chatsfield, and Mr. Veeriswamy already were…"

"A couple, yes, long before they married. Of course, they had to keep quiet about it, because it would have been a terrific scandal. But they had known each other almost their whole lives. Mr. Veeriswamy and his father had come from India with Lady Chatsfield's father, who was an administrator in the British colony. Your Mr. Veeriswamy was raised partly as a servant, partly as a member of the family. Rather like Henry Watson, really."

"Was Henry their kid too?" Brandon asked. Anything seemed possible now.

The Professor shook her head. "No, no, only Sarah. I think Lady Chatsfield just gave Henry the same sorts of privileges and opportunities that she remembered Mr. Veeriswamy having in her home when they were children. And, of course, she missed her two sons, who were taken from her. Henry was a sort of substitute son, just as you, Alex, were for Mr. Thornhill."

"That's all very interesting," said Hannah. "Not that it has anything to do with me."

After a long pause, the Professor said "All right, there is something else. Hannah, do you remember Jessie's grandson, John? He was the father of Brandon's Mr. Gordon, the dentist in Balesworth."

Brandon gasped, but Hannah wasn't impressed. "No big. I mean, that's kind of… So what? I never said more than two words to John. He was a filthy little monster."

"Never mind," said the Professor hurriedly, as though she regretted mentioning it. "Forget I said anything. I don't think it does matter."

"Except," Brandon said, "that's one more connection to Balesworth, isn't it?" He looked the Professor in the eye. He sensed, not for the first time, that the Professor knew far more than she was letting on.

"It may be," said the Professor noncommittally. "But I suppose you will all want to know what became of Mr. Thornhill? Shortly after he returned to Georgia in the fall of 1851, he visited his other family. While he was on the plantation, he suffered a bout of malaria. It didn't kill him, but it did weaken him, and so, when he had a heart attack a few days later, he didn't have the strength to pull through. He knew he could not legally free his second family, so while he lay dying, he wrote travel passes for his partner and their children, so they could escape. His wife and children looked white, so nobody challenged them on the journey north, and they settled in New York… I'm so sorry, Alex. I know you became fond of him and he, in turn, was fond of you. He was shocked when you vanished from Balesworth Hall, along with Hannah and

Brandon. He didn't really think that his treatment of Jupe would upset you, because you had admitted to him that Jupe's company had been dumped on you. To him, black people were put on earth to make white people's lives better. He assumed that you thought the same way, just as a lot of English upper-class people thought in much the same fashion about the white working-classes in England. Mr. Thornhill didn't care about Jupe any more than Mr. Sutherland cared about Hannah. Jupe was a convenient pawn in his game with his wife."

"So was I," said Alex bitterly. "Wasn't I? He just needed me to do stuff for him, and to make her jealous that he had replaced her sons with me."

The Professor looked troubled. "No, I don't think that's true at all. He was devastated when his sons died, and meeting a clever young man like you gave him some sort of hope for the future. He knew that the children in his second family couldn't inherit his business from him, and he rather hoped that you would. He liked you, and enjoyed your company."

Hannah looked at Alex, and saw that this news had not made him happy. If anything, he seemed sadder than ever. He had tweaked a blade of grass and was rubbing it between his fingers.

Brandon asked, "What happened to Lady Chatsfield and Mr. Veeriswamy after Mr. Thornhill died?"

"Oh, they led a very quiet life. Because he died, there was no need for a divorce, and they got married. Mr. and Mrs. Veeriswamy moved into what would eventually become Verity and Eric's house. The new Viscount Chatsfield was a good man, and he made a present of Weston Cottage to them, so that they owned it outright. Kintyre Plantation produced enough money to live on. They married and had two more children, whose last name was Veeriswamy."

"One of them must have been the ancestor of Mr. Veeriswamy from the train!" exclaimed Alex.

The Professor nodded, smiled, and continued her story. "Their marriage caused quite a scandal, but, anyway, the new Mrs. Veeriswamy had lost so much respectability by her late husband's actions that she was now considered only middle class. Sarah was bitterly angry about everything that happened. You see, she believed that Mr. Thornhill was her father, despite the evidence of her own brown hair, brown eyes, and olive skin. She kept the name Thornhill, and she never forgave her mother for lying to her. The family's loss of prestige and income also harmed her own chances at marriage. But she did all right for herself. She was pretty and charming, and she married a man called Edward Hughes. After their wedding, they moved to the next county, Bedfordshire, and Sarah never spoke of or to her parents again."

"That's where I met her when she was an old lady," Brandon said, "when Mrs. D. and her kids were living with her. She was kind of uptight. "

The Professor smiled. "Sarah Hughes rejected her past, and became the very model of the proper Victorian lady. Her children never knew anything of their grandparents. If Mrs. Devenish or her sisters asked, they were told that those grandparents had died a long time ago, and eventually, they got the hint and stopped asking. Mrs. Devenish received Weston Cottage as an inheritance from her mother, but she never knew that it had once belonged to her grandmother."

Hannah said, "But why would the Veeriswamys give the cottage to Sarah when she never even spoke to them?"

"I've wondered the same," said the Professor. "I think it was Emma's, Lady Chatsfield's, one last effort to mend her relationship with her daughter. She thought it was all her fault, you see, everything that had happened. Anyhow, both she and Mr. Veeriswamy died in the early 1880s, and Sarah rented out the house for many years. When Mrs. Devenish, and her husband moved in, people in Balesworth mentioned that the house had once belonged to Mr. and Mrs. Veeriswamy, or to Lady Chatsfield and her Indian butler. But such stories never meant anything much to the Devenishes, because they had no idea they were related. All Mrs. D. knew about her grandparents was that they were named Mr. and Mrs. Thornhill.

"That house made a huge difference to the Devenishes' fortunes, though. Mrs. Devenish never had to pay a mortgage or rent, and so even after she was widowed, she could afford expensive schools for her daughters. During the First World War, she moved in with her mother in Bedfordshire, and rented out Weston Cottage, so she could save on living expenses and volunteer as a nurse. That's when Brandon met her, in 1915, when she was living with her mother and Flora."

Hannah shuddered. "Tell me it's not the same Flora I worked with..." But she already knew the answer.

Alex changed the subject. "What about the calculator? Why wouldn't you take back the calculator from me?"

The Professor paused for a moment before she answered. "The calculator was never supposed to be in 1851 to begin with. But I learned that it had some sort of role to play before I could remove it. It was important that I didn't take it before Time was ready."

"How did you manage to lose it in a field, anyway?" asked Hannah peevishly.

The Professor laughed. "Oh, it wasn't anything dramatic. I was just running some numbers before I bought the land from Emma Veeriswamy. I knew she didn't want to own Kintyre. So I offered her a pretty low price, and she took it."

Hannah was appalled. "So you cheated Lady Chatsfield and you became a slaveowner? That's evil!"

The Professor waved aside Hannah's outrage. "No, it's not. I didn't plan to make a profit, and I paid Emma and Sanjeev Veeriswamy the most I could afford. I bought it from them at the end of the Civil War in 1865, when slavery had ended, and the South was in ruins. It was still a lot of money, believe me. I simply hoped to recover some of that money by selling the land later. But I have never figured out the best time to sell. So, technically, I still own it, which means that I own a large part of Snipesville. Nobody knows that but us."

She got to her feet. "I'm going for some more barbeque. It's really very good. Back in a minute."

But she did not return. When the kids finally went looking for her, she had vanished. Nobody knew who she was, and nobody remembered seeing her.

Even Hannah noticed how quiet her brother was. It had been three days since their return, and Alex spent even more time than usual playing on the computer. When he wasn't staring at a screen, he was lying on the sofa staring into space. It wasn't like him.

After she had mentioned her concern to their dad, Mr. Dias asked Alex if he was okay. Alex replied that he felt fine, and Mr. Dias, who was having a really busy week at work, was happy to let the subject drop.

Not satisfied, Hannah now cornered her brother. "Look, I'm really sorry about how things worked out with Mr. Thornhill, but…"

Alex cut her off. "I don't want to talk about it, okay?"

Hannah hesitated. "The thing is," she said carefully, "I just got this in the mail."

She placed a large manila envelope on the computer keyboard. Alex looked at it for a moment, as though deciding whether just to brush it away. But then he slowly picked it up, opened it, and slid out the contents. It was a color photograph of him with Mr. Thornhill, taken in front of the Crystal Palace.

"Did they have color photographs in 1851?" Hannah asked.

"No," Alex said, still staring at the picture. He blinked, and returned the photo to its envelope, then handed it back to Hannah. All he said was, "I'd rather have one that showed me with Jupe." Then he returned to his computer game.

Upstairs, Hannah carefully stored Alex's new photo in the album that the Professor had sent him after their first adventure in 1940. Then she went to her room, and pulled out her own album. She had a manila envelope, too, and hers contained a color photo taken with Mina and Maggie on the day of the creeling. How the Professor had got that shot, she had no idea. But she was glad of it.

ACKNOWLEDGMENTS

I extend my warmest thanks to the following fans of The Snipesville Chronicles who helped make possible the publication of A Different Day, A Different Destiny.

Anon.
Brenda Dartt
Cynthia Frost
Yvette Gordillo
Norma Nicol Hamilton
Jack & Joyce Howard
Marky Lloyd
Nancy Malcom
Sharon McMullen
Rebecca and John Murray
Katie Olson
Cathy Skidmore-Hess
Wendy Turner
Rebecca Ziegler

Big thanks also to the following kids and adults from both sides of the Atlantic who read and commented on drafts of the manuscript at various stages: Miriam and Ellie Bryant, Rebecca and Alex Gordon, Julia Griffin, Joyce Harper, Fielding Keeley, Becky Laney, Sophie Lichtman, Bryan and Alec Ogihara, Laura Shelton, Cathy Skidmore-Hess, Annie Stevens, and Rachel Thomas.

Once again, Kelley Callaway and Deborah Harvey gave of their time and talents to design this book. I am delighted and touched by their support.

As ever, I owe many thanks to many academic historians, museum curators, archivists, and other kind folk for information on arcane topics. Although this is a work of fiction, it relies heavily on the work of professional historians: This book took me so long to write because I realized early on that I had forgotten (or never knew) so much Victorian history. Please support academic scholars and their work, because without them, the Snipesville Chronicles would not exist!

For your convenience, I will post the links below on my website at www.AnnetteLaing.com

Georgia

It's a weird thing to say, but I enjoyed a wonderful May afternoon at Whitaker Funeral Home in Metter, Georgia. Many thanks to the delightful Shaunta Ellis-Rivers for an informative and (dare I say it) entertaining tour. I'd like to make it clear that while the building of Clark and Sons Home of Eternal Rest, Inc. bears more than a passing resemblance to Whitaker's, Shaunta and Aunt Morticia could not be less alike! I also thank the owners, Larry and Brenda Gould, the son-in-law and daughter of the founders, for their warm reception. As I told Mrs. Gould, I absolutely want them to bury me. Not now, of course.

Dr. Jon Bryant is a goldmine of knowledge about nineteenth-century Georgia history, and I have exploited him shamelessly. He and Dr. Lisa Denmark, both former colleagues of mine at Georgia Southern University, answered my hapless questions about Victorian Savannah and its hinterlands.

As I made clear in the first book, the Snipesville I describe is nothing to do with the *real* Snipesville, Georgia, a hamlet near Hazlehurst. Thanks, however, to Dusty Snipes Gres, a descendant of the founder of the real Snipesville, for her support.

Visits to the Owens-Thomas House, the Green-Meldrim House, the Andrew Low House, and the Isaiah Davenport House, all in Savannah, helped me in constructing a mental picture of Mr. Thornhill's home.

The Kintyre Plantation house's appearance is based on the Tullie Smith Farmhouse at the Atlanta History Center, should you care to visit. The Museum is one of the finest in the South.

London

Andrea Tanner, archivist for Fortnum and Mason, kindly looked up info about that amazing clock on the ground floor of the Food Hall. When my Georgia study abroad students and I popped in fifty pence in 2007, it played *Dixie*. But I learned from Andrea that the clock plays a variety of tunes at random, and that it was purely coincidence that it played *Dixie* for us....Or was it?

Charles Babbage's pickled brain, and a working version of his Difference Engine, are among the many fascinating exhibits in London's Science Museum.

I enjoyed a lovely summer's day in 2007 at the Kensal Green Cemetery Open House, in the agreeable company of my student Shannon McLeod, not to mention the ladies of the WRVS and a crowd of Goths. The Friends of the cemetery gave an informative and truly creepy tour of the Anglican Chapel catacombs, and also of the main grounds. It was a uniquely British day out for Shannon and me. I also owe the Professor's details about Kensal Green to the

Friends of Kensal Green Cemetery Web site, http://www.kensalgreen.co.uk/

Fiona Cormack in the archives at the Museum of London Docklands told me about Dundee Wharf in Limehouse, in the East End of London, which was leased or owned by the Dundee, Perth and London Shipping Co. It was next to Buchanan's Wharf, where tea was handled. Neither dock exists today. However, it turns out that Hannah's ship would have docked at the DPL's earlier London base, Hore's Wharf in Wapping, a fact I discovered in Graeme Somner's book on the DPL (see bibliography, below.)

The Thames Tunnel still exists, and remains part of the East London Line of the Underground (subway) system, which at time of writing is closed for major renovations.

After the Great Exhibition ended, the Crystal Palace was moved to a new site in south London, where it was enlarged and remained a popular attraction and venue. It burned down in 1936. It is still memorialized by Crystal Palace railway station.

Some of the exhibits from the Great Exhibition formed the starting collection for the South Kensington Museum, opened by Queen Victoria in 1857, and later renamed the Victoria and Albert Museum. If you visit the V&A today, you can see some of the original pieces from the Crystal Palace.

Thanks to Dr. Jon Bryant for loaning me a working replica of the revolver exhibited by Samuel Colt at the Great Exhibition. I still can't work it.

New Lanark

Aynsley Gough, Education and Access Officer for the New Lanark Conservation Trust, diligently researched the sanitary arrangements at the beautiful New Lanark Mills in the mid-nineteenth century. Talk about a loo with a view… Hannah should have been more grateful.

My family and I enjoyed staying in New Lanark at the SYHA hostel on Wee Row, although we imagine that our digs, however Spartan, were a little better than conditions at Mrs. Nicolson's. Thanks to the staff of this superb industrial museum.

The Midlands and the Black Country

Heather and Bob Salway, and their kids, Hannah, Daniel and Michael, graciously—and perhaps foolishly-- loaned me their house in Walmley, West Midlands, while they were away on holiday. It made a splendid base for visiting the Black Country and the Midlands, and I was also able to make serious strides on the first draft while sitting in their living room! Many, many thanks.

My son, Alec, and I spent two splendid days at the Black Country Living Museum in Dudley, eight months apart. Both visits were a great deal of fun. Brandon's coal mine was inspired by visits to the impressive reproduction 1850 mine here, and to the drift mine at Beamish Open Air Museum, near New-castle and Durham. We also enjoyed our canal boat ride at the Black Country Museum.

Joyce Harper has a fine command of the English language, and, indeed, was my public speaking coach at school, more years ago than either of us would care to recall. Her skill with standard English is especially remarkable since her first language is the tongue-twisting dialect of England's Black Country, the area to the west of Birmingham (and very definitely separate from it, as Black Country folk never tire of telling us…) Many thanks to Joyce, a native of Netherton, who corrected my misuse and abuse of Black Country dialect, and so helped me devise a modified version of the Real Thing that would nonetheless be intelligible to my readers. All the inaccuracies are entirely my doing.

The song sung by the miners is The Miner's Petition, quoted in Jon Raven, *The Urban and Industrial Songs of the Black Country and Birmingham* (Broad-side Books, 1977)

Roma, splendid guide at the National Trust Birmingham Back-to-Backs, answered my questions and objections without wincing. The NT effort to pre-serve working-class housing is commendable, although, as I said on the day, it needs to be less Trustified and precious.

The Southwell Workhouse of the National Trust was a great example of the innovative approach the NT has taken toward adding to its portfolio of buildings in recent years. It was a fascinating and memorable tour. Thanks to the welcoming staff. Oh, and by the way, Americans? It is shameful that our version of the NT is so tiny, and far more pompous. C'mon, we have historic buildings, too, and we need to stop being so stuffy about history.

Alec and I spent a lovely time in the stunningly beautiful village of Stoke Bruerne, where we had a delicious pub lunch, visited the National Waterways Museum, rode in a canal boat, and watched several narrowboats pass through the traditional lock (a process I found very hard to describe!) Today, canal boats are floating RVs, and we were tickled to see the pretty gardens some boat own-ers had planted on the roofs of their floating homes! The village is close to the M1 Motorway, and well worth a detour: http://www.nwm.org.uk/stoke/

Dundee
I have set part of my book in the very real city of Dundee, Scotland, and I

am standing by to receive complaints from the large number of local historians who have chronicled its history. Most of the parts of Dundee that I describe are long gone, demolished in the name of slum clearance and not-always-successful urban renewal. I relied on old photos and drawings for my descriptions, along with my knowledge of urban conditions in early and mid-Victorian Britain, and imagination. The Royal Arch, which was completed in 1851 to celebrate the visit of Queen Victoria many years earlier, was torn down in the 1960s to make way for an exit road from the new Tay road bridge, a loss which Dundonians still mourn many decades later. In other acts of civic vandalism, the Town House and the houses behind it, including the Vault and Castle Lane, were demolished to build Caird Hall and the underwhelming city square. To get a sense of what Dundee was like in the 19th century check out the photographs of early twentieth-century Dundee at the city's Photopolis site at: http://www.dundeecity.gov.uk/centlib/photopolis/index.html

Fiona Sinclair, senior curator at Dundee's McManus Galleries and Museum (formerly known by what I shall always consider its proper name, the Albert Institute, named for the creator of the Great Exhibition), helped refer me to other sources of information while extensive and disruptive renovations are carried out on the building.

Eileen Moran and Deirdre Sweeney proved unflappable when I descended on them unannounced one August day in 2008 at the Dundee City Library Local History Room. They quickly assembled material, both from my requests and their own suggestions, for what proved to be the most productive and enjoyable few hours I have ever spent in an archive. Thanks to them, my descriptions of Dundee and its people drew much more on mid-nineteenth century sources than would otherwise have been the case.

My great-grandfather, James Harris, kept a grocery store in Dundee in the early twentieth century, so I borrowed his name. Hope he wouldn't mind.

I was gobsmacked to learn that the Dundee, Perth and London Shipping Company is still very much in business, and still headquartered in Dundee, almost two hundred years after its founding. I am grateful to Alasdair Chalmers and his secretary Ann Bain for information about the time it took for a company paddle steamer to make the journey from Dundee to London, and the likely conditions onboard. Alas, they were unable to help with a description of the steamers' passenger accommodations, so I have improvised, based on contemporary accounts. Hannah's ship would most likely have been the Perth.

Jessie Gordon and her weaver daughters were inspired by a photograph I have of my great-great-grandmother with her husband and their six weaver daughters (and one son), taken in 1927. The family story is that the daughters were all able to become weavers because my great-great-grandfather, John Simpson, was a supervisor at Caird's Mill. Mina Simpson was a union organizer. Two of her sisters emigrated to New York with their husbands, one of whom was a pierrot, or seaside entertainer. Oh, and the youngest sister, Barbara, was my great-grandmother, who died in 1992. The Simpsons were far more respectable than most of their fictionalized Gordon selves, but by the time they were born, the Scottish upper working classes had become thoroughly Late Victorian.

According to the 1851 Dundee census, Whitehall Close, where Maggie lived, was among the worst slums in a city notorious for the worst housing in Britain. It was inhabited mostly by immigrant Irish laborers who, without capital or connections, and facing anti-Catholic discrimination, had small chance of getting out of poverty.

Hannah's riot was inspired by a news item in the *Dundee, Perth and Cupar Advertiser* in 1851. The two ads for voyages to San Francisco and Dundee really did appear on the same page of the *Dundee, Perth and Cupar Advertiser* on April 11, 1851.

The information about Moon and Langlands' shop was drawn from the 1850 Dundee City directory.

Please do visit Dundee, my birthplace and arguably the most Scottish city in Scotland. I go there every year to visit family and touch base. There is still much lovely Scottish architecture, despite all the demolitions. You can also check out Verdant Works (the museum of the now-departed jute industry), and the soon-to-reopen city museum at McManus Galleries (a magnificent Victorian Gothic building, originally known as the Albert Institute, in honor of the prince). Don't miss the fabulous bakeries of Fisher & Donaldson and Goodfellow & Stevens, who have sold Dundee's (and Britain's) best cakes and pies for decades, including the meat pies and rhubarb pies of which Hannah and Maggie were so fond. The meat pies, in 1851, would have been made from mutton: Today, the usual filling is ground beef, and they are to die for. Take home some freshly-roasted coffee from J. Allan Braithwaite, who have been selling from the same location and even the same shop fittings since the 1860s! Poverty continues to plague Dundee, but Dundonians remain among the friendliest people to visitors, and you will be charmed by the accent and the attitudes. If you liked Mina, you will love Dundee.

Balesworth

Distant Writing, Steven Roberts' exhaustive online history of early Victorian telegraphy companies in Britain, was extremely helpful: http://distantwriting.co.uk

Once again, Barry Attoe, Archives Officer at the British Postal Museum and Archive, helped make sure I didn't reveal my ignorance of the postal system.

You won't find Balesworth Hall in Hertfordshire, or on the National Trust's web site at nationaltrust.org.uk, because, like Balesworth itself, it doesn't exist. What I had in mind was an amalgam of historic manor houses I visited in the run-up to the book, including Sudbury, Hanbury Hall, Audley End, and so many more. The Chatsfield peerage, as well as its allied titles, is entirely fictitious, as are the members of that family: The "Chats" part of the name was an unconscious nod to Joseph Paxton, architect of the Crystal Palace, who based his design on the greenhouses he built for the Duke of Devonshire at Chatsworth. If you are embarked on a serious study of aristocracy and land inheritance, please do NOT use this book as your starting point: I bent the rules a bit.

Thanks to Wikipedia for the quick look-ups: If there are any mistakes, blame me for using Wikipedia.

SELECT BIBLIOGRAPHY

Just a few of the books I consulted. I recommend only the most readable, but let me reiterate that my work would not be possible without that of academic historians, including their more boring stuff.

New Lanark

Donnachie, Ian L. and Hewitt, George, *Historic New Lanark* (Edinburgh University Press, 1993)

Dundee

Lewis, George, *Impressions of America and the American Churches* (Edinburgh: W.P. Kennedy, 1845);

Rice, Alan J. and Crawford, Martin, *Liberating Sojourn: Frederick Douglass and Transatlantic Reform* (Athens, GA.: University of Georgia Press, 1999)

In the 1840s, Reverend George Lewis of Dundee really did visit the American South, including Savannah, to solicit contributions for the new Free Church of Scotland. What's more, Frederick Douglass really did visit Scotland, including Dundee, on a triumphant tour of Britain. He explained to Dundee people that the contributions to Rev. Lewis had come from the proceeds of slavery. Of the warm reception he got, Douglass wrote home from the Royal Hotel, Dundee, "It is quite an advantage to be a 'nigger' here." (quoted in William S. McFeely, *Frederick Douglass* (New York: W.W. Norton, 1995))

Miskell, Louise, Whatley, Christopher, and Harris, Bob (eds.), *Victorian Dundee: Image and Realities* (East Lothian: Tuckwell Press, 2000)

Somner, Graeme, *The DP&L: A History of the Dundee, Perth & London Shipping Co. Ltd and Associated Shipping Companies* (Kendal: World Ship Society, 1995)

London and The Great Exhibition of 1851

Auerbach, Jeffrey A. *The Great Exhibition of 1851: A Nation on Display* (New Haven: Yale University Press, 1999)

Drew, William Allen, *Glimpses and Gatherings During a Voyage and Visit to London and the Great Exhibition in the Summer of 1851* (Augusta, Maine: Homan & Manley, 1852)

My description of 1851 London, and of the Thames Tunnel especially, is primarily dependent on Drew's super account. I am grateful to the Wikipedia contributors who made me aware of it, and to Google Books for making the entire text available.

Leapman, Michael, *The World for a Shilling: How the Great Exhibition of 1851 Shaped a Nation* (London: Headline Publishing, 2002)

Pamela Pilbeam, *Madame Tussaud and the History of Waxworks* (London: Hambledon & London, 2006)

Savannah

Jones, Jacqueline, *Saving Savannah: The City and the Civil War* (New York: Knopf, 2008)

This splendid and readable account was an invaluable source of information about pre-Civil War Savannah.

About the Author

Dr. Annette Laing was born in Scotland, raised in England, spent many years in California, and now lives in rural Georgia. For many years, she was a professor of early American and British history before resigning in 2008 to concentrate on her work for children's history. She is director of Imaginative Journeys, a program that runs creative day camps for kids in South Georgia.

To learn about Annette's books, summer camps, school visits, and consultancy, please visit www.AnnetteLaing.com.